THE RAKEHELL
THE GRAND SAGA OF THE GREAT CLIPPER SHIPS AND OF THE MEN WHO BUILT THEM TO CONQUER THE SEAS AND CHALLENGE THE WORLD!

Jonathan Rakehell—who staked his reputation and his place in the family on the clipper's amazing speed.

Lai-Tse Lu—the beautiful, independent daughter of a Chinese merchant. She could not know that Jonathan's proud clipper ship carried a cargo of love and pain, joy and tragedy for her.

Louise Graves—Jonathan's wife-to-be, who waits at home in New London keeping a secret of her own.

Bradford Walker—Jonathan's scheming brother-in-law, who scoffs at the clipper and plots to replace Jonathan as heir to the Rakehell shipping line.

THE RAKEHELL DYNASTY

The bold, sweeping, passionate story of a great New England shipping family caught up in the winds of change—and of the one man who would dare to sail his dream ship to the frightening, beautiful land of China. He was Jonathan Rakehell, and his destiny would change the course of history.

The Rakehell Dynasty

Michael William Scott

WARNER BOOKS

A Warner Communications Company

WARNER BOOKS EDITION

Produced by Lyle Kenyon Engel

Cover art by Tom Hall

Warner Books, Inc., 75 Rockefeller Plaza, New York, N.Y. 10019

Ⓦ A Warner Communications Company

Printed in the United States of America

First Printing: July, 1980

10 9 8 7 6 5 4 3 2 1

For
Marla and Lyle Kenyon Engel

The wind that sighs before the dawn
  Chases the gloom of night,
The curtains of the East are drawn,
  And suddenly—'tis light.

—Sir Lewis Morris

THE
RAKEHELL
DYNASTY

Voyages of the

Arctic Ocean

Russian Empire

Russian America

North West Territories

Mongolia

Peking

Oregon

Tibet

China

Japan

Mexico

India Burma

Canton

Formosa

Siam

Bangkok

South China Sea

Phillipine Islands

Sandwich Is.

Pacific Ocean

Equator

Ceylon

Singapore

Djakarta

Dutch East Indies

Indian Ocean

Australia

Fiji

New Zealand

Pearl River Delta

Pearl River

Canton

Whampoa

mud flats

The Bogue

Hong Kong Is.

deep water channel

mud flats

Macao

Ron Toelke 1980

Pearl River Delta

Flying Dragon

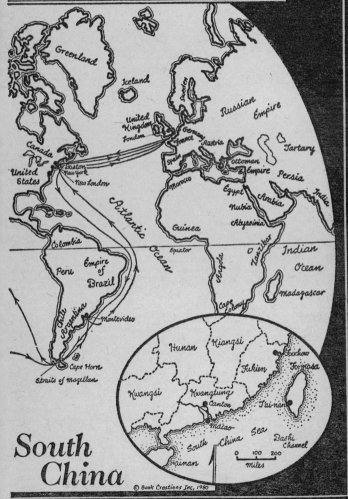

South
China

© Book Creations Inc, 1980

Book
I

I

She was even lovelier than Jonathan Rakehell had imagined, and he fell in love with her at first sight.

Never in the thousands of years that men had gone to sea had there been another ship like her. Halting his horse on the shore, Jonathan stared in fascinated concentration as the extraordinary vessel, long and lean, crowded with more sail than anyone had ever utilized previously, cut through the clear green-blue waters of Chesapeake Bay. All the rumors and stories that had reached the yards of Rakehell Builders and Shippers in New London, Connecticut were true, more than true.

Her designer, Kennard and Williamson of Baltimore, who had built her for merchant Isaac McKim, called her a clipper, presumably because she clipped over waves rather than thrusting through them, and just watching her under full sail was enough to confirm the legends she was already creating. The young man was enthralled. She resembled a great, flying cloud that seemed to float above the sea rather than slice through it. Her speed was dazzling, and she maneuvered with an elegant grace that not even a barracuda could match.

As far back as the American Revolution, there had been brigs and schooners built in Baltimore which were exceptionally long, low, and extremely fast. Many of them had served as privateers. The ship now before him, their descendent, was beautifully slender. She was a flush-decked vessel, with three main masts, her sails square rigged.

Curbing his excitement, Jonathan sat back in his saddle and studied the *Ann McKim* with the cool professionalism that only a fifth generation Rakehell could achieve. He had first gone to sea as his grandfather's cabin boy at the age of nine, and two years later his father had handed him an adze made for a small boy and had put him to work in the yard during his summer holidays. Now, five years out of Yale College at the age of twenty-five, he was totally devoted, in the Rakehell tradition, to the building and sailing of ships.

Last year, in 1833, he had first heard of the revolutionary new vessel, and now he had come to the yard of Isaac McKim specifically to see her. Well, she was splendid far beyond his expectations.

Her most unusual feature was her very sharp-raked bow, the better part of it above water, and Jonathan immediately understood that she owed her speed, in part, to the fact that less of her hull was in contact with the water than were those of ordinary merchantmen. His hazel eyes narrowing as he analyzed her, he saw that her beam, or widest portion, was located far toward the bow. This, he knew instantly, gave her great stability and was partly responsible for her ability to achieve such speed. As nearly as he could judge at a distance, her length was about five times that of her beam, far more than the usual ratio of three or even four to one. No wonder she was unique.

What astonished Jonathan more than anything else was the vast number of square-rigged sails she carried. She had three principal masts, and as he looked at the billowing white canvas on the mainmast, set forward of amidships, he automatically began to count upward. At the bottom, naturally, was the course, with the lower and upper topsails, then the topgallant. Craning slightly, he looked up at the royal, then shook his head in wonder. Good Lord! There was still another sail above the royal, and he wondered what it was called. As to the fore-and-aft sails on the jib, extending from the prow, he counted four, no, five! And there were three spanker sails at the stern.

Of course she looked like a cloud, and with the wind behind her she almost literally flew across Chesapeake

16

Bay. Obviously she would reach her berth before he got there, and he spurred forward.

An hour later he reached the shipyard and was escorted to the office of the short, stocky Isaac McKim. The middle-aged man looked him up and down quickly. Well over six feet tall and rawboned, Jonathan was slightly awkward on land, but the Baltimore merchant knew his type and suspected that he came into his own at sea.

"So you're Jeremiah Rakehell's son," he said. "Welcome. Your father wrote that I could expect a visit from you, but I gather he didn't approve too highly of your journey here."

"Papa doesn't hold with new-fangled notions," Jonathan replied, his grin infectious as he ran a hand through his crisp, dark brown hair. "But if he'd seen the *Ann McKim* under sail, as I have today, I daresay he'd be a convert."

"You like her, then."

"There's no doubt in my mind, Mr. McKim, that the clipper is the ship of the future." Jonathan became solemn. "My mind reels when I think of what a fleet of clippers could accomplish."

The *Ann McKim*'s owner smiled in satisfaction. "We're in agreement. Her crew has come ashore, so I can't take you for a sail until morning. But between now and the time Ann gives you one of her oyster and crab pies for supper, we can go aboard and inspect her, if you like."

Jonathan jumped to his feet and started toward the door. They walked together through the yard to a dock where a boat transported them to the clipper. "She looks to me as though she displaces about five hundred tons. Am I right, sir?"

"She has a gross displacement of ninety-three," McKim replied. "Her register is deceptive. Her bottom isn't flat, you see, but is V-shaped, like the under-fin of a fish."

"I see. To what extent does that cut down the storage capacity of her holds?"

"That space is reduced by approximately one-half."

Jonathan shrugged. "Obviously sacrifices must be

17

made for the sake of speed, although I can't help wondering if her bottom could be modified somewhat."

"You're free to experiment as you wish, young man."

"I intend to do just that. What is her speed?"

"She averages fifteen knots," McKim said proudly.

Jonathan whistled softly. No ship constructed at the Rakehell yard had ever achieved an average of more than ten knots per hour.

They crossed a gangplank and stood on the main deck. "You'll note, Mr. Rakehell, that we've used seasoned oak for planking rather than the heavier teak. Wherever possible we've utilized lighter wood. That and precision in the overall distribution of her weight are two of her secrets."

Jonathan and McKim paused, scarcely aware that they had halted, and for a time they discussed a number of technical matters. They talked about economy of running, crewing, and handling, earning power per voyage, and the potential employment to capacity each year.

They spent the rest of the afternoon making a detailed inspection of the *Ann McKim*. Everywhere, space was at a premium. The master and mates had their cabins under the poop, and the saloon, where they ate, was there as well. The crew had bunks under the forecastle-head. The cargo was carried in hatches along the upper deck, covered with tarpaulin and held by ropes.

Boats were carried on deck. A portion of the space in the forepart of the ship was allotted to what was known as "eatable livestock," including cows and pigs, sheep and poultry.

Jonathan was surprised to learn that the *Ann McKim* had a complement of only three officers and eleven seamen, including the boatswain. The men had to go aloft to set the sails, of course, but the clipper handled so well that she could carry fewer men than the far bulkier standard ships of the day.

His head reeling after the inspection, Jonathan said, "Just one more question, sir. For the moment. What do you call the sail above the royal?"

McKim grinned. "The builders and I went round and round on that one. We finally decided to call it a skysail."

Jonathan couldn't help wondering if yet another sail could be placed above the skysail, giving the vessel even greater speed and maneuverability. But he refrained from voicing the thought, not wanting to look foolish. The problem was one he could solve only on his own drawing board.

Isaac McKim took the visitor off to his house for supper and to spend the night. Mrs. McKim, as promised, served a seafood pie, followed by a huge steak. Jonathan was ravenous and ate accordingly, politely answering Ann McKim's questions about his family. His father was well, thank you, but had shown no inclination to remarry since his wife's death a decade earlier. "He's too busy, ma'am. He spends day and night at the yard."

"And your sister and her family? They stayed with us several years ago when they were traveling to Virginia."

"They're fine, thanks." Jonathan didn't realize he spoke curtly. He loved his older sister, Judith, and was very fond of her two small children. But his brother-in-law, Bradford Walker, was not one of his favorite people. Oh, Brad was all right, in his way, but ever since Papa had made him General Manager of Rakehell Builders and Shippers two years earlier, also giving him a seat on the board of directors, Brad had grown pompous and enjoyed throwing his weight around. It was particularly irksome that Jonathan, who would inherit his father's place as president and principal proprietor, needed Brad's approval for every move he made, approval that was rarely forthcoming.

Sensing that something was amiss, Mrs. McKim dropped the subject and led the way to the parlor for coffee. She should have known better than to pry. When she had met Bradford Walker she had learned he was ambitious, and she suspected he didn't particularly like working with a young brother-in-law who would some day be his superior, particularly when Jonathan's interest in clipper ships revealed that he wasn't cast in the traditionally conservative Rakehell mold.

That night Jonathan slept lightly, and early the next morning, after a hearty breakfast of fish and hot bread, he accompanied his host to the yard. A quarter of an hour later they went aboard the *Ann McKim,* where the crew was already assembled, and Isaac McKim took the command himself, with Jonathan standing beside him on the quarterdeck.

"Loose and make all plain sail!" McKim ordered. Then, with the anchor catted and the jibs hoisted, he called, "Haul aft the sheets!"

The sails snapped in the breeze as they filled, their cracking sound like that of rifle shots, as the clipper began to glide through the water. Jonathan drank in every detail of the operation. Having spent more than the required seven years at sea since he had started his apprenticeship, he himself held a Master's ticket and was qualified to command a ship at sea.

"Man topsail sheets!" McKim shouted. "Haul taut! Let fall tops'ls and courses," he called to the topmen, who were laying out along the yards. "Sheet home!"

The clipper was before the wind, or "on a wind," as the seamen said, and the lower yards were braced up to about an angle of twenty degrees with the fore and aft line. Large sails, such as the courses, were braced up at a sharper angle than the yards of smaller sails.

The *McKim* gathered speed.

"Ease the helm down," McKim told the quartermaster at the wheel, then ordered, "Haul over the boom!"

The spanker boom was hauled amidships to bring the bow nearer to the wind.

"Helm's a-lee," the quartermaster reported.

"Let go head and foresheets," McKim directed. This would take the wind out of the jibs. "Head braces." The sharper the yard was braced, the more effect the sail had to bring the bow round when the sail was once aback. "Raise tacks and sheets! Let go to'gallant bowlines."

Jonathan admired the crew's precision. These seamen knew their business.

"Main brace—mains'l haul! Head braces!" McKim was cautioning the men to come from the main tacks and sheets to the weather head braces. "Of all haul!"

The lee head braces and head bowlines were let go, the head yards were braced round, and the foresail was set on the other tack.

"Brace up the mainyard!"

The tacking operation was completed, and the clipper was beating to windward.

"She's slack in stays," Jonathan said, indicating that she was slow in going from one tack to another, with her head in the wind.

McKim explained that the one weakness of a clipper was her tendency to "buck like a stallion around a young mare" when she sailed with her head in the wind.

The sailing technique, that of coaxing more and yet more speed out of the ship, was unlike any that Jonathan had known, and for almost three hours he watched in fascination, himself testing the wind and then mentally ordering changes in the ship's course. He managed to keep pace with the orders that McKim gave.

Isaac McKim sent a sailor below for mugs of coffee for his guest and himself, and after they had been emptied, his eyes gleamed. "Now you'll see what she can do," he said, and ordered the crew to come about. Maneuvering with rapidity and grace, the ship reversed her direction.

Her many sails filled again, and within moments she was slicing through the whitecap-ruffled water.

Jonathan caught his breath. Never had he known such an extraordinary experience. Never had a sailing ship achieved such blinding speed as she did moving downwind.

Scarcely aware of what he was doing, he removed his hat and allowed the wind to ruffle his hair. The taste of salt was on his lips, and as he looked at the shore to judge the *Ann McKim*'s speed, he was astonished as the land slid past him. The clipper was performing superbly.

Only a bird could experience a similar sensation, Jonathan told himself, and had to curb a desire to shout aloud in sheer, exuberant joy. He had given his heart to the clipper, and she was living up to his faith in her. Glorying in the sea spray, relishing the steady pace of the vessel, pitched and tossed only slightly as she cut a path through the sea, he knew she was moving far faster than fifteen knots.

A man who took full advantage of the prevailing winds that blew from east to west in the northern hemisphere, from west to east in the southern hemisphere, could take such a ship anywhere on earth, vastly reducing customary sailing schedules.

His head almost bursting with the thoughts that rocketed through it, Jonathan Rakehell made a private vow: for as long as he lived he would give his complete fidelity to clipper ships, and he was certain they would never betray that trust.

His saddlebag crammed with naval architect's sketches of the *Ann McKim,* Jonathan wasted no time on his return trip to New England. He spent his days from dawn until dusk in the saddle, pausing briefly only when it was necessary to eat and rest his mount. As exuberant as he had been sailing downwind on the clipper, he mentally made and refined plans, changing and discarding, starting again and retaining only the best features of the schemes gradually taking form in his mind.

No Rakehell ever slighted or ignored the demands of immediate business, to be sure, so he spent a necessary two days in New York. There he called on the merchants and traders who sent their products to England, Continental Europe, and the West Indian islands of the Caribbean in merchantmen owned by the family company. When he left the city and rode toward the northeast through Westchester County, he carried enough new orders to satisfy even his father and his carping brother-in-law. Regardless of what they might think about clippers, he had more than justified his absence from New London.

After he crossed the state border into Connecticut, Jonathan's euphoria began to fade, and a sense of caution pervaded him. Certainly he needed no reminder that he would be dealing with arch-conservatives who were inclined to regard him as something of a reckless, flamboyant radical. After all, he was the only member of the family who had not only refused to become an active member of the Whig party but had actually voted two years earlier for the re-election of President Andrew Jackson. In vain he had argued that Jackson was the worthy successor of Thomas Jefferson and was trying to fulfill the ideals of Jeffersonian democracy. The Rakehells preferred what

Papa called the "sound" policies of John and John Quincy Adams.

How Papa and Brad Walker would react to the idea of building and sailing clipper ships might depend on his presentation, at least to some extent. But Jonathan knew he faced an uphill battle, at best. He would need facts and figures at his fingertips, and under no circumstances could he allow himself to lose his temper when Brad followed his tactics of prodding, then denigrating everything he proposed.

It was late on Saturday afternoon when Jonathan finally reached the bustling seaport of New London, so late that the shipyard had already closed for the Sabbath, so he rode directly to the house of his ancestors on Pequot Avenue, facing the water where the Thames River widened and flowed into Long Island Sound. The dwelling stood on the site of the house built by the first Jonathan Rakehell early in the 18th century, and a few of the original rooms were still in use, but succeeding generations had made many additions to the place. It faced the water on its own beach, but even from the road, which was at the rear, it was oddly handsome and impressive, a rambling, three-story structure of white clapboard, as solid as the shipyard that was the foundation of the family fortune.

Glancing across Pequot Avenue at a house only slightly smaller, Jonathan caught a glimpse of Dr. Martin Graves, lighting oil lamps in the parlor. Well, he would wait until tomorrow, when he would join the Graves family for dinner after church, before he saw Louise. Martin and Naomi Graves didn't like anyone, not even the young man who was unofficially betrothed to their daughter, to drop in unexpectedly and unannounced. They and Jeremiah Rakehell shared the same values, the same sense of dignity and respect for protocol, but that wasn't surprising. Dr. Graves's father had been a business associate of Grandpa Rakehell, building his mansion across the street from his friend's home, and the two families had been close for decades.

Papa's housekeeper hadn't expected Jonathan to return this evening and was surprised. "I'll have cook fix you a pick-up supper," she said. "Your father and

Mr. Walker had to go up to Rhode Island on business, and they won't be home until Monday."

Jonathan instantly decided he could use the intervening time to his advantage. "Don't bother, Miss Nan," he said. "I'll beg supper from my sister."

The substantial Walker house stood a few doors away on Pequot Avenue, and Judith Walker was pleased to welcome her brother, as he had known she would be. Seven years his elder, she was still pretty and trim at thirty-two. She was dressed in a high-necked gown of English wool, which befitted a Rakehell, and she wore her dark brown hair in a bun at the nape of her neck in the style favored by her late mother, but her long-lashed hazel eyes were mischievous and spirited. Not even an overbearing husband, Jonathan thought, could stifle her.

"Where are Judy and Braddy?" he asked as she led the way to the sitting room she preferred to the formal parlor.

"Don't shout or you'll wake them up," she said. "They wore themselves out on the beach this afternoon— while I sat in constant attendance on them. So I had them bathed, fed, and put to bed, and if the Almighty is compassionate, I won't see them again until breakfast tomorrow morning. Help yourself to a drink. None for me."

He poured himself a small glass of the sherry wine that the Rakehells imported from Spain. "What are Papa and Brad doing in Rhode Island?"

"Something to do with a ship built at the yard that's being sold at an auction because the owner went bankrupt." Judith shrugged. "Nobody told me details, and I didn't ask."

As usual, he thought, she wasn't too much concerned with what happened at Rakehell Building and Shipping, but that was a woman's prerogative. His mother's interest in the business had been limited, too.

"Tell me about your mysterious trip, Jon."

"There was no mystery. I went to Baltimore to see a new kind of ship. A clipper."

"Oh. Brad made it sound mysterious." She glanced

24

into the dining room, saw that supper was being served, and beckoned.

"I'll tell you all about it," he said cautiously, waiting until the right moment to launch his tale about the wonders of the *Ann McKim*. His sister's support would be enormously helpful, although he had never known her to oppose her husband at a board of directors' meeting.

"I'm more interested in you and Louise. When is your engagement being announced?"

Jonathan's broad shoulders rose and fell, but he did not reply until the servingmaid placed steaming bowls of clam chowder before them and left the room. Menus at the Walker house were identical to those served at home. "Dr. Graves and Papa," he said lightly, "will make that decision in their infinite wisdom."

"I should think you and Louise would want a say in something that important to you."

He grinned, and there was no malice in his voice when he replied. "Both families have taken it for granted ever since we were Braddy's and Judy's ages that we'd marry. So Louise and I are in no great rush. We're obedient children who will do what's best for posterity."

Judith looked sharply at her brother and raised an eyebrow. "May I ask you a very personal question? You can tell me to mind my own business, if you prefer."

He returned his sister's gaze, then made a circle of his thumb and middle finger.

She immediately recalled the gesture from his early childhood as a pledge to tell the truth. "Are you and Louise in love?"

"Did you love Brad when you married him?" Jonathan countered.

"I do now!" Judith said hotly.

He grinned at her. "The spouses of Rakehells, like royalty—or blooded cattle—are chosen for the sterling qualities their children will inherit. Dr. and Mrs. Graves are pleased because Louise will marry into a family of standing and means. Papa is happy because Louise is healthy, comes of good stock, and has an even disposition. It doesn't hurt that she's quite pretty, but since I have

25

brains, Papa doesn't care what she thinks. Or whether she thinks."

They fell silent while the soup bowls were cleared away and the maid placed a platter of the inevitable Saturday night boiled beef, cabbage and potatoes, onions and carrots on the table.

"If you and Louise both feel that way," Judith said at last, "I'm surprised you don't tell Papa and Dr. Graves that you refuse to go through with the marriage."

Jonathan became serious. "You misinterpret me," he said. "I'm never afraid to speak my mind, as you know."

"Only too well."

"I don't have an interest in anyone else, and neither does Louise, to the best of my knowledge. Surely you can't have forgotten how I was brought up. The way you were. The family and the company—which are one and the same, indivisible—come first in all things. Louise will be a good wife. She'll entertain customers from New York and Boston and Providence in the right way. She'll call regularly on the families of our yard workers, just as you do. And most important of all, she'll bring a sixth generation of ambitious, healthy Rakehells into the world, boys who will take their assigned places in the dynasty."

"You sound bitter," Judith said uneasily.

"I'm not!" her brother retorted. "The future of the company and the family mean as much to me as they do to Papa. As much as they did to Grandpa and his father. Louise and I get along fine, we're comfortable with each other, and both of us know what's expected of us. So I can't imagine any good reason we shouldn't marry."

She shook her head and sighed. "Please pass the horseradish sauce."

"My coming marriage is the least of my worries," Jonathan said, and plunged into an impassioned account of his visit to the clipper ship.

Rakehell women knew more than most men about ships, so Judith was able to grasp most of what her brother told her, even though her mind occasionally wandered. She listened to his recital as best she could and did not interrupt until he paused for breath. "Jon, why are you telling me all this?"

26

"So you'll be prepared in advance," he said. "I'm going to ask Papa to call a directors' meeting for the purpose of establishing a new policy."

"You want to build a clipper."

"Oh, I'm going to build and sail them for the rest of my days. I'm convinced we'll double our business and treble our profits. And that's a conservative estimate. I'm just hoping Papa and Brad will share my enthusiasm."

Judith believed otherwise, but kept her opinion to herself. "I can't speak for either of them," she said carefully.

"No, but you can speak for yourself. What's your reaction to what I've told you?"

She became still more cautious, knowing the commitment he wanted but feeling she could not offer him support automatically. "When you've built your first clipper," she said, "I hope you'll take the children and me for a sail."

"You know I will," Jonathan said, "just as you realize that's not what I want to know."

Judith felt compelled to match his candor. "Papa's attitude is certain to influence me," she said. "And certainly *you* realize I'll never vote my shares of company stock in opposition to any position my husband takes. I love him, so it should be obvious that I have faith in him as a man, as a shipbuilder, and as someone who is devoted to my best interests."

"I'm not anticipating a conflict," Jonathan said after the main course was followed by bread and raisin pudding. "I'm hoping that Papa and Brad will share my vision of the future." He dropped the subject and thereafter discussed matters of little consequence.

The following morning he felt the need for physical exercise, so he walked several miles to the Anglican church on downtown State Street, arriving just as Judith and her children were entering the family pew. He paused to bow to Louise Graves and her parents across the aisle, and always conscious of his conduct when he knew people were watching him, he did not smile.

Louise, looking even prettier than usual in a flower-printed dress, with her wheat-blond hair tucked under a

27

wide-brimmed straw hat, responded to his salute by nodding solemnly. But he thought he saw her lower an eyelid in a suggestion of a wink. He should have told Judith last night, when he had discussed his relationship with Louise, that they also shared a sense of humor their elders regarded as unusual.

After church he did what was expected of him by joining the Graves family at their carriage and riding back to their house with them. The talk on the drive consisted mostly of Naomi Graves's light gossip about people she had seen at church. Her husband pretended to listen to her, but Jonathan and Louise heard nothing new or startling, so their minds drifted elsewhere.

Jonathan pictured himself standing on the deck of the *Ann McKim* as the clipper sailed downwind as though pursued by demons, and he couldn't help wishing he were on board the trim vessel at this very moment.

He wasn't the only dinner guest. The first to join the Graves family was Ruth Halliburton, Louise's close friend since early childhood. Jonathan had known her all of his life, too, as her father was the chief carpenter at the Rakehell yard, and she was so vivacious that he was pleased to see her. Her presence was guaranteed to lessen the dull solemnity of dinner at the home of a couple to whom dignity was all-important.

As Ruth removed her hat and allowed her dark blond hair to tumble down her back, she averted her face for a moment, but Louise caught a glimpse of the bright expression in her eyes and felt sorry for her. Poor Ruth! She had been infatuated with Jonathan since childhood, and it was evident that her feelings hadn't changed, even though she knew her dear friend would marry him. Ruth had known her cause was hopeless, that a Rakehell heir would not marry the daughter of a shipyard employee, but she had never been taught the self-control that Louise practiced. Only someone who had been reared on the principle of discipline knew it had to be utilized at all times and under most circumstances.

Looking obliquely at Jonathan, who had been handed a small glass of wine by her father, Louise knew he still had no idea that Ruth long had imagined herself in love

28

with him. It was unlikely that he would ever know, in part because he would have rejected the very idea of a romance with the daughter of his father's chief carpenter, and partly, too, because he had also grown up under strict discipline and would have squelched any feelings other than comradeship.

Looking again at her future husband, Louise felt a trifle smug. Their backgrounds were so similar that she knew how he felt about most things most of the time. And what she didn't know she could guess from her own reaction.

The girls chatted with each other in low tones and were sympathetic to the plight of Jonathan, who was forced to listen to one of Dr. Graves's interminable medical stories about a patient whose symptoms he had diagnosed correctly. Certainly the doctor deserved his reputation as eastern Connecticut's leading physician, but all of his stories were alike, and it was difficult to distinguish one from the other.

The atmosphere brightened somewhat when the last guest appeared. The short, stocky Edmund Barker, a native of New Haven, had been Jonathan's classmate at Yale and had his friend to thank for his current employment as second mate on a Rakehell schooner that sailed between New London and the islands of the West Indies. The old friends were delighted to see each other, but Edmund reddened when he bowed to Ruth Halliburton.

Louise, who fancied herself as a matchmaker, smiled quietly. As she had long suspected, Edmund had a definite interest in Ruth, and she herself was not adverse to the idea of seeing Ruth safely married. Even though Jonathan respected conventions, it was dangerous for someone as attractive as Ruth to remain at large. Safety, Louise believed, lay in planning ahead.

"When did you get back, Eddie?" Jonathan wanted to know.

"We docked at the State Street pier at noon yesterday," Edmund Barker said. "Our hold was so crammed with logwood from Jamaica for dyes that we rode low in the water all the way home."

Mrs. Graves announced that dinner was ready, and

they went to the table. Here, as at home, there were no surprises, and Jonathan knew in advance that the meal would consist of clam broth, corn on the cob as a separate course, roast leg of lamb with potatoes and vegetables, and a peach trifle for dessert.

He knew, too, that Mrs. Graves would discuss that morning's sermon in detail. As it happened, the topic had been the indignity of human slavery, and Edmund Barker had a major contribution to make to the conversation.

"I saw slavery on the British islands in the West Indies again, and it's a disgraceful condition." Aware that he had Ruth's full and sympathetic attention, he felt his natural shyness assert itself and began to stammer. He had suffered from the affliction all of his life, but manfully tried to ignore it. "The s-slaves on some of those islands live like an-animals," he said. "But it's a c-condition that won't last. It can't."

"We contribute to the abolition movement regularly," Mrs. Graves said, and her husband nodded.

"We give, too, but it's a waste of money," Jonathan declared. "It's easy enough to believe as we do here, in the free states, but slavery is such an institution in the South that I doubt it will ever be uprooted in the United States."

"I quite agree," Louise said.

"Well, ma'am, I don't!" Edmund was unexpectedly emphatic.

Ruth applauded him.

He was so intense that he forgot his stutter. "There's a rising tide of feeling against slavery in the West Indies," he said. "You see it everywhere, and even the plantation owners know the end is coming. I predict that slavery will be abolished there in five to ten years, no longer."

"That's as it should be," Ruth declared.

Jonathan knew it was bad manners to argue at the dinner table, of course, but he couldn't help saying, "What should be is far different from what really exists in this world. We'll need a major upheaval before slavery is abolished in America."

"You're right," Louise said. "We read abolitionist

tracts, but what good does that do? We already believe what they tell us. Show me a plantation owner in the South who reads them!"

"That's beside the point," Dr. Graves declared. "They should."

The pronouncement by an older man ended the direct discussion of the subject, and the young people fell silent, allowing Mrs. Graves to return to the fine points of the sermon.

After the meal came to an end, the quartet adjourned to the porch that looked out onto the Rakehell property across the street and, beyond it, the estuary of the Thames River. The girls sat side by side on a sofa-swing that creaked slightly when it moved, and the two young men perched on the railing. At last Jonathan felt free to talk about the matter that consumed him. "I've just come back from Baltimore," he said, directing his remarks to Eddie but taking care to include the girls. "I not only saw the *Ann McKim,* I went for a sail in her!"

Edmund was not impressed. "I think these new clippers are over-rated."

"I don't know much of anything about ships," Ruth said, "but my father believes that clippers are freaks."

"Your father is wrong," Jonathan said, "and so are you, Eddie." He launched into a glowing account of the *Ann McKim.*

Louise listened dutifully but made no comment.

"I've come home with one goal in mind," Jonathan concluded. "I'm going to build and sail clippers!"

"What does your father think?" Louise ventured.

"He doesn't know yet. When he gets back from Rhode Island tomorrow, I'm going to ask him to call a directors' meeting, and I'll lay out my plans there."

Louise had known her future father-in-law all of her life and understood him as well as she did Jonathan. "Don't set your heart on it," she warned. "Mr. Rakehell doesn't much care for innovations, and he can be stubborn."

"So can Mr. Rakehell's son," Jonathan said, his jaw jutting forward.

The others looked at him in shocked silence, and even Ruth Halliburton, who believed he could do no wrong, was startled. Edmund retreated carefully, not wanting to get caught in the middle of a dispute developed between his employer and the friend who had done so much to launch his career.

Louise felt that, as a future Rakehell, she had to say something. "I'm sure I needn't urge you to be diplomatic," she murmured. "Perhaps, instead of calling a directors' meeting, you might break your father in to the whole concept of clippers, a little at a time."

"The longer I wait," Jonathan replied, "the longer the lead others will have. Isaac McKim is already having a second clipper built. It won't be long before yards in New York and Marblehead and Boston will be following his example. We'll be left far behind. Look yonder!"

They followed the direction of his long, jabbing forefinger and found themselves staring at a brig that had just emerged from the Thames and, under full sail, was pitching and rolling as she headed for the open Atlantic beyond the eastern end of Long Island Sound.

"As of today," Jonathan said, "ships like that are the backbone of the British, American, and French merchant fleets. The Dutch and Swedes, too. About ninety-five percent of the whole world's merchant marine."

"My father," Ruth said proudly, "was the master carpenter in the building of that brig."

"As it happens, I've sailed on her myself," Jonathan said, "and you'll notice she flies the Rakehell eagle. So it pains me to tell you that tomorrow that brig—and thousands like her—will be obsolete, reduced to carrying cargo between American ports. The seven seas will belong to the bold and the swift—and that means clippers!"

Louise Graves sighed inaudibly. She had been brought up to believe that a woman never argued with a man or contradicted him in public, but she had never heard Jonathan express such positive convictions or show such unyielding determination. But his father, assisted by Bradford Walker, had the final word in every decision made by the Rakehell company, and she was afraid that serious trouble loomed ahead.

Senior employees familiar with the large office that occupied one end of the second floor of the headquarters building that overlooked the shipyard swore that all Rakehells looked alike, and there was a measure of truth in the joke. The portraits of four generations that stood on the wall could have been made of the same man. The newest, only recently completed, was of Jeremiah Rakehell, whose son bore a strong resemblance to him. Energetic at fifty-four, Jeremiah's hair was gray at the temples, his face was lined, and he had more than a suspicion of a paunch, but otherwise he could have been Jonathan's older brother.

The president of Rakehell Building and Shipping sat behind his gleaming mahogany table, adjusting his spectacles slightly as he scanned the new contracts that Jonathan had secured in New York. "You weren't idle, I must admit," he said at last, removing the hated spectacles. "You did well."

Papa's compliments were rare, and Jonathan bowed his head in thanks.

Jeremiah studied him across the desk, a hint of amusement in his eyes. They were so alike, yet so different. The father admittedly was old-fashioned and still wore coats with long tails and pewter buttons, knee breeches and shirts topped by stocks that swathed the throat. Under no circumstances would he be seen in long trousers like his son's, much less coats without tails or the high, standing collars that caught a man under the chin.

But such differences were only surface manifestations. In his own youth, Jeremiah had rebelled against the authority of his father, too, and had been hauled in line for his pains. Now the battle of the generations would be fought again. He had a shrewd idea of what was in his son's mind, and he felt almost sorry for the boy. He held all of the controls in his own firm hands, and he had no intention of relinquishing them. Unfortunately, it was time Jonathan learned a lesson.

Loving him, the older man gave him a final chance to back out gracefully. "You're quite sure you want a directors' meeting called for this afternoon, Jon?"

"I'm positive, Papa."

"It might be easier to discuss whatever you have in mind informally with Brad and me first."

Jonathan shook his head.

Jeremiah sighed, reached for an ivory-handled bell, and rang it. "If you please," he told the clerk who answered the summons, "go to Mr. Browne at the bank and ask him if he'll mind attending a directors' meeting as soon as he can get here. You might remind him he holds the proxy votes of Lady Boynton."

The clerk closed the door behind him, and then he started to run. Jeremiah Rakehell expected orders to be obeyed promptly.

"Your sister may have other plans for the afternoon, Jonathan."

"I think not, Papa. I've already alerted her."

Jeremiah shook his head. The youngster was forcing a showdown. So be it. Perhaps he would be a trifle wiser after he was chastened. "Join me in the board room in an hour," he said.

Too restless to concentrate on the paper work piled on his desk in his own small cubicle, Jonathan left the building and began to roam through the yard. He paused for a few minutes at a maze of scaffolding to watch the construction in progress on a new schooner, and as he listened to the familar cacophony of hammering and sawing, he felt a wave of nostalgia for his own past. Exchanging a wave with Cliff Halliburton, Ruth's father, he directed his attention to what the chief carpenter was doing. Wielding an adze, a tool that resembled a hatchet but had a curved head, Halliburton was truly an expert, Jonathan had to admit. Grandpa Rakehell had claimed that skilled workmen could build a ship with no tool other than an adze, and Jonathan's first toy had been a miniature adze. He was proud of his ability to handle the tool, but he wasn't in a class with Halliburton.

Continuing to make his way across the yard, carefully avoiding mountainous piles of seasoned lumber, Jonathan lingered behind one such pile when he caught a glimpse of a man he disliked. Captain Davis Hartley was one of the senior masters of the Rakehell merchant fleet and certainly he enjoyed Jeremiah's trust. Why, then, was

Jonathan going out of his way to avert a harmless exchange of greetings with the man? He was damned if he knew. Perhaps it was because Hartley had become friendly with Brad Walker. That was it! There was no love lost between him and Brad, and they were civil to each other only for Judith's sake. No, that wasn't true, either. They made it their business to maintain a semblance of a cordial relationship because Papa would not tolerate open hostility between his son and son-in-law.

Glancing at the gold pocket watch he had inherited from his grandfather, he again rehearsed what he would say to the directors as he sauntered back in the direction of the headquarters building.

"Ho, there! Jonnie!"

Jonathan halted, then grinned when he saw the man who had hailed him and was approaching him, his walk the rolling gait of a sailor. Grimshaw was a veteran seaman in his late forties, a grizzled bear whose two gold teeth picked up the sunlight. The senior boatswain in the Rakehell fleet, he had been Jonathan's first instructor at sea, and they had sailed together on a dozen voyages.

Grimshaw enveloped the younger man's hand in a clasp of iron. "I thought ye was too high and mighty for the likes o' me, Jonnie."

"The day I behave that way, you have every right to punch me in the jaw," Jonathan said, and meant it.

"I thought you were on the *Arabella,* bound for England."

Grimshaw's smile became broader. "I had me a few words with your pa, and he let me off'n that assignment. I'm sick o' the English run."

"You're staying sober, I trust."

The boatswain scratched the graying stubble on his chin. "Some days I am," he said, "and some days I ain't. When I start drinkin' more than is good for me, I'll ship out on the first brig your pa has available. Come along, and I'll treat ye to a pint o' ale. There's a new tavern on Bank Street I ain't tried yet."

Jonathan excused himself, explaining he was obliged to attend a meeting. A few minutes later he reached the board room, its walls lined with paintings of ships built and operated by Rakehells for more than a century. The others were gathering, too, and he eased his long frame into a wooden armchair at the foot of the polished oak table.

The group was small. Amos Browne, the head of the local bank, a wizened man with a surprisingly sharp sense of humor, was present as the representative of Jeremiah's sister, Jessica, who owned ten percent of the company's stock. For more than a quarter of a century she had lived in England and was the wife of Sir Alan Boynton, the principal owner of a British shipping company closely associated with the Rakehells in the trans-Atlantic merchant trade.

Bradford Walker, always meticulous in tailored suits and silk shirts, exchanged a cool nod with his brother-in-law, looked for a moment at his highly polished boots, and then glanced through a stack of papers beside him. In his own right he owned only five percent of the Rakehell stock, a gift made to him by his father-in-law, but for all practical purposes, as Jonathan knew only too well, he controlled his wife's ten percent. As Judith herself had said on Saturday night, she could never cast a vote contrary to her husband's wishes.

Jonathan himself owned only five percent, which had been left to him by his grandfather. The remaining shares were owned by Jeremiah, and presumably his son would inherit a controlling interest one day. But not if Brad had his way, Jonathan thought. In the past couple of years Brad had made it plain that he hoped to succeed to the top spot himself.

Judith sat demurely, her hands folded in her lap, and all at once Jonathan felt sorry for her. He had placed her in a difficult position by requesting her loyalty. But that couldn't be helped. The issue at stake was greater than personal considerations.

Jeremiah Rakehell entered the board room from his adjoining office and took his place at the head of the table. "Under the by-laws of this company written by my great-grandfather," he said, "any stockholder may ask that the directors convene. Such a request has been made by Jonathan Rakehell. Inasmuch as this is a special meeting, we will dispense with the reading of the minutes. What's on your mind, son?"

Jonathan looked slowly around the table, holding his enthusiasm in check. "First," he said, "I'd like to tell you about an extraordinary experience I enjoyed two weeks ago." Speaking as dispassionately as he could, he explained his brief voyage on the *Ann McKim* in detail, describing the clipper in glowing terms. Then he distributed the naval architect's designs for the ship. "Before I proceed, I hope you'll look at these."

There was a long silence as the prints were passed from hand to hand.

"Because of the incredible speeds a clipper can attain," Jonathan said, "I'm convinced she is the ship of the future. Therefore, I propose that this board authorize the construction of a clipper and place her in service."

Bradford Walker cleared his throat. "If I read these designs accurately," he said, "a clipper can carry one-third less cargo than a standard merchantman."

"The hold is reduced to almost fifty percent," Jonathan said. "But I believe that by modifying the V-shape of her bottom—without slowing her speed—she might carry as much as sixty percent of a standard ship's cargo."

"Obviously impractical," Brad said with finality. "What would it cost to build a clipper?"

"About five thousand, I estimate," Jonathan said. "I have figures here—"

His brother-in-law waved them away. "Never mind. It would cost us a thousand to fifteen hundred more than we spend on building a ship we know will make money. What kind of cargo do you propose to carry in one of these fancy clippers?"

In spite of his brother-in-law's derogatory tone, Jonathan did not lose his temper. "Until now, Rakehell has concentrated her shipping in voyages to England, Europe, and the Caribbean. A clipper, the first of the fleet, would enable us to enter the China trade."

The others were stunned.

Even Jeremiah lost his poise. "For the sake of the record," he said, nodding to the clerk who sat beside Jonathan, taking notes, "my brother-in-law, Sir Alan

37

Boynton, has been engaged in the China trade out of London for the past three and a half years. Alan and I have been in frequent correspondence on the subject, and he assures me his trade there is highly profitable. For one reason only. His ships pick up opium in India and take it to Canton, where they sell it for silver. Jonathan, are you suggesting that Rakehell should enter the opium trade?"

"No, sir. I am not. Under no circumstances would I deal in a habit-forming drug that destroys human beings. Rakehell has never engaged in slave trade shipping, and I regard the opium trade just as evil, if not worse." Jonathan was emphatic.

Bradford Walker became sarcastic. "If the Boyntons, with all of their long experience, can show a profit in China only by selling opium, how would we earn money there?"

"There is a tremendous potential market in the United States for tea and for silks," Jonathan said. "Look at the sales figures for the tea we import from Great Britain —most of it from China. And at our tea imports from Indonesia, by way of Holland. The English and the Dutch skim off the cream, and we get only what's left. As to silk, let me ask the one lady present. Would you and your friends buy reasonably priced silks from China?"

Judith hesitated for a moment, then spoke reluctantly. "Of course," she said.

Jonathan smiled.

But his brother-in-law was persistent. "What goods would you sell to the Chinese?"

Here was the one weakness in Jonathan's argument, but he was prepared to meet the objection candidly. "I have that matter under intense study," he said. "I've opened correspondence with two Boston merchants who are already in the China trade, and I've also written a long letter to my cousin in England, Charles Boynton. I'm not yet prepared to say what I'd sell to the Chinese, but I hope to have definite information in hand long before our prototype clipper is launched."

"Keep in mind, please," Bradford Walker said sarcastically, "that your cargo space would be severely limited."

"I can assure you I'm not forgetting those limitations." Jonathan turned to the others. "The British and French are entering the China trade on a large scale. Several companies in this country are preparing to do the same thing. *Now* is the time for us to start! If we wait, we'll be left out in the cold! There are tens of millions of people in China, and she's just beginning to open her doors to the West. We have the opportunity of the century!"

"We've prospered in traditional trade," Brad replied.

"You're forgetting the speed that a clipper can achieve," Jonathan said. "I've been making careful calculations, and I estimate that a clipper can sail from New London to Canton in three months, more or less."

His brother-in-law laughed aloud. "Ninety days?" he demanded, his tone mocking. "No ship could reach China in that time, ever! You'd require far more, not less. And even assuming you can find suitable cargo the Chinese might be willing to buy, you well might lose money on your first voyage. Have you taken that into consideration?"

"Naturally." Jonathan remained seemingly unruffled. "I'd allow for a deficit in the budget of five thousand dollars, which is generous."

"In all, then, we'd be ten thousand out of pocket. A small fortune." Brad hooked his thumbs in his waistcoat pockets and looked around the table in smug triumph.

"I don't accept the probability of a loss," Jonathan said. "In fact, I regard it as a very slight possibility. I'm counting on showing a substantial profit on our initial voyage, and more on each succeeding voyage. You keep forgetting the element of speed. I've actually sailed on the *Ann McKim*—"

"For a few hours," his brother-in-law interjected. "You're asking us to squander ten thousand dollars because you enjoyed a sail in Chesapeake Bay!"

Jeremiah entered the discussion. "I think we've heard enough to reach a decision. Brad, you've made your position eminently clear."

"You bet, sir! I'm opposed to this idiocy!"

"Amos?"

The banker removed his spectacles and polished them. "Even allowing for the exuberance of youth," he said cautiously, "it may be that Jonathan has some valid arguments. I've read press accounts of the *Ann McKim*'s sailing records, and they're staggering. On the other hand, I don't know that I'm willing to incur a ten thousand dollar debt on Jessica Boynton's behalf. If clippers are so fast and efficient, Sir Alan Boynton would be using them in his China trade."

"I doubt if he's even heard of them as yet," Jonathan said. "They're a totally new kind of ship!"

"You're out of order," Jeremiah said, and turned to his daughter. "Judith?"

The young woman could not look at her brother as she murmured, "I must agree with Brad's reasoning, so I vote against the building of a clipper ship."

Jeremiah folded his hands across his paunch and leaned back in the only leather-covered chair at the table. "I am obliged to cast the deciding ballot," he said, and after glancing at each of the directors in turn, he directed his remarks exclusively to his son. "This company has done well, in good times and bad for more than a century, because it was founded on principles from which it has never wavered. In the days of the first Jonathan Rakehell, the company made and operated only brigs. A rage for sloops developed, but not one was launched here until the administration of Joseph Rakehell, who knew he was not putting funds into a passing fad."

He paused and sipped a glass of water. "In my own day I've heard competitors in Massachusetts and Rhode Island call us old-fashioned, hopelessly behind the times. Those competitors have gone bankrupt, but we show handsome profits, year after year."

Jonathan knew what was coming and braced himself.

"I admit," Jeremiah said, "that I am curious about clippers. I admire the ingenious design of McKim's ship, and I have little doubt that other, newer clipper ships will establish speed records in the years ahead. But I am reluctant to break the conservative traditions that have caused Rakehell Building and Shipping to prosper. It is possible that, ultimately, after clippers have proved their

40

worth, perhaps when they have been redesigned to carry larger quantities of cargo, we will build them. Until then, however, we shall continue to do what we know and do best. Therefore I must regretfully reject the proposal presented to us today. The meeting stands adjourned."

The clerk left the board room, quickly followed by Judith and Bradford Walker, the latter's steady smile indicating that he was savoring his victory.

Jonathan slowly gathered the naval architect's sketches.

"I'll want a copy of the minutes so I can send them to Jessica," Amos Browne said.

"You shall have them no later than noon tomorrow," Jeremiah replied.

The banker hesitated for a moment, then grasped Jonathan's shoulder before leaving the room.

"Wait for me, Jon," Jeremiah said. "We'll walk home together." As he went into his office for his high-crowned hat and gold-headed walking stick, he failed to notice that his son's jaw was set.

A few minutes later they started on the walk along the riverfront that would take them home. Only in the worst of foul weather would a Rakehell think of riding when the distance was less than two miles.

"Don't take my decision too hard, Jon," Jeremiah said. "I quite agree that the clipper may become the ship of tomorrow, but I can't invest a large sum of money in what may be a gamble."

"Of course I'm disappointed, Papa, but I'm not really surprised," Jonathan said. "So I've already made my contingency plans. When Mama died she left me a nest egg, and with the interest I now have something more than ten thousand dollars in the bank. I'm going to use that money to build and sail a clipper ship." He spoke quietly, but there was a metallic ring in his voice.

The older man stopped short and stared at him. "My God, son! You can't!"

"I'm of age, sir, and the bequest wasn't conditional. I don't believe I'll be gambling with that money."

"But your betrothal is being announced soon, and in another year you'll be married. Unless you and Louise are planning to live with me, in which case you're more than welcome, you'll want to build a house for her, buy her furniture, a team of horses, and a carriage. You'll have good use for your inheritance!"

"I've got to live with myself before I live with Louise," Jonathan said as they resumed their walk. "And I know I won't be satisfied until I build a clipper. I'm already spending my evenings working on designs, and unless you object I'll have them analyzed by the Rakehell architects before I start the actual construction."

It took one Rakehell to understand another, and Jeremiah knew his advice would not be accepted. "By all means," he said, "show your plans to our architects."

"I'd like to ask one more favor, but don't grant it if it embarrasses you. If I must, I'll go up to Rhode Island and rent an independent yard. But I'd prefer to build the ship here, at home, and hire workmen from our own force who aren't otherwise occupied. I realize I'm defying you— challenging you, actually—but I'm still a Rakehell, and I'll be much happier if I can build our first clipper in our own yard."

Jeremiah had to admire his stubborn tenacity. "Your request is granted," he said gruffly, "and if you prove me wrong I'll be the first to eat crow. I just hope you know what you're doing."

Jonathan's quick grin was unexpectedly boyish. "So do I," he said.

They walked the rest of the way in a silence that suggested an armed truce.

"I'll join you for supper," Jonathan said when they reached the house. "But right now I want a word with Louise."

His father watched him as he crossed the street, his youthful stride buoyant and self-confident. The risks he would be taking in building and sailing a vessel like the revolutionary *Ann McKim* were enormous, and the odds against him indicated almost certain failure. All the same, Jeremiah had to admit to himself, grudgingly, that if anyone could bring off the feat, his son would do it. In spite of his own conservatism, he couldn't help wishing that Jonnie would succeed, but that was something he could never admit aloud. To anyone.

"I'd like to speak to Louise on a matter of considerable importance," Jonathan told Naomi Graves.

His manner was so solemn that Mrs. Graves didn't question him as she admitted him to the house.

A few moments later a worried Louise joined him in the parlor, holding her full skirt closely around her as she walked.

Jonathan bowed to her, then told her about the directors' meeting and its aftermath.

The girl's frown deepened as she listened to him.

"You and I have known, almost as far back as we can remember," he said, "that some day we'd marry. Our future was decided for us, so I've never proposed to you, never given you the chance to accept or reject me."

"I hadn't thought of it that way," Louise replied, her frown giving way to a slight smile.

"Well," Jonathan said, "my decision to use my inheritance to do what I believe is right changes all that."

"Do you mean you're leaving your family's company?"

The idea shocked him, and he shook his head. "No, I'm taking what you might call an informal leave of absence. First I'll build my ship, and if I can find the right master, I'll send him to sea with her. But my father is making no attempt to stop me from spending the money my mother left me. That means I won't have a penny for a house, furniture, or a carriage for you."

"I see," she said uncertainly.

"Eventually I'll go back on the Rakehell payroll, probably around the time we're actually married. And I will be earning a couple of thousand dollars a year on my small share of the company stock."

Louise's pretty face cleared. "That makes everything all right, then."

"It does and it doesn't. We may have to live with my father for a spell—"

"I just love that house!"

"—and if my clipper doesn't earn money as I think it will, we may be poor for a few years. That's why I've got to give you the chance, right here and now, to tell me good-bye. If that's what you want."

43

The girl would have preferred to discuss the situation with her parents before giving him an answer, but he was waiting for her reply. "You aren't really breaking with your father."

"No ship could come between us," he replied. "And some day that company will be mine." No matter how much Brad Walker wants it for himself, he added silently.

Louise made up her mind. "The way I see it, nothing is really changed. And I honestly wouldn't mind being poor for a few years."

He realized that, never having known poverty, she didn't know what she was saying. In all fairness to her, however, he had never been poor, either. "That's settled," he said, then added gallantly, "will you marry me, Miss Graves?"

"With pleasure, Mr. Rakehell." Her smile widened.

He extended a hand, drew her to her feet, and for the first time since they had stolen behind the barn as teenagers, he kissed her. She was the only lady he had ever held in his arms—certainly he didn't include the trollops he had known and occasionally visited in New Haven and New York—so his kiss was tentative, restrained.

Louise responded with gingerly circumspection, then hastily withdrew from his embrace and looked embarrassed.

"Seeing that I'm going to be on my own for a long time," Jonathan said, "maybe we ought to set our wedding date ourselves and then tell our families to announce our engagement."

"Oh, that wouldn't be right," she replied. "My mother and father would never forgive us if we didn't leave that important a decision up to them."

For two months the construction of Jonathan's clipper ship proceeded at a maddeningly slow pace. He drew his own plans with infinite care, changing them from time to time, until at last he submitted his prints to the Rakehell naval architects for analysis. "You'll note that her bottom doesn't come to as sharp a V-point as the bottom of the *Ann McKim*," he said.

The senior designer was complacent. "You'll be

sacrificing no speed, and you will gain hold space. The Lord knows you'll have little enough!"

"You'll also see that I'm adding still another sail above the skysail." Jonathan grinned. "I've tentatively decided to call it a moonsail."

The designer filled several sheets of paper with mathematical calculations. "Well," he said at last, "you've come up with something new, no two ways about that. As nearly as I can figure it, you won't be so top-heavy that you'll turn turtle. But you know as well as I do that there's a heap of difference between doing arithmetic on paper and sailing a ship in a storm."

"I've satisfied myself that a moonsail won't be too dangerous," Jonathan said.

The naval architect, interested in the revolutionary design in spite of himself, could only nod.

"You'll also see that I'm going to have six sails on my jib and that I'm increasing the size of my spanker."

"You'll have so blame much sail," the designer declared, "that you're likely to blow your ship clean out of the water!"

"Almost, but not quite," Jonathan said. "That's the whole idea!"

According to his final plans, his clipper would be twenty-three feet longer than the *Ann McKim*, with her length almost six times that of her beam, and her gross displacement burden would be five hundred and fifty tons. Her profile would be even more rakish than that of Isaac McKim's ship.

Only the finest of seasoned oak was used for her hull, and in order to obtain precisely what he wanted, he scoured Connecticut, Rhode Island, and Massachusetts, selecting the timber himself. His keel would be curved because her draught was deeper aft than it was forward and because his mainmast would be stepped so far toward the sharp-raked prow. This forced him to break with convention again, and rather than use a single log for his keel he selected several, which were heavily braced when they were laid.

Older workers at the Rakehell yard like Halliburton would not participate in the construction of a "Satan ship" that defied so many rules of shipbuilding. So Jonathan hired younger carpenters who were doing nothing between assignments. Gradually they became imbued with his own enthusiasm, and they were further encouraged because he spent his own days on the keel blocks, too, laboring shoulder to shoulder with them.

He had not forgotten the art of wielding an adze, his hands became callused and he strengthened muscles whose existence he had virtually forgotten. Executives, members of the office staff, and the crews of merchantmen returning from sea often gathered to stare at him, marveling that a Rakehell would spend hour after hour on the blocks. Jonathan invariably grinned and waved, understanding their curiosity about his strange vessel, but his face became wooden whenever he saw his brother-in-law pass below.

Bradford Walker made a point of ignoring him in return. "It's wrong for a member of the family to lower his dignity that way," the company's general manager complained to Judith. "The one thing I can't understand is why your father doesn't become upset. He just laughs at me when I tell him that Jonathan is injuring the family's stature."

Little by little the long, lean vessel took shape. An ordinary brig or schooner required approximately four months to build, but Jonathan's clipper was going to require twice that long.

"Your brother is mad," Brad told Judith. "He's throwing his money into a sewer."

At the insistence of Dr. Graves, the announcement of his daughter's betrothal to Jonathan was delayed. "I have nothing against the lad," he said. "On the contrary, I admire him for having the courage of his convictions. But I want him to get this clipper ship insanity out of his system and rejoin the mainstream of Rakehell shipbuilding before he marries Louise. Then he'll be able to concentrate on his wife and his proper life's work, as a bridegroom should!"

Jonathan offered to name his ship for Louise and have a figurehead in her likeness made for his beakhead, but she demurred. "It wouldn't be appropriate when our

46

engagement hasn't yet been announced," she said. "People would talk, you know, and some of them would think we've—well, that we've already been intimate."

Under the circumstances he decided to break with convention again and have no figurehead carved. His ship, he told himself, would create her own destiny, just as he himself was doing, and at the right time the right idea for a figurehead would suggest itself to him. Until then the beakhead would remain bare.

Six carpenters went to work finishing off the interior of the vessel, while Jonathan and three others continued to work on the exterior. Again he went off on a trip to select the finest masts he could find, and after he returned he was delighted to see that only a few more days of work remained.

The deck planks, of white pine, had their seams caulked with cotton and "payed" with hot pitch. The seams of the hull planking were sealed in the same manner. Below the waterline the hull was sheathed in copper.

The clipper was launched without fanfare from the stocks via a slipway and was hauled to her fitting out berth. There the masts would be stepped, a delicate and complex operation, and Jonathan decided to supervise the stepping of the mainmast himself.

First the heel was squared off and fitted into steps in the keelson of the ship. Then it was secured in place by shrouds, running from masthead to chainplates on the ship's side, and by stays, which ran from masthead to deck level fore and aft. The yards were crossed, or sent up on the mast, from which they were held in position by lifts.

The job began at daybreak one morning and continued without pause until mid-afternoon. The winter weather had been cold and raw, with layer after layer of leaden clouds overhead. Now, with the mainmast in place, he sent the carpenters off for something to eat while he remained behind so he could look at the mast and enjoy the feeling that his initial task was coming to an end.

He peered up at the stout pole, shivering slightly in the cold and raising the collar of his sailor's pea jacket to ward off the sharp wind that blew from the west. Suddenly the sun broke through, the black clouds began to dissipate and were replaced by an endless series of white clouds that raced across the sky.

The sun shining down on the mainmast was an omen, Jonathan told himself solemnly.

One problem that plagued him was his inability to find the appropriate name for his ship. He thought of many, but discarded each in turn and began to wonder if he was being stubbornly foolish when he refused to seek advice from members of his family. Perhaps. But just as the ship was his creation, her name would be his, too.

That night, at supper, he was more silent than usual, conversing only when necessary as he sat opposite his father. Jeremiah, as usual, occupied what had come to be known as "Uncle Fred's chair." Uncle Fred had been his mother's eccentric bachelor brother, who had lived off an inheritance and had died young of dissipation. His one claim to fame had been a trip around the world that had lasted for three years, and after that journey Uncle Fred, an accomplished woodworker, had carved an oak chair as a memento of his experience. That task had taken him another year.

The centerpiece was a square of ivory, which he had obtained in India. One of the very few foreigners ever to visit China, or the Middle Kingdom, as he insisted on calling it, he had carved a dragon with huge wings out of the ivory to commemorate that visit. The square fitted into the inside back of the chair and was its most prominent feature.

Jeremiah realized his son was preoccupied, so he did not force table talk. But when they had finished eating he asked, "Coming into the parlor with me?"

"I'll join you there, Papa." Jonathan stared at the chair his father vacated, and it was so familiar to him that he did not really see it. Then something stirred in the back of his mind, and he began to focus his attention on the winged dragon. When he had been a very small boy, Judith had teased him after he had misbehaved by telling him the dragon would "fly up the stairs and spank you."

Now he studied the carved ivory figure at length. Neither he nor anyone else in the family had ever seen any Chinese art, so he had no idea whether the dragon was an

48

authentic representation of work done in the Middle Kingdom.

But there could be no doubt in his mind that Uncle Fred had been an accomplished artist. The dragon, long and lean, its expression appropriately ferocious, appeared to be flying with ease through the air. Its body was graceful and arched and was almost dwarfed by the spread of its white wings.

The white, winged dragon, powerful and sleek, would soar and swoop for centuries to come on the back of the chair.

All at once Jonathan knew he had found the right name, the only name for his ship. Strange that he hadn't thought of it previously, inasmuch as he hoped to employ his clipper in trade with China. Yes, it was perfect.

He would name her the *Flying Dragon*.

II

Ships' captains from Great Britain, Europe, and the United States who managed to sail their ships through the maze of the Pearl River Delta swore, with good cause, that there was no other waterway on earth like it. A-shaped and forty miles wide at its mouth, emptying into the South China Sea, the delta was flanked on the southwest by the tiny peninsula called Macao, where the existence of a small colony of Portuguese and other Fan Kuei, or foreign devils, was barely tolerated by the imperial authorities in distant Peking. At the northeast end of the delta lay the lush semi-tropical island of Hong Kong, separated from the mainland Middle Kingdom of China by a narrow channel and uninhabited, although it possessed one of the finest deep-water harbors on earth. Scattered across the wide entrance to the delta lay a string of bleak islands on which only scrub vegetation grew. These islands were so barren that even the countless smugglers and pirates of the area regarded them as useless.

The delta itself was the despair of the unwary. Studded with islands, some of them filled with the shacks of fishermen and others avoided even by gulls and other birds, the delta's sides frequently gave way to peninsulas of varying, odd shapes and sizes. In places, the waterway was so deep that the largest warships on earth could sail through it with ease, but it was filled with treacherous sandbars, and in other places it was so shallow that a man could have stood in waist-high water, provided he didn't sink in the soft, sticky mud.

At the inner end of the A-shape was a spot called the Bogue, behind which stood a series of low-lying hills. Sailing past it into a deep channel for a distance of thirty miles, the ships of the foreigners, surrounded by the saucer-shape, high-hulled junks and tiny sampans of the Chinese, came at last to Whampoa, where the Fan Kuei were compelled to drop anchor and remain, by order of His Celestial Divinity, the Manchu Tao Kuang Emperor.

Here were the only foreign buildings allowed on Chinese soil, the offices and sprawling warehouses, the homes and churches and the jointly operated hospital of the English, French, Dutch, Swedes, Spaniards, and Danes. Here, too, were the recently established consulates of the commercial nations.

Behind Whampoa, where foreigners were forbidden to go except under extraordinary circumstances, lay the great walled city of Kuang-chou, better known as Canton, the capital of Kwangtung Province. Sailors who climbed to the crows' nests of the foreign merchant ships were awed when they gazed out at an endless vista of tiled roofs which stretched as far as they could see toward the high hills that ringed the city, the monotonous scene of closely compressed humanity broken only by the tops of graceful pagoda temples that rose here and there.

In fact, Canton had grown far beyond its walls, and no census ever having been taken, no one, not even the Tao Kuang Emperor or his viceroy for Kwantung, the august Teng Ting-chen, knew the city's population. It was the guess of Peter Snow, the United States Consul, that one and a half million people made their homes in Canton, but the British thought his estimate was low.

Canton lay seventy-five miles from the sea, but only the favored few who lived on the heights at the inner end of the city, just inside the walls, enjoyed an overall view of the teeming metropolis and its surrounding countryside. At the crown of the highest eminence, appropriately, stood the palace of the imperial viceroy, Teng Ting-chen. Below this imposing compound, guarded day and night by soldiers carrying long, curved swords and matchlock muskets, were the dwellings of the mighty.

The mandarin, or ruling class, was divided into nine levels. Those at the very top of the order, distinguished scholars, did not deign to live in Canton and instead made their homes at the Middle Kingdom's great universities and other institutions of high learning. It was said that the mandarins of the first class were so erudite and refined that they were able to communicate only with each other. Mandarins of the second class held the highest posts in the imperial government, so the few who had been born in Canton had gone off to Peking, the seat of all power, to bask in the aura of the Manchu ruler himself.

Therefore, for all practical purposes, the highest-ranking residents of Canton were mandarins of the third class, who were so wealthy and powerful that ordinary people prostrated themselves before them in the classical kowtow that was still practiced everywhere. No member of this class was more powerful than Soong Chao, and none enjoyed greater universal respect.

Born into a family that had been prominent for generations, he had more than trebled its wealth because he held the imperial appointment as principal hong. Only he and the handful of merchants who comprised the co-hong, all of them far lower on the mandarin scale, were permitted to engage in trade with the foreign devils. So, in effect, he was China's chief merchant, making his headquarters in the one port at which foreign ships were permitted to dock. He owned his own warehouses at Whampoa and a half-dozen others that were still larger were located inside the city gates.

Soong Chao's home reflected his stature. Located at the crest of the second highest hill in Canton, a short distance from the viceroy's palace, it was surrounded by a wall of brick that stood twelve feet high. Stationed at the ornately worked iron gate were men of his own guards, dressed in uniforms of purple and carrying ku ming, perhaps the most distinctive of Chinese weapons. Seven feet long, with a metal shaft, the ku ming had a spear at one tip, but it was the other end that was unique. Its most prominent feature was a curved, double-edged blade, either side so sharp that it could decapitate a man, and at the inner end of the knife was a barbed hook four inches long.

The significance of the ku ming was not lost on the people of Canton. The weapon was used in only one other household, that of the viceroy, and any prowler who entered the grounds knew he would be shown no mercy by Soong Chao's majordomo, Kai.

Inside the compound stood a succession of gardens, each encircled by a wall lower than that beyond it. Here flowers bloomed in artful profusion, and there were waterfalls, lily ponds, and miniature rivers, complete with tiny bridges, to delight the eye. At the core stood the nine buildings that comprised the heart of his domain, all of them handsome pagodas of varying, carefully graduated sizes. These buildings of stone and wood were painted in brilliant colors, their floors and connecting, covered paths were made of intricately designed tiles, and the slanted roofs were fashioned of thick tiles that kept the interiors cool during the sub-tropical summers and warm in the raw months of winter.

The largest of the houses was Soong Chao's personal dwelling, and he sat cross-legged on a cushion before a low table of brilliant porcelain, dipping his brush into ink and forming his characters on a sheet of parchment with a quick, sure hand. Dressed in an embroidered, ankle-length gown of the purest silk, he was an imposing figure, tall and broad-shouldered. His ancestors had been northerners, and thanks to careful breeding over the generations, the Soongs still towered over the short, slender Cantonese.

Soong Chao's face was that of a man long accustomed to power and its uses. Relatively youthful at fifty, he wore his thinning hair in a pigtail, and his eyes, behind heavy-rimmed glasses, were cool and shrewd, quick to appraise, slow to judge. The few who knew him well also realized that his eyes frequently gleamed with amusement, as though he were enjoying a private joke.

Filling one sheet of parchment, he began to write on another, but paused, then removed his glasses as a tiny, gray-haired woman came into the room.

Sarah Applegate, her face as stern and uncompromising as the rocks of her native New Hampshire, held the unusual distinction of being the only Westerner who lived permanently in Canton. The widow of a Yankee sea captain who had died at sea, she had been taken into Soong Chao's household nineteen years earlier to act as his baby daughter's governess, and in those years she had become a fixture. The many members of the houeshold staff well knew that her power was second only to that of the master.

Attired in a traditional silk cheongsam, with a high collar and a skirt slit on both sides to facilitate walking, she took care to open the conversation in Mandarin, as she always did. "You sent for me," she said, making a statement of plain fact.

He elected, as he always did, to reply in English. It was one of their favorite games. "Is she prepared, and will she do as I've requested?"

Sarah Applegate slid easily into English, too, speaking with a sharp New England accent. "Really, Chao! You know very well that she is always prepared."

Soong Chao grinned at her, secret amusement creeping into his eyes. "You didn't answer my full question."

"It can't be answered. You don't need me to tell you the girl has a mind of her own!"

The man who controlled all of China's trade with the West remained mild-mannered. "As a rule she listens to you."

"When she wishes." Sarah was curt. "When it suits her convenience. I've tried to tell you for years that she's been granted too much freedom, and now the chickens are coming home to roost."

Soong Chao didn't understand her colloquialism, but he nevertheless knew what she meant. "If I must," he said, "I shall be forced to deal very firmly with her."

"I wish you good luck," Sarah said dryly. "Do you want to see her now?"

He glanced at the stone and jade sundial outside the window behind him. "If you please. I have very little time."

The woman turned and left the room without further ado, and he resumed his writing.

A short time later he heard the familiar, light footsteps of leather-soled high-wedge sandals and looked up in anticipation. When the girl came into the room he couldn't help beaming at her.

Soong Lai-tse lu was exquisitely beautiful, breathtakingly lovely by any standards, those of the East or those of the West. Standing head and shoulders above the young women of Canton, her height was further accented by the high wedges of the shoes she almost always favored. Her slender, supple body, perfectly proportioned, was encased in a silk, dragon-embroidered cheongsam that left little to the imagination, yet was still demure. Her breasts were high and full, her waist so tiny that her father could have spanned it with his hands, her buttocks and thighs firm. And her skirt, slit to the knees on both sides, revealed legs that were long and flawless.

Unlike many girls of her class, her feet had never been bound. Soong Chao was an enlightened, highly educated man who, assuming complete control of his only child's destiny when her mother had died in childbirth, had refused to abide by the ancient, cruel custom.

Lai-tse lu's thick, blue-black hair, straight and shimmering, descended to her waist, and a fringe of bangs covered her high forehead. Long teardrops of an unusual shade of green jade fell from her small ears, and her features were so symmetrical that her face might also have been carved from jade. Her nose was straight, her lips full, the touch of coloring she had added gave them just a hint of sensuality, and her chin was firm, with clean lines.

But her eyes were the most remarkable feature. Set beneath delicate brows and fringed with thick lashes, they were liquid and pure, so large and overpowering that strangers could not tear their gaze from them. But there was more than beauty in her dark eyes. They reflected an intelligence that was rare in any Middle Kingdom woman of her era and revealed a wisdom far beyond her twenty years. But there was far more in her eyes: she had wit, determination, and cunning, and she had inherited her father's subtle sense of humor.

She pressed her hands together in front of her breasts, her brown-lacquered, long fingernails touching in a gesture of respect for her father. Then, abruptly reverting to her natural state, she seated herself in a low stone chair with carved lions' heads on the arms. Deliberately playful, she addressed him in Dutch, one of the many languages of the Fan Kuei that she had mastered. *"Ik vrees, dat ik u derangeer."*

Chao tried to look severe as he replied in English. "There is no need to fear you are disturbing me. On the contrary, as you well know, I have been waiting for you."

Lai-tse lu's quick smile was mischievous. "I would be guilty of filial disrespect if I disputed the word of my father."

"I hope you'll remember that." He removed his glasses and looked hard at her. "I go shortly to present my petition to the viceroy. First, I want you to listen well, and tell me if you detect flaws in what I say."

"I listen," she said.

Chao lapsed into Mandarin. "I will request that I be permitted to build another warehouse, larger than all the rest. I will explain that I will replace the homes of those whose houses I must tear down and that their new homes will be much superior to those that will be destroyed."

Her nod indicated her approval.

"Now, as to the need for a warehouse. A tidal wave of English, Americans, and Europeans who wish to trade with China is striking the Middle Kingdom. So far, we have felt only the froth of the wave's edge, but in the years ahead we shall be inundated. The greed of the white devils is so great that we cannot keep them out." He paused for breath.

"Why not?" Lai-tse lu asked, instantly taking the role of the viceroy. "Do you deny that our soldiers and sailors are courageous?"

"Their courage would be wasted," Chao declared, immediately picking up his daughter's thought. "Our junks will be like sheets of paper when they face the great warships of the West. Our cannon are ancient and ornamental, their cannon are as huge and efficient as they are ugly. Our archers and those who fire our matchlocks are no match for their soldiers, whose rifles cannot miss their targets."

The girl raised her hands over her head and applauded him.

"Besides, we should trade with the Fan Kuei," Chao continued. "We have much to learn from them. They have goods and many inventions that would be useful to us. And we can become wealthy at their expense. They want our tea, our silk, and our porcelain. Let them pay for these products. Since we cannot bar our door to them, let them become our teachers, and let us line our purses with their gold and silver." He halted and looked at his daughter.

"That is all you will say?" she wanted to know.

"It is enough," he replied testily. "Teng Ting-chen has visited this house often enough for you to know he dislikes long speeches."

Lai-tse lu looked radiant. "He is my friend. Often I have played Mah-jongg with him."

"Yes," Chao growled, "and the last time you had the ill grace to beat him!"

She giggled, then sobered. "Take me with you," she begged, "and allow me to speak with him, too."

She was renewing the argument she had presented so forcefully at dinner the previous evening, and as usual, she refused to give up. "It would not be seemly," he said sharply. "Women are inferior beings who do not present petitions to the imperial viceroy!"

Lai-tse lu raised her head and replied succinctly. "I am inferior to no one!"

"I grant that you are right, my daughter, but only behind the walls of our own home. You know far more than most men, and your mind is better tuned. In you is accumulated the wisdom of our ancestors. You and I know it, but the world does not. You would create a scandal if you appeared at the court to present a petition."

The girl shrugged. "People would talk, my father, but there would be no scandal. The sister of the Tao Kuang Emperor does not remain hidden in the quarter of the Forbidden City reserved for wives and families and concubines. She has her own throne only a few feet from the Celestial Throne itself."

"She is the sister of the emperor," he admitted grudgingly.

"At the great university in Nanking there are three young women, all of a lower mandarin class than the

58

Soongs, who are students learning the wisdom of the ages. In Tientsin a woman operates the shipping company that belonged to her late husband, and she earns a far larger profit than he ever made. In Honan Province the niece of the viceroy has written a play that many companies of actors perform. In Chungking—"

"Enough," Chao roared, his patience exhausted. "In Canton the daughter of Soong Chao obeys the orders of her father, as the women of our family have obeyed the orders of their men for tens of generations. You will not come with me to the court! That is an order!"

Lai-tse lu rose effortlessly to her feet and pressed her hands together in a sign of subservience. Then, not speaking again, she walked out without another glance at her father.

He shook his head and rang a tiny bell of carved ivory to summon his palanquin bearers.

The girl took her time strolling down the tiled, covered path that led to her own house. She paused to admire a chrysanthemum blooming in a rock garden, then sniffed a budding black rose appreciatively.

Sarah Applegate awaited her in the living area, and the woman's face was grim. "Well?" she demanded.

Lai-tse lu's eyes were innocent. "My father forbade me to accompany him to the court. But he did not order me to stay at home," she said.

Sarah was outraged. "You have the guile of a viper and the tongue of a snake. Have you forgotten the legend of the merchant's young wife who was transformed into a water buffalo by the gods of wind and rain because she twisted the truth to suit herself?"

"That was just a legend," the girl replied airily. "Besides, I am no man's wife."

"May my God and your gods take pity on the poor man who marries you!"

Lai-tse lu giggled, then walked into her adjoining bedroom and opened a drawer in an intricately carved chest of ebony.

Sarah followed her and watched her suspiciously. "Now what are you doing?"

The girl found what she wanted and held it in the

palm of her hand. "It is only a Mah-jongg tile," she said, wide-eyed.

Her governess stared at her. "There is a story behind that tile, but I can't remember it."

Lai-tse lu remained unruffled. "You told the cook to prepare a pot of Hangchow seaweed soup for you," she said. "It will be tasteless if it simmers too long."

Sarah stamped out, her back rigid, and muttered unintelligibly under her breath.

The girl immediately became busy. Daubing liberal quantities of a lotus and musk scent behind her ears and in the crooks of her elbows, she used a tiny brush to enhance the green line around her eyes and another to touch up the sheen of her lips. After combing her hair she stared at her reflection in a mirror set in jade, and then, still clutching the Mah-jongg tile, she went hurriedly to the smallest house in the compound, slowing her pace to a near-crawl as she approached it, and tapped lightly on the door.

Kai, the majordomo, a burly man in his late thirties with a scar on his face that extended from one temple to the corner of his mouth, was concentrating on sharpening a long, curved knife with an ivory handle. "Come in," he growled in a deep voice, then rose quickly to his feet when he saw his visitor.

Lai-tse lu's radiant smile would have melted a stone dragon. "Do I disturb you?" she asked.

"Never!" Kai slid the knife into his broad belt, then tugged at his tunic of padded cotton to smoothe it.

"I have been told," the girl said as she leaned indolently against a wall lined with rice paper, "that you have many powerful friends in Canton, Kai. I have been told that no door you wish to enter can be closed to you."

"My lady Lai-tse lu hears too much," the giant muttered.

She ignored his comment. "I know why the story is true," she said.

"Whoever may have told you that tale exaggerates!"

Again she paid no attention to his protest, but she took care to lower her voice. "It is said that Kai is a member of the Society of the Oxen."

"The teller of that tale lies!" he shouted.

She well understood the reason for his agitation. Secret societies had been forbidden for centuries by the Manchu rulers of China, but they nevertheless existed in defiance of the law. The Society of the Oxen was particularly suspect at the imperial court because it was an organization of patriots who regarded the Manchu, correctly, as foreign invaders who had captured the throne.

"As we are told in the old myths," the girl said sweetly, "oxen first lived only in heaven, but the Ox Star made an error and allowed them to come to the earth. Here they devote themselves to helping man, even though they are abused for their efforts. So it must be with the Society of Oxen."

She was so sharp-witted and had come so close to the truth that Kai became even more uncomfortable. "I deny that I belong to any society," he insisted.

"I challenge you to prove that you carry no tattoo mark on your left shoulder!" Her steady smile took the sting out of her words.

"What would your father think if I dared to remove my tunic in your presence? And what would Missy Sarah do? She'd have me skinned alive."

"I have reason to believe," Lai-tse lu went on, "that Lo Fang, the majordomo in the household of the imperial viceroy himself, also is a member of the Society of Oxen. That makes him your brother."

Kai's eyes glittered dangerously. "He who talks out of turn about secret matters has his throat slashed!"

"Oh, no one told me these things," she said, her fluttering hands indicating her feminine helplessness. "I see people. I watch them. I listen to them. Then I put pieces together, as one fits parts of a box puzzle together."

Kai inhaled, then exhaled sharply. Had she been anyone but the beloved daughter of the master he was sworn to protect and honor, he could have throttled her with his huge, bare hands. But Lai-tse lu was a very special person and, he and his friends were convinced, only one who was favored by the gods could be so lovely and at the same time so intelligent.

"If you wished," she said softly, "you could gain

61

admission for me to the audience chamber of Teng Tingchen."

"For what purpose?" he demanded, not realizing he was admitting he could accomplish the virtually impossible feat.

Lai-tse lu became even more innocent. "My father today presents a petition to the emperor's viceroy, and I helped him to prepare the words he will speak. It is my dearest wish in all this world to hear what he will say."

Kai's mind functioned slowly, so it took him a long time to weigh the request.

The girl displayed monumental patience, seemingly undisturbed by the silence.

The request was unusual because women never attended the viceroy's audiences, but she seemed to have no ulterior purpose in mind. "You would need to be masked to hide your identity," he said.

"Of course. I will wear the same mask I wore when you escorted me the day I went shopping in the Street of the Beggars."

"You would also need to stay at the very rear of the audience hall and not call attention to yourself."

Lai-tse lu nodded with what appeared to be breathless eagerness.

It didn't occur to the majordomo that she really hadn't agreed to his condition. "Well," he said at last, "I suppose it would do no harm."

"Please, Kai," she said beseechingly, and touched his arm.

He thought of the fable of the stone dragon that melted and felt the same way. "All right. But first I'll need to have a word with Missy Sarah."

"You'll find her in the dining pavilion," Lai-tse lu said at once, her manner becoming crisp. "I shall meet you in a quarter of an hour's time at the Coral Gate. My chair bearers should not wear the uniform of the house of Soong because it would be too easy to identify me."

Kai nodded and hurried off to the pavilion.

For a small woman Sarah Applegate had a prodigious appetite, but she never gained an ounce. Now she sat, happily dropping liver dumplings into her Hangchow seaweed soup and eating them with relish.

"You'll get indigestion," Kai said as he joined her.

"Watch your own plate," she told him, reverting to an American expression.

"I have none," he replied logically, then told her about his conversation with Lai-tse lu, omitting only any mention of the Society of Oxen.

"That girl!" the exasperated Sarah said. "She can twist you around her little finger."

He smiled sheepishly. "It is the loveliest of fingers," he said.

"You've promised to take her to court?"

"Well, I agreed. I wouldn't call it a promise."

"Then there's nothing I can do to stop either of you. Very well." She tapped her curved, broad porcelain spoon on the tiled dining table to emphasize her words. "The wrath of Soong Chao will descend on your head and that of the girl. Not on mine. I think you've lost whatever tiny common sense you ever possessed."

Kai was puzzled. "Why should Soong Chao become angry? The girl does as she pleases, as all of us know, and he treats her more like a business partner than a daughter."

"Nevertheless, she *is* his daughter," Sarah said primly, pausing to eat a spoonful of the steaming soup. "She claims her father forbade her to go to the court with him, but that he did not forbid her to attend it herself. She may be technically correct. She almost always is in such matters. But he'll be furious if she creates a disturbance and mortifies him. Teng Ting-chen is his friend, to be sure, but he would lose face if he should be embarrassed in the presence of the court."

"I'll be right there, myself," Kai said. "I'll stand close to her, and I won't allow her to create a disturbance."

"You?" Sarah laughed. "My friend, you are as bumbling as the mythical Phan-ku, who was so enormous he filled all of the space between heaven and earth. Lai-tse lu is as delicate as the bird-goddess that inhabits bamboo groves. She will act as she pleases, and she'll be done with it before you even know what has happened. But enough!

I've warned you, and I can do no more. Go, so I can enjoy my soup!"

Kai left the pavilion and summoned six chair bearers, telling them not to change into uniforms from their solid gray cotton tunics and trousers. They followed him to the Coral Gate at the third of the inner walls, but he saw no sign of the girl.

Lai-tse lu stepped out from behind the gate, the upper part of her face covered with a mask of black silk, the conventional disguise of high-ranking ladies when they were carried on shopping expeditions in the city's seamier neighborhoods. He was satisfied that no one would know her.

While the bearers lowered her palanquin to the ground and waited until she seated herself in it before lifting it to their shoulders, Kai hurried back to his own house for his long, double-edged sword, a massive curved blade so heavy that only someone endowed with his great strength could wield it.

Lai-tse lu closed the curtains of knotted cotton that permitted her to see without being seen. So far her little scheme was working to perfection, but it had required more time than she had estimated, and she hoped to arrive at the court before her father presented his petition.

Kai strode beside the palanquin, and the bearers made their way down the hill, then climbed the higher slope, trotting in unison and taking care not to jostle or shake their rider.

A short time later, having pushed through the ever-present crowds of pedestrians who clogged the narrow, winding streets, they reached the high, thick walls of the palace. Here the bearers halted, and Kai, without identifying himself, asked the officer of the guard to send for Lo Fang.

Lai-tse lu smiled to herself behind the knotted curtains. Her guess about the Society of the Oxen had been right.

The viceroy's majordomo was even taller and huskier than Kai. His nose had been broken in a fight years earlier and seemed to spread across his face; his entire head was shaved, which emphasized his oversized ears, and his skin was pockmarked. The girl shuddered slightly and thought he was the ugliest, most menacing brute she had ever seen.

Kai and Lo Fang exchanged hand signals so quickly that Lai-tse lu couldn't quite make them out. Then the bearers started forward again, with the majordomos on either side of the palanquin. Her great adventure was about to begin, and her pulse raced, but she managed to look cool and self-possessed.

The palace gardens were many times larger and far more elaborate than those at her father's house, and there were so many walls, so many gates through which they passed that she stopped counting them. Soldiers in dusty yellow uniforms, armed either with ancient matchlocks or swords, seemed to be everywhere.

They passed a huge fountain and came to the massive, polished doors of a pagoda at least as large as Canton's biggest temple. The building was completely surrounded by smartly uniformed imperial guards in black, red, and yellow, each standing at rigid, unmoving attention, each gripping a deadly ku ming. The weapon was effective, the girl remembered Sarah telling her years earlier, only if the curved blade of the larger end was sharp enough for a man to shave his face with it.

One of the doors opened noiselessly on oiled hinges, and the bearers lowered the palanquin to the ground. Lai-tse lu stepped out and, taking a deep breath, walked into the pagoda in which viceregal audiences were held. The burly majordomos remained close at her sides.

At least one hundred imperial guards armed with ku mings lined the inner walls, and some of them blinked when they saw the cheongsam-clad girl, but they were so disciplined that not one moved.

Lo Fang tapped Lai-tse lu on the shoulder and indicated with a gesture that she was required to halt. Her hand, tightly closed around the Mah-Jongg tile, felt clammy.

Seventy or eighty men, some of them academicians in black, others in colorful silk gowns that indicated they were wealthy merchants or prosperous professional men, a few in the cheap cotton tunics and trousers of humble artisans, all stood with their backs to her, all facing the jade and peacock feather throne on the dais at the far end of the chamber, as protocol demanded. A number of gowned officials of the court stood in the intervening open space, among them the Tea Taster, the Cup Bearer, and the Fan Holder. In spite of their quaint, ancient titles, these nobles were mandarins of high rank and held positions of great responsibility and authority.

Nearest the throne, also facing it, holding a staff decorated with a tiger's tail of silk in one hand and a sheet of parchment in the other, stood the first assistant to the viceroy, the chamberlain.

Seated on the throne in a gown embroidered with pearls, with a pearl-studded, square hat on his head, sat Teng Ting-chen, the Deputy and Personification of His Celestial Majesty, the Tao Kuang Emperor. Only a few years older than Soong Chao, the viceroy looked very regal, very distant, little resembling the cherubic, smiling man with whom Lai-tse lu had joked, eaten meals, and played Mah-Jongg. Her heart beat still faster.

If her presence displeased him, she knew, her family would be so badly disgraced that she would be banished to their country house in the hills and would be compelled to remain there, a virtual prisoner, for at least two years. There would be such a blot on the name of Soong that her father would never forgive her, and no eligible bachelor would ever step forward to claim her as a bride. In fact, she would be lucky if some high-placed nobleman paid her father for her services as a concubine, a prospect that made her blood run cold.

She could leave at once, she knew. No one had seen her here, no one would ever believe she had actually engaged in such a mad escapade. But she wasn't breaking tradition for sport. She had come here for a specific purpose, and if it proved necessary to make her presence known she would do what had to be done. Her legs trembled slightly, but her face, behind the silk mask, remained expressionless.

The chamberlain called the name of her father, and Lai-tse lu knew that, whatever might become of her, she could not leave now.

Soong Chao advanced on the tile floor to the outer end of a long, rich rug that stood below the throne, then lowered himself to it in a ceremonial kowtow, his forehead touching the floor three times.

The viceroy ordered him to rise.

He stood, and glancing occasionally at the parchment on which he had made his notes, he delivered his speech.

Teng Ting-chen's face was wooden, and it was impossible for the girl to read his reaction.

When her father stopped speaking, there was a silence.

Then the viceroy spoke. "We regret," he said austerely, but with a hint of sympathy for his friend, "that the facts as presented to us do not warrant the granting of the petition."

He continued to speak, but Lai-tse lu heard no more. The time had come for her to act! Now, instantly!

She drew a deep breath, steadied herself, and turned to Lo Fang. Her manner patrician, she nevertheless addressed him in the dialect of the Cantonese lower classes. "Take this to the viceroy," she whispered, pressing the Mah-Jongg tile into his hand.

The viceregal majordomo blinked at her in astonishment.

"At once!" she commanded fiercely.

She never knew whether her beauty, her manner, or a combination of both sent Lo Fang forward.

Kowtowing even before his master stopped speaking, the majordomo handed him the little oblong of bamboo and ivory, then muttered something to him that no one else in the hall could hear.

Lai-tse lu held her breath. Her fate, her entire future would be determined in the next few seconds.

Teng Ting-chen turned the tile over and over in his hand, his expression bemused. All at once he chuckled aloud.

The girl was so relieved she was afraid, for a moment, that she might faint.

"Two months ago," the viceroy said to the assemblage, "it was our great pleasure to play a game of chance with a friend. A remarkable friend, one who was too honest to lose a game deliberately because of our high station." He held up the counter so everyone could see it. "We gave this tile to our friend, whom we told to present it to us if ever the time should come when we could grant a special favor. The tile has been presented to us at this moment. Ever mindful of our word, we ask our friend to step forward."

Lai-tse lu's legs felt shaky, but she held her head high as she threaded through the crowd, smashing a precedent as old as the Middle Kingdom itself.

The petitioners were so amazed they began to murmur to each other, and the officials of the court gaped when they saw the young woman approach.

Soong Chao recognized his daughter instantly in spite of her mask. He grew pale, and a white line formed around his tightly compressed lips, but he did not dare intervene. The matter had passed out of his hands.

The chagrined Kai recalled what Missy Sarah had told him and cursed himself because the little she-devil had outsmarted him.

Lai-tse lu halted when she reached the carpet. Women did not kowtow, but she lowered herself to the floor, sinking onto the rug with her legs crossed in front of her, her back erect, and her shoulders squared, somehow managing to accomplish the feat gracefully in spite of the handicap created by her tight-fitting skirt. Pressing her palms and fingertips together, she raised her head and looked at the viceroy.

Teng Ting-chen's smile indicated that he was thoroughly enjoying the unique experience that, he well knew, would create countless legends. "Rise," he said, "and remove your mask, so that all in the Middle Kingdom may learn the identity of a lady who is courageous as well as bold."

The girl's sense of the dramatic impelled her to take off the silk mask very slowly.

Her beauty was so great that the men stared even harder at her.

Soong Chao looked as though he were on the verge of a collapse.

"What is the favor you seek, Soong Lai-tse lu?" the viceroy asked.

"If it please Your Celestial Highness," she said in a clear, musical soprano, "I would like to present aspects

68

of the last petitioner's request that might cause Your Celestial Highness to change his mind."

Teng Ting-chen was delighted, but curbed a desire to laugh aloud. "You may proceed," he said gravely.

"The Middle Kingdom," Lai-tse lu said, the volume of her voice rising, "suffers great agonies, thanks to the wickedness of foreign devils. Men and women become skeletons because of the opium that is smuggled into our land. Men and women die by the hundreds and by the thousands, thanks to the curse of this vile drug. The foreign devils break the laws of the Tao Kuang Emperor when they sell this drug. But the Chinese who buy it and sell it to our people also break the law. The foreign devils are right when they say they sell to us only because we ourselves create a market for the opium."

The viceroy recognized the validity of what she was saying, and many in the crowd nodded emphatically. But no one knew where she was leading or what the connection might be with the petition her father had presented.

"Your Celestial Highness does much to stop the traffic in opium, but you do not succeed. Soong Chao tries, too, but he also fails."

Men looked at each other. She was telling the truth, to be sure: the viceroy was making valiant efforts to choke off the drug trade, yet opium continued to pour into the country. Surely this inexperienced female had to realize it was dangerous to inform the deputy of the emperor that his policies were a failure! People had been tortured to death for less!

"But not all foreign devils are wicked," Lai-tse lu went on. "There are many who obey our laws and offer us merchandise that is legitimate in return for the tea and silks and porcelains they crave. So it is we ourselves who are to blame when we do not buy these goods. In the house of my father I have heard men say, just as Your Celestial Highness has heard it said, that China has no need for foreign products. I have heard it said that we have all we need here for our happiness. That is nonsense! Sheer rubbish!"

Teng Ting-chen was no longer smiling and watched her intently, his eyes guarded.

"The ships of the Fan Kuei," she continued passionately, "are larger and faster than our junks. Their guns hit their targets, while our matchlocks often explode in the hands of our soldiers. Their cloth of cotton and wool is finer than that of China because they have better looms. It was we who invented printing, but they make books that are superior, and they produce them in larger quantities. Their physicians use modern medicines that cure the sick, when all too often our sick do not recover because our physicians still use ancient remedies that should have been discarded long ago. The foreigners have countless factories, and in them they make so many things we need. Tools for our farmers. Tools for our carpenters and masons. Warm clothes so our people do not freeze to death in winter!"

By now the viceroy was leaning forward on his throne, listening to every word.

"We must stop refusing to trade with the Fan Kuei," Lai-tse lu said. "If we buy what we need from them and sell them what they want, it will become easier to stop the sale of opium in return for our silver. We need more merchants, more warehouses filled with tea and silks and jade and porcelain. Let the Fan Kuei prosper. We shall prosper, too." Again she sank to the floor and pressed her hands together.

There was a long silence. The viceroy remained immobile, no one spoke, and a man's quiet cough sounded like a shout.

Soong Chao gripped the handle of the ceremonial dagger so hard that his knuckles turned white.

At last Teng Ting-chen spoke. "The argument that Soong Lai-tse lu has presented to us is of great interest," he said. "As we have learned to our sorrow, there are so many islands in the Pearl River Delta that it has proved impossible to prevent the smuggling of opium into the Middle Kingdom, even if we were to forbid all traffic with the Fan Kuei. Now it is argued that if we increase our legitimate trade with the foreigners, the demand from us for their products and their demand for our products will be so profitable that fewer and fewer men will be willing to risk their lives and lose all their silver for a drug that vanishes in smoke. Soong Lai-tse lu, we applaud your rea-

70

soning. You have a wisdom beyond that of our court and our official advisors. The petition of Soong Chao is granted. May your new warehouses help our people and make us more prosperous!"

The tea-smoked dish of Szechwan duck was a sophisticated masterpiece that had taken the principal Soong cook and his assistants two days to prepare. A plump duck had been rubbed, inside and out, with a mixture of spiced salt and saltpeter, then left in a shady place to dry for a day and a night. Today a combination of black tea, sugar, rice, and the peels of lemons, oranges, and limes had been placed in a pot to boil, and ultimately a quantity of brown rice wine had been added. Then the duck had been placed on a rack over the pot and had steamed for several hours before being cut into bite-sized pieces and fried in peanut oil to crisp it. Served with the rice from the pot, it was a meal fit for the emperor himself.

But the three people who sat at the dinner table had little appetite. They ate in a gloomy silence, and there was no sound in the handsomely furnished room but the occasional clicking of ivory chopsticks.

"The fault is mine alone," Sarah Applegate said at last. "It was I who filled the girl with the spirit of American independence. It was I who gave her the writings of Jefferson and Madison to read. But not even in the United States would any woman be so lacking in filial respect that she would defy her father and make an exhibition of herself. I'm ashamed. Not for her, but for me." The woman from New Hampshire had not wept since the day she had learned her husband had been lost at sea, but she was on the verge of tears now.

"I would have lost face if my petition had been rejected," Chao said, speaking with slow emphasis. "Now, instead, thanks to the warehouses I shall build, my profits will be doubled. No man in all of Kwantung other than the viceroy himself will be wealthier. But I pay a great price for the gold and silver I shall earn. The name of my daughter is already on every tongue in Canton. Soon the stories will reach the Forbidden Palace in Peking itself. Only the gods of our fathers know what wild tales will be whispered

71

into the ear of the Tao Kuang Emperor. Oh, I am sure his sister who sits on her own throne near his will approve. So will all of the young people who are abandoning the ways of our ancestors."

Lai-tse lu sat with downcast eyes, neither moving nor speaking.

"If I had been allowed to do as I wished," her father continued, "I would have sent her to the country with a square wooden stock, each side four times the span of a man's hand, around her neck. For one month she would have been forced to sleep either standing or sitting on a stool. The next month, after removing the stock, I would have had chains of lead placed around her ankles and wrists for a month. The third month . . ." His voice trailed away. "But I may do none of these things. The viceroy ordered me to stay behind after the petitioners were dismissed and commanded me to inflict no punishment on my daughter for her conduct. He delights in her and says she is unique."

"Oh, she's unique," Sarah said. "No one can argue that!"

Lai-tse lu's gentle sigh sounded like the rustling of willow branches in a light breeze. "I alone am to blame for what I did," she said. "If I bring discredit to my father and dishonor the proud name of my ancestors, it is I who must pay the penalty."

Chao picked up a sliver of duck with his chopsticks and ate it reflectively. "What I cannot understand," he said, "is how you talked Kai, who is faithful to me in all things, to take you to the court. Or how you persuaded that brute, Lo Fang, to admit you to the audience chamber."

The girl made no reply, fighting hard to curb the giggle that threatened to well up in her.

Even though her face was lowered, Sarah became aware of her surreptitious smile. "I daresay she blackmailed them," the woman declared.

"Is that true?" Chao demanded.

"Kai is my friend," Lai-tse lu said. "And Lo Fang was kind and generous. It is enough that they do no wrong. They are loyal to their masters, and they love their country above all else."

Her father guessed she had learned or divined that the two majordomos belonged to one of the secret societies. For his own sake he wanted to know no details because it would place him in a difficult position if the viceroy or his staff ever discovered that he had failed to report that a member of his household belonged to one of the forbidden organizations. He was a patriot, himself, and had no love for the Manchurians who claimed the throne and brought their own troops to the Middle Kingdom to protect them.

The girl breathed a trifle more easily when she realized her father was dropping the subject.

Suddenly Chao smiled and began to eat with greater appetite. "Our situation could be far worse," he said. "No one was killed today. I saved face, and I shall need new strongboxes to keep the additional money I shall earn. What's more, the argument that my daughter presented to the viceroy really does have merit. As our people engage in more and more legitimate trade—and gain by it—the more reluctant they will become to risk execution for importing opium."

Sarah picked up her chopsticks, too. "People always gossip about something. That's as true in the world where I lived as it is here. Soon there will be a new sensation somewhere, and today's incident will be forgotten."

The relieved Lai-tse lu reached for her own chopsticks. She was being forgiven, and tea-smoked duck, after all, was one of her favorite dishes. What was more, she was ravenously hungry now that the day's tensions were dissipating.

Again they ate in silence for a time.

Suddenly Sarah exchanged a meaningful glance with Chao. "What will become of her, do you think?" She spoke as though the girl were not present.

The urbane merchant shook his head. "No mandarin of the first three classes whom I have ever known would allow his son to marry someone of greater intelligence and shrewdness than her husband." He took it for granted that under no circumstances would she ever marry anyone of a lower mandarin class.

"The thing that troubles me," Sarah replied, "is that

73

she's not only beautiful, but she uses her beauty. She knows how powerful a weapon it is. If I hadn't wanted to box Kai's ears, I could have felt sorry for him today."

Lai-tse lu could no longer control the mirth that rose within her, and she laughed aloud.

Her father shook his head. "Just listen to her, Sarah! She is incorrigible!"

"Only the Almighty I still worship knows what deviltry she'll perform next."

The girl swallowed her laughter. "I'll behave myself, you'll see," she said demurely.

"For the moment," her governess declared. "Until you think we've forgotten today's episode."

Lai-tse lu did not reply, but she turned to face the older woman for a moment, and there was more than a suggestion of a challenge in her eyes.

Chao, unaware of the byplay and thoroughly enjoying his meal now, remained immersed in his own thoughts. "It may be that in a place as remote as Chungking," he said, "there will be an upper level mandarin—with a son eligible for marriage—who will not hear of what took place today."

His daughter looked at him reproachfully. "Have I become so repugnant to you, my father, that you would marry me immediately to some clod from a distant province who smells of the manure from his father's barns and cannot distinguish between jade and quartz?"

"Not at all," he replied, his sincerity genuine. "But I am worried about you. On your next birthday you will be twenty-one, ripe for marriage, but the reputation you have been acquiring will prove to be a great handicap."

"I will marry," Lai-tse lu said, her manner suddenly lofty, "only when I meet the man who will love me as much as I love him."

"Romantic piffle," Sarah said with a sniff.

Chao became coldly dignified. "In this house we are not as modern as all that. Because you succeeded in defying me today, do not think you can do so in matters of even greater importance. At the appropriate time I will choose your husband for you, and you will marry him in accordance with my wishes."

Suddenly submissive, she bowed her head and mur-

74

mured, "Yes, my father," but he could not see her tightly clenched fists beneath the table.

Sarah laughed dryly. "Chao," she said, "you create an issue where none exists."

He nodded unhappily. "I fear you are right. Nowhere in the Middle Kingdom could we find a man willing to marry a girl of such great beauty—whom he could not control."

"Nowhere in all the world is there such a man," Sarah said. "Not unless he took leave of his senses!"

III

Gas lamps flickered, their shadows playing on the Greek columns and gleaming white paint of the stately mansions that lined Belgravia Square in one of London's most fashionable districts. Not for another two hours, when dawn broke, would armies of cooks and housemaids and butlers begin to appear in kitchens and go about the business of preparing multi-coursed breakfasts for the noble, distinguished, and wealthy whom they served.

An oil lamp was burning in a third-floor bedchamber in the house of Sir Alan Boynton, baronet and chairman of the shipping company that bore his name, but even if a neighbor chanced to awaken and see the glow he wouldn't have been surprised. The bedchamber was that of Charles Rakehell Boynton, Sir Alan's son and principal heir, and everyone who was anyone in London knew he was a Rakehell in more ways than one, his conduct more than matching his mother's maiden name. The unsurprised neighbor would have assumed he was living up to his reputation and had just returned from a night at the gaming table or in the bed of an attractive wench.

No one, particularly those who knew him best, would have believed the truth. Charles had retired immediately after eating dinner with his parents and adopted sister, had slept soundly, and was now preparing swiftly and efficiently for a new day. A bath would have made too much noise, as the new indoor plumbing recently installed in the mansion was inclined to be temperamental. So he washed in his own room, shaved with greater care than usual, then dressed in the clothes he had laid out the previous night. A black suit of fine worsted, black stockings and boots, and a black cravat. Only his shirt of expensive lawn was white.

He combed his blond hair, as pale as that of little Elizabeth, and thought it small wonder that strangers automatically assumed they were brother and sister by birth. Then he clamped a square-crowned bowler hat onto his head, saluted himself with a pair of black gloves, and for a moment studied his reflection in the pier glass, the expression in his light blue eyes ironic.

Ruggedly handsome, thanks to his mother. Obviously a Rakehell, in spite of his fair coloring, although he bore a resemblance to his father, too. What a waste. "We who are about to die salute you," he said softly and, leaving the room, crept down the corridor.

A floorboard creaked beneath him, and Charles cursed silently but fluently. He'd never manage to leave the house if his mother or father awakened. He continued to grope in the dark as he made his way to the landing.

Just before he reached it, a door opened, and a little girl, clad in a nightgown and robe, blinking in the light of the candle she had just lit, gazed at him with sleepy eyes. "Wherever are you going, Charles?" she asked.

He waved her frantically into her room, followed, and closed the door behind her. "You'll awaken the whole house with those bloody great shouts. Do lower your voice."

The child giggled, but continued to peer at him.

Ordinarily Charles held the advantage, thanks to his twenty-four years, and he tried now to utilize it. "Child," he said severely, "you'll catch ague, running about in bare feet. Go back to bed at once, if you please."

Elizabeth did not remove her gaze from him as she stepped into a pair of slippers. Wide awake now, she had no intention of following his orders. "You haven't told me where you're going."

"If you must know," he replied in a conspiratorial whisper, "I'm driving out to Windsor Castle and taking Princess Victoria to supper."

"Silly. Just because you went to her garden party doesn't mean she'd accept an engagement with you. A girl who is going to be queen is allowed to go out only with kings and princes and dukes."

"If you say so, dear child," he replied with exaggerated condescension as he started to edge back to the door.

"Oh, no you don't," Elizabeth said. "I am not your dear child, so that settles it. Either you'll tell where you're going at this hour—and tell me the truth—or I'll wake up Papa. No, I'll do even worse. I'll call Mama."

"How happy I was all those years before you came into my life, you little toad."

"Tell me, you great toad," she replied, standing up to him.

Charles looked at the pocket watch Grandpa Rakehell had given him and then sank into a chintz-covered chair with a sigh. "Rick is coming for me, so I have only a few minutes. First you must swear never to repeat what I'm going to tell you. Unless—I don't show up at the office later in the morning."

She saw he was serious now and was impressed. "I swear, so get on with it."

"The other night," Charles told her, "I became involved in an argument—a stupid, senseless argument—over a girl."

"Who?"

"Elise."

"How could you? Everyone knows she's a harlot."

"Children of your age aren't supposed to know of such things. Besides, I've already told you the argument was idiotic."

The way the little girl tapped her foot was reminiscent of Jessica Boynton when she lost her patience.

"Well, one thing led to another," Charles said lightly, "so right now I'm off to Richmond Park to fight a duel."

"Elise isn't worth the risk of your life. Have you thought of that?"

"I've thought of many things. But my honor is at stake, which you may or may not be able to understand."

Elizabeth placed the candle-holder on her bedside table, turned to him, and threw her slender arms around his neck. "Be careful, Charles! You're the only brother I've ever had, and I'd miss you awfully if you didn't come back!"

He kissed her on the forehead, then disengaged himself. "I'll come back," he said grimly, then softened. "No tears now, and don't forget. Mum's the word."

She nodded solemnly, too choked to speak.

He let himself out of her room, then walked as quietly as he could down the broad marble steps. What a dear little tyke, young for her age in some ways, strangely adult in others. He supposed her background was responsible for all that. Actually the daughter of his father's junior partner, she had been adopted at the age of three when her own parents had been killed in a freakish carriage accident. She was ten and a Boynton now, although she was no blood relative, and some day she would own a minority interest in Boynton Shipping in her own right. When that time came, and even before it, she'd be one of England's most eagerly sought heiresses. He hoped he'd be on hand then, so that he could protect and advise her.

He hoped he'd be around? He'd damned well make it his business to be here!

Closing the front door behind him, he walked quickly down the cobblestones of Belgravia Square to a corner, where a phaeton pulled by a team of two horses was drawing to a halt. Charles sprinted to it and climbed in beside the driver, a young man of his own generation. "Morning, Rick."

"There's a jug of coffee under the seat if you haven't yet had any," his friend said. "But don't drink too much of it. You'll need a steady hand and a sharp eye."

"Don't you worry about my hand and eyes. You've brought a pair of blades?"

"Of course. But Nelson is the challenged party, remember, so I'll be surprised if he doesn't elect to use his own swords. The choice is his."

Charles fell silent, and as he drank the hot, black coffee, he became immersed in his thoughts. Obviously, this was the time for reflection, so he'd make the most of it.

For the past three years, ever since he had come down from Oxford and had spent fourteen months as the mate on a Boynton schooner, he had been tearing off London's roof. Oh, he hadn't neglected his work at the company, and even his father would admit he had done well. But his evenings had been devoted to gaming, wenching, and drinking, not necessarily in that order. And he had been lucky. Thanks to a recent winning streak, he was slightly ahead at cards. Not one of the many assorted wenches he had bedded had become pregnant or given him the French disease. And because of something in his physical nature, perhaps his rugged constitution, he was always clear-headed after a night of heavy drinking.

But the games of chance he had played made him realize that the odds would turn against him sooner or later. The time to change was right now, before a catastrophe of some kind overcame him. The day would come when Boynton Shipping would be his company, and he would also inherit a baronetcy and his mother's interest in Rakehell Building and Shipping. The business fascinated him, and he was seething with ideas, but he could do little if he should be incapacitated and nothing if he were killed.

Charles knew he could explain his self-disgust in one word. Elise. With her flaming red hair, her full scarlet mouth—and her wanton ways. Little Elizabeth had been so right when she had said Elise wasn't worth the risk of fighting a duel.

Well, there was no honorable escape, so he put everything except the immediate future out of his mind. He loathed his opponent, so he warned himself not to allow Nelson to provoke him into losing his temper. If he remained cool, he was certain to win; he was too accomplished a swordsman to lose, even to a captain of the Grenadier Guards. Nelson knew, of course, that he had a well-deserved reputation as a hothead, so Charles realized he would be teased and prodded in the hope he would explode. Well, that wouldn't happen. Not today.

They left London behind them, and after the better part of another hour's drive they came to Richmond Park, a vast royal preserve comprising hundreds of acres. The trees were just beginning to bud. Rick paid a small boy tuppence to keep watch on his horses and carriage and, with Charles beside him, walked into the forest.

Ever since the time of Henry VII, Charles thought, young bloods had been settling their quarrels with pistols and swords here. This was his first duel, but it would also be his last. He had promised himself he would reform, and he intended to keep that pledge.

The pair reached a clearing deep in the forest just as dawn broke, and Charles was pleased. His dramatic timing had been perfect.

Captain Nelson, also dressed in black civilian clothes, stood at the far side of the clearing with his second and deliberately turned his back when his opponent arrived.

Three men came forward to shake hands with Charles and Rick. The referee was an old acquaintance, the physician was a fellow member of the club to which Charles and his father belonged, and the third member of the trio, who would keep watch for royal game wardens and tip them to keep them from the scene, had known Charles at Oxford. All were cordial but grave.

"There is no need to show me your swords," the referee told Rick. "Captain Nelson has already decided to use his own."

Charles nodded calmly and said to his second, "Please be good enough to fetch my blade."

Rick returned with it, and Charles grasped it, balancing it in his hand and then swishing it experimentally. It was rather heavy for a dueling sword, almost as heavy as a rapier. Trust a Grenadier Guardsman to choose such a weapon. Not that it mattered. Charles removed his coat, waistcoat, and cravat, turned down his fashionably high collar for comfort's sake, and rolled his sleeves above the elbows, taking care not to crumple the cuffs too much. Then he practiced with the sword again and was satisfied when it no longer felt too heavy.

The middle-aged referee moved to the center of the clearing. "Will the principals join me here?" His voice was casual. "The seconds will remain at the sides of the area."

Charles walked slowly toward the center and saw that Captain Nelson, who was doing the same, was glaring at him. Their eyes met, and Charles's expression remained bland, almost indifferent. Let the fellow scowl and glower all he pleased. This was one morning when Charles Rake-hell Boynton utterly refused to lose his temper.

"Gentlemen," the referee said, "I am required by custom to inquire whether you will be reconciled without the shedding of blood. Let me make only a few comments. Not only is dueling illegal, but the present government is determined to uphold the law, so both of you could suffer fines and imprisonment if you are apprehended. Allow me to add that words exchanged in anger after a fair consumption of alcohol often appear trivial in a subsequent light. Captain Nelson, will you be reconciled with your opponent?"

The officer stared hard at Charles, then sneered. "I will not, sir!"

Charles knew for certain that his foe was trying to arouse his ire.

"Mr. Boynton?"

Two could play at the game. "Under no circumstances, sir, am I willing to be reconciled with Captain Nelson."

"Very well." The referee became crisp. "Both of you are accomplished swordsmen, so I needn't rehearse the rules with you. I shall remind you only that the honor of both parties will be regarded as fully satisfied the instant first blood is drawn." He raised his voice. "I shall not permit the duel to continue beyond that point. If either principal persists, I instruct both seconds to intervene and use every means at their command to halt the fight. I trust I make myself clear, gentlemen. I shall not tolerate needless bloodshed."

Charles nodded curtly.

Captain Nelson's laugh was harsh. "I intend to skewer the lad very quickly."

Feeling a knot of anger forming in the pit of his stomach, Charles willed it to dissipate. Nelson was clever, but would be taught a rather special lesson in good manners.

"You may stand ready." The referee raised his own sword to shoulder height and extended it, separating the contestants.

Charles took two steps backward, then went through the elaborate ritual of saluting his opponent. Nelson was doing the same, and for an instant their eyes met. Nelson was glaring again, but Charles smiled amiably. So far his self-control was good.

"En garde!"

The duelists raised their blades, their feet separated, and were ready to start.

"You may begin, gentlemen," the referee said, still casual, and quickly retreated to the side of the clearing.

The officer had planned his strategy with care, and he attacked instantly, furiously, thrusting repeatedly at his opponent's face and chest.

The intensity of the assault startled Charles, who was forced to take a defensive position, parrying repeatedly. Now he knew why the captain had threatened to skewer him. The boast had not been idle, and his foe wanted to kill him, at the very least to wound him badly. The realization lighted another torch to his temper, but he forced himself to put out the flames. The man was a better swordsman than he had given him credit for being, and it would be difficult enough to stay alive and healthy.

Nelson was relying on his greater experience to win the day for him, and he continued to press his attack, his thrusts so strong that his opponent was forced to move backward warily around the clearing, parrying repeatedly.

What the captain had failed to take into consideration, however, were the quickness of Charles's responses and his remarkable sense of balance. His quick eye, combined with an ability to react instantly to a critical situation, was something he had inherited through his mother, who had told him as a child that Rakehell men had an instinct for self-preservation. But he owed his balance to his many voyages on Boynton ships; even in the past three years, since he had occupied an office at the company, his father had insisted that he spend six weeks at sea annually.

A man who could battle with wildly flapping canvas over one hundred feet above a rolling deck in the teeth of a Cape Horn gale, Charles reflected in grim satisfaction, had little to fear from a swordsman who, although strong, relied neither on surprise nor his own agility. Enough! Aware that his arm was tiring and his responses soon would be slowed, Charles's defense became more vigorous.

Nelson tried hard to maintain his advantage, but could not.

Charles laughed deliberately, just loudly enough for his opponent to hear him, squandering precious breath in order to infuriate the man. The ruse was effective, and color rose in the captain's face.

Now! Charles delivered a lightning thrust that cut a long, thin line on Nelson's cheek.

Blood had been drawn, so Charles was careful to obey the referee's instructions. Lowering his blade, he retreated several paces.

But the enraged captain leaped forward and slashed viciously. If his blow had found its target it might have decapitated his foe.

Charles's instinct for self-preservation did not desert him, however, and he raised his own sword just in time to knock the other's blade aside.

The referee and the two seconds raced toward the center of the clearing. Only Rick had the presence of mind to approach Nelson from the rear, leap on him, and, pinning his arms to his sides, bear him to the ground.

Now, at last, Charles was able to give vent to his own anger. He had been attacked unfairly, and there was nothing to prevent him from running Nelson through. Under other circumstances he could be accused of committing murder, but he had been assaulted with a deadly weapon after the duel had ended, and the courts would exonerate him.

Taking a firm grip on the handle of the heavy sword, he took a step toward his fallen opponent.

Before he could strike, however, a strange feeling took hold of him, something he had never before experienced. If you are a man, an inner voice told him, behave like a man. Because your enemy behaved dishonorably is no excuse for you to follow his example.

Slowly lowering his arm to his side, Charles discovered he was perspiring.

The disarmed Nelson was helped to his feet. He had regained his senses and, ashamed of his outbreak, stared down at the ground. Blood was oozing from his cut, and the physician attended him.

"Honor has been satisfied," the referee declared.

Charles relinquished his sword and turned away abruptly, looking at Grandpa Rakehell's watch. The sun was rising, and he would be on time at the office if he didn't dally, but he was so hungry that he and Rick would have to stop somewhere for a hearty breakfast. If he was lucky, his father might not notice that he was late.

Sir Alan Boynton, white-haired and impeccably tailored, looked every inch the baronet and shipping magnate as he sat behind his oversized teakwood desk. In his early fifties, he looked older than his years because he was overweight, but he radiated an air of cheerful self-satisfaction, and with good cause. He had climbed the ladder of success through his own efforts and had become sufficiently prominent, sufficiently well-to-do to have been honored with a baronetcy by the Crown.

Not that he was complacent. Although the huge and powerful East India Company had what was virtually a monopoly of the Far Eastern trade, his firm was already growing rich, thanks to its links with China and its share of the Atlantic markets. Sir Alan had good reason to dream of the day when he could buy a country estate as vast as that of an earl, and when he retired he would keep one of his sleek sloops as a pleasure craft. He had earned—and was continuing to earn—his place in the world.

His clerk came into the office, interrupting his reverie. "Mr. Charles has just arrived, Sir Alan."

Glancing at the handsome chronometer that stood on the mantel over the fireplace at the far side of his office, the shipping magnate concealed his relief. "Tell him I'd like a word with him—at his convenience," he said dryly.

As he had anticipated, his son came into the room promptly.

Charles was ill at ease, but tried to compensate for his feelings by taking the initiative. "Good morning, Father," he said. "Sorry I missed you at breakfast, but I left the house early today."

Sir Alan was equally determined to gain the upper hand at once. "The *Rose of India* is taking on the last of her cargo and will sail on the afternoon tide for India and

China. I'd like you to make the final inspection and give her clearance."

"Yes, sir." The task involved considerable responsibility, and Charles was pleased. This would mark the first time he would be going alone to approve or disapprove a sailing.

"You'll need the better part of the day, so you'd be wise to cancel any luncheon engagement you might have at the club."

"I was hoping to eat with you today, Father. There's a matter I very much wanted to discuss with you."

"I suggest we talk now." Sir Alan sat back in his chair and obviously had no idea he looked forbidding.

"I—ah—wanted to tell you why I missed breakfast with you at home this morning."

"Oh, that. Your mother squeezed the truth out of Elizabeth, who let just enough slip to indicate she'd seen you before you crept out of the house. You know what a terrier your mother can be when she thinks information is being withheld from her."

Charles swallowed hard and braced himself for the storm. "Yes, sir," was all he said.

"As a matter of fact," his father said casually, almost too casually, "I knew of your duel four or five days ago."

"You did?" Charles was dumbfounded.

"There's nothing more difficult to keep secret. I was told about it—in the strictest of confidence, to be sure—by at least a half dozen fellows at the club. Actually, I was a bit hurt that you didn't confide in me."

Charles faced the issue squarely. "I didn't think you'd approve, Father."

"I don't. Dueling is one of the more barbaric privileges of the bluebloods. Along with gaming, wenching, and drinking. I never allow myself to forget our origins are rooted in the middle class, so I avoid diversions that might interfere with hard work."

"I work hard, Father, but you're right, of course." The rebuke was deserved, so Charles faced the issue squarely. "I've already resolved to change some of my less attractive habits."

"For your sake, I hope so. You'll be sitting behind

this desk some day." Sir Alan raised an eyebrow. "I gather you won the duel?"

"Yes, sir."

"Splendid!" Sir Alan smiled broadly. "I've never met young Nelson, but if he's like his father I can't feel much sympathy for him. General Nelson is not only a crashing bore, but quite nasty. You didn't inflict too severe an injury?"

"A scratch." Charles thought it best not to elaborate on the unethical attack his foe had launched after the duel had ended.

"I won three guineas by placing a wager on you, so I shall have to treat you to a bottle of good claret the next time we lunch together."

His father had actually bet on him! Charles made no attempt to hide his surprise.

"I try to deal realistically with the world. But I warn you to expect trouble with your mother this evening. She not only disapproves of dueling on moral grounds, as I'm sure you know, but I glean she entertains a very low opinion of the young lady who was the cause of your dispute with Captain Nelson."

"I'm compelled to agree with Mother," Charles said. "The lady in the case is no lady, and I was stupid to let myself become involved. Now the wench will regard me as her champion, and I shall have the devil's own time trying to avoid her." He rose and started toward the door.

"Serves you right," his father said with a chuckle.

Charles thought it wise to make no reply. His father was letting him off lightly, and there was nothing to be gained by prolonging the talk. He returned to his own small office for his hat and gloves, then went to the stables for a horse. He was entitled to use one of the company carriages when engaged on official business, but he didn't want to appear ostentatious. He was already under a handicap when dealing with his father's employees, so he tried to maintain a modest profile whenever he could.

The Boynton docks and warehouses were located in Southwark, on the far side of the Thames, and as Charles rode there he was glad he had stopped for breakfast on his way to the office. He'd have no chance to eat again before evening.

The *Rose of India* was a lumbering schooner of two thousand tons, and like all Boynton ships she had undergone an extensive refit, so that her paintwork sparkled and her transom and figurehead were picked out in gold leaf. It was unlikely that she would return from her long voyage to the East in less than two years.

Charles halted after riding through the front gate and returned the watchman's salute. Friends who knew him only as a drinking and gaming companion would have been surprised by his watchful and knowledgeable attitude. He had not only made many voyages on Boynton ships, but he had spent a number of holidays working in the vast, single-story warehouses, too, and every inch of the complex was familiar to him. He checked automatically to make certain that the doors of storage buildings were closed and that guards were on duty outside each of them, in accordance with company regulations. Several dockworkers who were sitting on the ground outside one of the warehouses, smoking pipes, glanced toward him. One recognized him, and in a moment all of them were on their feet, scurrying back to work. No wonder his father made several surprise inspections here each week.

Two large, squat brigs were unloading cargo at the wharves, and Charles knew that one had just returned from India while the other had come home from the West Indian islands. If he had time he would visit them, too, before he left at the end of the day.

All of the *Rose of India*'s hatches were open, and dockworkers were loading the last of the cargo piled high on shore into her holds. Charles's experienced eye told him the task should be completed with ease at least an hour before she would sail on the afternoon tide. So far so good. He dismounted, looped his reins over a post, and strolled toward the schooner, whose crew members were busy bending sails to the yards.

The cabin boy saw him approach, and as Charles went on board, the ship's master appeared. Charles had sailed with Captain Whittaker on two voyages, first as an apprentice and much later as third officer, so they were well acquainted and shook hands with pleasure.

"I've been sent to clear you, Captain," Charles said.

The squat, broad-shouldered ship's master grinned at him. "You really are moving up in the world," he said. "Soon I shall be calling you Mr. Boynton."

"Never," Charles replied as they made their way down the main deck toward the captain's cabin. Just because he was a Boynton didn't mean he would ever put a distance between himself and old friends.

"Well, it's a shame that a natural-born sailor like you should be wasted in a shore berth," Whittaker said. "With your talents you should be at sea."

"Tell that to my father," Charles said.

"I have, often. But he says he can't spare you for two and a half years. I'd take you on in a minute as my first mate if you'd say the word."

"I wish I could," Charles replied, and there was a measure of sincerity in what he said. It was true that he longed for a return to the sea, which he loved. What he refrained from mentioning, however, was that his father was right. A voyage that would last anywhere from two to two and a half years was far too long to absent himself from the mainstream of the Boynton business. Besides, he thrived on challenges, and he lacked the patience that would be required of him on board the slow-moving schooner.

They entered the spacious cabin, and as they sat in easy chairs bolted to the bulkhead, the captain handed him a sheaf of papers. "Here's the manifest."

"I've already noted that you're traveling light," Charles said as he scanned the document.

"On the first leg of the voyage, yes," Whittaker replied. "We're taking as much general cargo to Calcutta as the market there will tolerate."

"How large is your crew?"

"Twenty-nine, including three officers."

Charles studied the manifest more intently, then did some mental calculations. "Depending on how long you're at sea, which is very difficult to estimate, you'll do well to break even on this leg. You can't possibly show a profit on what you're taking to India, Captain."

Whittaker smiled and nodded. "Quite right. But you don't see me worrying, and your father isn't losing any sleep, either."

Charles looked at him questioningly and raised an eyebrow.

"The *Rose* will earn a fortune by the time she returns to London. Take my word for it."

"How so?"

The captain's smile grew broader. "Oh, we'll pick up a cargo of tea in India on our return from Canton. Not that there will be all that much room for tea, you understand. Chests of silver are very, very heavy."

"Silver!" Charles's complacency vanished, and his pale eyes seemed to grow darker. "You're picking up a cargo of opium in India and taking it to Canton," he said, his disgust evident in his tone.

"That's the real profit in a voyage to the East these days, as everyone knows," Whittaker said, his manner becoming defensive.

"There isn't a word about opium in these manifests!"

"Nor is there in any of our ships that trade in the Orient. You know that!" Whittaker sounded aggrieved.

"I've suspected it, but I haven't known for certain," Charles said slowly. "Now I begin to see why more and more of our ships are being taken off other runs and are sailing to India and China."

"You'll hear no complaints from the directors and the other stockholders," the captain said.

There was nothing to be gained by arguing with him, Charles knew, so he held himself in check. Whittaker shared in the profits earned by his voyages, so he had a great deal to gain by engaging in the opium trade, but he had no voice in the establishment of company policy. Only the managing director, who was also the principal stockholder, determined such issues. Instead of cutting the present conversation short, however, perhaps there was something to be learned from the captain that might prove useful as ammunition.

"You make the trade sound so easy," Charles said.

"There's nothing simpler. The government of India collects a tax on the sale of opium, so the poppy is grown, processed, boxed, and sold openly."

"But you must smuggle it into China."

Whittaker shook his head. "It isn't smuggling in the way French wines are landed on the Cornwall coast in the dead of night. In Canton everything depends on the viceroy of the moment. If he's lenient, the cargo is unloaded openly at Whampoa. If a ship's master learns when he stops at Macao that a new imperial viceroy is being sticky, you just drop anchor in the Pearl River Delta and wait for the traders to come to you. Which they do. They take off the opium chests and pay you the going rate in silver, which is also boxed. All we do is make the opium available. The Chinese do the rest, no matter what their government's policy of the moment may be. Who could ask for a better arrangement? We take no risks, we break no laws, and we earn staggering profits."

Charles nodded, not daring to speak for fear he would lose his temper, and then suggested that he begin his inspection of the ship. For the rest of the day he immersed himself in work.

He stayed at the dock until the *Rose of India* cast off her lines, weighed anchor, and set sail. Watching her as she sailed sluggishly but majestically down the Thames on her interminable voyage, Charles finally started for home. Traffic on all three of the bridges that crossed the great river was so congested that he did not reach the mansion on Belgravia Square until long after nightfall.

Seeing no one as he hurried to his own room, he bathed in the tub of hot water the maids had already poured for him, shaved for the second time that day, and, following the Boynton custom, dressed in formal black for the evening.

He was just placing a pearl stickpin into his black cravat to keep it in place when a light tap sounded at the door.

An abashed Elizabeth, wearing an ankle-length white dress trimmed in pink lace, slid into the room. "I'm so sorry," she said, "but I told on you this morning. I didn't mean to, honestly, but I couldn't help it because—"

"I know," Charles said, putting the little girl out of her misery. "I've heard that mother hammered at you, so I can't blame you for tattling."

The child's enormous eyes shone with gratitude. "You're sweet, Charles."

"Not at all. I have something on my mind far more important than a stupid duel, and if you have any sense you'll stay out of the discussion." She had an annoying habit of supporting any position he took and often landed in parental hot water for being outspoken. "Just remember mother's saying."

The little girl's sigh was exaggerated. "Children should be seen but not heard," she said, and grimaced, then looked up at him in concern as they walked together down the broad, curving stairs. "You aren't going to have another of those beastly quarrels with them, are you?"

"I hope our talk won't develop into a quarrel," he replied grimly. "But I can't guarantee it."

"Oh, dear."

"The best I can do is wait until we've had our sweet. Then, if the conversation becomes a trifle warm, you can always ask to be excused from the table."

"Thank you." She stared at him. "Why do you fight them so often, Charles?"

"As you well know," he said, patting her on the shoulder to soothe her, "we're taught in this family to stand up for our convictions. Often I'd prefer to keep silent, but I can't do it when my silence is construed as consent."

In spite of her youth Elizabeth had developed mature powers of observation. "Sometimes," she said, "it appears to me that you go out of your way to create controversies."

"Sometimes," he said as they reached the second floor landing and headed toward the sitting room where the family congregated, "my sense of honor requires me to speak the truth as I see it."

Sir Alan, in attire similar to his son's, was sipping a pre-dinner glass of whiskey.

Charles poured some wine for Elizabeth, diluting it with water, then measured a small quantity of whiskey into a glass for himself.

"The *Rose* sailed on schedule?" his father asked.

"To the minute. I'll bring the copy of the manifest, the final sailing list, and the other papers with me to the office in the morning."

Both men rose as Lady Boynton came into the room, and Elizabeth jumped to her feet, too.

Lord Palmerston, one of England's more astute political leaders, had remarked several years earlier that Jessica Rakehell Boynton never made an inconspicuous entrance and invariably sailed rather than walked into a room. Even in the privacy of her own home, with no one but her immediate family on hand, she made her presence known instantly. Still slender in her late forties, her bearing majestic in a gown of dark gray silk taffeta, she paused on the threshold, smiling at her husband, son, and adopted daughter, and then came into the sitting room.

Sir Alan poured his wife a small glass of sherry, Charles held his mother's chair for her, and Elizabeth waited to place the sherry glass on a small side table. Rituals assumed great importance in the Boynton house.

"I had hoped to invite a guest to dine with us this evening," Jessica said blandly, "but I thought I'd speak to Charles first."

Her son braced himself.

"Perhaps I'll send her a note in the morning and ask her to join us tomorrow evening."

Charles knew what was expected of him. "Who, Mother?"

"Elise, of course."

He winced. "Don't bother for my sake."

"Oh? It seems to me," Jessica said slowly, "that when a young man is idiotic enough to risk his life for a girl, to place his whole future and that of the family company's future in jeopardy, the very least he should want is to spend as much time as possible with the young lady."

Charles felt himself flushing. "Some men profit by the errors of others, but some of us, being dim-witted, seem to learn only from our own mistakes."

Shrewd eyes appraised him, and then his mother smiled. "I would have been grievously disappointed if you had lost the duel," she said.

It was small wonder, Charles reflected, that many people assumed she was responsible for her husband's success. Her drive, her demand for perfection, her inexhaustible energy were inherited Rakehell traits that she had passed on to her son.

He grinned at her. "It was bad enough that I fought," he said. "I had to win. I wouldn't have dared to come home if I had lost."

Sir Alan's chuckle ended the tensions.

The butler appeared in the entrance. "Dinner is served, milady," he said.

Jessica walked down the stairs to the ground floor dining room on her husband's arm. Elizabeth fell in behind her and took her brother's arm, even though she had to reach up for it. The gentlemen held the ladies' chairs for them before seating themselves, and Sir Alan's nod indicated that it was Elizabeth's turn to say grace. Ritual having been duly observed, two serving maids brought in the first course.

The meal began with prawn cocktails, served with a horseradish sauce that was part of Jessica's American heritage. It was followed by a thick, rich oxtail soup; then came filets of sole broiled in lemon butter. The main course was a roast of lamb, served with boiled potatoes and several vegetables. Next came a salad of lettuce and watercress, always called "Italian greens," although no one in the family knew the reason.

The elder Boyntons ate sparingly, as was their custom, and so did Elizabeth. Only Charles, whose appetite knew no bounds, did justice to the meal.

As the time for the sweet approached, Elizabeth glanced apprehensively at her brother. So far he had behaved himself, but she expected an outbreak at any moment.

"We had a fascinating letter from my brother today," Jessica said.

Charles and Elizabeth looked at her expectantly. Sir Alan corresponded regularly with his brother-in-law, but such communications were confined exclusively to business. "I do hope Uncle Jeremiah has invited us to come over," the little girl said. "I haven't seen Jonathan in ever so long."

"There was no mention of that, dear." Jessica turned to her son. "Jonathan has defied the Rakehell directors and is using his inheritance to build something called a clipper."

95

The news was electrifying. "Good for Jonathan!" Charles said.

Jessica smiled wryly. "You approve of Jonathan's defiance, do you?"

That aspect was irrelevant, so Charles confined himself to the heart of the news. "From what I've read," he said, "clippers are going to be the most extraordinary ships in the world. According to one prediction, they'll sail from New York to England in about two weeks and will travel from China to England in less than four months, perhaps as little as three and a half."

Elizabeth snickered.

There was laughter in Jessica's voice when she said, "Two weeks to sail from America to England would be miraculous. As to coming here from China in three and a half months, I hope you realize we're speaking of a distance of approximately sixteen thousand miles!"

"The author of the article," Charles said, "was the naval correspondent of the *Times* of London."

His father did not join in the laughter. "I've found some of the claims on behalf of these ships totally incredible myself, but we shall soon have an opportunity to judge. Jonathan is bringing his clipper here on her maiden voyage."

Charles was so excited he almost forgot his distress. He and his cousin had spent three long summers sailing together and had become close friends. Certainly Charles realized, as he was sure Jonathan did, that they would be doing business together for decades to come. "I don't know what speeds Jonathan may claim for his ship," he said, "but I'll wager a gold sovereign that he'll live up to any claim he makes."

"I thought you were done with gambling," Sir Alan said.

His son waved cheerfully. "This is different."

The maids cleared away the salad dishes and served the sweet, a deep-dish pear pie.

"I'm willing to be convinced that a clipper can establish new speed records," Sir Alan said. "Not as extreme as the claims that are being made, surely. But suppose they reduced the voyage to China by a month. What a boon to our trade that would be! Yes, I shall be very much interested in Jonathan's ship."

The mention of China trade sparked Charles's discontent anew. He had found a logical opening for the discussion he craved.

Elizabeth saw his eyes harden and intervened quickly. "Why is it," she asked, "that Rakehells have names that begin with the letter J? Jonathan and Judith and Jeremiah and Joseph and—"

"It's a family tradition, dear," her mother explained. "It's just a way of reminding everyone in the family that our founding father was the first Jonathan Rakehell."

The child already knew the answer, but was determined to keep talking. "Why don't the Boyntons do the same thing. Charles could have been called Andrew, for instance, and when you adopted me you could have changed my name to Ann. Or Alberta."

Sir Alan laughed and shook his head. "For one thing," he said, "I happen to have been the founding father of this family, and I'd be a most uncomfortable ghost if my descendants, for generations to come, were given Christian names beginning with the letter A." He turned to his wife. "I trust you'll forgive me, my dear, if I observe that the Rakehells are all a bit mad. Present company excepted, of course."

"They're men of high principle," Charles said stridently. "They wouldn't accept profits earned out of the sorrows of suffering people."

Elizabeth quickly finished her deep-dish pie and asked to be excused.

Jessica waved her from the table and studied her son. "Your father has consistently refused to take part in the slave trade, if that's what you mean."

"It isn't," Charles said, and couldn't blame Elizabeth for her hasty flight from the austere dining room. His parents well knew he was challenging them. "In the past year and a half we've taken ship after ship off other runs and sent them off to India and China."

"The Crown is encouraging our trade with the East, and so are both parties in Parliament. For the simple reason

97

we earn larger profits. Surely you don't think it accidental that our stockholders include two members of the Royal Family!"

"I'm sure it isn't accidental," Charles replied, "but it's shameful."

He inherited his Rakehell temper from his mother, and Jessica was quick to take offense. "Shameful? That's rather strong language, Charles."

"If I could without cursing in your presence, Mother, I'd make it even stronger," Charles replied. "It disgusts me that we're earning money from the opium trade."

"Ah, so that's your problem." The deep furrows in Sir Alan's forehead eased. "Surely you don't think the East India Company—which rules half the sub-continent—would engage in opium trade if there were something terribly wrong with it."

"Of course they would! Their directors and stockholders are earning money faster than they can count it! All from the opium trade!"

"All? That's an exaggeration of fact," his father said, becoming sharper. "It is also a fact that at no time has Parliament ever made a law forbidding any company to trade in opium."

"Laws usually follow a public outcry," Charles said. "The lawmakers are behind the times."

His parents exchanged tolerant, faintly amused glances.

"Selling opium is immoral," he said.

"One moment." Sir Alan looked at the savory that had just been served, oysters wrapped in bacon and broiled on toast, but he had no appetite for this final dish. "The British government places no restrictions on the sale of opium, be it abroad or here at home. The government of India freely permits the growing and sale of opium. In fact, the East India Company's Board of Control actively participates in setting the annual price, depending on the size and quality of that year's Indian crop."

"The government of China specifically forbids the importation of opium into that country, Father."

"The Chinese," Sir Alan said, "are among the most backward, barbarian people in the world. And their government is corrupt. Their officials close their eyes when they're bribed small sums, and they make no serious attempt to halt the flow of opium into their country."

"Then why does their government forbid it?"

"For the same reason that foreigners are allowed to engage in trade nowhere in China other than Canton. They try to kep their borders sealed from the outside world. They want no contact with outsiders. They've been a closed society for thousands of years, and they're so backward they want to remain ignorant."

"They're advanced enough to have invented gunpowder," Charles said. "And paper. And printing. And—"

Jessica became impatient and cut him off. "No civilized nation on earth forbids the trade of opium," she said.

"That's correct, my dear," Sir Alan added. "Don't think for a moment that we British are unique. The United States permits its merchant ships to carry opium to China, and the only reason their trade isn't larger is because they must buy it in the Dutch East Indies. India will sell only to us. The French trade in opium. So do the Dutch, obviously. And the Danes. And the Swedes. And every other nation that boasts a merchant fleet, large or small."

"You don't understand," Charles said.

"Perhaps you can enlighten us." His mother became icily disdainful.

"I'll try. The smoking of opium is dangerous. The drug ruins the smoker's health. He becomes dependent on it and must have larger and larger quantities of it. He loses his appetite, he lives in a dream world, and eventually he wastes away. If he smokes or chews it long enough, opium will kill him."

"That's nothing but conjecture," Sir Alan said briskly. "I've seen the same lurid articles that you've obviously read. But I've yet to hear of a reputable physician at a medical school where research is done—Edinburgh, for example, or Harvard—who substantiates the claim you've just made. I'll grant you that many people feel as you do, including Jeremiah Rakehell. And Jonathan, no doubt. But the facts they claim haven't been proven scientifically."

"They will be," Charles said. "When people here and in the United States start dying because they're addicted to opium, when hospitals are filled with people who can't survive without doses that then will kill them, the physicians will get busy fast enough. They'll find the proof. And then the lawmakers will get busy."

"How long do you suppose all that will take?" Jessica demanded.

"Who can say? It may take another ten years."

Jessica sighed in exasperation.

"In that case," Sir Alan said, "you'll forgive me if I spend the next ten years earning profits infinitely larger than I can acquire in any other way."

Jessica controlled herself. "Charles," she said, "you're still young enough to be idealistic. But men who are in business can't afford to be that way."

"Precisely," her husband said. "The silver is piling up in China, waiting to be taken, and if I don't earn it, someone else will. Never do I allow myself to forget that I have an obligation to my stockholders. And I urge you to remember it, too. The man who operates a shipping line can't afford to be governed by rules of false sentiment."

"The Chinese have already discovered what other nations haven't yet learned, that opium is as dangerous as a loaded pistol!" Charles realized his parents weren't really listening to him, but his conscience wouldn't permit him to fall silent gracefully.

"If the government of China truly wanted to stop the sale of opium, they'd find ways to do it. Our captains tell me that Canton is filled to overflowing with soldiers, customs officials, and constables. If they truly wanted to halt the traffic, they could do it overnight. The situation there is that simple."

"If it were simple the trade would have stopped!" Charles retorted. "There are greedy men everywhere, including China. Customs officials and constables can be bribed, just as they are in other countries. And there's so much money at stake in opium dealing that our people offer them bribes they can't resist. I defy you to call that simple!"

His father was fighting a losing battle to control himself. "Again you're wrong. We bribe no one. Our ships—that just happen to be carrying opium—drop anchor offshore. The Chinese come to us, make their deals, and take the opium away in their own boats, paying us silver

100

in return. If there are bribes being paid, the Chinese dealers are paying them. Boynton crews don't even go ashore in Whampoa while there's as much as an ounce of opium on board a Boynton ship. Our hands are clean."

Charles's temper exploded. "I hope your conscience is as clear as your hands are clean! Mine certainly isn't!" He pushed back his chair and began to pace up and down the length of the thick Indian rug.

Sir Alan stood, too. His own patience was exhausted, and for the first time he began to shout. "How dare you question my conscience? Obviously you have no understanding of our profits. You fail to grasp the reasons for our marvelous growth. Why, the very food you've eaten this evening, this splendid house that gives you shelter, and the expensive clothes you love to wear have been bought with profits we've earned from the opium trade. It brings us more in a year than we made previously in five years!"

Jessica felt they were going too far, that soon they would be saying things they would regret. So it was up to her to restore order, if not harmony. "Sit down, please!" she said, a metallic ring of command in her quiet voice.

Her husband was the first to obey. He was descending to his son's level, and he was ashamed because he knew better.

"You haven't had your glass of port, Charles," Jessica said, "and you haven't been excused from the table."

A lifetime of his mother's discipline forced Charles to resume his seat. But he was determined to have the last word in the dispute, and he steadied himself so his voice would not tremble. "If I've offended you, Father, forgive me," he said. "All the same, if I sat in your office today— if Boynton Shipping were mine to control—we'd never sell another grain of opium!"

Book
II

I

Flying Dragon lay still in the quiet waters of her berth. Her bow, even finer than that of the *Ann McKim,* her convex stern and rounded main transom, her raked masts and gleaming hull—even tied up to the wharf with her canvas furled, like the closed wings of a resting bird of passage—made her a picture of grace. She was a real beauty, Jeremiah Rakehell had to admit, and he privately admired his son's tenacity and courage. Even if the ship failed to live up to his impossibly high expectations for her, his determination to prove the superiority of a clipper remained undimmed.

Jonathan stood beside his father in the latter's office, and as he gazed out at *Flying Dragon,* admiring her now familiar lines, he felt a surge of suppressed excitement.

"I hear your trial runs didn't live up to your expectations," Jeremiah said quietly.

His son reflected for a moment, then worded his reply with care. "I wouldn't put it quite that way, Papa," he said. "I'm learning that what Isaac McKim told me was true. A crew can't just step on board a clipper and sail her, as seamen can do on other ships. They need practice in working together. She really has to be worked, Papa. Her extended stem, faired with the hull, gives her the ability to cut the water clean and true, when the man at the wheel understands fully how she must be humored. That means training. Under a bo's'n who is sensitive and quick to learn the ways of a clipper."

"I see." Jeremiah thought he was fooling himself, but withheld comment.

"One of the problems is that I don't have the right bo's'n." Jonathan hesitated. "I wonder if you'd consider loaning me Grimshaw. He isn't at sea right now, and he doesn't appear to be scheduled for any voyage in the near future. He's the fellow I need to help me whip my crew into proper shape."

His father smiled. "Oh, Grimshaw could do it—if any bo's'n could." Perhaps it would be wise to permit the crew chief to work on the clipper. Only when Jonathan ran out of rationalizations and excuses would he be able to admit to himself that his new type of vessel, although admittedly beautiful, was no faster than the standard brigs and schooners the company built and sailed. "All right," he said at last. "Take Grimshaw, and let's see if he can help improve your speed."

"I'm sure he can!" Jonathan replied as the excitement in his voice surged to the surface. "Now I can enter the contest the postmaster general is sponsoring!"

Jeremiah was startled. The United States Post Office Department was intending to issue new contracts for the carrying of mail between Boston and England and would not only award the lucrative run to the winner of a race to London, but would pay a cash prize of one thousand dollars to the ship that came in first. "I hope you realize that a Rakehell schooner is already entered in the contest."

"I know, Papa. But that's no reason for me to hold back."

Jeremiah was hurt. "You mean you'd compete against a ship flying the family flag?"

"Certainly not, sir!" The very idea was shocking, and Jonathan spoke emphatically. "There's no limit on the number of ships any one company is being allowed to enter in the race. If you'll give your permission, I intend to fly the Rakehell pennant, too!"

A sense of relief flooded Jeremiah, who felt slightly ashamed of himself for doubting his son's loyalty. "That puts a far different face on the matter."

"Then you'll give me your approval?"

"Not so fast. There's a complication that may not have

occurred to you. In your trial runs you've been acting as your own master."

"Of course." Jonathan was puzzled.

"There are a half-dozen captains in New York and Boston who are known to put speed above everything else. None of them can be hired by any of the competitors in the race. Only ships' captains who have held their masters' tickets as employees of a competing company for at least twenty-four months are eligible to act as captains. You've had your ticket as a Rakehell master for only a year and a half. So you're six months shy of being eligible."

"That means we'll have to use someone else as the master, and the best I can do is sail with him as first mate."

"Correct. I'll have to assign one of our regular captains as master of *Flying Dragon* if you enter the race under our house flag."

"Fair enough, I guess," Jonathan said. "I don't suppose you happen to know which of our masters might be available."

His father shook his head. "Brad is in charge of personnel assignment. He's done a competent job, so I've had no reason to interfere. I'll tell him to allow you to take on Grimshaw as your bo's'n, but you'll have to leave the assignment of a master up to him."

Jonathan felt uneasy. He disliked the idea of being at Bradford Walker's mercy. On the other hand, all Rakehell captains were veterans who knew their business, so any one of them would be satisfactory. At the outset, to be sure, he couldn't expect any master to share his belief in the superiority of a clipper, but *Flying Dragon* was certain to create her own converts to her cause.

"I'll write to Jessica and tell her to expect you in London," Jeremiah said. "The Boyntons will be pleased to see you."

"No happier than I'll be to see them. Charles and I don't correspond as much as we should."

Jeremiah was pleased, as always, by the reminder that the Rakehell and Boynton heirs were close friends. The relations of the two companies would remain solid for another generation. "Will you need to drop anyone from your crew when you take on a new, temporary master?"

"No, sir. During the trials Edmund Barker has been my only mate, and he'll fit in automatically as second mate. After I show you—and the world—what *Flying Dragon* can do when she kicks up her heels between here and England, I hope to sail her myself for a time. And I'll need a new first mate. But I'll have no problems finding the right man when I've broken the speed record."

His father wanted to provide a cushion for him. "The present record on a Boston to London run is three weeks. What sailing time are you anticipating?"

"I'll give you my most conservative estimate, Papa," Jonathan said with a quick grin. "Twenty-one days. Actually, I hope to make the run in twenty days—or even less."

The prediction was absurd, in Jeremiah's opinion, but he didn't want to discourage his son. "For your sake," he said, placing a hand on Jonathan's shoulder, "I hope you break the record and make the Rakehell schooner look like a wallowing tub."

As Jonathan left his father's office he told himself there was no way he could express his gratitude for that encouragement. This was the essence of the spirit that bound members of the family together and made it possible for the great Rakehell traditions to be passed from one generation to the next. Humbled by his father's generosity, Jonathan could only hope that he would prove as tolerant to his own sons.

Bradford Walker was away from his desk, but his assistant gave Jonathan the address of the boardinghouse where Grimshaw lived, and the young builder went there at once. There was no time like the present to acquire the boatswain he needed. The race to England would start in another two weeks, and Grimshaw would need every day of that brief period to whip his crew into shape.

The boatswain's dwelling was an unpretentious boardinghouse located less than a mile from the Rakehell yard. The landlady, a crusty New Englander, looked sourly at the visitor when he asked for Grimshaw. "You don't look like one of his drinking friends," she said.

"I'm his employer," Jonathan said politely. "My name is Rakehell."

The woman's attitude changed instantly, and she motioned the visitor into her small, stuffy parlor.

Jonathan sat uncomfortably on the edge of a mohair-covered chair that was too short for his long legs.

"Grimshaw don't mean to be bad," the woman said. "It just seems like he can't help getting hisself into mischief when he has too long a spell between voyages."

Jonathan smiled. "What has he done now? Or should I let him tell me about it himself?"

"He ain't here right now, that's for certain," the landlady declared, then peered at the young gentleman. "You won't discharge him if I tell you what little I know?"

"Certainly not. There isn't another seaman in this area as competent."

She hoped he could be trusted and was comforted by the knowledge that he was a Rakehell. Everybody in New London knew that members of that distinguished family were honest and kept their word. "Grimshaw ain't been here for three days now, going on four," she said. "The other boarders won't talk about it, but I can put two and two together. I heard tell there was a terrible hullabaloo the other night at the Black Whale."

"There often is," Jonathan said.

"Well, Mr. Rakehell, Grimshaw ain't come home since that night. So I got me a strong suspicion he was drunk and that the constables picked him up. There have been other times he didn't have the cash to pay his fine, so the sheriff let him work out his time in jail. I got me an idea that's where he is. Again."

"Then I'll have to bail him out."

"But you won't throw him out of work?"

He could understand the woman's anxiety. "He's too good a seaman and too much of a rogue. I'd let him spend a month in jail if I thought he'd learn a lesson. But he won't. And I need him."

Jonathan left the boardinghouse, went to the harbor in the heart of town, and then began to climb the State Street hill behind the waterfront. The jail was located behind the Anglican church, and the New London county sheriff sat in his tiny office, playing cards with a friend.

He looked up at the tall visitor and chuckled. "I

109

figured you'd be moseying around when you found out Grimshaw is a guest here, Mr. Rakehell."

"How much is his fine this time, Sheriff?"

"Ten dollars. Plus three dollars and fifteen cents damage to the bar and two lamps at the Black Whale."

Jonathan whistled under his breath. "He must have torn the place apart. Never mind. I'll pay the whole amount. But I'd like a word with him before you release him."

"Glad to oblige." The sheriff picked up a bunch of keys, walked down a long corridor, and unlocked a door of heavy oak at the far end of the row.

Grimshaw was sitting on a bunk, engaging in earnest conversation with his cell-mate, a short, black prisoner in his twenties. But the moment he saw his visitor he slumped, held his face in his hands, and moaned. "Ah, Jonnie," he said, "I'm a miserable sinner. I don't deserve the sympathy o' the likes o' you."

Jonathan managed to keep a straight face. "You're right. You deserve no sympathy from anyone. This is the third time in a year that I've been forced to bail you out."

Grimshaw's manner changed instantly, and his grin revealed the gaps between his yellowed teeth. "Bailin' me out, are ye? Jonnie, ye be a prince among men!"

"Not so fast," Jonathan said. "I'd leave you here to rot if I thought it would do you any good, you old reprobate. Why did you take to drink again?"

"The same reason as always." The boatswain's face became conveniently contrite. "When I'm at sea I'm strong and fit, and the very idea o' raisin' a cup o' rum to my mouth makes me sick. But let me linger on land for a long spell, and the dry rot seeps into my bones."

"Enough." Jonathan well knew the man found prolonged life on shore intolerable; when he had work at sea there was no one more sober, more responsible. "You have a new assignment. Today. You're the bo's'n of *Flying Dragon.*"

Grimshaw seemed somewhat less than overjoyed. "The new clipper. Be ye sure she ain't so top-heavy she'll turn turtle in a gale?"

"Find out for yourself."

"The smell o' salt air is better than the stink o' this

place, even if I drown on that new-fangled ship. Mr. Rakehell, meet my friend Oliver."

The young black man rose, and although he was painfully thin his handshake was strong and firm.

"Why are you here?" Jonathan asked.

"I was slave in Carolinas. Run away."

"He's waitin' for the Abolitionist Society to raise the funds that'll set him free," Grimshaw volunteered.

Jonathan nodding, knowing the system well. When the Abolitionists paid fifty dollars for an escaped slave, the man was freed. If the sum was not raised, however, he was returned to his owners.

"Bail Oliver out, too, Jonnie, and if ye must, take the fee out o' my wages, a bit at a time. I'll vouch that he's a fine lad, and it may be ye'll have a place for him in your crew."

In spite of the boatswain's weakness for drink when he was ashore for any length of time, he was a shrewd judge of men. "Are you a sailor?" he asked the black man.

"In land of my birth," Oliver said with simple dignity, "I was *zhonga* of dhow owned by father."

"He means he was the captain," Grimshaw said.

Jonathan studied the little prisoner. A dhow was a type of ship seen in the waters off the eastern coast of Africa, usually single-masted with a huge mainsail, lateen-rigged. At best it was a difficult vessel to handle, and if the man was telling the truth, he was necessarily an accomplished seaman. "How many in your crew?"

Oliver held up five fingers.

"How many years did you sail?"

"Whole life until Arab traders sell as slave."

"How many years were you a *zhonga?*"

Oliver raised six fingers.

He could prove a valuable addition to *Flying Dragon*'s crew, and at worst Jonathan would have done his duty as a man with a conscience. Under no circumstances could he allow the prisoner to be returned to slavery. "I'll pay the fee," he said, "and you'll have your chance to win a berth. Send him aloft today, Grimshaw, and put him through his paces. We'll soon find out if he's a true sailor."

Oliver's eyes shone as, folding his arms so they crossed and touched his shoulders, he bowed low from the waist. "You make Oliver free man?"

"Completely free. Whether you win a place on my ship is another matter, but as fast as I can give the sheriff the money to send off to the Carolinas, you're no longer a slave."

"*Zhonga* Rakehell not be sorry," the little man said softly. "Oliver your friend."

Citizens of substance and standing were seen at the Black Whale on New London's Bank Street only late in the evening, when a man might want one of the trollops who frequented the place, and a wary gentleman always took care to use the side entrance. At noon only a few customers sat at the bar or at one of the small tables of unpainted wood. The only food ever served by the proprietor consisted of sandwiches of fried ham or grilled sardines. Only on a rare occasion did a sailor, inevitably a foreigner, order the greasy food.

As Bradford Walker approached the side entrance, his hat pulled low on his forehead, he regretted having chosen the place for his meeting, and when the stench of ham, sardines, and fat assailed his nostrils, he felt even sorrier. But he could not turn back. It was impossible to hold the meeting in his office or at his home.

The proprietor had been waiting for him and immediately conducted him to one of the curtained booths that, at night, was used for assignations.

Brad sank into the long hardwood bench. "My friend will join me momentarily," he said. "So you may bring us two mugs of rum, to which you will add equal portions of water, with half of a lime in each mug. Mind you, I want the best rum that's made in the Danish islands of the West Indies. And don't try to pass off that raw slop you sell to sailors. I know the difference."

The proprietor's bow was deferential. Members of the gentry were never addressed by name here, but he recognized the powerful son-in-law of Jeremiah Rakehell, who sometimes came here late at night for other purposes. "You can depend on me, sir," he murmured.

Soon after the drinks were served, Captain Davis Hartley joined Brad in the booth. Husky and broad-shouldered, he seemed to fill the cubicle. "I haven't set foot in this hole," he said with a bemused smile, "since I was promoted from bo's'n to third mate. That must have been twenty years ago. I was that surprised when I received your note suggesting that we meet here, Mr. Walker."

"No names, please," Brad replied sharply. "And I hope you destroyed the note, as I requested."

"I always follow orders from the front office," Captain Hartley said.

Brad's smile was tight. "To your health," he said.

Hartley sipped appreciatively. "This is first-rate rum. I didn't know the Black Whale kept it in stock."

"They do now," Brad said, and offered no explanation. Never one to waste time on small talk, he plunged into the subject that was uppermost in his mind. "What's your opinion of these new clipper ships?"

The captain tried to reply honestly. "I watched *Flying Dragon* sail up the river to her berth the other day. God knows she's graceful. She's skinny as a toothpick, of course, and whether she's seaworthy with that narrow a line I wouldn't know. Just as I'd hate to venture a guess as to whether she's top-heavy in a stiff wind."

"It's my view," Brad said, his voice becoming harsh, "that any ship costing twice the price of a schooner to build, but carrying only a little more than half of a schooner's cargo, isn't worth the wood that went into her hull."

Hartley had heard there was no love lost between Walker and his brother-in-law, and it appeared that the rumors were accurate. Long accustomed to tacking in order to pick up a favorable breeze, Hartley made the necessary adjustments now. "Oh, she's a handsome ship, all right, but I was about to add that I can't see a clipper ever paying her way. She just isn't practical in these days when trade is growing and every foot of cargo space is badly needed."

"Precisely my objection," Brad said, and offered him

one of the special *cigarros* that he imported from Spain's New World capital, Havana.

The captain didn't smoke, but became even more alert. Walker was known among Rakehell employees for being a pinch-penny, so it became clear, when he offered a *cigarro* worth at least six or seven cents, that he had something important on his mind.

Brad took his time lighting his *cigarro,* then changed the subject. "Ever since our company was founded," he said, "the president—being a seafaring man himself—has kept the title of commodore of the line. All that will be changed when I take charge. Because I'm no sailor."

Hartley concealed his surprise. He had always assumed, as had everyone else who was familiar with the business, that young Rakehell would succeed his father some day. But here was Walker saying in so many words that he stood first in line.

"It's very possible that we won't need to wait for a change of command at the top to institute a new policy and appoint the best of our senior captains as commodore."

Hartley didn't want to betray his own fierce ambitions, but he couldn't help leaning forward in his seat. Obviously Walker hadn't summoned him to this unlikely place for an inconsequential chat. "May I ask why the—ah—present head of the company might change his mind?"

"For one thing, he never goes to sea himself any more. He's saving the title for his son. But this clipper ship is such a wild venture that the son well may be discredited in his father's eyes. And if that should happen, I predict the policy regarding a commodore could be changed overnight. I can guarantee the change, because I'd take action on it myself."

"I see." The captain saw nothing as yet, but waited with as much patience as he could muster.

Again Brad appeared to be changing subjects. "Too bad you haven't been scheduled for the mail-run race."

Hartley shrugged. "It couldn't be helped. Captain Bowen has seniority almost equal to mine, and when Mr. Rake—when the head of the company decided to enter the *Jean K.*, that finished my chances. Bowen has been the master of that schooner for the past seven years, maybe longer."

"We're going to have another entry." Brad prolonged the suspense by pulling a bell-rope, and when the proprietor answered the summons, he ordered another round of drinks, then remained silent until they were served.

The captain tried hard not to fidget.

"*Flying Dragon* is being entered," Brad said at last. "But the young man who has conducted her sea trials doesn't hold a certificate as one of the company's masters, so he's disqualified for the race. The rules of the Post Office Department are very strict. That means we'll need a temporary captain, someone already one of our senior masters."

Hartley wished he could loosen the cravat at his throat so he could breathe more easily.

"I wonder if you'd care to take the assignment," Brad said. "You come to mind first whenever I think of the commodore I intend to appoint, so I've come to you before going to anyone else."

The captain tried to stifle the alarm that rose within him. "I've never sailed a clipper," he said, "so I just don't know what kind of a performance I could coax out of *Flying Dragon*. I might not win, and I wouldn't want you to be disappointed in me."

Brad spoke very slowly. "I wouldn't expect you to win. In fact, I'm quite positive in my own mind that the *Jean K.* will establish a better sailing record. A freak ship called a clipper—no matter what has been written in the press—simply cannot compete with a reliable, sturdy schooner."

Hartley stared at him, his mind churning. If he understood Walker correctly and put together the pieces of the puzzle properly, the man didn't want him to win the race. He could be offered the title, prestige, and greater pay as commodore of the Rakehell shipping line *if* the ship Jonathan Rakehell had built failed to make an impressive run. In that event his father would become so disgusted that he would approve the appointment of an outsider as commodore. And—of course!—Walker would move a step ahead of his brother-in-law and would be the next head of the company.

The whole idea was so startling, so daring, that Hartley wanted to make sure he wasn't jumping to the wrong conclusion. He groped for a delicate way to ask several questions.

Brad sensed his uncertainty and realized he'd have to spell out his scheme even more clearly. "I'm staking my own future," he said, "on the unalterable conviction that *Flying Dragon* cannot and will not win the mail contract race to England. I'll go even farther. I'm certain the *Jean K.* will reach England ahead of the clipper."

Hartley's last doubts vanished, and a slow smile lighted his face. "I'm glad we've had this talk, sir," he said. "I can promise you won't be disappointed in me."

"Before you agree," Brad said, "it's only fair to tell you that you'll encounter complications."

"Oh?"

"The crew is small, but the men have been selected with care, and with the exception of a black man, a former slave, who was added a couple of days ago, all of them have worked for us for years. I know of no merchant ship anywhere with a better crew."

"That doesn't worry me."

"Grimshaw has been appointed bo's'n."

"Grimshaw has sailed with me. I can handle him."

Brad paused for a long moment and took a swallow of his drink. "The ship's builder, who has been conducting his own sea trials, will sail on the clipper as first mate. Young Barker is her permanent second mate."

"I'm not worried about Barker." Hartley wiped a film of perspiration from his forehead. "But the builder could cause a lot of trouble. I'd find it hard to forget that he's the son of the company's principal owner."

"I see no problems for you if you're firm," Brad said. "Certainly he's been at sea enough to know that the captain is the master, and his decisions aren't open to question. But if he forgets, I daresay you'll remember."

Captain Hartley's face became set. "I'll have no trouble remembering," he said.

"Not that I anticipate problems for you. After all,

the young man has been subjected to discipline at sea all of his life. He'll have his own ideas, and if I know him, he won't be reluctant to express them, but he'll be in no position to insist."

"Indeed he won't."

Brad smiled as he extended his hand, and his guest left without exchanging another word with him. He ordered the drinks charged to his regular bill, and his walk was jaunty as he made his way back to the Rakehell yard. His mission had been totally successful, and soon— far sooner than he had dared to hope—Jonathan's reputation would suffer permanent damage. After he assumed control of the company, he reflected, he would change its name to Rakehell-Walker.

"I'm going to be at sea for about six weeks," Jonathan told Louise Graves, "and I expect to spend at least a week visiting my relatives in London. So I don't see why there's a need for a delay of almost two more months before our betrothal is announced. We'll still have another year to wait before we're married."

The girl's pretty face became clouded. "I know that Papa and your father have had some talks, and they seem inclined not to make an announcement yet."

"Why not?"

"I—I haven't asked," Louise said. "You know how my father hates having his decisions questioned."

"This is a decision that directly affects your life and mine." Jonathan stood, towering over her in the Graves parlor. He knew he could discuss the situation with his own father, but that wouldn't be right. The final word was up to Dr. Graves, so he had to take matters into his own hands. "Do you or do you not want to marry me?" he demanded.

The idea of not marrying him hadn't occurred to her, and she was startled. "You know I do!"

"Come along, then. We'll get this settled right now." He grasped her hand, helped her to her feet, and continued to hold her hand as they walked down the corridor to the study, where Dr. Graves was at work on his medical records.

Ordinarily no one was allowed to interrupt him when his door was closed, but Jonathan was in no mood to temporize, and he rapped on the door with greater strength than he knew.

"Come in." Dr. Graves sounded annoyed, but his expression became quizzical when he saw the young couple holding hands. "What's this?"

Louise started to speak, but stammered.

"Sir," Jonathan said firmly, "I'm going to be out of the country for almost two months, and the longer we put off announcing our engagement the longer it will be before we're married. Everyone in town knows that Louise is going to become my wife, so we're wondering if there's any reason the announcement can't be made before I sail."

The physician carefully placed his quill pen on his desk, sighed gently, and waved the couple to the small settee opposite him. He and his wife had been unofficially betrothed for two years prior to the full year of a formal engagement that custom demanded, but these days young people were always in a hurry.

"Your father and I have discussed the matter, at some length," he said. "We thought it might be appropriate, if your hopes for this clipper ship of yours should be justified, to make the announcement after you return from England. The atmosphere will be celebratory, so to speak, so we thought that would be the right time."

Jonathan was in no mood to tolerate further delays, but realized he needed a logical argument. "People love to gossip," he said, "and if we wait until then, it will be whispered around town that Louise is marrying me because I've enjoyed another Rakehell success. It would be far preferable to make the announcement now, before the mail contract race. For Louise's sake. For your sake and that of Mrs. Graves. It would show you have confidence in me, no matter how I fare in the race. Then no one would have cause for gossip." He believed he had struck the right note. Dr. and Mrs. Graves were very sensitive to the opinions and attitudes of their friends and other social peers.

The physician became lost in thought and tapped his pen lightly on the desk.

Louise tried to free her hand, but Jonathan grinned at her and tightened his grip. It was essential that she appear to be supporting his position.

"You've made an interesting point," Dr. Graves said at last. "I hadn't thought about gossip, and you may well be right. I'll let you know."

Jonathan knew he had won, but not until much later did it occur to him that he felt no elation, that he wasn't actually all that eager to make Louise his wife. Why had he been so insistent when he and Louise weren't in love with each other? He had to admit that his reason didn't make him proud of himself. His destiny and Louise's had been settled by their parents, and there was no way either could back out without creating a scandal. As the day would inevitably come when he would be expected to marry Louise, Jonathan's loyalties to her as well as to his family demanded that he fulfill his obligation as soon as he reasonably could. That was the honorable way, and to a Rakehell honor was paramount. Besides, any long wait, no matter what the cause, annoyed Jonathan because he lacked patience. Delays irritated him, and he knew the trait was a character weakness he would have to overcome. A major problem of being a Rakehell was one's unyielding inner demand for self-improvement, and he could sympathize with those who married into the family. Their lot was not easy.

The ceremonies marking the betrothal took place a few nights before *Flying Dragon* was scheduled to sail for Boston to participate in the mail contract race. The Graves house was crowded with guests, and the engaged couple greeted well-wishers in the formal parlor. Louise, wearing a gown of pale lilac, looked even prettier than usual as she stood with one hand resting lightly on Jonathan's arm. On the fourth finger of her left hand she wore the modest diamond that had been his mother's engagement ring. He looked solemn and dignified in a suit of black worsted, and he rarely smiled, even when chatting with old, close friends like Ruth Halliburton and Edmund Barker.

As Jeremiah Rakehell observed privately to Dr. Graves, the young couple had taken each other and their relationship for granted, but now, for the first time, they were beginning to understand the true nature of their new partnership.

Jonathan indicated this awareness soon after the guests departed. "I've held off having a figurehead carved for *Flying Dragon*," he said to Louise, "because I haven't thought of a symbol that will be right for her. Now, I think, you must have the privilege of deciding the question and supervising the carving of the ornament."

She looked up at him helplessly. "But I don't know that much about ships." According to Rakehell tradition, the ship's owner determined the subject of the figurehead, so Jonathan was extending her a rare privilege. But the significance of the gesture escaped her.

"You'll learn a great deal about ships in the years ahead," Jonathan replied with a smile. "I've been told that Rakehell men think of little else."

The girl was already conscious of his obsession and had no intention of telling him she hoped she could cure him of it and broaden his interests after they were married.

"Take your time making a decision," he said. "All I ask is that you give me some idea of the ornament you'll want before we're actually married."

Louise's mind was blank, but she was reluctant to admit that she really didn't care what prow ornament he had made. Selecting her trousseau and linens would keep her fully occupied in the months prior to their marriage.

Among the last to leave the reception were Ruth Halliburton and Edmund Barker, who had asked for the right to walk her home. The spring night was balmy and they strolled slowly, with Edmund very much aware of the lovely girl beside him.

The silent Ruth knew she was bad company tonight, but she could not force a gaiety she didn't feel. Somehow, for more years than she cared to recall, she had kept alive the remote hope that Jonathan would take notice of her, fall in love with her, and marry her. From the outset she had known, of course, that her dream was unrealistic. A Rakehell couldn't marry—would not be allowed to marry —the daughter of his father's chief carpenter. The wives of Rakehell men were chosen with great care to insure that the next generation would live up to the family's exacting standards.

Edmund was only remotely aware that the girl walking with him was not talkative. His own mind was seething, and although he was a placid man most of the time, he felt exceptionally nervous.

As they approached the modest Halliburton frame house on Montauk Avenue, a short distance from the Graves mansion, he cleared his throat, then broke the silence. "May I come in for a few minutes? There's something I want to discuss with you."

Ruth's mind was still elsewhere. "Of course," she said.

Her father had retired early, as he always did, because he reported for work at the Rakehell yard shortly after daybreak. A single candle was burning in the modest parlor, and Ruth busied herself lighting a pair of oil lamps. "Would you like something to eat or drink?" she asked, remembering her manners.

Edmund shook his head. "No, ma'am, thank you. We had plenty at the party."

She sat in one of the chairs her father had made, then gestured toward its twin. "Sit down, Edmund."

"I—I'd rather stand right now." He sucked in his breath, and the words came out in a rush. "Ruth, I—I'd like the right to speak to your father."

She had known for a long time that he loved her, so his request didn't surprise her. But tonight, of all nights, it upset her. She had just lost Jonathan forever, and the knowledge that he had never been hers to lose was no consolation. She wanted to race off to her own room and bury her face in a pillow. Instead, however, she had to handle this situation.

Sensing Edmund's tension, she had no desire to hurt him, and smiled up at him as she considered her reply.

"I have loved you," he said, speaking with difficulty, "for a long time."

"I know," she murmured.

Edmund squared his shoulders. "I earn a decent living as a second mate at Rakehell, but that's only the

121

beginning. In a couple of years I'm sure to be promoted to first mate, and eventually I'll be a captain."

"I've never been worried about money," Ruth said, still not certain how to answer him.

"The worst of being married to a sailor," he said, "is that I'll be at sea for long stretches. I know that isn't good, but it can't be helped. The sea is my life."

Many women in town were married to sailors, and she needed no one to tell her they led lonely, complicated lives.

Edmund paused, then became bolder. "Just say the word, and I'll go straight to your father. Right now, if he's awake."

A sense of recklessness stole over Ruth. Now was the moment to forget Jonathan. Now was the moment to concentrate on the real future that lay within her grasp. Edmund loved her. He was sober, ambitious, and gentle, so it was possible that in time she might learn to care for him. Until then she would be protected by marriage, and that shield would help her forget Jonathan Rakehell.

"If there's one thing I can't tolerate," she said, surprised by her own comment, "it's a long betrothal. I'd hate to be engaged for a whole year!"

She seemed to be encouraging him, and his hopes soared.

"We aren't society folk like the Rakehells," Ruth went on. "Nobody cares how long an engagement lasts, or whether there's even a formal betrothal." She steadied herself, then took the plunge. "Yes, Edmund. By all means—speak to my father. But on one condition." She paused.

His eyes clouded.

"I insist," Ruth said, "that we marry as soon as you come home from England!" The sooner the better, she thought, because then the nightmare might come to an end.

For a moment Edmund looked at her in stunned disbelief. Then his face cleared and he took a step toward her.

Ruth leaped to her feet, uncertain whether she was laughing or crying, and threw herself into his arms. Perhaps his kiss, his embrace, would overcome the feeling of desolation that still gripped her.

A small crowd gathered at Rakehell Wharf number three to bid farewell to the officers and men of *Flying Dragon*. Ample quantities of food and water had been taken on board for the voyage to England, and the crew would not go ashore the following morning in Boston, prior to the start of the race on the afternoon tide. The *Jean K.* had already sailed for Boston, so the adjoining berth was empty.

Jonathan was busy on board, occupied with his duties as first mate. The supplies of food, water, and wood for cooking had been in place for days. The gear of the seamen, the crew having been enlarged to twenty for the sake of efficiency, was neatly stowed in the cramped forecastle, and when he descended to the hold he made certain that the burlap sacks of corn being carried to England were secure. Captain Hartley had thought it might be preferable to carry no cargo, but had relented when Jonathan had told him that a clipper could attain her sailing potential only when she carried enough ballast. Besides, there was a great demand in England and on the Continent these days for corn, known in the Old World as maize, and no Rakehell could sail empty-handed when he knew there was a market for the merchandise he could carry.

He wished he could rid himself of his dislike for Hartley, and he reflected that he had no grounds for his uneasiness. No Rakehell master was more experienced, and the man enjoyed Jeremiah's trust. That had to be sufficient. Hartley was a reasonable man and surely would take advice from a mate who had built *Flying Dragon* and had sailed her himself.

When Jonathan climbed through the hatch onto the deck, he saw Oliver aloft, at work on the standing rigging, and he smiled quietly. Grimshaw's judgment of men had been right: the escaped slave was a natural-born sailor, and when he became accustomed to the peculiarities of a clipper, he was certain to develop into one of the most valuable members of the crew.

Glancing toward the shore, Jonathan waved to Ruth Halliburton, who was talking to Edmund, and as he waved he thought Edmund was lucky to have won her. She would make him a devoted wife.

Only two of the seamen were still on shore, bidding farewell to relatives. Jonathan inspected the two small cannon mounted fore and aft, then asked Grimshaw to open the ammunition locker. The flares fired by pistols as distress signals and shot were snug in their respective compartments, and he was pleased. His last stop was the tiny cabin in the after part of the ship that he and Edmund would share, and he nodded when he saw their foot lockers lashed to the bulkhead. It would be strange not to occupy the adjoining master's cabin that he had used during the sea trials, but he had no complaints. During his apprenticeship his only "home" at sea had been a hammock slung just inches from those on either side of him.

Coming out on deck again, he saw his father approaching with Louise and Judith, so he hurried ashore, kissed his sister lightly on the cheek, and, after a moment's hesitation, greeted Louise in the same way.

Jeremiah handed him a letter to be delivered to Jessica and a bulkier parcel for Sir Alan. "You're already familiar with most of the matters that relate to Boynton Shipping," he said, "but you may want to look through these papers before you land. Alan is certain to bombard you with questions."

Jonathan grinned. Uncle Alan had a mania for sniffing out details that the Rakehells left to subordinates.

"Brad asked me to wish you a safe voyage," Judith said. "He's sorry he couldn't see you off himself, but he had to go to a meeting of the merchants' association in Norwich."

"Thank him for me, please," Jonathan replied politely. He well knew—and he suspected his sister knew, too—that the meeting in Norwich, twelve miles up the river, could have been postponed with ease. At least Bradford Walker was no hypocrite. He thought the building of *Flying Dragon* had been a foolish venture, he had made it plain that he had no faith in clippers, and had he made an appearance today, it would have been a strain to offer encouragement.

Captain Hartley appeared, the sun gleaming on the silver braid of his bicorne hat, a small valise in his left hand. His own sea chest had been delivered earlier in the day to his cabin. He was alone, his wife and children having said their farewells to him at home because his voyages were no novelty to them.

Jonathan and Edmund automatically saluted him, and he returned the gesture, then raised his hand to his hat again as he greeted Jeremiah.

"Do you think you can win the race in this strange ship, Captain?" the head of Rakehell Building and Shipping asked genially.

"I've never sailed her, sir, so I don't know. I'll be in a better position to answer your question a month from now."

They would reach England in far less than a month, Jonathan told himself, but refrained from expressing himself aloud. His position in the weeks ahead would be delicate.

"I wish you fair seas and lively winds," Jeremiah said, offering the master the traditional farewell.

"Thank you, sir." The captain turned to his mates. "Take your time, gentlemen. We're in no hurry today."

As he approached the ship, Grimshaw bawled an order, and the boatswain's mate piped the master aboard.

Jonathan reacted to the shrill sound like a mastiff straining at a leash. "We'd best go on board, too," he said. He kissed Louise again. "Think about that figurehead while I'm away."

"I'll try," she said, but made no promise.

He turned to his sister, and then, on sudden impulse, kissed Ruth on the cheek, too. He was too preoccupied to see her face redden.

Jeremiah stood apart for a final word with his son. "All I ask is that you prove me wrong," he said. "Win this race, and everyone in shipping will know what a clipper can do!"

He was sincere, and as Jonathan gripped his hand he realized anew that his father was a magnificent, generous person. He didn't believe in the future of clipper ships, but he nevertheless wanted his son to triumph. No man could ask for greater generosity.

As soon as the two mates reached the quarterdeck, Captain Hartley gave his first command. "Bo's'n, you may cast off your moorings. Set your loose flying jib and send hands to braces."

"Aye aye, sir," Grimshaw replied, and raised his voice in a bellow.

Flying Dragon soon slid away from her berth and, gathering speed slowly, began to move at a moderate pace toward the mouth of the Thames and the open waters beyond it. Jonathan and Edmund turned to wave, and the little shore party responded.

Jeremiah Rakehell removed his square-crowned beaver hat and held it high in the air until his arm grew tired. Soon the shore party faded from sight.

The master set a course that would take the ship past the western tip of Fisher's Island, and then, following the traditional route, he would sail past Montauk Point at the tip of Long Island and head for Boston through the open Atlantic.

"Gentlemen," he said, turning to his mates, "we have all of today and most of tomorrow to reach Boston, so I intend to exercise the crew. In that way we'll become accustomed to each other."

They had a stiff beam wind as they headed out to sea, perfect weather for a clipper, and Jonathan wished the master would add more sail, much more sail. "Sir," he said after a moment's hesitation, *"Flying Dragon* performs best in weather like this under full sail."

"Thank you, Mr. Rakehell," Hartley said coolly, "but I have taken the precaution of studying this vessel's characteristics. Rest assured that if I require additional information at any time I shall ask you for it."

The message was clear, and Jonathan was forced to swallow the rebuke. The captain was in command and wanted no gratuitously offered advice, not even from the man who had built the clipper and acted as her master in her trials. Aware that he had been dismissed, he saluted and went to the main deck, then went forward to the prow.

By now, he told himself gloomily, the topgallants should have been raised, and as soon as they caught the wind, the royals above them should have been set as well. The breeze was as lively as any master could have wished, *Flying Dragon* cut sharply through the swells of a moderate sea, pitching and rolling only slightly, and as Jonathan planted his feet apart, adjusting to the ship's rhythm, his spirits sank.

Had he been in command, he soon would be raising the skysails and moonsails, adding all of his jibs and spankers, and *Flying Dragon* would be slicing through the water like a barracuda. The crew needed the incentive of a very fast run to Boston so they would gain confidence in themselves and in the ship. Instead, the clipper, capable of attaining far greater speed, was sailing at a stately pace of eight or nine knots, which was suitable for a heavy schooner or an ungainly brig.

What he would have to remember—at all times—was that he was not the master of *Flying Dragon*. Captain Hartley held that position because the ship was flying the Rakehell ensign, and the first law of the sea declared that only one man issued commands. No matter what the consequences, Jonathan knew, no matter how thoroughly he thought he understood his ship, on which his own future depended, he still was required to subordinate himself to the will and judgment of Davis Hartley.

Seventeen American and British merchantmen, most of them schooners and sloops, sailed out of Boston Harbor in ones and twos, and then, barely inching their way eastward, formed in a parallel line. A sloop of the United States Coast Guard moved up and down the line, shepherding the contestants into position, and when her captain was satisfied, he ordered the firing of a nine-inch gun on her foredeck. That shot signaled the start of the transAtlantic race, and the competition for the Boston-London mail contract was under way.

Flying Dragon held a place between the *Jean K.* and a British ship, and had Jonathan been in command, he would have shown both his heels. Certainly the clipper sailing weather was perfect. The all-important tailwind was brisk, clouds high overhead were scudding toward the east, and there were whitecaps on the waves that rose about three feet from the surface of the sea.

But *Flying Dragon* sailed at the same pace as the *Jean K.,* in a sisterly show of affection, and together they edged ahead of the British sloop. Other vessels were spreading out, and in less than two hours the Boston shoreline vanished on the horizon.

Jonathan stood alone on the deck, muttering to himself. "Hoist your royals and inner jibs! Raise your skysails. Hoist your moonsails. Hell and damnation, Hartley! Why are you loitering?"

Edmund came up beside his friend and clapped a sympathetic hand on his shoulder. "I know how you feel," he said, "but don't be impatient."

Jonathan stared at him with hard, cold eyes. "You understand sailing, Eddie. You don't need me to tell you that although prevailing winds in the northern hemisphere are from east to west, the North Atlantic is the exception. Here they run from west to east. Just feel that westerly! It's superb! *Flying Dragon* should be doing just that—flying to England. We ought to be under full sail whenever possible. We shouldn't be losing one minute of one day. Not only are we in a race, but we're trying to show the world what a clipper can accomplish."

Knowing he was right, Edmund nevertheless tried to calm him. "We've hoisted our topgallants," he said. "It seems to me the captain is feeling his way."

"Wearing blindfolds."

Edmund shook him. "Remember what Professor Kimberly at Yale always told you? Patience, young man! No ship can cross the Atlantic in a day, you know. Captain Hartley is familiarizing himself with *Flying Dragon* and the crew."

"He should be driving them a damnsight harder, the way we did in her trials."

They fell silent when Hartley appeared, sauntered to the quarterdeck, and leisurely tested the wind. He, like his mates, knew that adjustments had to be made, but he took his time before giving the necessary orders.

"Lee braces, Mr. Rakehell."

At last! "Aye aye, sir. Hands to the lee braces, bo's'n—haul taut! Square mainyard!"

The clipper responded at once, so Jonathan was momentarily mollified. But Hartley was not taking advantage of the ship's real capabilities, and he continued to brood.

He had no opportunity to complain again until he and Edmund were off duty and retired to their cabin. Then, the master's lackadaisical attitude still eating into him, he could keep silent no longer. "There's only one way to sail a clipper, and if Davis doesn't know it he should."

His friend was gentle but firm. "That's your way. Because, except for Isaac McKim, you know more about clippers than anybody on earth. But it isn't Captain Hartley's way, obviously. Like it or not, he's in command. I'm sure we'll win the race, and that's all that matters."

"We're doing no better than ten knots, and we could come close to doubling that speed when the winds are astern. We've lost sight of all the other ships, even the *Jean K.,* and I think I may be losing my mind."

Edmund laughed. "They're all astern somewhere. Get control of yourself or you'll be a nervous wreck by the time we reach England. Above all, take care not to criticize the master, or you'll cause trouble for yourself."

Jonathan tried hard to follow his friend's advice, and for a time he managed to curb his anxieties. He realized his own eagerness to demonstrate his ship's capabilities was responsible for his attitude, and common sense told him it was only natural that a captain who had sailed ordinary merchantmen all of his life wouldn't understand a clipper's potentials.

By the fifth day of the voyage, however, with the weather still fair and the following wind invariably brisk, his patience became wafer-thin. The final blow was an unexpected accident: a topgallant mast was carried away, crippling *Flying Dragon.* Jonathan decided to seize this opportunity to speak to Hartley. He waited until Edmund took the watch and then went to the master's cabin.

Davis Hartley glanced up from the log in which he was writing, looked at his first mate's face, and braced himself for the coming storm. He had known from the out-set that such a scene would take place sooner or later, and this morning's episode inevitably made it come all the sooner. Hartley well knew, as Jonathan did not—and as no man could ever prove—that the loss of the mast had been anything but accidental. Hartley had been guilty of deliberate bad steering, but his maneuver had been so clever that he could not be accused of sabotage. He had set the ship by the lee—that is, when she was running free—and the wrong order had brought the wind across her stern and on the lee side of her sails, thus laying them aback. He had known that the maneuver could easily bring down an upper mast in a ship carrying a great deal of canvas, and that was precisely what had occurred.

Now Rakehell was standing before him. The young man was not only his employer's son, but the builder of the *Flying Dragon*. Of course, Hartley was confident that his maneuver had been subtle enough so that its true intention could not be detected. Accidents often happen at sea, and even the most experienced of masters were sometimes guilty of faulty judgment, particularly when sailing ships that were unfamiliar to them. Nevertheless, Hartley knew he would have to be careful to play his cards right. "Sit down, Mr. Rakehell," he said.

"Thank you, sir," Jonathan lowered himself into a small chair bolted to the bulkhead.

"I daresay you're a trifle upset by this morning's unfortunate incident."

"Well, yes, I am, sir."

"No one regrets the accident more than I do," Hartley said, "but I'm afraid that's a penalty I've had to pay when I'm commanding a new-fangled ship. This never would have happened to me on a brig or a schooner. I'm making a full report in my log, of course."

"I'll grant you that accidents can happen to anyone, sir," Jonathan replied graciously. "All the same, there's something deeper that's been nagging away at me. Let me just say first that I realize there are risks involved. There could be more accidents. But there are times when risks have to be taken, and this is one of them." Then he hesitated.

"Speak up, Mr. Rakehell," the master said. If he could placate Jeremiah's son sufficiently to quiet him, his logs would provide ample justification for his actions, should trouble arise after he returned home.

"With all due respect, sir, we're in a race. And I can't help wondering whether there's some reason you've never used our sky and moon sails."

"Yes, I do have a reason," Hartley replied, treading carefully. "I've spent more decades at sea than I care to count, and in all that time I've never known a ship that's carried so much sail."

"She was built for that purpose, sir."

"I must be honest with you, Mr. Rakehell. *Flying Dragon* has an exceptionally narrow hull, and her V-bottom is unlike that of any ship I've ever sailed. I'll grant you that she should move like a streak of lightning when she's sailing on a wind. But you know as well as I do that winds are fickle. They're shifting constantly, a few points one way or the other. Faster than any officer of the watch and helmsman can make adjustments. Let the wind unexpectedly shift several points, as it undoubtedly will, and this fine ship will keel over. Drowning all hands, you and me included, not to mention destroying a safety record it has taken me a lifetime to build."

Jonathan shook his head vigorously, but took care not to raise his voice. "There's no chance we'd keel over or turn turtle, sir. The true secret of a clipper's construction is her extraordinary balance. I built *Flying Dragon* and I know. What's more, I experimented with small-scale models before I laid her keel. There's no ship anywhere, not even the prototype *Ann McKim,* that can match her potential performance in fair weather or foul."

Hartley knew the moment had come for him to give in gracefully—for a time. His experience-sharpened instinct told him the weather would change by morning, so this was precisely the right time to appear accommodating. "I can't and won't argue with you, Mr. Rakehell. Do I assume that you'll have no objection if I make a notation in my log to the effect that you've assured me this ship will remain upright, no matter what the weather?"

131

"Please write it in capital letters, sir. I'll be glad to sign the log statement, if you wish."

"No, that won't be necessary. Tomorrow, when you have the watch, pile on all the sail you want, and we'll find out how she will behave."

Jonathan was elated, but his euphoria was short-lived. When he awakened early the next morning, he could hear rain beating on the quarterdeck over his head. A glance out of the square window beside his bunk told him *Flying Dragon* was moving at a snail's pace in a fog so thick it was impossible to see farther than a few yards.

He donned his oilskins, then stamped up to the quarterdeck to relieve Edmund, and his mood became even more sour when he realized the wind had died away and had been reduced to a gentle, almost imperceptible breeze. He ordered all of his jibs and spankers hoisted, which increased the clipper's speed by a knot, perhaps a trifle more, but his superb, unique topsails were useless. What was more, it was too dangerous to increase her speed too much in the fog. He could come upon an iceberg or another ship so quickly that he would have no opportunity to veer and avoid a collision.

Oliver brought him a mug of scalding, black coffee and several chunks of freshly baked bread.

Jonathan grunted his thanks, tugged the brim of his storm hat lower, and chewed on the bread. He was behaving like a spoiled child, he knew, but his disappointment was so great it overwhelmed him.

The former slave continued to stand nearby.

Jonathan looked at him in irritation. "Is there something you want?"

"When weather like this," Oliver said softly, "gulls no follow ship. In bad fog, bad rain, bad wind, even birds no fly."

The observation was so sensible that Jonathan felt foolish, and grinned. "You're right, Oliver. And we're not going to fly, either. We can't control the weather, so we'll have to make the best of things. Thank you."

Oliver slipped away and vanished into the fog on the main deck.

The weather remained miserable for the next four

days and nights, which was typical of the North Atlantic in the spring. The night the weather cleared Jonathan charted the ship's position and knew that, after more than nine days at sea, she had not yet reached the halfway point on her voyage. Unless he could coax *Flying Dragon* to perform miracles and could persuade Captain Hartley to do the same when he held the watch, the chance that she would beat the speed record for a trans-Atlantic crossing was becoming dim.

In mid-morning, when he relieved the master, he saw the sky had cleared, the wind behind him had freshened, and the sea was moderate. Sailing conditions were ideal.

"Sir, do I have your permission to see how fast we can travel?"

Hartley was secretly satisfied that the weather, until now, had been cooperating with him. "Do what you please, Mr. Rakehell," he replied. Instead of going below he lingered on the quarterdeck to see what happened.

"Bo's'n, all hands on deck, if you please."

"Aye aye, sir," Grimshaw replied with his toothless grin.

Feet pounded on the deck.

Second Mate Edmund Barker realized what was taking place and hurried to the quarterdeck, too, hastily donning a pea jacket and trying to blink the sleep from his eyes.

Thanks to the foul weather, the ship had been under only topsails and jibs. Her courses had not been set, and now the topmen eagerly went aloft to increase sail.

The braces were manned, and Jonathan ordered, "Set to'gans'ls!"

As the ship began to respond, he directed the helmsman, "Meet her!"

This stopped the clipper from swinging any further round.

"Keep her so!" he told the helmsman.

Sail after sail cracked and billowed, and the clipper, living up to her breed, started to slash through the water with the agility of a porpoise.

"Nothing off!" Jonathan told the helmsman.

Flying Dragon continued to increase her speed as a

sea of white canvas opened high above the deck on the three principal masts and caught the wind.

"Set skys'ls!" This was the first time the order had been given on the voyage, and Jonathan's pulse raced as the boatswain roared the command and the topmen worked in unison.

Captain Hartley peered in open-mouthed wonder as the skysails were unfurled. The jury-rigging had been effective, and the temporary top portion of the mast broken five days earlier held firm. This was the first time Grimshaw had ever seen skysails, too, and he shook his head. The other members of the crew, with the exception of Oliver, were old hands after the sea trials, and none were impressed. The former slave nodded solemnly, then began to chuckle in obvious approval. It was evident that he was enjoying the unique experience.

"Set moons'ls!"

The sails at the very top of the masts cracked like rifle shots as they opened.

This was the moment for which the clipper had been created. Her body lean and lithe, her sails seemingly filling the sky, she resembled a majestic cloud as she cut through the blue-green water of the Atlantic, her varnished hull gleaming in the sunlight.

Again she picked up speed, and for a moment Jonathan felt a surge of exhilaration. He had made his dream come true.

But something was amiss, and his sense of joy faded. Certainly *Flying Dragon* was moving far more rapidly, but she felt strangely sluggish underfoot. Having known the sensation of flying on board the *Ann McKim,* Jonathan realized he was experiencing no similar sensation now.

Craning his neck, he studied the great sails methodically. All were filled, and the ship was sailing smartly. But not smartly enough. The problem that plagued her on her sea trials was recurring. Jonathan had hoped she would overcome the difficulty when the crew learned to function together, but today their teamwork had been faultless.

He was puzzled and studied the registering dial of a streamlined rotator that would tell him the ship's speed.

This device, known as a "log," had been developed early in the century by an inventor named Edward Massey, an Englishman, and consisted of a line, with knots in precise spacing that was towed astern.

The instrument told him the clipper was sailing at a speed of fourteen knots. A respectable speed, to be sure, but it wasn't too much to hope that, under full sail in ideal conditions, she might reach a speed of twenty knots. Why, even a sloop, if handled properly, could work up to a speed of fourteen knots for brief periods.

"Mr. Barker," Jonathan said, "I'll be obliged if you'll relieve me for a short time."

"Very good, sir." Edmund took the watch.

Jonathan inspected the mizzenmast, then moved to the mainmast and finally to the foremast. Everything seemed in order and, his bewilderment increasing, he removed his boots and stockings. He climbed via the shrouds to the mainmast crosstrees, then to the topmast or upper crosstrees, and made his way to the crow's nest, where the lookout was stationed.

Flying Dragon slashed through the swells, pitching and tossing only slightly, and the sails remained filled. Everything seemed to be functioning perfectly, even when he looked down at the sea and watched the clipper cutting through the water.

He stayed aloft for a half-hour or more, making and rechecking calculations, and when he finally climbed down to the deck again, Captain Hartley joined him.

"What's wrong, Mr. Rakehell?" The master's concern seemed genuine, and he took care not to gloat.

"I'm damned if I know, sir. All I can tell you is that she isn't responding as she should."

"She appears to be handling well enough, in my opinion," the master said. "I'd be reluctant to use anywhere near this much sail in anything but a direct beam wind, but I can find nothing wrong with her performance."

"She should be traveling four or five knots faster, Captain." Jonathan frowned.

Hartley raised an eyebrow. "Four or five knots? I think you ask the impossible of the ship, Mr. Rakehell. No vessel that uses sails can attain such speed!"

"This ship can, sir. And will." Jonathan returned to the quarterdeck and relieved Edmund. For the rest of his watch he continued to observe and ponder, and at one point he summoned the boatswain. "Grimshaw," he said, "I want you to study *Flying Dragon*'s behavior, and when the men have nothing better to occupy them, I want them to do the same. One of you may be able to pick up a clue that I'm missing."

"You mean she can do better than this, sir?"

"Far better—even when we're jury-rigged," Jonathan replied emphatically.

A short time later he saw Oliver climbing to the crow's nest, making his way up the lines with agility. He stayed there for an hour or more, remaining motionless for long periods, his face expressionless and his eyes half-closed. Perhaps, Jonathan thought bitterly, he had found a convenient excuse to take a cat nap.

Edmund was concerned when he returned to the quarterdeck to take the next watch. "Any luck?"

Jonathan shook his head. "None."

"It's strange."

"I could have sworn that all my calculations were accurate, Eddie. I went over them so many times I knew them in my sleep. There's no way we can break the record, and we'll be fortunate if we don't disgrace ourselves."

"Does this mean you may have to rebuild her?"

Jonathan's Rakehell jaw jutted forward, and at this moment he bore a remarkable resemblance to the portraits of his ancestors. "If I must," he said, "I'll strip her plank by plank and tear her down to her keel. Yes, and I'll even replace the keel if that's what is causing our problem. I'll go into debt. I'll do anything that's necessary to prove that clippers are the ships of tomorrow!"

He stamped off to his tiny cabin, where he had to sit on his sea chest after he found pen and paper. He filled page after page, drawing sketches of the ship from memory, then checking and rechecking the calculations he had made while building her. He could find nothing wrong, and an unfamiliar feeling of despair came over him as he tried to force himself to sleep for a few hours.

Late in the afternoon he awakened with a start when

he heard pounding feet and shouted orders. *Flying Dragon* was wearing because the wind had veered to the nor'nor'-east and had reduced her speed again.

The frustrations that welled up within Jonathan were overpowering but he fought hard against them. Somehow he would find the cause of the clipper's sluggishness. Somehow he would persuade Captain Hartley that it was safe to utilize full sail under virtually all weather conditions. How Brad Walker would laugh at him if he failed! The very thought of his brother-in-law's smirk steadied him, and he promised himself he would allow nothing to prevent him from attaining his goal.

In spite of his determination, however, he encountered continuing difficulties he could not control. The wind, although it continued to blow from west to east, was variable during the next week, and the master, unconvinced by his first mate's renewed arguments, exercised his prerogative of insisting that *Flying Dragon* operate under reduced sail.

On the few occasions when he permitted the sky and moon sails to be set for brief periods, the clipper still did not live up to her potential. After spending twenty-one days at sea, Jonathan knew he was fighting a battle he could not win.

On the twenty-third day the lookout's cry of "Land ho!" heralded the first sighting of Land's End, at the westernmost tip of Britain. Jonathan paced the main deck incessantly when he was not on watch. By now his neck was sore from peering upward.

Suddenly he halted. *Flying Dragon* was not using her three top sails, but even under course, topsails, and topgallants, she should be doing better than nine or ten knots per hour. Captain Hartley's ultra-conservatism had cost the clipper days at sea, but a fundamental structural error of some kind was equally responsible.

Oliver lowered himself to the deck from the crow's nest, and Jonathan, who hadn't known he was aloft, was surprised.

The former slave approached him diffidently. "You save me, so you my friend," he said. "Now I help you and be your friend."

Jonathan nodded absently, but remained polite.

"Bowsprit too short," Oliver said.

For a moment Jonathan was incredulous, and then the pieces of the puzzle began to fall into place. A longer bowsprit, fitted at a different angle, would lift her head when she was running. This relatively simple correction could make a difference in her speed and stability.

"What makes you think the bowsprit should be lengthened and raised?" he asked.

Oliver shrugged modestly. "Same on dhow," he said. "Dhow go fast, too. Not as fast as clipper, but plenty much fast for ship with just one sail."

"If you're right," Jonathan told him, "I owe you a promotion, a fine dinner, and the most handsome suit of clothes a London tailor can make."

Jonathan went quickly to his tiny cabin and set to work with a vengeance. His lack of patience tended to make him sloppy, so he deliberately slowed his calculations, taking his time as he waded through the mathematical formulae in which stresses were related to speed, balance, and weight. He became so engrossed that he lost count of the passage of time until Grimshaw tapped at the door.

"Mr. Barker's compliments, sir, and he wants to know if ye'll be takin' the watch."

It was inconsiderate to be tardy for watch relief, but Jonathan felt no guilt as he raced to the quarterdeck. "Sorry I'm late, Eddie," he said, "but I think I've finally located the trouble, thanks to Oliver. If I'm right we'll put *Flying Dragon* into dock in my uncle's yard, and the problem can be corrected in a few days."

Shortly before noon on the twenty-fourth day of her voyage from Boston, the clipper finally put into a berth in the Royal Mail complex of docks just below London Bridge.

The final leg of the voyage seemed interminable and stressed what Jonathan and all of the other competitors in the race well knew, that the rules of the contest weren't really fair. The Thames was tidal for part of its length, but the distance from the tidal flats at the Nore, off Sheerness, to London Bridge was more than forty miles, as the crow flies. So the wind, if favorable for a ship heading down river to the Estuary and the English Channel, had to be unfavorable for a vessel heading for London Docks. Consequently a laggard, meeting a favorable wind and in-coming tide, easily might have overtaken a ship that had been far ahead of her.

What was more, the river was vastly congested, with ships from all over the world entering or leaving port. The docks were literally a forest of masts, and the Thames itself was a maze of shipping of all sizes and destinations. Hence she had to be navigated with great caution, her masters and crews always dependent on the vagaries of the wind, which no man could control.

As it happened, *Flying Dragon* was well out of the competition, regardless of the difficulties that she, like the other contestants, encountered in the last hours of the voyage.

Three of the others already rode at anchor, and Jonathan was deeply embarrassed when he learned that the *Jean K.,* which had arrived the previous evening, had been declared the winner. Rakehell would be awarded the mail contract, and the schooner's master had won the prize of one thousand dollars.

What compounded Jonathan's chagrin was the fact that a British sloop had come in second and an American sloop had been third. The clipper, supposedly the fastest of vessels afloat, would not even be given an honorable mention.

Flying Dragon's sluggishness had been partly responsible, of course, but if her master had crowded on full sail through the voyage, she still could have won handily. No excuses would be offered, but Jonathan felt that the captain deserved a share of the blame.

He found it odd, however, that Davis Hartley was not perturbed by the clipper's failure. He accepted the victory of the *Jean K.* with equanimity and seemed to be delighted that the master of the schooner had been granted the large cash prize.

As nearly as Jonathan could judge, Hartley actually seemed pleased and relieved that he had lost. His attitude made no sense.

II

Commodore Sir William Alexander, Knight of the Bath, was not only a high-ranking officer in the Royal Navy, but he looked every inch the part of the commander of the China Seas flotilla. Tall and spare, his gold-laced blue uniform immaculate, his hair graying at the temples, his stern, lean face somewhat relaxed, he sat beneath a canopy on the aft deck of his flagship, the seventy-four gun H.M.S. *Valiant,* and composed a letter to his wife. As always, he was cool and remote, impervious to the bedlam around him.

The *Valiant* rode at anchor in the deep water channel of the Pearl River Delta, about two miles below Whampoa, a gun crew standing by near a quarterdeck gun as other vessels moved toward Canton. Any strange ship that approached the harbor was required to halt and identify herself.

On the port side the owners of eight or ten small sampans jockeyed for position near the fantail, vying with each other as they tried to sell the commissary lieutenant their melons, Chinese cabbages, and white carrots. All were shouting simultaneously, trying to drown each other out, but Sir William did not hear them.

Hovering nearby were three high-decked junks of the Imperial Chinese Navy, each with a mammoth human eye painted in bright colors on her squat prow. These symbols were supposed to ward off evil spirits and make the junks invincible in battle. But the ancient cannon lashed to the decks of the junks were so feeble, so inadequate for the task assigned to them that they were ludicrous. And the sailors who wore padded cotton uniforms in spite of the heat and who crowded the decks, staring at the great British warship, resembled an undisciplined rabble.

Sir William rightly ignored the junks and their crews. A few well-placed shots would send all three to the bottom, and their guns would explode before they could inflict any damage on an enemy. His mind uncluttered by his surroundings, the commodore wrote in a neat, well-formed hand:

> You will never know, dear Molly, how much I miss you and the children. I've spent almost two years on this godforsaken station, relieved by only one voyage to Calcutta, and the admiralty gives me no hope that I'll soon have a successor. In fact, Admiral Gilbert has written to me from India, hinting that I shall be forced to remain here for at least another year. No doubt I'll be promoted to rear admiral for being a good boy, but I don't know that the stars on my epaulettes are worth the endurance of this dreary place.
>
> Some senior officers have brought their families out here, but without exception they regret it. Everyone in the little foreign colony at Macao knows everyone else's business, and the gossip there flows as swiftly as the waters of the Pearl in the rainy season that, the Lord be praised, is now coming to an end. The mosquitoes, flies, and other flying pests are as bloodthirsty as the two-legged gossips of Macao, who would lose no time sinking their fangs into you. After all, my dear, you are the wife of the vicious villain, Alexander, who is made of cast iron and has no conscience.
>
> Unfortunately, I do not jest. That is how I am universally regarded. I do my duty, upholding the interests of the Crown and obeying the di-

rectives of the admiralty to the letter. No one realizes that I loathe my work, but have no choice in its execution. I would give five years of my life to be walking hand in hand with you in the garden of our Sussex home.

Tonight I shall dine with Soong Chao and his lovely but strangely unorthodox daughter, and I look forward to the occasion. They are among the only truly civilized people in this strange world, and in their company I do find respite from my cares of office.

A lieutenant approached the table, stood at attention, and saluted.

The commodore finished a sentence before looking up. "Yes, Mr. Foster?"

"The master of that Dutch merchantman has been brought aboard, sir, and he's very indignant."

Sir William carefully placed his unfinished letter in a leather folder, placed his quill pen in a jar of sand, and sighed. "I'll attend to him in short order. Has his ship been searched?"

"Not yet, sir."

"Order the search made while I question the fellow. You may bring him to me."

A few moments later a bearded, red-faced Dutchman in rough sailor's attire was hustled forward by two husky Royal Marines in scarlet tunics and blue trousers who grasped his arms.

"Welcome," Sir William said, a hint of irony in his voice. "Won't you sit down, Captain?"

The marines shoved the Dutchman into a canvas chair opposite the commodore.

"May I see your identity papers, please?"

"You have no right to see them!" the Dutchman shouted. "These are not British waters! I have been abducted from my own quarterdeck, and—"

"Come, now," Sir William cut in quietly. "The Royal Navy has the right to do as we please because we take that right. Give me your papers voluntarily, or they shall be removed from you forcibly."

The Dutchman looked up at the burly marines, knew he was trapped, and surrendered a packet of papers that he removed from an inner pocket.

The commodore inspected them in a leisurely manner. "Ah, so you are Henrik van der Groet, master of the *Zuyder Zee,* a barque of twenty-one hundred tons. What are you doing so far from home?"

"The same as dozens of other masters. Trying to earn a living in honest trade."

"The honesty of that trade is the reason we're holding this little chat. What cargo do you carry?"

"Spices from the Indonesian islands. There's a great demand for them in Canton." Captain van der Groet became surly. "You'll find my complete manifest among my documents."

Sir William was silent for a few moments as he scanned the papers. Then he asked gently, "Are you quite sure you carry no opium?"

"Are you mad, Commodore?" The Dutchman became even more annoyed. "Everyone in the Orient knows how you *verdammte* English behave at Canton. You have no right of seizure, but you stop and search every foreign ship that puts in here. You confiscate all the opium you find, and then you beat the master and his crew to teach them a lesson. And why? Because you want all the opium trade for yourselves. You allow the Americans and French a trickle because their governments protest so vehemently when their citizens are molested."

"If you're innocent, Captain van der Groet, you will have nothing to fear from us. You'll be free to go on your way and sell your fine, fragrant spices at Whampoa." The commodore's smile was almost pleasant. "Even as we chat, your ship is being inspected."

"You dare?"

"His Majesty's Navy dares," Sir William said flatly.

"You are not afraid I will complain to my own government?"

"Complain all you please," the commodore replied gently. "Even if you sail straight back to Holland with a cargo of tea, let's say, you won't arrive there for six or eight months in a ship as slow as a barque. Suppose your government listens to you and makes representations to London. The Foreign Office will send an inquiry to the Royal Navy, which will refer it to me. Or my successor," he added under his breath. "Another six to twelve months will have passed. Our records here will show you were suspected of carrying opium. The Royal Navy has taken it upon itself to insure that no opium is smuggled into China. It is in Great Britain's best interests to make certain the laws of the Chinese emperor are obeyed. Only in that way can we maintain our trade here, you see."

His sophistry was almost too much for the Dutchman, who made a strangling noise in his throat.

"So, my dear van der Groet, in yet another year to a year and a half, the Foreign Office will receive our report and will communicate with the government of the Netherlands. Regardless of whether you are innocent or guilty, the protest will be rejected. The Royal Navy is doing its duty."

The young officer drew near and saluted. "There's no opium on board the *Zuyder Zee,* sir. Our inspectors say her manifest is accurate, so they've given her clearance."

"Thank you, Foster. There, Captain van der Groet, you see? All that fuss for nothing. I wish you a pleasant and profitable stay at Whampoa. But don't try to go into Canton itself. I give you a friendly warning. The Chinese are very quick to cut off the heads of foreigners who enter their territory."

Van der Groet struggled to his feet. "You are very smug, Commodore, very sure of yourself. But you assume responsibilities you have no call to take. You usurp the rights of the Chinese themselves. They hate you and all your kind, Commodore, and one of these days it will be your heads they will sever!"

"See Captain van der Groet back to his ship," the commodore told the two marines. "He's innocent of wrong-doing, so I want him to suffer no harm."

The marines dragged the Dutchman away.

Sir William felt sorry for the man, but his own harsh attitude had been deliberately assumed. The next time van der Groet came to Canton he would think very carefully before trying to smuggle in a cargo of opium for

145

which he would make a far larger profit than his spices could earn.

Lieutenant Foster still stood at attention.

"What now?" the commodore asked plaintively.

"A British schooner, the *Mermaid,* has dropped anchor below us, sir, and her master craves the indulgence of an interview with you to obtain clearance to enter Whampoa."

"Quite so. I'll see him, naturally." Sir William was relieved. The Royal Navy policy was many-sided, and British masters, unlike foreigners, were treated with great consideration. The interview would be brief, giving him ample time to finish his letter and bathe before going ashore to dine with Soong Chao.

A tall, shabbily attired man, the gold braid on his bicorne tarnished, a stubble of beard on his face, shambled forward and extended his hand. "Captain Frederick Flint of the schooner *Mermaid,* Commodore."

Sir William was forced to shake his hand, but did not rise. "Welcome to China, Master Flint."

"Thank you kindly." The Englishman dropped into the canvas chair without an invitation. He looked at the commodore for an instant, then glanced away. "What do you need to know about me and my ship?"

"Very little. The Royal Navy expects British merchant masters to be honorable and truthful."

"Of course." Flint's gaze continued to shift constantly.

The commodore's long experience in the South China Sea had taught him a great deal about the civilians with whom he dealt, and he felt certain the *Mermaid* was carrying a rich cargo of opium. But his own hands were tied; he needed what the admiralty called "good cause" to inspect a British ship. "File a copy of your manifest with my principal clerk, Master Flint. That's the long and short of formality."

A slow smile spread across the man's face.

"By the way, what cargo are you carrying?"

Frederick Flint shifted in his chair. "Oh, a little of this and a bit of that. Goods from Birmingham and York and Sheffield."

"You didn't happen to pick up any cargo in India,

146

I presume," Sir William said, making an obvious reference to opium.

"Never!" Flint looked horrified.

"I'm pleased to hear it. Should you be carrying drugs, you'd be wise to sail closer to the mouth of the delta. The Chinese smugglers would lose no time coming to you on their junks, and your hands would be clean."

"Commodore, I'd never—"

"One moment." Sir William interrupted curtly. "I'm obliged to offer you an explanation, Master Flint. If you land opium at Whampoa, you'll be breaking a Chinese law. A law they consider so important the edict was signed by the emperor himself. If you should be caught, the viceroy of the province would send troops to seize you and drag you into Canton. You'd be lucky if they executed you quickly. Their customary routine is to place a condemned man in a cramped basket, suspend him in the air for days without food or water, and torture him to death very slowly. Their concept of justice is far less merciful than ours."

Frederick Flint shuddered. "That's one good reason I'd never allow opium on the *Mermaid*," he said piously.

"I'm glad to hear it because there is literally nothing I could do to help you. And don't fool yourself into believing you've developed a foolproof smuggling system. They've all been tried. Whampoa crawls with spies and informers, and if you smuggled in a single pound of drugs, that fact would be reported to the viceroy's palace within an hour."

"Commodore, I swear to you on the memory of my dead mother—"

"No swearing is necessary," Sir William replied with distaste. "Give my clerk a copy of your manifest, and the rest is up to you." He reached for the letter in the folder and dipped his pen into a jar of ink.

Flint needed a few moments to realize he had been dismissed summarily. He started to speak, thought better of it in the presence of this austere Royal Navy officer, and rose to his feet. As he turned away he pushed his hat back on his head and wiped beads of sweat from his forehead.

It was cool under the awning, and Sir William reflected that he had never seen a man trying harder to conceal something from the authorities. He was willing to wager almost any sum that the *Mermaid* was carrying many chests of opium in her hold. Well, Flint was on his own now. If he should be apprehended and punished, to be sure, the navy's directives would require that a formal protest demanding his immediate release be sent to the viceroy. Sometimes, after repeated, urgent requests, a foreign prisoner was released, but on other occasions he was tortured in public for as long as a fortnight before he died in captivity. No one could predict the moods of Chinese officialdom or divine the reasons for their erratic responses.

It would be helpful, of course, to hold a face-to-face meeting with the viceroy, but the commodore had long abandoned that hope. The Chinese were adamant in their demands that all foreigners, regardless of their status, kowtow before the personal representative of the Celestial Emperor, and no self-respecting Englishman, much less a flotilla commander who had been knighted for valor in battle, would be willing to abase himself so.

Sir William dipped his pen into his ink jar and resumed his letter writing, shutting out his surroundings. The stench of rotting vegetation and human refuse was ever-present in the delta, and now it mingled with the odors of garlic and onions, peanut oil and frying fish on board the nearby war junks as the Chinese cooks prepared their evening meal. But the commodore's self-discipline was so great that, as he wrote to his wife, he imagined he could smell the honeysuckle that climbed the walls in his Sussex garden.

Meantime, Frederick Flint, hiding his elation, was rowed back to his own ship in a Royal Navy gig. He swaggered as he made his way to the quarterdeck, then winked at his worried first mate. "All's well," he said succinctly. "Weigh anchor and we'll put into port."

Soon the *Mermaid* was inching up the channel toward the unique complex at Whampoa.

The community faced toward the south on the river,

where more than thirty docks and jetties jutted out into the water. Most were made of wood and had been hastily built, but those owned by the East India Company, Boynton Shipping, and other British concerns had been constructed of stone. Directly behind the waterfront stood the Chinese Customs House, where foreigners were required to file copies of their cargo manifests.

The area was so crowded and space was so precious that all trees and shrubs had been removed. At the western end of the complex stood the "cow yard" where the animals jointly owned by the foreigners grazed, and near the eastern end stood a vegetable garden owned by the British and maintained by their local help.

Standing in a long row and stretching out for a distance of almost three-quarters of a mile were the ugly, huge warehouses of the Chinese hong merchants and the foreigners. All were cavernous, oblong structures made of stone and wood, and all were two or three stories high. Two were the property of Soong Chao, and three others were owned by lesser Chinese merchants.

Those buildings that belonged to the foreigners, called "factories" for some reason that no one knew, were extraordinary. Vast quantities of merchandise were stored on the first and second floors, and the managers and their assistants had their living quarters and dining halls on the top floors. Approximately two hundred white men lived and worked in the thirteen foreign factories, served by an army of Chinese. There were no women or children in Whampoa. In front of each warehouse-dwelling the flags of the various nations represented there drooped listlessly in the late afternoon air, the breeze having died away. France, Spain, and Denmark, the United States, Sweden, and the Netherlands each owned one factory. The rest were British.

No foreigners remained confined in Whampoa for more than six months. Canton was closed to them, the forbidding city walls behind the compound excluding them, and only a favored few, among them the commander of the British flotilla, were allowed to go through the Petition Gate and enter Canton itself. The bleak life

149

that men lived here tried their nerves, and twice each year they went off to Macao for a rest of several weeks. In no other way could Whampoa be endured.

But there were some who found ways to make the best of their isolation, and no one was more ingenious in devising escapes from boredom than Owen Bruce, the burly owner and manager of one of the independent British warehouses. He had spent the last eight of his forty-three years here and had learned the art of making himself comfortable. There were no reminders of the Orient in his parlor and bedroom, every stick of his heavy furniture having come from England. He refused to eat Chinese food, having taught his cook how to prepare British meals, and his favorite drink was the whiskey he imported in large quantities from his native Glasgow.

His face was ruggedly ugly, and there were scars on his chest and shoulders as he donned a thin shirt of loosely woven silk. Owen Bruce knew how to live well. Stuffing the shirt into his trousers, he wandered into the parlor, which was the cooler room, and picked up the stiff drink that had just been poured for him.

The young woman who sprawled indolently in an easy chair, the high heels of her shoes resting on the carpet that had been loomed in Leeds, was the only reminder that this was indeed China. Thanks to the thigh-high slits on either side of her cheongsam, which revealed her bare thighs, and her very heavy cosmetics, she was flamboyantly attractive. Her name was Wong Ai-li, but her foreign clients knew her as Alice Wong, and her services were in great demand. Her fees were exorbitant, but her customers agreed she was worth every penny they paid her.

She, too, held a glass of whiskey in her hand. It was half-empty, and Bruce had no idea that, before he had come into the room, she had poured the contents into his house plants. Her clients often liked her to drink with them, but that wasn't part of her bargain, and as she loathed alcoholic beverages, she disposed of them in her own way.

Alice barely glanced in Bruce's direction, peering at him for an instant through lashes stiff with blackening. He, too, had dressed, so she assumed he wouldn't want her again today and soon would pay and dismiss her. Unlike some of the younger foreign devils, Bruce tired after one session.

Bruce glanced at his pocket watch, muttered something under his breath, and then smiled slightly when a loud tap sounded at the door. "Come in!" he called.

Master Frederick Flint entered the room, removing his hat out of deference to the prosperous factor.

"I heard you were docking," Bruce said. "I've been expecting you for the past three weeks." Not bothering to introduce the young woman, he poured his visitor a drink.

"I was delayed at Calcutta," Flint said, looking uneasily at Alice. "My—ah—special merchandise required special packaging."

"You had no troubles with our local saint, the commodore?"

"Not really." Again Flint looked at the girl.

Bruce waved negligently. "She doesn't understand a word of English," he said, then addressed her in the Cantonese dialect. "You may go when you finish your drink."

A pouting smile played on her heavily rouged lips, and she extended a delicate hand.

The factor reached into his pocket and placed a gold coin in her palm.

She looked at it, but did not move.

Bruce paid her a second coin, murmuring a curse, then turned back to his guest. "So your merchandise is intact."

"Every last ounce of it," Flint said. "The junks and sampans of local dealers swarmed all around me when I entered the delta. But I followed your orders and told them I had nothing to sell them."

Alice stretched and walked to the nearest open window, her drink in one hand. The men were paying no attention to her, so she allowed the better part of the contents to trickle down the outer wall. If she could, she wanted to linger for a few more moments. Her ability to understand English, French, and Dutch was one of her most closely guarded secrets. She had never revealed this to any of her foreign clients, except for a favored few

151

whom she liked and trusted—and Bruce was not among these. His conversation was fascinating, in any case, and she wanted to delay her departure as long as she dared.

"You won't regret it," Bruce said emphatically. "The prices for goods landed here are almost fifty percent higher than the dealers in the delta will pay. Because the risks are reduced."

"How so?"

"That's my business," Bruce said curtly. "After dark my dockworkers will bring your cargo here for storage, and within a week you'll be paid."

"We split the proceeds? Fifty-fifty?" There was a whining note in Flint's voice.

"That's our agreement," Bruce replied angrily. "I always keep my bargains."

Alice had heard enough. Placing her glass on a table, she walked slowly to the door, her hips swaying provocatively as she took tiny steps. "You will want me to come here the first day of next week at the usual time?" she asked in Cantonese.

Bruce grinned at her. "Aye," he said.

Frederick Flint moistened his lips. He had seen how much the factor had paid the wench, but his profits from his cargo would enable him to give her an outrageous fee, too. He hadn't had a woman in a long time, and this Chinese girl was luscious.

Alice's walk became purposeful, and she increased her pace when she reached Thirteen Factories Street at the rear of the compound, just inside the Canton Wall.

Two soldiers in uniforms of drab yellow cotton halted her briefly at the Petition Gate.

Their expressions were long familiar to her. It was plain they wanted her themselves, even though they hated her for selling her body to the Fan Kuei. She hailed the head of a team of palanquin bearers, and before closing the bamboo curtains, she told him her destination in a low tone too soft for the soldiers to hear.

The end-of-the-day traffic was heavy, and not until three-quarters of an hour later did the bearers deposit the girl at one of the side entrances to the palace.

Alice reached under her collar and drew out a thin

chain, to which was attached a jade medallion with two oxen carved on it.

The officer in charge of the detail looked at the medallion, the expression of contempt and lust vanishing from his face, and his manner became deferential. He bowed low, then conducted the young woman into the palace, leading her through a labyrinth of tunnels and corridors.

Obviously the route was not new to Alice. She knew where to turn without being directed, and her step was confident. It was not accidental that they encountered no one else on the walk.

The private chamber of Lo Fang was starkly simple. Rows of swords, spears, knives, and firearms, including Western-made pistols, stood in holders on the walls, which had no other decorations. The floor of inlaid woods was bare, highly polished, and the only furniture consisted of a pallet, with a rough woolen blanket over it, a table of plain wood that stood about a foot off the floor, and a small chest of drawers.

The viceroy's majordomo was sitting cross-legged on the floor, reading a bulky document when the girl came into the room. His face expressionless, he placed his reading matter face down on the table, then motioned her to the pallet.

Alice was careful to arrange her skirt as decorously as she could before she spoke, and then she launched into an account of the talk she had overheard.

Lo Fang's eyes bored into her, but he did not interrupt, and when she finished, he said quietly, "Tell me again."

She repeated her story.

He nodded, helped her to her feet, and patted her clumsily on the shoulder. "You have done well," he said. "Go, and speak of this to no one. And for the next two days do not return to the concession of the Fan Kuei. No one must suspect the role you have just played."

"What will become of the opium?" she asked as she rose to her feet.

His smile resembled the grin of a skeleton and was humorless. "Fear not. No one will smoke a single pipeful."

"What will become of the pigs, Bruce and the ship's captain? How I would love to see them lose their heads in the Square of the Great Temple!"

Lo Fang's expression became thoughtful. "If I had my own way," he said, "I would strangle one, then the other with a thread of strong silk." He sighed and shrugged. "Do not concern yourself with such matters. Leave them to those who know best how to deal with them."

The girl lowered her head in resignation, then departed at once.

Lo Fang immediately climbed a flight of stairs to the viceroy's inner sanctum, a tiny room crowded with statues, wall banners, and bric-a-brac. The air was thick with the scent of incense burning in two bronze lion's head pots, and although evening had not yet come, a pair of oil lamps were lighted behind a pile of cushions heaped on the floor. Teng Ting-chen, the divine manifestation of the Celestial Emperor, sat on the cushions, clad in a shapeless old gown of faded silk and embroidered slippers that had seen better days.

He pushed his metal-rimmed spectacles onto his forehead and laid aside the handsome, hand-printed book of one thousand year old poetry he had been reading. "Your face tells me there are problems, Lo Fang. Am I never to have an hour I can call my own?"

Wasting no time on preliminaries, the majordomo repeated what Alice Wong had told him.

The viceroy took off his spectacles and removed an almost invisible fleck of lint with the long nail of his little finger. "The man Bruce is a respected member of the English community who owns his own factory and has become wealthy here. What do you know of the sea captain?"

"He is nothing, Excellency," Lo Fang said with unconcealed disgust. "Another greedy foreign devil who deserves to lose his head after he has been subjected to the Torments of Fifty Days and Nights."

"I know you. I am sure you would have me send troops to Bruce's factory, seize the opium, and arrest the guilty."

"Of course, Excellency. They are deliberately breaking and defying imperial law. Such brazen conduct cannot be tolerated."

Teng Ting-chen absently cleaned his spectacles with the tail of his long gown. "I am told by Soong Chao, whose word I trust, that Sir William Alexander is a civilized and compassionate man. Nevertheless, he commands a squadron of many powerful warships. Until recently there were only three at anchor in the delta. Now there are five, and their guns could kill thousands of our people, setting fire to countless homes, if they bombard Canton. Surely Alexander will be forced to do this if we move into Whampoa and remove two British subjects. He obeys the orders of those who stand above him, just as I obey my master, the emperor. Alexander's many letters have warned me of what he will be obliged to do if I apprehend Englishmen, no matter what offense they have committed."

"You would let these Fan Kuei go unpunished, Excellency?"

Teng Ting-chen took a joss stick from an ivory holder, broke it into four pieces, and dropped them into the incense burners. "For the present my hands are bound with thongs of silk and shackles of iron. China is too weak to make war with the English. Their great ships make a mockery of our war junks. The accurate fire of their soldiers' rifles will decimate the ranks of our poor troops before they fire a single shot with their ancient blunderbusses. The court in Peking knows, I well know, and only you fail to understand, Lo Fang, that the Middle Kingdom would be badly beaten in a war with the English."

A vein pulsed on the crown of the majordomo's shaved head. "Then no harm may come to these evil Fan Kuei who dare to defy the edicts of the emperor?"

"For the present they may not be touched."

"No accident will befall them?" There was a pleading note in Lo Fang's voice.

"There will be no accidents," the viceroy replied firmly, and betrayed his agitation only by removing the guard from his long nail, then replacing it.

"What of the opium that is being smuggled into Whampoa, perhaps at this very moment?"

"Ah, the opium! Enough of it, I am sure, to make slaves and paupers of many hundreds of our benighted people." Teng Ting-chen picked up his book of poetry and fingered it lovingly. "Under the law I have every right to seize and confiscate it, to throw it into a pond, and let it soak there until it becomes useless. And kills my favorite goldfish. But it is a delicate matter to take official action in a matter such as this. If I become involved, Sir William Alexander will also become involved."

Lo Fang bared his teeth in a grimace. "There are other ways this problem could be handled, Excellency."

"You are too quick and nimble for me, Lo Fang. Remember your place hereafter, and allow me to make the suggestions."

The majordomo accepted the rebuke and, lowering his head, mumbled an apology.

The viceroy smiled. "As I was about to observe," he said brightly, "I have read of a cook at the Forbidden Palace in the time of Ming who knew more than one thousand ways to prepare the skin of a duck. All were succulent and delightful."

Lo Fang's dark eyes burned. "I understand, Excellency. Rest assured that your orders will be obeyed."

"Not my orders!" The viceroy sounded faintly annoyed. "I have been told nothing of this load of opium. I have never heard of its existence. But in a land such as ours, crowded with the poor, such a cargo would be a rich prize for the many brigands, thieves, and robbers who are bold and fearless."

"Of course, Excellency. Brigands have long been the curse of the Middle Kingdom."

"Let me know the outcome tomorrow, no later than the hour when I drink my first cup of tea," Teng Ting-chen said. "Brigands are noted for striking swiftly when the purse they will cut is heavy with silver."

Sarah Applegate had made herself several Western-style dresses, and it didn't matter that they were fashioned of the special, soft silk that came from Shantung. She didn't care, either, that they were full-skirted with square necklines, in the style Dolly Madison had made popular two decades earlier, when she had been First Lady of the United States. Sarah always wore one of her Western gowns when a foreign visitor was being entertained.

Sitting opposite Soong Chao at the tiled table, she had supervised every aspect of the meal's preparation, and now she faultlessly directed its serving. The banquet began with dim sum, tiny dumplings filled with an astonishing variety of meats, fish, seafood, and vegetables. Then came a spiced fish dish from Chekiang, redolent of shredded ginger root, which was followed by a Cantonese specialty, stirred eggs with bean-thread noodles, to which ground pork was added. A dish of assorted vegetables, including bean sprouts, water chestnuts, and snow peas, enabled members of the party to clear their palates.

Only Lai-tse lu refused the warm rice wine, which was served in gold-trimmed lacquered cups. Ever since childhood she had disliked alcoholic drinks, so she abstained deliberately and instead drank an aromatic, almost colorless tea which she poured for herself from a pot colored and shaped like a peacock. Dazzling in a cheongsam of lilac, with frogs of a deeper shade of purple, she wore nail lacquer and eyelid coloring that matched her gown.

Tonight she had chosen to assume the role of the diffident daughter of the household, leaving the bulk of the conversation to her father, Sarah, and the guest. As she well knew, this attitude caused the gallant Sir William Alexander, who had daughters of his own, to address most of his remarks to her in the hope of drawing her out. She was enjoying her little game, even though Sarah, wise to her as usual, glared at her from time to time.

The main dish, steak kew, also Cantonese, was a triumph. The meat had been cut into bite-sized cubes and, after cooking with at least a dozen condiments, had been served with a rich oyster sauce. It was accompanied by pickled asparagus.

Lai-tse lu always ate sparingly and soon finished a small portion of steak. The others were still busy with their chopsticks, so it suddenly amused her to become more talkative. "Sir William," she asked suddenly, "do you suppose China and Great Britain will ever become friends?"

"I believe our relations are amicable right now," the commander of the British flotilla replied diplomatically.

She could not resist chiding him. "Come, Sir William! You know that's not true. The only reason we trade with your merchants is because your great cannon menace us."

Chao and Sarah were distressed. The unpredictable girl was violating a basic rule of hospitality by making a guest uncomfortable.

"I mean real friendship," Lai-tse lu continued. "I wonder if the time will ever come when an Englishman will be able to travel where he pleases in the Middle Kingdom, and whether a Chinese may go anywhere in your country."

"You're free to do so right now," he said.

The girl shook her head. "I wouldn't dare. I was enough of an object of curiosity when my father and I dined with you on the *Valiant*. How your sailors stared and gawked at me!"

Sir William laughed heartily. "That, my dear, is because you're an uncommonly attractive young woman."

Now Lai-tse lu was embarrassed, and Sarah joined in the laugh.

Kai came to the door, and Chao excused himself, then conversed at length with his majordomo in low tones.

"It seems to me," Lai-tse lu said thoughtfully, "that there can never be true friendship between us until the vile traffic in opium is ended for all time."

The commodore sighed. "I am compelled to agree with you. Unofficially, of course. But I'm afraid it will continue as long as there is a market for the drug—and men can earn huge sums of money in return for little labor."

"But if all governments worked together, couldn't the trade be stopped?"

"I think not," Sir William said. "China is the center of attention at the moment because most opium smoking is done here. It won't be long before the disease spreads to my part of the world, and the curse will be difficult to eradicate there, too. It's so easy at the moment to brand us as villains and the Chinese as innocent dupes, but soon we'll all be in the same boat. The trade will stop when the markets dry up, but that won't happen until people everywhere learn that opium can kill them."

Chao returned to the table, obviously disturbed by his talk with his majordomo. He soon recovered, however, and guided the conversation into another channel, the differences between Chinese and Western forms of opera.

The meal ended with the serving of chrysanthemum soup, made of beef stock with slivers of fried pork, and floating on the top were large, white chrysanthemum petals. Lai-tse lu ate all of her soup because it wasn't fattening.

When they left the table, the girl and Sarah bade the visitor farewell, and Chao retired to a sitting room with his guest for further talk over tiny thimbles of mao tai, a sorghum-based liqueur. As Lai-tse lu approached her own building, a figure loomed up ahead on the walk, and she saw Kai, dressed in black from head to toe, with a finger pressed to his lips.

She motioned him into her suite and closed the sitting room door behind them.

"I thought your dinner talk would never end," Kai said. "I've been waiting for you. I need your help, if you have the courage."

The prospect of adventure delighted her.

"Certain people," he said bleakly, "have learned that a large cargo of opium was landed at Whampoa tonight and is being stored in the factory of an English Fan Kuei named Bruce."

The girl was shocked. "They've actually brought it to Whampoa? And they're hiding it in a factory next door to one of my father's?"

The burly majordomo nodded. "The words I have spoken are true. Teng Ting-chen has been approached, but he cannot punish the evil-doers or confiscate the drugs."

She nodded. "I understand. That would cause too

many problems with the English. Sir William is our friend, but he would not hesitate to blow up our factories if he thought it was his duty."

"The opium will be removed," Kai said grimly, "by certain people."

"I see."

"I have spoken to your father about all this, but for one who is so wise he is sometimes blind. He does business with Bruce, and he does not believe the man would be stupid enough to store opium in his factory. But if you told him it is true he would believe you, and he would not do business with Bruce again."

"Oh, I believe you, Kai," Lai-tse lu said, "and I'm sure the Society of the Oxen—ah—certain people will attend to the matter. But I don't know how to persuade my father that what you tell him is true. He can be very obstinate when he wishes."

"He will believe you," Kai said, "if you see the boxes of opium with your own eyes and watch it burn after we steal it."

She clasped her hands. "You want me to come with you?"

"I have brought you the clothes of a boy," he replied, thrusting a bundle at her. "Until the very last, when we will be busy, Lo Fang and I will be at your side. I give you this also," he continued, handing her a tiny bamboo whistle on a silver chain. "This will summon help if you need it. But you will be in little danger if you do as you're told and keep silent, so no one will know you are a woman."

The idea of taking part in the raid thrilled her. "I'll go with you," she said, "and I'll do everything I'm directed to do."

"You must also swear an oath on the spirits of your sacred ancestors," Kai said sternly, "that you will never reveal—to anyone—the identities of those whom you will meet tonight."

"I swear it!"

He was satisfied. "Hurry or we'll be late. When you're ready, just tap on the window of your bedroom and I'll lift you out. If Missy Sarah sees you, that will be the end of the night for you!" He left, closing the door silently behind him.

Lai-tse lu cleaned off her cosmetics with lotus-perfumed sesame oil, then scrubbed her face with soap and water. It amused her to arrange a portion of her long hair into a pigtail, braiding it so it resembled a man's. Then, after donning the black cap Kai had given her, she changed into the black trousers and tunic. They not only fitted her reasonably well, but the tunic was loose enough to conceal her feminine figure. Now she needed shoes and finally found a black pair with cork soles. They would be quiet, and she could move rapidly in them if it became necessary.

She was ready now. No, not quite. She opened a seldom-used drawer in a graceful, high chest decorated in mother-of-pearl and removed a small, silver-handled knife which she thrust into her belt beneath the tunic to conceal it. The act of bravado made her smile; she couldn't imagine using the blade in earnest.

Lai-tse lu tapped lightly on the window, then opened it, and strong hands closed around her waist, then deposited her gently on the ground. Lo Fang stood behind Kai and apparently was not overly pleased that she would accompany them. But he made no comment.

No one spoke as they left the Soong compound, and the two burly men ranged themselves on either side of the girl as they made their way through the crowded streets to the far side of the city. Windows of the small houses were open, and men and women stood in open doorways or leaned out of the windows to chat with passing friends. Old people sat in rickety chairs placed against the walls of their modest dwellings, and children, knowing they were under the scrutiny of their elders, played decorously in the streets.

No one paid the slightest attention to Lai-tse lu, which was a new experience for her. All at once she realized, too, that she was actually mingling with the citizens of Canton. Throughout her entire life she had been carried in a palanquin whenever she passed through the districts occupied by the poor, but tonight was different, heightening her sense of adventure.

It did not occur to her to be afraid of what might

take place later; the proximity of the always dependable Kai and the surly Lo Fang was a guarantee of her safety. All the same, she had to remind herself that this was no mere lark for its own sake. The men were engaged in a serious enterprise, feeling compelled to perform a task that the imperial viceroy was afraid to order officially because of the Middle Kingdom's military weakness. And she had her own important role to play.

It seemed strange to her that her father should find it difficult to believe that Owen Bruce would deliberately defy an imperial edict. On the other hand, in spite of his wisdom and business acumen, her father judged his peers as he would judge himself. She was more fortunate, Sarah Applegate having brought her up to believe that every individual, regardless of his wealth or race, had to be regarded strictly as an individual. So she was approaching the adventure with an open mind.

The silent Kai seemed concerned over the girl's ability to maintain the steady, rapid pace that he and Lo Fang set, but at the same time he did not defer to her. Had she faltered, she supposed, the pair might have moved a trifle more slowly, but she was determined to keep up with them. Their immediate destination appeared to be the Petition Gate, and as they drew nearer to it, Lai-tse lu gradually became aware of something unusual that was taking place without fanfare. Other grim-faced men, also dressed in black, were appearing in ones and twos out of nowhere and were walking directly ahead of the trio or falling in behind them. No greetings or signs of recognition were exchanged, but the girl knew that these newcomers undoubtedly were members of the Society of Oxen who were taking part in the raid.

An officer who carried a long, curved sword in his belt and four soldiers armed with ancient matchlocks were stationed at the Petition Gate. Lo Fang moved ahead, and the officer, catching sight of him, suddenly turned away as he addressed his subordinates. He and they seemed not to notice the approach of the raiders, and after Lo Fang opened the gate partway, the members of the party slipped through it into the foreign concession. Lai-tse lu had no way of knowing whether arrangements had been made in advance or whether the officer, perhaps, also was a member of the secret Society of Oxen.

As soon as she stepped through the gate, Kai handed her a hood of black silk, with small openings for her eyes and mouth. He indicated with a gesture that she was to don it, and she obediently slipped it over her head. The others put on masks, too, and when they paused the girl made a quick, rough count of their numbers. To her surprise there were at least thirty men in the group. No, she was wrong: there were more than forty!

Lo Fang moved to the head of the column, and Kai guided Lai-tse lu to a place directly behind him as the entire company moved silently down Thirteen Factories Street. She had visited her father's warehouses here on a number of occasions and had been treated with the respect due the daughter of the wealthy and influential Soong Chao. Now she was an interloper, taking part in a mission that lay outside the law, and her pulse quickened.

As nearly as she could judge, her companions were unarmed. Again she was mistaken, she told herself. They were carrying black-handled knives in their belts, but it was curious that none had brought firearms or crescent-shaped lances. Then it dawned on her that the omission of such weapons undoubtedly had been deliberate. If white men were killed in the raid, there would be complications, and the British Navy would feel compelled to intervene in order to protect what it regarded as its honor. The girl began to develop an appreciation of the delicacy of the operation.

Lo Fang halted in the dark outside a warehouse window, and Lai-tse lu assumed that this was the factory of Owen Bruce. She had no way of identifying it herself.

A short, wiry man, no taller than Lai-tse lu, edged forward as Lo Fang silently pried the window open with the blade of his knife, performing the act so quietly that the girl could hear only a few faint, scraping sounds. Then the window was raised about two feet, and the small man squirmed through the opening.

The others waited in silence, and they seemed to be standing forever, but no one spoke and no one moved. At last the window was opened wider from the inside, and members of the party climbed into the warehouse. Lo Fang was one of the first, and Kai picked up the girl, then handed her to his comrade, who placed her on her feet again with surprising gentleness.

Men were moving inside the building through the window rapidly, spreading out, and heading in different directions as they entered. It appeared that each had been given his assignment in advance and knew precisely what needed to be done.

Kai's mask moved close to Lai-tse lu's ear. "Stay here," he whispered. "Go no farther. Say and do nothing. Watch, and you will see all that is needed."

She nodded.

He vanished without another word.

There were no lights burning inside the cavernous building, and it was impossible for the girl to see more than a few feet in the almost impenetrable gloom. As the members of the Society of Oxen entered, they sped away again, each on his own errand, with none seemingly noting her presence. She could hear nothing, either, and the silence was eerie.

Gradually, as her eyes became more accustomed to the dark, she was able to pick out bulky shapes, and after a time she could make out rows of barrels and crates. The nervousness that had been building within her dissipated somewhat, and she was comforted by the familiarity of the place, which resembled the interior of her father's warehouses.

A thrill of horror crept up Lai-tse lu's spine when she saw the body of a man lying on the floor no more than ten feet away from her. He was one of the English guards, and he had been bound hand and foot, then gagged, and a blindfold had been placed over his eyes. Occasionally he moved slightly, trying to break his bonds, so it was plain that he was conscious, and she guessed he was unharmed. Her skin felt prickly, and she rubbed her arms.

Her companions did not return, and she couldn't imagine what might be delaying them. Perhaps they hadn't yet found the boxes of opium they were intending to steal.

Somewhere in the distance a light began to glow faintly, and it moved closer very slowly. Lai-tse lu was fascinated, and trying to put the nearby bound guard out of her mind, she watched the approaching light. She realized it was an oil lamp, and in its glow she was able to see two other English guards, each carrying a leaded club, each with a pistol in his belt. She shrank against the nearest barrels, instinctively reaching beneath her loose-fitting tunic for the little knife she had taken the precaution of placing in her belt.

The loud voice of a man broke the silence. "I told you something odd is 'appening! That window is open!" One of the pair spoke in a Cockney accent.

Lai-tse lu scarcely dared to breathe.

The men moved more rapidly now, approaching the window, and suddenly one of them caught sight of the slender, black-clad figure. " 'ere, you!" he called. "What you doing in this place?"

She knew she had been seen, and they were bearing down on her rapidly, making escape impossible.

"Oho! Wearing a mask, are you?" One of the guards reached out toward Lai-tse lu.

In sudden panic she slashed at him with her knife, and he leaped backward to avoid being struck. Not until much later was she grateful for the realization that she had not harmed him.

The other guard drew his pistol.

In spite of her fright, the girl suddenly remembered the bamboo whistle suspended on a chain around her neck. Fumbling for it, she backed away, rounding a corner as she fought for a few precious seconds to summon help.

"You! Chinee fella!" the guard called. "Come out chop-chop!"

A familiar scent assailed Lai-tse lu's nostrils. Tea! She had moved into a section of the warehouse in which tea intended for export was being stored. In spite of the gloom, in spite of the two Englishmen pursuing her she became steadier. This was no terrible cave filled with evil spirits, but was merely a warehouse like the many her father owned.

Lai-tse lu raised the whistle to her lips, and a piercing sound, high and thin, echoed through the vast structure.

The two guards were startled and for the moment were immobilized by the blast.

Then things began to happen so quickly that Lai-tse lu was bewildered. First, a husky figure hurtled out of nowhere, a bulky black streak who leaped at one of the guards and sent him crashing to the floor. At almost the same instant, another burly man in black climbed through the window, astonishing Lai-tse lu, who had assumed that all members of the raiding party had actually entered the building. Unseen by the second guard, the Society of Oxen member reached for the oil lamp with one hand, while simultaneously striking the Englishman a blow on the back of his neck with the edge of his hand.

Lai-tse lu well knew there were techniques, utilized for almost countless generations, in which an unarmed man could fight in deadly combat. Such methods were never written on paper, instead being passed from fathers to sons and teachers to pupils. Never before had she seen such fighting, and she marveled when the single blow, seemingly delivered without force, sent the second guard sprawling.

His assailant lost no time binding his wrists and ankles with strands of silk, stuffing a cloth into his mouth, and blindfolding him.

Meanwhile, the giant who attacked the first guard lost no time trussing his victim, too. Leaping to his feet with agility, the masked man came to the girl, and not until he spoke to her in a low tone did she recognize the voice of Kai.

"You have done well," he told her. "These two were missing, but you found them for us. Now, if you please, be patient for just a little longer. All who could cause danger for you are now harmless." He disappeared again into the gloom.

The anticlimax made the girl feel weak in the knees, and she leaned against a high stack of tea cases, the scent soothing her. Only now, feeling relatively safe and secure, did the enormity of what she was doing strike home.

She had risked her father's displeasure when she had appeared unbidden before the viceroy, but on that occasion she could justify her act. The grounds for tonight's escapade were far flimsier. Oh, she was performing a service for which her father ultimately would be grateful, but he would know, as she herself did, that it would have been easy for her to avoid taking part in the raid.

Certainly if her role should be discovered, which had almost happened just moments ago, she would have brought genuine disgrace on her father's head, tarnishing an ancient and honorable name. The keystone of Chinese society, regardless of one's class, was filial respect. One obeyed one's father, and someone of her intelligence didn't need to be told what to do and what to avoid. She had allowed a desire for excitement to lead her beyond the bounds of propriety.

Lai-tse lu had to admit, however, that the experience truly was the most exciting and unpredictable she had ever known. Her guilt mingled with her feeling of pleasure, and she giggled nervously.

The sound died in her throat when the black-clad members of the Society of Oxen materialized out of the gloom, walking silently, each man balancing large, square boxes on both shoulders. Their prodigious physical strength stunned her. The boxes were similar to those used for packing tea, and she guessed that each weighed one hundred pounds, according to the English and American system of measuring weights. So every man was laden with a burden of two hundred pounds, but all walked upright and easily.

One by one they went to the window, handing the boxes to unseen comrades, and not until all of the boxes had been removed did the men themselves begin to leave.

Kai touched Lai-tse lu's arm, and she went with him to the window. He passed her to waiting hands outside, and she breathed the odors peculiar to Whampoa, the combination of sea air and rotting vegetation, the smell tempered by the very faint scent of tea.

The last to leave Bruce's factory was Lo Fang, who carefully closed the window behind him. Picking up a box, he moved to the head of the line, and the company retraced its steps. Lai-tse lu was the only member of the party who was not carrying at least one square box; many of the men were still burdened with two.

The officer and soldiers at the Petition Gate took care to avert their faces again, and the entire group moved inside the city walls. They continued to wear their masks now, and walking in single file, they headed toward the heart of the city.

The residents of Canton melted away at their approach. Gossiping women took cover, the elderly left their chairs and went indoors, men who were chatting took to their heels, and the children followed their elders into the houses. No one knew the meaning of the strange procession, and no one lingered to ask questions. The mere fact that all members of the group were hooded meant that they belonged to one of the dreaded secret societies, organizations whose power was reputedly as great as that of the emperor himself. Rarely did any secret society make a display in public, even when hooded, so people preferred to take no chances and moved out of the path of these silent men.

Lai-tse lu, walking beside Kai, who was carrying two boxes, was surprised when the procession proceeded to Great Temple Square. Ancient, magnificent pagodas, each of them repeatedly enlarged through the ages, stood on three sides of the square, and the scent of incense that emanated from them was strong. Although it was almost midnight, a large crowd was gathered on the fourth side of the square, where several huge lichi trees stood, their branches forming a canopy. The juicy interiors of the lichi fruit, sweet and pure white, were encased in dark red hulls, and although these nuts, as they were popularly called, were favored by almost the entire population, no one ever picked the fruit of the trees in Great Temple Square. Indeed, even when a ripe, red shell fell to the ground, it was allowed to remain there until it rotted. These lichi trees were regarded as sacred, and no one, no matter what his class, dared to defy the gods and the spirits of his ancestors by eating one.

The attitude of the hooded men was not menacing

toward the crowd, so the throng did not dissipate. People withdrew to places beneath the lichi trees and stared in silence as the men in black deposited their burdens in neat piles.

Huge quantities of dried bamboo had been deposited at the side of one of the temples before the raid, and Society of Oxen members retrieved the brush, laid it on the ground in the center of the square, and then arranged the stolen boxes on top.

Lo Fang went into the largest of the buildings, the Temple of Heavenly and Earthly Peace, and emerged with a glowing joss stick he had taken from one of the many altars inside. He stood for a moment, motionless, his eyes piercing as he gazed at the crowd through the slits in his hood. Word was spreading, and the crowd under the trees was growing. A single wave of Lo Fang's brawny arm would have sent people scurrying off to their homes, but he did not discourage their presence.

In almost no time, as Lai-tse lu watched, the crowd seemed to double, then double again. So many men and women, most of them poor, the men in faded cotton robes, the women in pajamas of age-rusted black, were pouring into the square that the stone steps leading up to the temple entrances were filled. Yet no one climbed onto the carved stone representations of the phoenix, a mythical bird as old as the Middle Kingdom itself, in order to obtain a better view. Not even the most curious wanted to run the risk of arousing the spirit of a phoenix, who might turn a mortal to stone.

The joss stick in Lo Fang's hand burned slowly. He descended the stone stairs of the Temple of Heavenly and Earthly Peace, the people nearest him shrinking away to avoid physical contact with him.

Kai raised an arm, and the hooded members of the Society of Oxen formed a hollow square around the high mound they had constructed. At last Lai-tse lu, standing beside her father's majordomo, guessed what would happen, and she was right.

Lo Fang went to the pile, then repeatedly thrust the joss stick into the brush at the bottom. The dry bamboo began to smoke, and after some moments it burst into flames. The boxes were made of dried wood, and they caught fire, too.

The contents glowed and smoldered, but did not flame. As they caught fire, however, they gave off a smell that was unique. The smoke that drifted around Great Temple Square was sweet and heavy, with a lingering effect that caused nostrils to sting and eyes to water. There were many in the gathering who knew the scent all too well. They muttered to others, and soon everyone present, even totally innocent, realized what was taking place.

Many hundreds of pounds of forbidden opium, worth a fortune to the illegal dealers who dared to handle the drug, were being destroyed.

Lai-tse lu felt great admiration for the Society of Oxen. Not only had a greedy English sea captain and a corrupt English factory owner been deprived of an enormous profit, but a warning was being served on the people of Canton. By morning everyone in the city would know that a powerful secret society was supporting the stand of the emperor and his viceroy. The message was as clear as the smoke of the burning opium was black and pungent: henceforth, even the man who bought and smoked the drug would be regarded as an enemy of the people.

Lai-tse lu no longer felt guilty over the role she had played. She was proud she had been associated with these patriots who were purging China of an evil as terrible as the plagues that sometimes swept across the country.

III

London was the most cosmopolitan and handsome city in the world. Jonathan Rakehell sat in the open, behind the driver of the phaeton he had hired, the clothing he needed for his stay with his aunt and uncle beside him in a sea bag. He looked around him, relishing the sights as he was carried to the Boynton mansion. He was familiar with New York and Boston and Philadelphia, the three largest American cities, but all of them were raw frontier towns by comparison. And even such picturesque centers as Spanish Havana and British Kingston in the Caribbean were relatively drab.

London had a pulse, an atmosphere, a flavor all its own. Few people tarried in the busy streets, but fewer seemed hurried. Pedestrians walked at a steady gait, coaches were driven sedately, and even young horsemen were considerate of others as their mounts' hooves clattered on the cobblestones. London might be burdened with a staggering population of almost two million, the largest in the Western world, but the innate courtesy of her people made her size tolerable.

Gentlemen in square-crowned beaver hats and suits of expensive velvet held their gold-handled walking sticks under their arms and made way for washerwomen laden with laundry. Great ladies gathered their skirts of the fine silk imported from China and stepped aside for roughly clad fishmongers and sooty chimneysweeps carrying the cumbersome tools of their trade. Coach drivers paused to allow larger vehicles to pass them, and all horse traffic halted at corners to permit pedestrians to cross.

Not that London was perfect, as Jonathan well knew from his previous visits to the city. Cutpurses and pickpockets mingled in the crowds, and some of the attractive young "ladies" who strolled nearby were trollops eager to separate a lascivious man from his money. London was a city for everyone, no matter what his taste, as Papa often said; to Jonathan it was a community that offered unrivaled opportunities for lucrative trade.

At the same time it was a great deal more. He felt a glow as he passed the Gothic bulk of Parliament, the world's first and foremost gathering place of the duly elected representatives who ruled a nation. The United States. proud of her democracy, owed a permanent debt to her former mother country. Off to one side stood Westminster Abby, where he would attend services on Sunday with Aunt Jessica and Uncle Alan.

Riding down Pall Mall, Jonathan looked at the huge stone buildings that housed various government offices, and seeing them made him realize anew that here was the heart of the British Empire, which was spreading steadily across the globe. Not since the time of ancient Rome had any nation become as powerful.

But there was far more to London than solemnity. In the Serpentine, part lake and part pond, Jonathan caught a glimpse of a young man and a girl in a curious small craft, about the size of an American rowboat, with a flat bottom and square ends. The man was propelling the boat with a long pole, which he dug into the muddy bottom. while the prettily dressed girl, lolling on a pile of cushions, watched him. They were lost in each other, oblivious to the world around them, unmindful of the stares of passersby.

At last the phaeton came to Belgravia Square, which to Jonathan typified the best of London. The houses of white with their Grecian porticos were solid but unpretentious. representing great wealth with typical English understatement. Brass door knockers and nameplates gleamed. and even the glass covers of the gas lamps in the street were clean and polished.

He paid the phaeton driver, then carried his sea bag to the front door.

A dignified, middle-aged butler in livery answered the summons, and a broad smile broke through his reserve. "Welcome, Mr. Jonathan! You're expected."

"It's great to see you again, Miller," Jonathan replied, shaking his hand.

"Will you go to your room, sir? It's been prepared for several days."

Jonathan winced at the reminder that *Flying Dragon* had not lived up to his expectations on her maiden voyage. "No, I think I'll just see who's around," he said, handing the butler his sea bag.

Miller shook his head as he carried the luggage up the broad marble stairs. Lady Boynton's informality was sometimes surprising, but that of her American relatives was startling. Certainly no English gentleman would wander through the living quarters of a house that wasn't his own without first being announced.

Jonathan thought, as he had so often in the past when visiting the Boyntons, that living here was like living in a palace—or a museum. There were paintings on every wall in room after room, marble statues and statuettes stood on pedestals, and the rugs Uncle Alan had imported from India were so luxurious they muffled all sound when one walked on them. The chairs, at least in the endless anterooms, were spindly, with gilt legs, and all of them looked uncomfortable. Come to think of it, he had never seen anyone sit in any of these rooms.

A door opened and closed, cutting short his reflections, and a little girl came toward him, her hair in pigtails, her dress a short-skirted school uniform of drab maroon. Jonathan stared at her for a moment, realized she was far taller than he remembered her, and shouted, "Elizabeth!"

Before she could reply, he lifted her into the air and planted a firm kiss on her cheek.

"How do you do, Cousin Jonathan." Elizabeth was so mortified she wanted to die. She had known he would be here at any time, and she hated herself because there had been no chance to change out of her ugly school uni-

173

form, with its cotton stockings of thick lisle and flat-heeled shoes. She hadn't even had the opportunity to comb out her hair!

Jonathan placed her on the floor again and grinned at her. "You've grown up so much I hardly knew you."

She knew her face was scarlet, and her fingertips crept to the place on her cheek where he had kissed her. He was so handsome and dashing she was afraid she would faint, and she could only hope her confusion didn't show. For as long as she could recall, ever since she had been about five, Elizabeth Boynton had been secretly, madly in love with Jonathan Rakehell. It was a secret so deep she wouldn't even confide it to the locked diary hidden at the bottom of the dresser drawer in which her camisoles were kept.

The secrecy, however, in no way deterred the little girl's unchanging ambition. Some day she would marry Jonathan. He wasn't her blood relative, after all, so no one could possibly object. Sometimes she daydreamed that he was proposing to her, and on these occasions her tension was so great she felt excruciating pains in her chest that made it difficult for her to breathe. Last year, after her most recent visit to America, she had decided that New England was too drab and plain, but she had worked that out to her satisfaction in her daydreams, too. Jonathan would be so dazzled by her beauty, wit, and charm that he would gladly consent to take up residence right here. Perhaps in this very house, which she adored.

Now, suddenly, Elizabeth faced the reality of the flesh-and-blood Jonathan. "You're looking well, too," she said. Her mind went blank, and she could only add, "Mama and Papa are in the library," before taking to her heels and fleeing.

Jessica Rakehell Boynton greeted her nephew with a warm hug and kiss, and Sir Alan pumped his hand. "Perfect timing, m'boy," he said. "You're just in time for a glass of sack."

Jonathan handed them his father's letters. "You should have had these a week ago," he said.

Jessica knew he referred to the mail contract race,

174

but she had more important matters on her mind. "You look scrawny and peaked," she said.

He shrugged. "I was plagued by problems during almost a month at sea, so I had little appetite."

"Then we shall see to it that you gain weight while you're here," she said. "You'll have desserts twice a day, and I don't want it reported to me that you've skimped on breakfast."

Only one answer was possible when a Rakehell woman gave orders. "Yes, ma'am. I'll do whatever you tell me."

Sir Alan grinned behind the pages of the letter from Jeremiah that he was already scanning. The lad would do as he pleased, as he had a right to do at his age, but he certainly knew how to handle his aunt. It was too bad Charles had never learned the knack. "Save the story of your voyage until Charles gets here," he said, "and you'll be obliged to tell it just once."

"Where is Charles?" Jonathan followed the Boynton custom of pouring his own drink, which was just as well. The cut-glass decanter with the solid silver top was handsome, but Uncle Alan's sack was too sweet for his taste, so he gave himself a very small portion.

Jessica frowned. "He should have been home an hour ago. He knew you'd be here today, so there's no excuse for his tardiness."

Jonathan came to his cousin's defense. "He doesn't need to dance attendance on me, Aunt Jessica."

She sniffed aloud. "I know of nothing more important than one's obligations to one's family," she said firmly.

She sounded remarkably like Papa, Jonathan thought. He was as devoted to Charles as he was to his own sister, to be sure, but he was hanged if he'd lift a finger for Brad Walker. But one didn't say such things to his aunt's generation of Rakehells. He found safe ground by chatting with her about Judith and her children while Sir Alan read his long letter.

The reaction of the managing director of Boynton Shipping to the letter was predictable. "After dinner, over port," he said, "I'll want you to clarify several matters your father mentions here."

Elizabeth slipped back into the room. She had changed into an ankle-length dress and white silk stockings, with her newest shoes, which had three-quarter inch heels. Her hair fell to her shoulders, and Jessica, looking at her, wondered if the little minx had put a touch of rouge on her cheeks and a bit of glistening salve on her eyelids. They would have words on the subject later. No, on second thought, she would say nothing. The child was showing a splendid sense of family obligation by trying to look adult for her cousin, so she deserved a commendation rather than a scolding.

Jonathan rose to his feet and bowed deeply. "It's astonishing how much Elizabeth has grown in this past year," he said.

The little girl could feel her face turning scarlet again and hated herself.

"As long as you're standing," Sir Alan said dryly, "perhaps you'll fix a drink for her serene highness. Half sack and half water."

Elizabeth was even more miserable. Jonathan would never think of her as a woman if everyone continued to treat her like an infant.

Jessica skimmed her brother's letter. "Congratulations," she said, handing the communication to her husband. "I hope you'll bring Louise with you on your next voyage to England."

"We'd like that, I'm sure," Jonathan said politely as he placed the child's watered drink on the table beside her.

Elizabeth stiffened. "Who is Louise?"

"You met her in New London, dear," Jessica said. "If I remember correctly, you sat next to her at a clambake on the beach one evening. She and Jonathan are betrothed."

The child dug her hands into the folds of her dress so no one would see her clenched fists.

Sir Alan offered his congratulations, too, then turned to Elizabeth. "Where are your manners?" he asked. "It's

176

customary to offer felicitations when someone becomes engaged to be married."

"I won't," Elizabeth said. "I don't like Louise." ·

Sir Alan and Lady Boynton laughed, but Jonathan remained sober-faced. "Why don't you like her?" he asked sympathetically.

Elizabeth was cornered, but had to wriggle out. "She's prissy and not very bright," she said. "And she lords it over younger girls."

Her parents laughed again.

But Jonathan remained gravely attentive. "I shall see to it," he said, "that Louise adopts a new attitude toward you the next time you two meet. She'll treat you with the dignity that only an adolescent deserves. You see, you weren't an adolescent the last time she saw you, but all that will be changed. I promise."

Elizabeth almost hated him at that moment, and never had she been so miserable. Only one solution came to mind. A new classmate, the daughter of the recently retired Governor-General of Jamaica, had been boasting that she was familiar with a form of magic practiced by the native West Indians. It was called obeah. Very well, Elizabeth would bribe her by giving her the cameo she had admired—and would hope Mama didn't notice its absence. And her friend, in return, would teach her the curse and secret ceremony that could cause a person to vanish from the face of the earth without leaving a trace. Louise's days were necessarily numbered. Because no one was going to marry Jonathan until Elizabeth grew older and he finally recognized her true worth. No one was going to spoil her favorite daydream, and that was that!

Charles burst into the room, and Jonathan was on his feet again. Whooping like Indians, the cousins pounded each other on the back.

Sir Alan was pained. His son, it seemed, behaved like a colonial savage when in the company of his American relative.

"I went to the Royal Mail wharves," Charles said, "but you had already left to come here. Ed Barker was on board and showed me through *Flying Dragon*. What a beauty!"

177

"You like her?" Jonathan was pleased.

"I've never seen a ship like her. What rotten luck you had, losing the race—"

"Enough!" Jessica interrupted forcibly. "Sometimes I wonder whether ships are the only subject ever discussed in this house. There will be no further talk of ships for one hour. I'm far more interested in other family matters."

Charles took out his pocket watch, peered at it, and, winking at Jonathan, announced, "We shall wait precisely one hour."

A few minutes later they went to dinner, and Jonathan was struck anew by the differences between English and American ways. He guessed that his father was every bit as well-to-do as Uncle Alan, but one would never know it. At home the service was plain and the meals were simple, but here the emphasis was always placed on elegance. The sterling silver was heavy and kept shined, the bone china was superb, the thin, rainbow-hued glassware imported from Bohemia was as fragile as it was rich. Even the table linen was obviously costly.

The meal matched the atmosphere. Served by two uniformed maids under the direction of the butler, it would have been regarded as a feast in New England. The first course consisted of raw oysters on the half-shell, somewhat thinner and considerably larger than those to which Jonathan was accustomed at home. The ox-tail soup with barley and vegetables was savory, and the poached sole that followed it was magnificent. The fish Americans called sole was actually flounder; genuine sole was found only in the waters of the English Channel and was Jonathan's favorite whenever he came here.

The roast of beef was a triumph. Crisp on the outside and sliced very thin, it was accompanied by Yorkshire pudding and roasted potatoes. Jonathan ate ravenously, his appetite matched only by that of Charles. Jessica smiled to herself as she watched the two young men accepting second and third helpings.

The salad of lettuce and cucumbers was crisp, and the dessert, huge strawberries over which rich, clotted cream was poured, was a dish unavailable in any other land. The meal ended with a savory, herring roe and bacon served on squares of toast.

Not until the roast was served did the conversation revert to ships. Charles looked again at his watch, grinned at his mother, and declared, "The restriction has ended. Tell me why you lost the race, Jonathan."

"We should have arrived days earlier than any other ship. But Captain Hartley was so cautious he wouldn't use full sail when weather conditions were less than ideal, and a clipper has been built to utilize all of her canvas. At all times. And my bowsprit needs to be lengthened and set at a different angle."

"That's what Ed Barker told me, but I find it hard to believe. You're already rather far forward of your stem."

"I've spent almost all of my time making calculations in these past few days," Jonathan said, "and I'm convinced that moving the bowsprit still farther forward will solve our problem. I hope to prove it on my westward voyage back to America. If you allow me to use a dry-dock in your yard, Uncle Alan."

"Help yourself, lad," Sir Alan replied. "I'm rather curious about clippers myself, and I'd like to inspect your new ship. Not that I believe the miraculous predictions about the sustained speeds that a clipper supposedly can maintain."

"I hope to prove you wrong, sir, just as I hope to prove my father wrong," Jonathan said quietly. *"Flying Dragon* and others like her soon will be crossing from America to England in less than three weeks and will make the return voyage in no more than three weeks."

His uncle's smile was indulgent. "What would you estimate as your sailing time to China?"

Jonathan was silent for a time as he did calculations in his head without allowing the process to interrupt his steady consumption of food. "I'm quite certain I could sail from New London, Boston, or New York to Canton in approximately one hundred days."

Sir Alan raised an eyebrow, and even Jessica leaned forward in her chair as her husband asked, "How long from here to China?"

"No more than three and a half months," Jonathan said flatly.

"Regardless of the season?"

"I wouldn't go that far, sir! But *Flying Dragon* will make better than twenty knots."

"I'm glad you recognize the problems of the monsoon season and the possibility of encountering typhoons in the South China Sea," Sir Alan said with a chuckle.

Jonathan's own smile faded. "There's always an element of luck in sailing, as I hardly need tell you, Uncle Alan. When there's no wind in the Doldrums, not even a clipper can perform miracles. And setting records depends on the weather at the Cape of Good Hope."

The older man's eyes narrowed. Every master who sailed around the Cape of Good Hope took his life and the lives of his crew in his hands. Not to mention the security of his ship. When storms howled around the Cape, a ship might be forced to wait for weeks before her master dared to make the passage safely.

"My predictions," Jonathan said, "are based on the assumption that the trade winds will be favorable, as they frequently are, that I won't float aimlessly in the Doldrums, and that I'll be spared a gale at the Cape. I carry enough sail to see my ship through the Doldrums—unless the winds die completely. Then I'm no better off than anyone else. As for the Cape, others have found fair weather there, so there's no reason to assume in advance that I won't be equally fortunate."

"You have the optimism of youth," Sir Alan said indulgently, then became serious. "If you're right, which I very much doubt, you'll revolutionize world shipping. Prove to me that you aren't daydreaming, and I'll order as many clippers as you can build for me, Jonathan."

Lady Boynton shook her head. "I find your predictions too much to swallow," she said.

Jonathan saw nothing to be gained by pursuing the argument. He would be required to demonstrate his assertions, and that was what he planned to do.

He received support from an unexpected source. "If Jonathan says he'll establish new speed records, he will," Elizabeth said.

He rewarded her with a broad grin.

To her dismay she felt herself blushing again.

Charles spoke quietly. "If I may, I'd like to offer my help. I presume you'll take her out to sea for trials before you sail back to America, even though you'll lose a great deal of time?"

"I may have more troubles with Captain Hartley, but I've got to put *Flying Dragon* through her paces before we cross the Atlantic again," Jonathan said. "I'll lose many days. but I want to make certain that lengthening the bowsprit will solve my problems."

Charles turned to his father. "If you please, sir, may I take a brief leave of absence to work with Jonathan?"

"Certainly." Sir Alan looked at his son, then at his nephew. "I don't want to discourage you lads. It's always the young who are responsible for new developments in any industry. But don't expect too much of your clipper ships. You're asking them to perform totally impossible acts!"

Early the following morning Charles accompanied Jonathan to the Royal Mail wharves, and the latter explained his intentions to Captain Hartley, who had spent the night on board.

The veteran master listened in silence. He had achieved the goal that Bradford Walker had set for him, and now he wanted his reward. Certainly he wanted no part in the lengthening of the bowsprit, and the prospect of the return voyage to New London on board *Flying Dragon* made him apprehensive. His delaying tactics had been effective on the voyage to London. but it would be difficult for him to use them again. Above all. he was inclined to suspect that young Rakehell might be right when he made outrageous claims on behalf of his clipper. Davis Hartley had spent enough years at sea to have gained a grudging respect for the strange new ship, and it was possible she might astonish the industry if allowed to travel at top speed.

"It seems to me," he said gruffly, "that any repair work should be done at the yard where the ship was built."

"I don't like to overrule you, Captain," Jonathan said. "But *Flying Dragon* isn't owned by Rakehell Building and Shipping. She's my personal property, and as her owner I choose to make the necessary repairs right here before we sail home."

There was no way the master could evade responsibility with good grace. "In that case," he said, "you'll have to sail without me. I agreed to sail your clipper here, but nothing was said about taking her home again. In my opinion it's dangerous to tinker with her."

"In my opinion it's a necessity!" Jonathan retorted.

"Then I'll return to New London on board the *Jean K.* as a supercargo," Hartley said firmly. "Do what you please with your ship. I just hope for your sake—and that of your crew—that she doesn't tear herself apart."

As the astonished Jonathan and Charles watched him, he stamped off to his cabin to pack his gear and have it transferred to the Rakehell schooner.

"That was damned odd," Jonathan said.

"He appeared to me to be finding an excuse to desert you," the equally puzzled Charles replied.

Jonathan shrugged. "I'll do better taking the command myself. We'll be short-handed, of course, but Edmund and I can sail her home without another mate."

A gleam appeared in Charles's eyes, but he kept his thoughts to himself for the present.

After Captain Hartley had gone, *Flying Dragon* sailed across the Thames to the Boynton yard at Southwark, using only her jibs and spanker for the purpose. Nosing past merchantmen that sailed to China and India, North America and the Mediterranean, the Caribbean and South America, she edged toward the entrance to her assigned dock, with shore workers hauling her into place.

The task of lengthening the bowsprit and changing its angle was basically a simple task when performed by experts, but it proved to be somewhat more delicate than Jonathan had anticipated. He and Edmund worked side by side with the Boynton yard workers, and Charles, after hesitating briefly, removed his coat, rolled up his sleeves, and pitched in, too.

The operation required three and a half days; the

seamen were given the weekend to do as they pleased, and Jonathan had enough provisions for a few days taken on board. The sea trials, which other owners might have regarded as unnecessary, but which he deemed essential, would begin on Monday.

On Sunday evening, after other members of the Boynton family had retired, Charles surprised his cousin by announcing, "I'm coming with you tomorrow, you know. You've said yourself that you need another mate, and this is an experience I wouldn't miss for anything in the world."

Jonathan took the master's cabin, and Charles moved in with Edmund. They went to work at once, and the clipper sailed slowly down the river choked with barges and the merchant ships of a score of nations. Late in the afternoon they passed the little town of Southend at the entrance to the Thames Estuary on the eastern coast of England and, using Foulness Island as a guide, added sail and headed into the open waters of the North Sea.

Jonathan remained on the quarterdeck himself, and the day was well advanced by the time he had threaded through small fleets of diminutive fishing craft. A southwesterly wind was blowing, but common sense told him to wait until morning before he put *Flying Dragon* to the test. His lack of patience got the better of him, however, and he exchanged swift glances with Charles and Edmund, who were standing together at the quarterdeck rail. Their expressions told him they felt as he did, even though only an hour of daylight remained.

Smiling in anticipation, Jonathan tugged at the brim of his bicorne hat. "Bo's'n," he called, "all hands on deck! Make all plain sail!"

"Aye aye, sir." Grimshaw knew what was coming and grinned broadly.

The crew members guessed what was in store, too, and needed no urging to hurry to their appointed places.

The clipper began to pick up speed when her topgallants were raised. Her royals were opened, and she surged ahead through the cold, blue-black waters of the whitecap-filled North Sea.

All was well, and Jonathan was confident he had

solved his problem. The ship no longer felt sluggish, and she reminded him of a horse that was desperately anxious to break into a full gallop. He ordered the skysails and moonsails unfurled.

Now *Flying Dragon* sliced through the water at a speed that no man on board had ever before known. His youthful exuberance too great to contain, Jonathan shouted at the top of his voice in joy.

Charles and Edmund were pounding each other on the back, and they, too, were shouting.

The seamen began to cheer, and the veteran Grimshaw, for the first time in his life, looked awe-stricken.

As the hubbub subsided, the three officers on the quarterdeck stared down at the water that seemed to be flashing past them, and Jonathan was reminded of an occasion in his boyhood when he had shot down river rapids in a canoe. He checked his Massey rotator, then said, "We're doing twenty knots!"

"Better than that," Charles declared. "I don't think there are instruments made that will tell us how fast we're really moving."

A sense of caution pervaded Jonathan. "At this rate we'd blame near reach the coast of Scotland by morning." There was no moon, he noted, so visibility left something to be desired, and with reluctance he ordered the boatswain to reef in the two top sails.

Edmund took the even watch, and the cousins retired to the master's cabin to eat a meal of cold boiled beef, bread, and apples that had been picked the previous day.

"Have you ever thought of going into the China trade with *Flying Dragon?*" Charles asked. "A ship that can achieve this speed could more than make a killing."

"I've more than thought of it," Jonathan replied with a rueful smile. "I had my plans all set. I had even made arrangements for a perfect cargo. I was intending to take a load of dismantled cotton looms to Canton. I've made a long study of the subject, and the finest looms anywhere are manufactured in Massachusetts. I've corresponded with various people who have been trading with the

Chinese, and they assure me that looms like ours would create a sensation there."

"Why looms?" Charles wanted to know.

"Because they're light in weight and they take up very small amounts of space when dismantled. Remember, I'm very limited on cargo space." Jonathan sighed. "It would have been a perfect cargo."

"Oh?"

"To be honest with you, Charles, I've almost run out of funds. I was counting on that one thousand dollar prize for additional capital, and if I had set a speed record I could have raised the rest of what I'd need without any trouble. As it is, I'm short. So I'll have to put *Flying Dragon* in the trans-Atlantic or West Indian trade for the next couple of years until I can accumulate a nest egg large enough to make a China voyage. I've made such an issue of being independent that I won't go to my father for help, as you can understand."

"That's natural. How much cash do you need?"

"About twenty-five hundred dollars, I'm afraid, to cover the pay of my crew, buy the cargo, and provision her for the voyage. Now you know the real reason I was so disappointed at losing the race. I could have wrung Captain Hartley's neck, even though he was doing what he thought best."

Charles picked up an apple and buffed it on the side of his trousers until the skin shone. "Have you thought of raising money by taking in a partner?" he asked quietly, then added with greater force, "Me."

Jonathan stared at his cousin.

"At the risk of embarrassing you," Charles said, his manner becoming diffident, "I have about seven hundred pounds in cash in my own private account. Five hundred of it—or twenty-five hundred dollars at the present rate of exchange—is yours. In return for a one-third interest in *Flying Dragon*."

"I'm overwhelmed," Jonathan said.

"Don't be. You're the one who'll be doing me a favor. Standing up on the quarterdeck and watching this ship cut through the water was the greatest experience

185

I've ever known. I'm selfish when I tell you I want a share in *Flying Dragon*'s destiny."

"You share my faith in her."

"More than that." In moments of emotional stress Charles, like all Englishmen of his class, seemed to become shy, almost reluctant to express himself. "I also have faith in you."

Jonathan felt tongue-tied.

"I have one additional condition on which I'm afraid the deal must depend."

"What's that?"

"You need a new first mate. Take me on, effective immediately," Charles said.

Jonathan looked at him, smiled, and extended his hand.

The moment was so solemn that neither spoke, but there was no need for words. Ever since they had been small boys they had talked of the day when they would control shipping companies and sail together to the far ends of the earth. Now *Flying Dragon* would be responsible for the realization of those childhood fantasies.

The sea trials lasted for three days, and the clipper continued to respond to every test. "We're on a zigzag course in a headwind," Edmund said. "It may be that the shortest distance between two points is a straight line, but Euclid never sailed a clipper. The fastest distance between two points in a headwind is to keep wearing and tacking!"

Jonathan and Charles busily used their free time to make long-range plans, and their first concern was the cargo they could carry to the United States. "There's a good market in America for the English saws made in Sheffield," Jonathan said. "They're superior to any saws manufactured in the United States, but I'm afraid I can't even think in such terms. They're too expensive."

"How much would a cargo of Sheffield saws cost?" Charles asked.

Jonathan worked with a pen and paper before replying. "We'd need four hundred pounds, so forget it."

"Not so fast. We can make a down payment with the two hundred I'll have left in my account."

"I'm afraid that won't do," Jonathan said. "The manufacturer will expect payment almost immediately after we reach the United States, and it well may be several months before we start getting an income from the sale of the saws."

"Leave that to me," Charles said. "I can almost guarantee you that we won't sail to New England with an empty hold."

Flying Dragon returned to London very late one night, and after she had slipped into a berth at the Boynton yard and had been made secure, Jonathan granted the crew several days of leave. Then he and Charles shaved and changed their clothes and arrived at the house in Belgravia Square just in time for breakfast.

They helped themselves to bowls of steaming Scottish oatmeal, smoked kippers, coddled eggs, and rashers of bacon from the sideboard, then returned for hot scones dripping with butter.

Sir Alan waited until they joined the rest of the family at the table before he asked, "How did the trials go?"

"I'm satisfied with *Flying Dragon*," Jonathan said.

"There's no other ship on the seven seas that's her equal," Charles declared. "Father, let the coachman drive Elizabeth to school this morning instead of taking her yourself. There's something I want to discuss with you and Mother."

"I suppose I'm too little to hear," Elizabeth said, her temper flaring.

Jonathan grinned and felt sorry for her. "It will do no harm to talk now," he suggested.

"I suppose." Charles looked at each of his parents, then drew in his breath. "I've bought a one-third interest in *Flying Dragon* for five hundred pounds."

"Doesn't that eat a rather large hole in your bank account?" Sir Alan asked dryly.

Jessica silenced her husband with a glare. "That doesn't matter in the least. Nothing could please me more than to know that my son and Jeremiah's son are becoming partners. Think of the family traditions these youngsters are continuing, Alan."

"I daresay," he replied. "Although they'd become partners soon enough, after Jeremiah and I have retired. Or died. But youth is too impatient to let natural attrition take its course."

"There's more to it than that, Father," Charles said as he added still more butter to a scone. "*Flying Dragon* is extraordinary, and I'd be missing the opportunity of a lifetime if I didn't share in her success."

Sir Alan dropped a teaspoon of sugar into his tea. "I just hope you aren't being rash," he said. "I've heard Jonathan's reasons for the clipper's failure to win the mail contract race, and they seem valid. But it strikes me Jeremiah would be far more interested in clipper ships if they had the future you lads claim."

Jonathan didn't want to intervene in a Boynton family conference, but he couldn't help saying, "My father has some surprises in store for him, Uncle Alan."

"I'm sure both of us would like nothing better than to be pleasantly surprised."

Charles steeled himself. "My partnership entails obligations that require me to ask for a two-year furlough from Boynton Shipping, Father. I want to sail to America as the first mate of the clipper—and then go on with her to China."

There was a moment of total silence, and even Elizabeth blinked.

Jessica spoke first. "I approve," she said briskly.

Sir Alan cleared his throat. "Shouldn't you and I discuss this in private first, my dear?"

"There's nothing to discuss, really," she replied with a Rakehell's characteristic bluntness. "Charles will learn as much from a voyage to the Orient as he will sitting at a desk in your office. And he's ready for his own sea trials, so to speak. Don't forget, Alan, that you spent three years on a quarterdeck of your own before we were married, and you've often said it was the best education you've ever had in the shipping business."

"But—"

"Charles has no responsibilities here. He's betrothed to no one, and the experience will be good for him. The best he could gain anywhere."

Sir Alan bowed to her wishes, as he always did when she took an adamant stand. "You've heard your mother, Charles. It appears the issue is settled."

"Thank you, Father." Charles exchanged a quick, elated grin with Jonathan.

Elizabeth, who had been eating bacon with her fingers because no one had been looking at her, took care to wipe grease from her mouth before she spoke. "Jonathan," she asked carefully, "will you marry Louise before you go to China?"

He shook his head. "No, a betrothal is supposed to last a year. I'll be home from China long before the year ends."

Sir Alan laughed. "Not unless your ship sprouts wings."

This was the moment for which Charles had been waiting, and he pounced. "Father," he said, "you simply have no idea what this ship can do. I told you I'd given up card playing, and so I have. But this is a rather special matter, so I'd like to make you a wager. I'll bet you two hundred pounds that *Flying Dragon* breaks the east to west speed record for a trans-Atlantic crossing from here to New London when we sail her to America."

Jessica started to protest.

This time, however, her husband insisted on asserting himself. "Be quiet, my dear. There's more than one way for the young to learn the ways of the world. Charles, I'm going to take your money and empty your bank account. In fact, I'm so confident you'll lose that I'll wager four hundred pounds to your two hundred that this miracle ship will break no record crossing the Atlantic!"

"Done, sir!" Charles leaned toward the head of the table and shook his father's hand, sealing the bet.

Jonathan was stunned. So this was how Charles had been planning to raise the money for a cargo of Sheffield saws! The rascal was being reckless, but he was shrewd, too. There was no doubt in Jonathan's mind, just as there was none in Charles's, that *Flying Dragon* was going to make history in the immediate future.

The next ten days were exceptionally busy. While Jonathan and Edmund inspected the clipper with infinite care, Charles made a trip to Sheffield, returning in triumph with the cargo of steel saws.

Jonathan supervised the stowing of the cargo in the hold himself, making certain not only that it was secure but that its weight was distributed evenly. No cargo, no matter how profitable, could be allowed to interfere with the operation of *Flying Dragon*.

Charles discouraged his parents from giving him a farewell party, and his new seriousness of purpose pleased Jessica. "He's growing up at last," she told Sir Alan. "Jonathan is a good influence, regardless of whether his ship performs wonders."

"Don't be too surprised," her husband replied in his usual dry manner, "if Charles succeeds in corrupting Jonathan before this association of theirs comes to an end."

After the cargo was loaded to Jonathan's satisfaction, a spring storm blew up out of the Atlantic, so the sailing was postponed until the weather cleared. Jonathan, who had been brought up on the principle that a ship owner should always pay cash and never ask for credit, was more concerned over his cousin's wager than he cared to admit to himself. If Charles lost the bet. the partners would be in debt and would not only need one thousand dollars to send to the Sheffield manufacturer. but would have to find two hundred additional pounds to pay Sir Alan. The desire to set a trans-Atlantic record had become a financial necessity.

On his last day in London Jonathan took time for a brief shopping expedition. Mindful of his obligations, he bought a gold locket for Louise Graves in a jewelry shop. Paying somewhat less for it than he had anticipated, he gave in to sudden impulse and bought a smaller version of the same locket for Elizabeth Boynton. The gift, he thought, would be a graceful way of thanking his aunt and uncle for their hospitality to him.

The night prior to the sailing, the cousins had their personal belongings taken to *Flying Dragon* and slept on board. Most provisions had already been delivered, but fresh produce and livestock were delivered at daybreak.

The crates and boxes of fruit and vegetables, which would last for only a few days, were lashed to the aft deck, and then Jonathan and Charles went off to the Boynton mansion for their final breakfast, their last meal ashore.

Jessica and Sir Alan were able to think only of the bleak fact that they might not see their son for as long as two years. But as members of a shipping family they concealed their sense of loss. Jessica smiled gallantly, and her husband revealed an unexpected sense of humor by telling several jokes, one or two of which made Elizabeth laugh.

The family intended to accompany the two young men to the yard for the sailing, and as they waited for the largest of the Boynton carriages to be brought from the stable at the rear to the front door, Jonathan quietly handed Elizabeth a small package.

"For me?" In her excitement she tore away the wrapping, then gasped when she saw the locket and chain resting in a satin-lined box. "This is the most wonderful gift I've ever been given," the enraptured child said. "I shall wear it every day, as long as I live."

The adults smiled indulgently.

Elizabeth insisted on wearing the locket at once and silently vowed that in the years ahead they would learn she meant what she said. Jonathan wasn't scheduled to be married for the better part of a year, which seemed like an eternity to her, so she wasn't too worried about his betrothal. She had already performed the Jamaican obeah ceremony that her friend at school had taught her, so she was confident that Jonathan would remain single until she was old enough to become his wife.

Rumors about the remarkable Yankee clipper had been spreading in London shipping circles since her North Sea trials, so several representatives of the press were on hand, along with two artists who were making sketches of the lean ship with the towering masts.

Jonathan modestly refused to make predictions regarding speeds that his ship might achieve. "Sir Alan will give me a signed certificate noting the date and time as we're ready to cast off," he said. "Thereafter I prefer to allow *Flying Dragon* to speak for herself."

The press representatives had to be satisfied with his reply. They would in any case judge the clipper for themselves later, since they would hire fishing smacks at Gravesend so that they could watch her at sea.

Jonathan wanted to give Charles a few final moments alone with his family, so he kissed a suddenly shy Elizabeth goodbye, then embraced and kissed his aunt.

"Godspeed," Jessica said. "You're a true Rakehell, all six feet and more of you!"

Sir Alan was gracious. "If you prove me wrong," he said, "I'll not only happily pay Charles four hundred pounds, but I'll remind you of my promise. I'll want as many clippers as you can build for me!"

The boatswain's mate piped Jonathan aboard, the first time he had been accorded the honor. He went briefly to his cabin, where he left the letters that Aunt Jessica and Sir Alan had written to his father, and then went to the quarterdeck, where Edmund greeted him with a formal salute and handshake.

"Bo's'n, all hands on deck." Jonathan was surprised that his voice sounded hoarse in his own ears.

"Aye aye, sir."

The eager seamen moved quickly to their places.

Jonathan watched the shore and saw Sir Alan sign the certificate that gave the date and hour of the ship's departure. Charles took the document, shook hands with him, and, after exchanging final kisses with his mother and sister, hurried to the ship.

The moment he stepped on board Jonathan gave the sailing orders.

As the awed correspondent of the *Times* of London would write after the fishing boat hired by the press at Gravesend followed *Flying Dragon* into the Channel, *"The clipper left our shores with the speed and urgency of a cannonball in flight. Whether she can sustain still higher speeds remains to be learned, but those who saw her as she catapulted westward in the Channel will never forget the sight."*

Edmund Barker took the watch as *Flying Dragon* made her way through the English Channel. The winds in this narrow body of water were unpredictable, changing constantly, and Jonathan, who remained on the quarter-deck, closely observed the clipper's every movement and response. A method of dealing with the winds they soon would encounter was already forming in his mind, and he was eager to test it.

When the clipper passed Land's End and moved into the open waters of the Atlantic, she headed into winds that would blow steadily throughout the entire voyage, and Jonathan surprised his officers and crew by taking the helm himself. Ordering full sail extended, he experimented for several hours, telling no one precisely what he was doing. During this time, however, the others noted that the clipper was easily maintaining a speed of at least fifteen knots per hour, sometimes moving even faster for brief periods.

Satisfied at last, Jonathan summoned his officers and all available hands to the quarterdeck. "I've learned the secret of how to sail a clipper into the wind," he said. "Obviously we must wear and tack. But the trick is to veer as little as possible, then hold her on course as long as we can. Never tack or wear sharply unless there's a sudden change in the wind. A gradual, gentle change enables us to maintain our momentum, and there will be no abrupt changes in our speed."

At his direction the other officers and the trained seamen who were assigned to the wheel took turns at the helm so they could gain the sense and "feel" of what he was telling them. Only when he was satisfied that every-one concerned understood what was required did he go below for a long-delayed meal and a short rest.

In a sense the voyage was anticlimactic. The spring weather remained fair most of the time, and the few rain squalls that blew up did not hinder *Flying Dragon*. When possible, the clipper moved under full sail day and night, reducing her speed only when visibility became poor. Jonathan set a grueling pace for himself and demanded the same from his mates and seamen. Even Grimshaw, the most experienced member of the crew, had never worked so hard or spent such long hours on duty.

193

But no one complained. Each day the men gained greater confidence in this strange new type of vessel, and Jonathan's enthusiasm was catching. The seamen were as determined as their captain to set a speed record. Various factors had combined to rob them of the mail contract on their maiden voyage, but they were determined to make history on this crossing to the west.

All that Isaac McKim had told the young New Englander in Baltimore was proving to be true. "No ship is better than her crew," Jonathan said to Charles and Edmund. "We'll keep as many of the present crew as are willing to sign up with us for the voyage to Canton, and we'll take great care in choosing replacements. The shape of a clipper and the huge amounts of canvas she carries aren't as important as the men who sail her."

Trans-Atlantic traffic was heavy at this season, with merchant ships of many nations plying between Europe and various American ports. Most followed the same routes, so at least once or twice each day *Flying Dragon* passed within sight of vessels sailing in the opposite direction. The reaction on board these schooners and brigs soon became predictable. Their crews lined the rails, their quarterdecks were crowded with officers, and everyone stared in stunned disbelief at the seemingly top-heavy clipper that slashed through the water at speeds never before achieved.

Jonathan kept two charts of the clipper's progress, reserving one in his cabin for his own use and posting the other on a bulkhead outside the galley. Each day, after he charted his position, the seamen went one by one to study the chart, but no one mentioned the possibility that the speed record for an east to west crossing might be broken. Sailors were superstitious, and no one wanted to put "Neptune's curse" on the voyage.

On the evening of the fifteenth day at sea, however, Jonathan felt sufficient confidence in their progress to mention the subject casually to his officers. "If the weather continues to hold," he said, "we'll be home in less than a week."

Land was sighted by the lookout soon after dawn on

194

the nineteenth day, and shortly before noon *Flying Dragon* swept past Fisher's Island. There was no longer any doubt that the record was being broken with days to spare. In fact, the voyage from Land's End to the United States had taken only eighteen days, and no ship sailing in the opposite direction could match that speed.

As the clipper approached the mouth of the Thames River, with the church steeples of New London already in view, Jonathan could not resist the urge to order the firing of both his small, deck-mounted cannon and the discharge of red, green, and white flares that soared high into the air. He was serving notice that something out of the ordinary was taking place.

Word on shore obviously spread quickly, and a crowd of more than one hundred people was gathered at the Rakehell Building and Shipping yard as *Flying Dragon,* gradually reducing her speed, glided toward an empty berth. Jonathan saw his father, with Bradford and Judith Walker standing beside him, and he raised his hat to them. Edmund was waving to Ruth Halliburton, but Louise Graves was nowhere to be seen. Perhaps, Jonathan reflected, she hadn't become familiar with the tradition that brought the families of returning seamen to the shore to meet a ship. There had been ample time for his sister to make an appearance, and he would have guessed that she would have explained the custom to Louise. In all fairness to his betrothed, however, it was possible that she had been away from home on some errand and therefore hadn't found it possible to come to the wharf.

After the clipper was hauled into her berth, the seamen were the first to break the news. "We've broken the speed record!" they shouted.

Jeremiah Rakehell, smiling broadly after seeing his son and overjoyed when he saw his nephew standing on the quarterdeck, too, spoke excitedly to Judith and Bradford.

Judith Walker's laugh and shrug indicated that she, like her father, was in the dark.

Bradford Walker's solemn expression remained unchanged.

Jonathan leaped ashore as the hawsers were being secured to bollards and went straight to his father. As soon as they had clasped hands, he took the certificate that Sir Alan had signed from his pocket and handed it to his father. "Papa," he said, "I'll be grateful if you'll note the present date and hour on this document. And sign it, please, to make it official."

Jeremiah automatically looked at his pocket watch, then stared at the paper. "This isn't possible," he muttered.

"You recognize Uncle Alan's signature, I'm sure," Jonathan replied quietly.

"Good Lord, son, this is extraordinary!" Jeremiah shook his hand again, then filled in the date and hour, signing the certificate with a flourish.

Judith looked over her father's shoulder, and when she realized a remarkable speed record for an east to west Atlantic crossing had been made, she impulsively hugged her brother.

Her husband offered Jonathan his congratulations, too, but even now he did not smile.

Soon the entire ship's company came ashore. Charles Boynton was warmly greeted by his relatives, Edmund embraced Ruth, and an impromptu celebration was held as news of *Flying Dragon*'s achievement spread. Jonathan was surrounded by people who offered him their felicitations, and one of the first to come to him was Ruth. "I've always known," she said, "that you'd do something like this."

Charles saw the expression in her eyes as she looked at Jonathan and was startled. Unless he was very much mistaken, this girl who was going to marry Edmund in the immediate future was in love with Jonathan. Hoping he was wrong, Charles nevertheless couldn't help wishing that his cousin showed a greater awareness of Ruth, whom he had always liked on his previous visits to America. For his taste she was far prettier, livelier, and more intelligent than Louise.

Jeremiah ordered a keg of beer brought to the wharf for the party that was developing.

Jonathan finally had an opportunity to speak privately with his sister. "I don't suppose you know where Louise might be?" he asked.

"Yes, she prefers to greet you at home. You know she hates crowds."

It was foolish of him, Jonathan supposed, but his triumph lost some of its savor.

IV

Jonathan remained at the wharf until his ship was made secure and a night watch was posted, so it was sundown before he finally reached the Graves house.

Louise, greeting him in her parents' parlor, was decorous as always and gave him her cheek to kiss.

"I've missed you," he said, knowing he wasn't speaking the literal truth, yet realizing their relationship demanded such a comment. "We broke the speed record for an Atlantic crossing."

The girl nodded. "So I've been told. I'm very pleased for you."

He knew her congratulations were perfunctory, but told himself he shouldn't have expected greater enthusiasm from her. Louise had little interest in ships, as she was the first to admit.

She came to life, however, when he gave her the gold locket and chain. "You're terribly extravagant," she said, "but this is lovely."

"I wanted to do better, but my funds were limited. By the time I'm ready to come back from Cathay, I should be able to bring you a keepsake worth having."

Louise was startled. "You're going to China?"

He told her in detail about his coming voyage, Charles's participation, and even the cargo he intended to carry.

Only one aspect was important to her. "Will we have to postpone our wedding?"

"Not if *Flying Dragon* behaves as she should and the winds are favorable," Jonathan replied cheerfully. "If you like, set a date, and I'll see to it that I'm back on time."

In spite of her lack of interest in ships, she was a member of a seafaring community and consequently was alert to its taboos. "That might bring us bad luck," she said. "We'll wait until you come home and then set the date."

"Fair enough." Like Louise, Jonathan felt no sense of urgency. He almost envied Edmund and Ruth, who had decided today that they would be married within a week. But he and Louise enjoyed a far more sedate, tranquil relationship, and he told himself their marriage would be solid because they would be subjected to so few emotional pressures. "Will you join us for supper tonight? Judy and Brad are coming over with the children because Charles is here with us. I know he's eager to see you."

"Thank you, Jonathan, but I wouldn't want to interfere at a family gathering."

He couldn't help laughing. "Interfere? You're going to be a Rakehell, too, you know."

Louise smiled shyly. "That's true enough, of course, but I'm not a member of the family yet, and I'd feel like an outsider."

He felt compelled to defer to her wishes.

"I'm sure Mama and Papa will want you and Charles and your father to come here for dinner tomorrow. They'll be in touch with your father." A sudden thought struck her. "How soon will you go off to China?"

It was difficult to explain that, although he was eager to leave at once, he and Charles had decided it would be wise to wait until their profits from the sale of the Sheffield saws was in hand. Their need for hard cash was urgent. "I'm not sure, but it'll be the better part of two months, I reckon. I'll be going up to Fall River for my looms, and they may not be delivered for some weeks."

Her eyes grew larger. "You're sure you won't be dealing in opium in the Orient?"

It was strange how little she really knew about him. "I'd rather see my clipper fall apart at the seams in a hurricane," he said. "And Charles feels precisely as I do.

There's a potential for so much legitimate trade with the Chinese that dealing in drugs would be immoral. What's more, it's contrary to Chinese law."

"I'm very glad," she said, walking to the door with him. "I'd feel awful if I thought you were making money out of human suffering."

"I have plenty of faults, but that isn't one of them."

Louise put a hand on his arm, and when he leaned down to kiss her, she offered him her lips.

Perhaps the gift of the locket had warmed her, or it may have been the stand he had just taken against opium. Whatever the reason, he was pleased—and somewhat shaken. Behind her docile, shy shell there lurked a passionate young woman, and the memory of her kiss burned into him. Maybe their relationship wasn't as tranquil as he had assumed, and he warned himself to exercise care and restraint during the weeks of his sojourn at home. It might be far easier to make love to her than he had imagined.

The Hartford *Courant* sent a reporter to New London to interview Jonathan, and an artist came to town, too, to make a sketch of *Flying Dragon* for the New York *Post*. "Isaac McKim deserves the credit for whatever a clipper accomplishes," Jonathan told the reporter. "I'm sure that in the decades ahead every speed record on the high seas will be broken, then broken again."

He was asked, "Would you care to predict the length of various sea run times in the next quarter of a century?"

"I wouldn't dare. My next clipper will improve on *Flying Dragon,* and other designers are bound to enter the field, too. All I can tell you for certain is that today we stand at the beginning of a new era. The world will grow smaller and is already starting to shrink."

A letter for Jonathan arrived without fanfare from Washington City and bore the seal of the President of the United States. The brief communication was written in the spidery hand of an elderly, ailing man:

When I retire to private life in a year and a half from now, I shall be consoled by the knowledge that young men like you will continue to carry forward the torch of greatness that is the mark of our beloved country. Accept my hearty congratulations on your accomplishment.

The signature was written in larger, bolder letters: *Andrew Jackson.*

The letter instantly became one of Jonathan's prized possessions, and he treasured it until the end of his days.

Jeremiah Rakehell, proud of his son, wanted to have a serious talk with him about the long-range future. But he decided to wait until the excitement over the record-breaking Atlantic crossing died away. Besides, he was troubled because there was something he failed to understand.

Certainly he was willing to admit he was mistaken about the potential that clipper ships might achieve. Provided he was really wrong. There were such discrepancies between the times of *Flying Dragon*'s two trans-Atlantic voyages that, as one who had spent his whole life in shipping, he was bewildered. He wanted to settle the matter in his own mind before he sat down with Jonathan.

As a first step, he called Bradford Walker into his office. "Brad, I need your help," he said.

Always deferential in his dealings with his father-in-law, Brad replied, "You know I'll do anything I can for you, sir."

"It isn't for me, it's for all of us. I assume that as a regular part of your work you've made a detailed study of Captain Davis Hartley's log of *Flying Dragon*'s maiden voyage?"

"Yes, sir." Brad instantly became wary. Hartley was demanding immediate payment after fulfilling his end of their bargain and couldn't seem to understand that the moment to seek his promotion to commodore of the line was inappropriate. Brad had explained to him that he would have to wait until the hullabaloo over Jonathan's achievement died away and better yet to be patient until Jonathan went off to China—and was half-forgotten.

"How does he account for his slow sailing time to England?"

"In his log," Brad said carefully, "he makes several

mentions of an unfortunate accident in which he lost a topmast. We know now, of course, that Jonathan lengthened a bowsprit and set it at a sharper angle at the Boynton yard in London."

"Anything else?"

"No, sir."

"Jonathan has been very careful not to criticize Hartley in any way, which is admirable of him. But there are omissions in his account of the west to east voyage that I find curious, and I wondered if Hartley notes any disagreements in his log."

"There are none." Brad decided to cover himself. "Hartley has been a loyal Rakehell employee for many years, of course, so I doubt if he'd even hint at the possibility there might have been any dispute with Jonathan." Brad allowed himself the luxury of a small smile. "Would you care to see the log for yourself, sir? I have a copy in my files."

"No, that won't be necessary," Jeremiah replied with a sigh.

His son-in-law left the office believing that a crisis had been averted.

But Jeremiah remained dissatisfied and continued to ponder. He waited for a few days, then decided to act on a morning when Brad was attending a merchants' association meeting in Norwich and Jonathan was busy at a rehearsal for the wedding of Ruth Halliburton and Edmund Barker. It was best, at the moment, that neither was aware of his acute discomfort.

"See if you can locate Captain Hartley, either in the yard or at his home," he told his clerk. "I'd like to see him at his convenience. This morning, if possible."

About an hour later Hartley appeared, wearing civilian clothes. "I'd have changed into uniform before coming in, Mr. Rakehell, but your clerk told me not to bother."

"Quite right. I just want to have a little chat with you." Jeremiah leaned back in the hand-carved oak chair that had been made for his great-grandfather. "You and I have been together for a long time," he said. "In fact, you came with the company as a third mate fresh out of your time, back in my father's day. I had just been graduated from Yale College myself and had come here full time."

"It has been a long time, Mr. Rakehell." Hartley wondered if he was about to be awarded the promotion. "There's only one master here who is senior to me."

"Yes, Jed Martin, who will retire at the end of the year. You'll stand at the head of the pack then, so you can pick and choose your assignments at will."

"Frankly, I'll like that."

"Of course you will." Jeremiah paused, and when he spoke again there was a subtle change in his tone of voice. He was still genial, but there was a hint of steel beneath the surface. "I mention all this because I know I can count on your cooperation now. Captain, how do you account for the slowness of *Flying Dragon*'s maiden voyage to England?"

The abruptness of the question jarred Hartley. "Well, Mr. Rakehell," he said, "there's the matter of the short bowsprit. I'm sure you're familiar with that."

"I am. I have the feeling that something else also may have been responsible, but I can't put my finger on it."

"Your son hasn't enlightened you?"

"I haven't discussed the matter with him." Jeremiah was sure now that he was on the scent of something.

Hartley squared his shoulders. "In a sense, Mr. Rakehell, I was responsible. Except for very brief periods I refused to use the two top sails."

"Why was that?" Jeremiah leaned forward, placed his elbows on his desk, and rested his weight on them.

Hartley was in a quandary. His conscience had been bothering him, and he was furiously angry with Bradford Walker, who had broken his end of a clearly understood agreement.

"Why was that?" Jeremiah repeated.

"Originally," the captain replied, speaking heavily and slowly, "I wrote about it at length in my log. I wrote exactly what I had told your son, that I was afraid the clipper would be so top-heavy that she'd turn turtle. But the argument seemed so weak to me that even before the voyage ended I tore the page out of my log and destroyed it."

Jeremiah suffered from the family trait, a lack of

patience. But he could see that the man on the far side of the desk was going through inner torment, and his long years of dealing with people made it possible for him to wait in silence.

Several face-saving devices occurred to Davis Hartley, but all at once he buckled. He was a simple seaman who had been cruelly used by a clever, sophisticated man taking advantage of his natural ambition, and he wanted to rid himself of the guilt feeling that weighed on his soul. Certainly he wouldn't be unhappy if he gave Walker a black eye in the process.

"Mr. Rakehell," he said, "you may discharge me after you hear what I have to tell you, and I won't blame you if you do." His voice occasionally faltering and his breath growing short, he related the deal he had made with Bradford Walker.

Jeremiah didn't lose his temper, as Hartley had expected, but instead looked pensive. "I suppose you know that I hold the title of commodore of the Rakehell fleet, although I don't exercise it as a command function. It's a family tradition, nothing more, and some day my son will inherit the title."

"I know it all too well, Mr. Rakehell, but I became convinced—"

"I know how you felt," Jeremiah interrupted him. "You saw an opportunity for advancement, and no seaman worth his salt would want to refuse the chance." He rose from his desk, walked to the window, and stared out at the busy yard.

He remained silent for so long that Hartley's shirt became soaked with perspiration.

"I'm grateful for your candor. It wasn't easy for you," Jeremiah said at last. "As it happens, there was no real harm done. The short bowsprit would have made it impossible to set a speed record."

The miserable Hartley could only nod.

"The thought occurs to me," Jeremiah said, "that perhaps I should make some changes within the conventions of my family traditions. At the end of the year, when you become the senior captain, I shall transfer some of the responsibilities of fleet commodore from the office of

Bradford Walker to you. I won't give you the title, but you'll be paid an additional fifty dollars a month for the added work load. Is that satisfactory?"

"Your generosity is far more than I deserve, Mr. Rakehell," Hartley said in a voice that shook.

"I trust we understand each other," Jeremiah said. "This has been a confidential conversation between you and me, and nothing that has been said here will be repeated to anyone. By either of us."

"I won't be disloyal a second time."

"I'm sure you won't." Jeremiah knew he was judging the man correctly and, rising to his feet, terminated the interview with a quick, firm handshake.

Captain Hartley closed the door behind him.

Jeremiah opened it again just long enough to tell his clerk he didn't want to be disturbed. Then he reverted to the habit he had formed during his years on the quarterdeck and began to pace slowly, his tread measured.

His first reaction was that Bradford Walker's perfidy shocked him, but that wasn't really true. He was saddened rather than surprised. For a long time he had been aware of Brad's carefully concealed hostility toward Jonathan, and he had guessed the reason. Unfortunately, his talk with Captain Hartley confirmed his suspicions.

It would be wrong, he decided, to give in to his righteous anger and send Brad packing. For one thing, the man was an exceptionally competent administrator who worked hard and who knew every phase of the business. He could be replaced, to be sure, but it would be a long time before his successor performed as efficiently.

Of far greater significance was the fact that Brad was Judith's husband and the father of her children. To reveal what he had done would either end their marriage or, if Judith remained loyal to her husband, cause a split in the family ranks, and that was unthinkable. The Rakehell strength lay in unshakable unity that every member of the family felt. They stood shoulder to shoulder no matter what the crisis, and as a consequence the company grew more prosperous for generation after generation.

Brad Walker had already come a long way in the world, rising from the position of clerk that he had held when Judith had married him. In some men ambition was an asset, but in Brad it was a liability. Craving power, he had behaved as no Rakehell would ever behave, and that was the heart of the matter. Brad Walker was not a Rakehell.

For the present, Jeremiah finally decided, he would take no action of any kind. He had been warned, so hereafter he would watch his son-in-law much more carefully. In the future Brad would neither fool him nor harm legitimate Rakehell interests. And Jonathan would go off to China with his mind untroubled, sure of his sister's love and loyalty. What was more, as a doting grandfather, it would not become necessary for Jeremiah to cut little Braddy and Judy out of his will. They had Rakehell blood, so they deserved shares in the company when they grew older.

Not that Jeremiah intended to allow Brad to go unpunished for all time. His God was a zealous God who loved justice, and at the right time, in the right way, the cause of justice would be served.

At present, thanks to Jonathan's imagination, courage, and skill, Rakehell Building and Shipping stood on the threshold of a new period in the company's history. The problems raised by the success of the new clipper ship were many and varied, and time would be needed to solve them. Jeremiah knew he was buying that time by temporizing, but he was satisfied.

He swore to himself that the day would come when he would force Bradford Walker to pay in full for his treachery.

Jonathan stood at one side of the altar in the Anglican church, beside Edmund, and watched the bridesmaids come down the center aisle. Louise, dressed in a gown of soft pink, followed them, and Jonathan studied her surreptitiously but carefully. He and she had been taking each other for granted, and that was their problem. It was astonishing, now that he had become aware of her hidden sensuality, that he hadn't recognized that quality in her all along. It was present in the way she moved her hips and thrust her breasts forward when she walked; he could sense it in the almost sleepy expression in her eyes, even in the way her lips parted slightly when she was unsmiling. She had been so completely dominated by her parents, he thought, that it was unlikely she knew herself well enough to realize there were deep passions stored within her.

Perhaps it was wrong, in church, at the wedding of a close friend, to allow his mind to dwell on Louise's physical attributes, but Jonathan knew he wanted her. He should have made an issue of pushing their wedding date forward; the better part of a year was a long time to wait.

Louise, as maid of honor, took her place at the far side of the altar, and for a moment her eyes met Jonathan's.

He smiled at her to let her know he was thinking of her.

Her expression remained solemn, but he was able to guess what was going through her mind. After he returned from his voyage to Cathay, they would be the principals in an identical ceremony, here in this same church. Apparently the realization made her somewhat apprehensive because she quickly averted his gaze.

The entire congregation stood as Ruth Halliburton, wearing a traditional white gown and veil, came down the aisle on the arm of her father. The Rakehell chief carpenter, smiling broadly in recognition of the presence of so many of his friends and colleagues, was unperturbed by his own old-fashioned attire, a swallow-tailed coat, knee breeches, white stockings, and shoes with pewter buckles. It was likely that he had not worn these clothes since his own wedding the better part of a quarter of a century earlier.

Charles Boynton, in the Rakehell family pew, stared hard at the bride, who was so vivacious that even now, on the most important day of her life, her eyes sparkled with warmth and humor. It was plain, even to an outsider, that she was thoroughly enjoying the occasion.

It was surprising to Charles that Jonathan, standing still at the side of the tense bridegroom, continued to look at Louise and paid scant attention to the bride. Edmund was the most fortunate of men, and Charles reflected that, had he been living in the United States, he would have given Edmund stiff competition for Ruth's hand.

Then his natural cynicism asserted itself. Never in his life had he thought seriously of marrying anyone, and the very idea of assuming such a responsibility was an anathema to him. So it was possible, he thought, grinning quietly, that he was pretending he could have developed an interest in Ruth because he knew she was no longer available. Charles was enough of a Rakehell that he couldn't allow his sudden romanticism to go unchallenged. Self-delusion, according to his mother—and Uncle Jeremiah—was a cardinal sin.

"Dearly beloved," the clergyman said, intoning the familiar words, "we are gathered here in the sight of God and in the face of this company to join together this man and this woman in Holy Matrimony. . . ."

The congregation was attentive, the children did not fidget, and a number of the ladies wept happily throughout the ceremony. At the appropriate moment Jonathan gave the bridegroom the thick band of plain gold, and Edmund fumbled for an instant before placing it on his bride's finger.

Ruth and Edmund led the procession out of the church, with Louise, on Jonathan's arm, directly behind them. As the congregation left the church, the members of the wedding party were offering their felicitations to the bride and groom. Charles saw Jonathan come up to Ruth and kiss her, and was sure he was not imagining things when he saw her avert her face slightly. The gesture was instinctive, and neither Jonathan nor the girl herself seemed aware of it.

His cousin, Charles decided, was thick-witted. He could have had Ruth had he paid court to her, but instead, he was settling for the pallid Louise Graves. Well, every man to his own taste. Charles knew only that he was thirsty for a stiff drink of the hard cider that was almost always served at New England wedding receptions.

Jeremiah Rakehell followed the principle of never discussing business at home because his late wife had protested so vehemently. So he refrained from mentioning the matters uppermost in his mind either at supper or at breakfast with his son and his nephew. They walked together to the yard, and only as they approached it did he say to Jonathan, "I hope you can spare me some time this morning for a chat. At your convenience, of course."

Jonathan instantly revised his day's schedule. "I'll come with you right now, Papa."

They walked in silence to the headquarters building, and Jeremiah closed the door of his office behind them. "I've been thinking a great deal about your future—and the company's," he said as he settled himself behind his desk. "First off, how are you and Charles fixed financially for your China venture?"

"We're much better off than we expected, Papa," Jonathan said. "The one-third interest Charles bought paid for our cargo, and we've had a lucky break. The dealer in Fall River who sold me the cotton looms has taken our entire cargo of Sheffield saws. He's not only paying the full sum in cash, but my profit is greater than I had estimated. As a matter of fact," he added with a chuckle, "we don't need the money that Charles won from Uncle Alan."

Jeremiah raised an eyebrow.

"Before we left London," his son explained, "we were so short that Charles made a wager with his father that *Flying Dragon* would break the east to west trans-Atlantic speed record. He put up two hundred pounds, and Uncle Alan was so confident he gave two to one odds. Well, the money came day before yesterday in a letter, and Charles is returning it. He's telling Uncle Alan he can't accept money on a bet in which there was no gamble involved."

"You boys have no doubts about your clipper's abilities."

"None, sir."

"I was intending to offer you an advance, if you had needed it," Jeremiah said.

"Thanks anyway, Papa. That's generous of you."

"I'm never generous in business," his father said. "I've been tempted to ask if you'd be willing to place *Flying Dragon* under the house banner on this voyage, but that wouldn't be fair to you. Or to Charles. You deserve the full profits yourselves. But I do want to come to a long-range understanding with you. What are your own thoughts?"

"It's important to me that I prove to the world what

a clipper ship can do on a voyage involving great distances," Jonathan said. "In spite of all the interest our voyage from England has generated, I'm sure many people in the industry believe we enjoyed some freakish luck. They'll change their tune. I'm taking great care mapping my sea route, and I honestly think I can cut a minimum of one-third off the sailing time from here to Canton."

"What route are you sailing?"

Jonathan sighed. "That question has been keeping me awake nights. I know the British, who send ten times as many ships to the East as we do, prefer the Cape of Good Hope. When a master is lucky he has fair winds all the way, even during the foul weather seasons. But the storms there can be so nasty that a ship can be held up for weeks. Charles tells me that one of the Boynton ships actually had to wait for seven weeks for the passage."

His father merely nodded.

"After searching my soul, I've finally made up my mind to round the Horn," Jonathan said.

"The Cape Horn weather isn't generally regarded as idyllic," Jeremiah replied, his tone somewhat caustic.

His son grinned at him. "The Lord knows I'm aware of that! But my reading tells me—and I've been reading everything I can find on the subject—that if I can hold to my schedule I should be reaching the Horn at a relatively good time of year. I'm not saying there are no gales, naturally. Just fewer gales. The big question is which is the lesser risk, Africa or South America. For better or worse, I'm casting my ballot for South America. Give me beam winds, and my clipper will set another record. Obviously, I've become a total clipper convert."

His father shook his head. "As you know, I was convinced it wasn't possible, but you're making a convert of me." Leaning back in his chair, he hooked his thumbs in his waistcoat pockets. "Let's say you succeed in what you're setting out to do and that you show a handsome profit as well. What then?"

"For one thing," Jonathan said, "I'll be pleased to add *Flying Dragon* to the Rakehell fleet."

"The company will buy her from you—at what you think is a fair price. I wouldn't accept her as a gift."

"That's the least of my concerns, Papa. Once I've smashed all the records between here and the Orient, there is going to be a tremendous demand for clippers. Other designers and builders will become involved, of course, not only here but in England and elsewhere. That's inevitable. But we'll have a head start. I estimate that at the present capacity of the Rakehell yard we can build three a year. One for ourselves, one for Uncle Alan, who will take as many as we can build for him, and one to be sold elsewhere."

Jeremiah nodded thoughtfully. "If we increase our capacity by buying that strip of vacant land adjacent to the present yard, we might raise the total output to four ships a year. That would give us two each year to sell to outsiders, and if you perform on your voyage as you expect, we can blame near set our own price. The demand for clippers will be insatiable."

"That's the way I see it, sir," Jonathan said. "I'll admit we face some nasty problems. There's a huge market for Chinese tea and silks, and it will be years before the saturation point is reached. So there's little doubt in my mind that clippers will come to monopolize the Cathay trade. But we've got to be more practical than that."

"What you're saying is that you want to see clippers dominate trans-Atlantic, West Indian, and other trade routes, too."

"Yes, sir." They understood each other completely. "And that means I've got to find ways to expand the clipper's cargo-carrying capacity without sacrificing her speed. At present she can carry only a fraction of the cargo that ordinary schooners, brigs, and the like can stow in their holds."

"How will you do that?"

"To be honest, Papa, I'm blamed if I know. All I can tell you is that I expect to be spending a lot of time at my drawing board sailing to and from Canton. I can't guarantee that I'll solve the problem, but I'll try. I have some thoughts, but I'd rather not talk about them until I can prove they're feasible."

Jeremiah smiled. "I see. But regardless of whether

you can increase a clipper's cargo capacity, you're proposing that Rakehell abandon the building of conventional ships and concentrate completely and exclusively on clippers."

"Yes, sir." Jonathan was firm. "Merchants and shippers all over the world are going to be clamoring for clippers—and more clippers—for the next half-century, which is as far ahead as anyone dares to look. Our annual profits will be doubled."

"I'll need to study the whole picture in depth—while you're away and after you come back—before I'll commit myself to a whole new program. I can't jettison what we've done for a long time in favor of something new until I know where we'll be headed. You understand my position."

"Of course, Papa. I'm in no rush. Clippers are going to be with us for a long time to come. And I want to keep improving them. I've already learned enough to know that my next will be faster than *Flying Dragon,* and once I solve the problem of increasing cargo space we'll be getting more orders than we can handle."

"That would be very pleasant," Jeremiah said. "But at the same time I'm reluctant to abandon building the ships that have put bread on our table for generations. I'll have to see what I can work out. It may be that we'll just use a portion of the yard to build clippers."

Jonathan's grin reflected his solid self-confidence. "The only trouble with restricted production is that we'll want a fleet of our own, and Uncle Alan will be pestering the daylights out of us for his fair share."

Jeremiah looked at him with mock severity. "Young man, I'm making quite a concession as things stand. I'm talking in terms of using a portion of our facilities for your confounded clippers when you haven't yet gone off to Cathay!"

His son laughed. "I'll let *Flying Dragon* talk for me."

"Good." Jeremiah nodded, then sobered. "You'll need to be wary on this voyage, son. I've never visited the Orient myself, but from all I hear, the business practices there are far different from what you've known in Europe and the West Indies. Every scoundrel on the high seas is

213

sailing to China in the hope of making a quick financial killing, and there's another snag, too. The Oriental ways of doing business aren't our ways."

"I'm well aware of it, sir. And there's something I want to check with you. I've asked all five of the people with whom I've been corresponding to tell me the name of the most reliable and honest merchant in Canton, and I'm encouraged because all of them have nominated the same man." He took a letter from an inner coat pocket and looked at it. "Soong Chao. Does the name mean anything to you?"

"I think every major shipping company in the West has heard of Soong Chao. All I can tell you is that he has a good reputation, but I have no specific information about him."

"Well, I'll go to him first to see if he wants to buy my cotton looms." Jonathan had to suppress the feeling of excitement that surged up inside him. "Papa, this trip of mine is going to be far more than a voyage in a merchant-man. There's so much at stake that it will mark the beginning of a whole new chapter in the history of the Rakehells!"

His claim was so sweeping that Jeremiah could only smile indulgently. Enthusiasm for his coming venture was one of Jonathan's most important assets, so it would be wrong to discourage him by warning him not to expect too much.

Only two members of *Flying Dragon*'s crew had to be replaced, and Grimshaw took charge of training the replacements, drilling them in raising and lowering the clipper's many sails until the art of handling the canvas became second nature to them. Oliver was promoted to boatswain's mate, his instinctive understanding of the great ship convincing Jonathan that he was capable of acting as crew chief in the event that Grimshaw became incapacitated.

The precaution was taken of putting the clipper into drydock, even though she had spent only a short time at sea. Edmund Barker returned from a week's honeymoon in time to supervise the painting of the ship and having a complete suit of sails made. No effort was spared to insure that *Flying Dragon* would live up to Jonathan's exceptionally high standards, and the young builder-owner-master was on hand himself when the dismantled cotton looms were stored in the cramped holds.

Great care was taken in ordering food for the voyage. *Flying Dragon* would carry larger quantities of pickled and dried beef than was customary. Livestock for butchering on the passage were also ordered in greater numbers than usual. Charles rigorously inspected the supplies, examining every side of bacon, every sack of beans, flour, and sugar. In the days immediately prior to the voyage he also put in lemons and limes that would ripen on board and that every member of the company would eat daily. Ultimately, of course, the clipper would put into predetermined ports for additional fresh fruit and for water.

The time for *Flying Dragon*'s departure rapidly drew nearer, and on the afternoon of the day prior to her sailing, Dr. and Mrs. Graves and Jeremiah Rakehell held a small party on the beach of the latter's home. The meal was a typical New England clambake and began with clams steamed in seaweed placed over a low fire. Then came the chowder, rich with cream. Steamed lobsters comprised the main dish and were served with corn that had been steamed in its husks. The feast ended with hot apple pie and coffee.

The older people sat in chairs from the Rakehell kitchen that had been carried to the beach, the children went swimming as soon as their dinner had been digested, and the younger adults congregated around the fire. Ruth Halliburton Barker sparked the conversation, bandying witticisms with Charles Boynton, who was at his effervescent best. Edmund, sitting close beside his bride, joined in occasionally and did his best to conceal his true feelings. He was deeply in love with Ruth, and the prospect of their long separation depressed him. Judith Walker was a member of the group, too, although her husband had elected to sit with the older people, and she, too, contributed her fair share to the talk.

Only Louise, attired in a dress of pale yellow that buttoned up the front, was virtually silent, and Jonathan, who sat next to her, said very little. His mind was seething, filled with countless details that would need to be settled between dawn and sailing time the following day. Besides, he was already all too conscious of Louise's proximity, and recognizing the dangers of giving in to his desires, he tried not to dwell too much on her.

That task became more difficult when twilight approached and Louise, sighing gently, leaned against him for support. Finally Jonathan gave in to the desire to place an arm around her shoulders.

There was virtually no breeze, and at nightfall mosquitoes appeared, driving the older people into the house. The Walker children were hungry again, so Judith went off to the pantry to make sandwiches for them. Edmund and Ruth needed no excuse to go off to the Halliburton house for their last night together.

Charles stood and stretched, then brushed sand from his trousers. "I'm a bit restless," he said. "If you two don't object too strenuously, I believe I'll go off for my last brisk walk on land for several months."

Jonathan waved him away with a smile. He suspected that his cousin actually intended to visit a brothel in town frequented by ships' officers. That was his privilege, of course.

Jonathan poured two goblets of wine and handed one to Louise, even though he knew that she rarely took more than a taste.

Louise made no move, and after the others had gone she continued to gaze into the fire.

"Why so pensive?" Jonathan asked lightly.

"All sorts of strange thoughts have been going through my mind," she replied.

"Would you care to give me an example?"

"All right." She hesitated for a moment, then quoted, " 'In Xanadu did Kubla Khan a stately pleasure dome decree.' " She paused. "That's all I can remember." She took a large swallow of her wine.

Jonathan picked up the poem. " 'Where Alph, the sacred river ran through caverns measureless to man, down to a sunless sea.' "

"I can't even remember the name of the poem or who wrote it," she confessed with a faint smile.

"*Kubla Khan,* by Samuel Taylor Coleridge, the English poet who died last year. What made you think of it?"

"Your voyage, Jonnie. You'll be going to such exotic, far-off places."

"And bringing you a priceless emerald or sapphire— or whatever precious stones they have in Cathay. If I can afford one," he added with a laugh.

"Please don't. I'd rather you save the money. I like jewelry, of course, but it doesn't really mean all that much to me." She stirred slightly.

Jonathan held her a trifle more tightly. "Any other strange thoughts?"

"More than I can remember. Looking at Ruth and Edmund a few minutes ago, it occurred to me they'll be spending their whole lives with him going off to sea for long periods. Is that the kind of life we're going to have?"

"Not really. Oh, I'll go to sea from time to time. But I'll be needed right here at the yard most of the time, particularly if my plans are realized."

She sighed. "That's good. I hate the idea of being alone." She drained her wine, although it was making her giddy.

"You never need be alone. Our families are here."

"That's different," Louise said. "When a woman is married, she's set apart, and it always depresses me when I see the temporary sea widows of New London keeping busy until their husbands come home."

"I've been thinking we should have been married before I leave, but maybe it's better that we're waiting for another eight to ten months."

"Much better," she said. "I'm in no hurry."

"Well, I am," he said harshly.

His tone surprised her, and she twisted in his embrace to face him. "Why, Jonnie?"

"The reason shouldn't be all that difficult for you to guess," Jonathan said, and his heart pounded harder.

"Oh, that," Louise said.

"I defy you to tell me you don't feel as I do!"

She made no reply.

Unable to hold back any longer, he lifted her face and kissed her. It was their first real kiss, not a token.

Louise stiffened, and at first she resisted him, but all at once she yielded, curling her arms around his neck.

The discovery that her ardor was as great as his own surprised Jonathan, and he cast aside all caution. This was their first intimate moment in all the years they had known each other, and now that the dam had burst there was no way the waters could be held back.

The fire was dying, and they stretched out on a blanket beside it, making love by its feeble glow. They no longer heard the distant sound of voices in the Rakehell parlor or the occasional pounding of a horse's hoofs on Pequot Avenue. No one else existed, and they were wrapped in their own cocoon, kissing feverishly, their hands exploring.

Jonathan knew he had to stop while he still could and tore himself away from the girl.

Louise sat up slowly, her eyes bright, her face suffused with color. She looked at the man her parents had selected as her husband. Then, very slowly and deliberately, she began to unbutton her dress.

The last of Jonathan's self-control vanished, and he reached for her, one hand plunging inside her opened dress as he kissed her again.

Later, when they thought about the incident separately, neither could recall the details of their lovemaking. Jonathan knew only that Louise, in spite of her lack of experience, was eager to consummate their union.

Her memories were even dimmer. Her physical reaction, as such, was curiously flat, but no one had ever told her how a woman might feel at this time, so she wasn't disappointed.

Gradually they emerged into the real world around them. Louise turned away from Jonathan as she dressed, and then, taking a small, silver-handled brush from her purse, she applied it vigorously to her hair.

By the time she faced him again her appearance was impeccable.

"How do I look?" she demanded.

"Wonderful. But you might want to put a bit of rouge on your lips before we go inside. They look—well, as though you've been thoroughly kissed."

"Which I have." Remarkably calm and collected now, she took a tiny pot from her purse, dipped her finger into it, and dabbed at her mouth.

Jonathan stood, then helped her to her feet. He knew he had to say something appropriate, that this was the moment he should declare his eternal love for her, but he couldn't form the words. Instead he said, "I suppose I should apologize, but I'm not really sorry."

Louise held her head high. "Neither am I," she said.

They wandered hand in hand up the beach toward the Rakehell house, their tranquility restored. Jonathan couldn't help wondering if their married life would be this serene.

Book
III

I

Flying Dragon faced her first test off Cape Hatteras, North Carolina, where she had to fight her way through an early summer storm. At best, the weather off Hatteras was unpredictable, rarely calm, and for a century and a half had been known as a graveyard for unwary ships. Now the mettle of the clipper and her crew were tried to the utmost. The winds were violent, blowing in gusts with a strength of forty-five to fifty knots. Sixty-three knot winds blew in hurricanes.

All hands remained at their stations, and Jonathan sent his vessel catapulting southward under reduced sail, tacking and wearing repeatedly as the winds changed. *Flying Dragon* reacted violently, pitching heavily and rolling erratically from side to side, with huge waves breaking over her bow and sending sheets of water cascading over her main deck. Officers and men lashed themselves into place at their posts so they would not be washed overboard. In spite of the extreme motion, the ship achieved such speed that the company found the experience exhilarating, and from that time forward no one was afraid of the weather.

Flying Dragon, with the bad weather far behind, picked up the sub-tropical trade winds while cruising past the West Indian Islands and was now so far ahead of schedule that Jonathan decided to wait until he reached Rio de Janeiro for water and whatever fresh foods he could buy. The winds became weaker as the clipper drew nearer to the Equator, and only a feeble breeze was blowing as she moved into the Doldrums. Vessels that carried less sail often became becalmed in these waters, and every seaman knew horror stories about crews that had died of thirst and hunger when a lack of a wind compelled them to halt for as long as four months.

But Jonathan crowded on every inch of available sail, and *Flying Dragon* sailed steadily toward the southeast, although at a painfully slow pace. For all of one day and night she managed to achieve a speed no greater than five knots. But no one complained; every man on board was grateful that she continued to move.

The next morning a fiery sun rose in a cloudless sky, and the heat and humidity were so great that anyone who came on deck stripped to the waist. The ship continued to inch forward, however.

Oliver was on duty in the crow's nest and soon called to Charles Boynton, who had the watch, "Deck there! Sail two points off the port bow."

Charles searched the horizon and made out a brig, her sails drooping listlessly, making it obvious she was barely moving. He immediately sent word to the captain, who had gone below.

Jonathan quickly reached a decision. "We'll close to hailing distance. . . . Luff round."

"Quartermaster, luff round," Charles ordered.

"Back your topsails to lose way."

"Aye aye, sir. Bo's'n, back your topsails!"

The maneuver was accomplished in the feeble wind, and *Flying Dragon* came within hailing distance of the other merchantman and hoisted the American flag.

After a few moments the national emblem of the Netherlands crept slowly up to the yardarm of the other vessel.

"What ship?" Jonathan called.

"Mieerneuw, out of Rotterdam," the master of the Dutch ship replied in a hoarse, weak voice. Middle-aged, with his face blackened by the sun, he was unshaven and his clothes were in tatters.

His seamen were sprawled on the deck, most of them looking across the water listlessly.

"*Flying Dragon* out of New London," Jonathan said. "Are you in trouble?"

"Bad trouble." The Dutch captain spoke English with a thick accent, but by straining it was possible for the crew of the clipper to hear him. "We've been becalmed for forty-six days. We're out of water and fruit. We'll all come down with scurvy, but I don't think that matters. A wind began to blow up this morning—faint, as you can tell, sir, but nevertheless a wind. I'm afraid we're too weak to take advantage of it."

Several of his men, looking like scarecrows, managed to haul themselves to their feet and staggered to the rail.

"I'll help you all I can," Jonathan said promptly. "What do you need other than water and fruit?"

"Nothing. We have salt pork, bully beef, and hardtack, but we haven't been able to eat because the food makes us thirstier!"

Jonathan immediately ordered a boat lowered, and it made several trips to the *Mieerneuw* with casks of water and a supply of fresh limes. He was generous with both the water and the fruit giving the Dutchmen half of what he had left.

The dehydrated seamen drank greedily, and after a time they gained sufficient strength to man the sails.

For the rest of the blistering day the two ships sailed side by side, both of them moving almost imperceptibly across the calm, glazed sea.

Night came, and when a three-quarters moon rose in a cloudless sky, Jonathan directed his officers to keep the other vessel in sight throughout the night.

Early the following morning, when the wind was picking up token strength, he returned to his quarterdeck and could see the Dutch seamen eating and drinking water at their duty stations.

The voice of the *Mieerneuw*'s master sounded less feeble as he called, "*Meinheer,* you have brought us back from the dead!"

Ordinarily Jonathan would have taken full advantage

225

of the strengthening wind, but instead, he remained near the Dutch merchantman throughout the day. Her men were moving with greater alacrity, and for the first time he believed they would come through the crisis unscathed.

The Doldrums had almost claimed another victim, but the generosity and prompt action of the Americans had saved the *Mieerneuw* and her crew.

At sundown the wind gathered additional force.

"Can you make out now?" Jonathan called.

"We'll be fine! Thank you, *Meinheer,* and may God bless you!"

Only now did Jonathan add more canvas and increase his speed to ten knots.

However, as he told Charles and Edmund, they had to pay a price for their kindness. "Our own supplies of water and fresh fruit won't see us to Rio," he said.

"What will you do, sir?"

Jonathan's smile indicated that he anticipated no serious problems. They were sailing a well-traveled passage route, and each day at noon he took sights with his sextant, then charted his previous twenty-four hours' run, so he knew his precise position.

"There are several coves and natural harbors along the unoccupied coast of South America where other ships have found water and ample supplies of wild fruit," he said. "I've collected data on all of them, so I'll study my notes after supper, and we'll put into the one that seems the best of them."

Neither of his mates mentioned the obvious fact that the encounter with the Dutch merchantman had put them off their schedule if they hoped to establish a new record.

But that question was always present in Jonathan's mind. "The customs and clearance procedures entering and leaving Rio are very complicated and incredibly slow," he said. "So we'll actually save time by helping ourselves to what nature offers us."

At the Equator, Jonathan knew, they had been near the mouth of the great Amazon River. By now, he estimated, he stood off the little town of Pernambuco at the easternmost tip of South America. The prevailing winds here blew from east to west, so it would be relatively easy for him to follow the coastline of the continent, which shrank toward the west.

The wind became brisk, and *Flying Dragon* soon was traveling at her customary speed of seventeen or eighteen knots. The shoreline was virtually uninhabited for a distance of many hundreds of miles, but Jonathan knew he would stand a better chance of obtaining wild fruit in the tropics than he would farther south, where it was winter now. So he studied his charts, then headed toward land, and without difficulty he found the mouth of the small, nameless river he was seeking.

The anchor was dropped in calm waters, and the entire company went ashore in the ship's boats, which carried all of their water casks. At Jonathan's direction every man carried arms. No Indians were known to live in this region, but it was best to take no chances.

Edmund Barker led a small party inland from a sandy beach that adjoined the mouth of the river, and the group returned to report the presence of a waterfall no more than three-quarters of a mile into the interior. "The water is muddy here," Edmund said, "but at the base of the waterfall it is so clear it sparkles. What's more, there's a fruit growing in profusion in hundreds of trees. It has a thick, green skin that yellows somewhat when it ripens. We tried one, and it has a tart taste that's delicious."

The entire party set out for the waterfall, with the men carrying empty water casks on their shoulders while the vanguard hacked a path through the thick jungle with their swords. Oliver, Jonathan noted, had made himself a blade similar to the weapon he had used in Africa. It was about twice the length of a long knife, and its curious handle of wood resembled an elongated egg. Oliver wielded it with great dexterity and cut away twice as much brush as did anyone else.

The weather was so hot and humid that the men rested when they came to the base of the waterfall. Jonathan was eager to resume the voyage as soon as possible, however, so they went to work with a vengeance, filling the water casks. They had to make two journeys back to the shore before all of the filled casks were taken on board the boats.

Then several volunteers, commanded by Charles, went inland again to obtain armloads of the citrus fruit that would prove so useful in warding off scurvy. Again Oliver proved himself the most adept, climbing into the upper branches with great agility and lopping off sphere after sphere.

Charles saw the former slave staring hard at him, and then, to the Englishman's astonishment, Oliver threw his long knife with all of his might. The blade sang through the air, landing only inches from Charles's feet. Indignant because he thought the man had tried to kill him, Charles was about to reprimand him when he saw something moving in the tall grass near his feet. To his horror he discovered it was the decapitated body of a snake, more than five feet long and as thick as a brawny man's upper arm.

Oliver's almost uncannily accurate blow had severed the reptile's head at its base. Its long fangs protruded from its mouth, and the Englishman knew the knife had been thrown just in time to prevent him from suffering a severe, possibly lethal snakebite.

"I'm in your debt," he told Oliver, who came down the tree and joined him.

The little man shrugged modestly, then added, "We go now. When find one bad snake like this, always another one near."

The sailors needed no urging and started back toward the beach with as many pieces of the fruit as they could carry.

As they were emerging from the thick brush they heard a rifle shot, then a second a short distance away.

Charles's first thought was that someone had encountered the second snake.

He was mistaken, however. Two or three men shouted in triumph, then appeared out of the brush with word that Edmund Barker had shot a wild boar. Three men had to carry the huge, ungainly beast, which weighed at least four hundred pounds. Now the company would have fresh meat as well as fruit to vary the monotony of their diet.

But no one was unhappy to return to *Flying Dragon*. The wilderness of equatorial South America obviously was an area hostile to civilized men unfamiliar with its hidden secrets. The company was relieved to be under way again, and for the next few nights they feasted on roasted boar meat and citrus fruit.

The winds were steady, and day by day the weather became colder. It was mid-winter in South America, and as the clipper moved through the temperate zone, the weather became so chilly that, for the first time on the voyage, the entire company had to don sweaters and pea jackets, mittens and knitted helmets. It seemed almost inconceivable they had been sweltering only a few days earlier.

Every man on board secretly dreaded the fate that might await the ship when it attempted to round the Horn at the southernmost tip of South America. But no one raised the subject. It was contrary to the traditions of the sea to discuss possible disasters, which superstition said might come true if they were mentioned aloud.

Jonathan realized, far more than did any of his subordinates, that he would need almost incredible good luck to sail through the treacherous seas without a mishap. He had tried to time the voyage so *Flying Dragon* would reach Cape Horn during what was known as the "July lull," a brief period in mid-winter when the winds became calm and storms were relatively infrequent. Only if he was fortunate enough to encounter such a lull would he be able to maintain his demanding schedule.

If his luck failed to hold, he knew, he would be required to put into a cove and wait out the storms. That period could last for many weeks.

The clipper drew nearer to the Horn, and all hands prepared for the treacherous seaway through the Straits of Magellan, the passageway between the Atlantic and Pacific Oceans, with the mainland of South America on its north and an island archipelago known as Tierra del Fuego on its south. Surprisingly, the weather did not become as cold as the crew or the master had anticipated. At no time did the temperature go below freezing.

The land, both on the islands and the mainland, was low-lying, with surprising evergreen forests spreading in every direction. A bright sun rose on the morning the passage would be made, and there were only scattered clouds overhead. Jonathan's apprehensions eased somewhat as he entered the Straits of Magellan.

Moving closer to the Pacific, the terrain on both the islands and the mainland changed abruptly, dramatically. Snow-covered peaks rose almost eight thousand feet, cliffs and fjords punctuated the landscape, and only moss grew on the plateaus. There was no sign of human habitation anywhere.

Horrendous tales were told of ships whose crews had been lulled into a false sense of security, and it was rumored that violent storms could blow up out of nowhere within a very short time when a ship was sailing through the Straits of Magellan. Jonathan had discussed the story previously with Charles and Edmund, and all three had agreed that the tales about such sudden storms probably were not based on fact.

All nevertheless remained nervous until they put the Straits behind them. Now, at last, they had reached the Pacific! Even the forbidding cliffs and the rugged mountains rising behind them looked welcoming!

Sailing northward again, along the west coast of South America, Jonathan took time to reflect on his good fortune, at having made such an easy passage through the Straits. He did not know, of course, just how lucky he had been; far more experienced captains than he had foundered in these waters.

Taking advantage of favorable winds, Jonathan piled on sail, tacking frequently. In a few days the weather began to grow warmer, and soon the clipper moved into the zone where the trade winds blew. No problems were encountered in the Doldrums, and when the ship moved past the Equator into the Northern Hemisphere, she picked up strong, steady winds. Heading toward the northwest at a latitude of approximately twenty-one degrees, Jonathan was killing two birds with one stone. He would be able to pause in the Sandwich Islands for water and fresh food, then would be able to sail at about the same latitude all the way to China.

Making the best time she had achieved on her voyage

to date, *Flying Dragon* swept through the balmy waters of the Pacific and reached the island of Oahu a scant sixty-nine days after leaving New London. No other vessel, either military or civilian, had ever achieved such a stunning record.

But he had no intention of revealing his exploit to anyone in the Sandwich Islands because he was afraid the ensuing festivities would force him to delay his departure.

The people of the Sandwich Islands, known to the natives as Hawaii, were ruled by their own king, but the monarchy was becoming corrupt under the influence of American, British, and French sea captains who were greedy for the products of the islands and ruthless in the pursuit of wealth. Merchant ships of all three nations rode at anchor in Oahu's natural harbor.

Protestant and Catholic missionaries who had been coming to the islands for a decade and a half were having an even greater effect on the population than the unscrupulous seamen. When Jonathan and his crew went ashore, they were surprised to see that the women, brown-skinned Polynesians, were covered in flowing garments from their necks to their ankles. Taverns and bordellos lined the waterfront, but clergymen stood under flowering trees whenever groups approached these establishments and delivered impassioned harangues on the evils of drink and licentious living.

The company of *Flying Dragon* had no time for frivolity, however. Jonathan led his men ashore soon after nine o'clock in the morning, and everyone went to work filling water casks. The produce of the islands was so plentiful that it proved possible to purchase large quantities of bananas, coconuts, papaya, and the mashed root of the local taro plant, called poi, for tiny sums of money.

To the astonishment of other crews, who had never seen a clipper, *Flying Dragon* weighed anchor again after tarrying for only four hours. Jonathan had registered his arrival-departure date at the royal navigation office, and that was sufficient for his purposes. Now he could prove he had stopped here on the day claimed in his log.

What mattered most was that he was poised for the

last long run across the bulk of the Pacific Ocean to Cathay. His arrival at Canton in record time would prove to the entire world that clipper ships were incomparable.

Lai-tse lu sat cross-legged on an embroidered cushion, her head bent over a low desk inlaid with mother-of-pearl as she repeatedly dipped her Western-style quill pen into a jar of ink. Conjugating French verbs was tedious labor, and the only task she despised even more was declining German nouns. Sarah was a merciless teacher and sometimes drove the girl to distraction.

Enduring the ordeal for more than two hours by the sun dial in the garden just outside her window, Lai-tse lu finally rebelled. Carefully wiping ink from her pen with a cloth, she placed it in a jar of sand. The stacks of paper piled up in front of her were proof positive that she had been conscientious. Now she looked guiltily over her shoulder, then relaxed when she realized that Sarah was no longer in the room.

Smiling to herself, the girl reached for the copy of Ivanhoe beside her and soon became engrossed in it. She could not admit to Sarah, much less to her father, that she preferred the fiction of England and America to the fables and tales of Chinese writers, who invariably stressed morals that were obvious from the beginning. English and American writers, as well as some of the French, seemed to delight in telling stories for their own sakes.

Even though Lai-tse lu became lost in the work of Sir Walter Scott, she remained aware of her surroundings, and when she heard soft footsteps approaching, she hastily closed her book and placed it beneath several textbooks. But she wasn't quite fast enough.

Sarah Applegate, as always, caught her in the act.

Offering no excuses, the girl handed her tutor the lessons she had been doing earlier.

Sarah glanced through them, frowning to herself, but gradually her features softened. "You did all I required of you," she said.

"I thought you would become annoyed with me for not doing extra work."

"It is enough that you are reading," Sarah said. "Soon

I hope to receive some books by an American author you will like better than Scott."

"Who is he?"

"James Fenimore Cooper. I haven't read his more recent books myself, but you'll find he is very exciting, and you will learn much about America from him."

"I can imagine no writer more exciting than Scott," Lai-tse lu said.

"We shall see. But not at present. Your father is coming here from his own workroom to see you, and he's badly upset."

"What about?"

Sarah shrugged. "All I know is what I've just told you. Kai is deliberately delaying him for a few moments with questions about the gardens. I wanted time to warn you so you would have time to compose yourself." Sarah peered at her, then asked sternly, "Now what have you done, Lai-tse lu?"

"Nothing!"

"I can't defend and help you—and find excuses for your conduct—unless I know what you've done."

"I swear to you in the name of Confucius, our greatest scholar, that I am innocent of all wrong-doing," the girl declared breathlessly.

She seemed to be telling the truth, and the woman removed a comb of translucent jade from her gray hair, then jabbed it back into place. "We shall soon find out. And I would rather not be here. Your father will send for me fast enough if there's trouble." Sarah opened a sliding door made of many layers of thick paper and painted with vermilion lacquer, then closed it firmly behind her.

Lai-tse lu had a clear conscience. Her life had been far duller than she wished since the night she had accompanied Kai and Lo Fang to the warehouse of the English Fan Kuei in Whampoa.

Soong Chao, attired in a long gown, his feet making no sound in silver-embroidered slippers, came into the room.

His daughter instantly slid from her cushion to the floor and inclined her head in a gesture of filial respect and obedience.

Chao was in no mood for even the tokens of humility. "Do you remember the fable about the frog who was a busybody?" he asked without preamble.

"Of course," his daughter replied. "The frog minded the business of everyone he knew until the gods became angry with him. To punish him they caused him to grow larger and larger, until he was as tall as the warriors of Honan. A mighty hunter saw him and cut off his head. And cooked him for dinner. But the meat was so tough it could not be eaten, so it was thrown into a rubbish heap and returned to dust. This is the fate of all who are busybodies. They come to no good end."

"It is so." Chao padded around the room restlessly, finally forcing himself to sit on a varnished window bench, its seat and back decorated with stylized paintings of flowers. Ordinarily he would have chosen another place to sit because he regarded the paintings as crude, but today his mind was elsewhere. Taking a square of pure silk from a robe pocket, he assiduously polished his eyeglasses.

Custom prohibited Lai-tse lu from moving until her father voluntarily offered his permission, but he seemed so lost in thought she was afraid she would remain on the floor for the duration of their interview unless she reminded him of her discomfort. "May I beg the right to move to a chair?"

His wave indicated a lack of concern with such matters.

The girl rose hastily and moved to a three-legged stool, covered with a cushion of green velvet. Sitting demurely, she arranged the skirt of her cheongsam so her legs would not show.

"Today," Chao said in his deepest voice, "a courier with spurs of gold on his boots, wearing a cloth-of-gold tunic decorated with a purple dragon, came to this house."

Lai-tse lu gasped. "An imperial courier from Peking?"

He nodded, then reached into one of his loose sleeves and withdrew a scroll covered with exquisitely formed characters. Only one who spent his whole life writing could make such superb brush-strokes. "Look at the seal," he said, opening the scroll and extending it for her inspection.

The seal of lavender wax showed a tiny dragon

crouching beneath a flowering lichi tree and bore only a few characters. "It bears the signature of An Mien," Lai-tse lu said, and stiffened. "The royal dragon. And An Mien! This must be a letter from the august sister of the Celestial Emperor himself!"

"It is so, my daughter." Chao unrolled the scroll and read it. "Her Serenity, sister of the sun, moon, and stars, requests that the daughter of Soong Chao be sent to Peking without delay. Her Serenity wishes to converse with this person. The daughter of Soong Chao and her retainers will dwell in the Forbidden City until Her Serenity has ended their talk."

The girl's head began to spin. "Why would the Princess An Mien send for me? How does she even know I exist?"

"Those same questions have come into my mind, but I do not know the answer." Chao handed her the scroll.

The document contained only the words he had read to her, and her bewilderment increased.

"As soon as I read the letter," Chao said, "I went to the viceroy, but he knows nothing of the matter. Her Serenity does not engage in the official business of the Middle Kingdom, and the viceroy concerns himself only with such business. Now you know why I asked you about the frog who grew. Have you been a busybody again?"

"No, my father! I swear I have done only that which you know and approve."

He sighed. "You realize, of course, a request from Her Serenity is a command that must be obeyed without delay."

Lai-tse lu nodded. "But why should she summon me to an audience?"

Again Chao shrugged. "I am somewhat consoled because you and those who will accompany you will be given quarters in the Forbidden City. Her Serenity wouldn't invite you as her guest if she intended to starve you in a cage, boil you in oil, or have your head removed from your body. Not even royalty would violate our ancient laws of hospitality."

"Princess An Mien," she said indignantly, "is known

as a woman of great culture. Surely she doesn't have people executed!"

Her father's smile was thin. "The Celestial Emperor and those of his blood make their own rules, and the laws laid down for others do not apply to them. An Mien may do as she pleases, and not one voice in all of the Middle Kingdom will be raised in protest."

"Well, we have no idea why she has sent for me, so I refuse to frighten myself by speculating on the evils that might befall me." Lai-tse lu sounded courageous, but nevertheless asked, "You will accompany me to Peking, my father?"

Chao shook his head. "I would not want it said that I used my daughter as a wedge to gain entrance to the Forbidden City. Missy Sarah will act as your chaperone, and Kai will escort you, taking as many men at arms as he needs to protect you."

His verdict was final, and she knew better than to argue with him. "I must find some rare silks so I may have new clothes made for my audience."

"No," he said. "You already have enough clothes so you could wear a different gown for fifty audiences. One does not delay when the sister of the Celestial Emperor commands. I have already ordered my best junk made ready for you, and you will sail when day comes tomorrow morning."

The thought of preparing so rapidly for the journey made the girl panicky. "But that is not enough time—"

"It will suffice," Chao said firmly. "You will go with my blessings and my prayers for your safe return."

She knew she would spend a sleepless night preparing for her departure.

Before dawn the next morning eight large lacquered boxes containing the girl's travel wardrobe, along with two boxes of Sarah Applegate's belongings, were carried on board the palatial junk tied to a wharf in front of one of Chao's factories. A small army had worked through the night, scrubbing and polishing, and a cook from the Soong household had supervised the loading of special food for the voyage. No greater care would have been given if the Princess An Mien had been making a journey.

The junk, *Scent of the Chrysanthemum Flower,* was painted yellow and black, its exterior resembling countless other commercial vessels. But this was the flagship of Soong Chao's fleet, the junk on which he himself traveled when business required him to make a voyage, and the interior was luxurious. The teakwood decks were polished, the fittings of burnished bronze gleamed, and the bulkheads, inlaid with ivory, mother-of-pearl, and semi-precious stones, were ornately decorated.

The two aft cabins, which Lai-tse lu and Sarah Applegate would occupy, were sumptuously furnished. Thick rugs covered the decks, the low beds were larger and more comfortable than the women used at home, and the table on which they would eat their meals was an antique heirloom made of eleven different rare woods, their natural colors blending as deftly as an arrangement of flowers growing in a formal garden.

Chao bid his daughter farewell at home, and the two women were carried to Whampoa in palanquins with bamboo blinds on all sides that shielded them from the gaze of passersby. The need for adequate protection rather than modesty was responsible for these precautions. Only the captain of the junk knew the identity of his passengers, and both understood they would be required to remain sequestered in their cabins until the ship reached the open waters of the South China Sea. Pirates preyed on the unwary in the Pearl River Delta, and the daughter of Soong Chao was a tempting target who could be kidnapped and held for an exorbitant ransom. So her presence on the *Scent of the Chrysanthemum Flower* was a closely held secret.

Any pirates who had the temerity to attack the junk would be surprised by her defenses. The twelve men at arms under Kai's command were experienced archers and lance-throwers who had also received rigorous training in the use of firearms. The two antiquated cannon on the fore and aft decks had been replaced with modern, nine-inch guns that Chao had purchased from a Danish trader, and the members of the crew were expert in the use of these weapons. Lai-tse lu would be more than adequately protected.

The junk put out far enough to sea to avoid the

coastal islands where pirate ships were known to lurk. The early summer weather was hot, but the sea breeze was pleasant, and the voyage was as comfortable as it was dull. Lai-tse lu and Sarah spent their days reading and chatting. Every afternoon they adjourned to a canopy-covered area on the aft deck, where they lolled on mounds of cushions, and only once did a shower send them below.

The voyage in the plodding junk lasted the better part of two weeks, but at last they saw the high stone walls of the fort that guarded the military garrison of Tientsin, the gateway to the north. Several war junks, each with a huge eye painted on its hull, put out to sea and escorted the *Scent of the Chrysanthemum Flower* to a berth directly below the scores of cannon that emerged from gun ports in the fort.

Before anyone was permitted to debark, a group of officials came on board, and Kai greeted them. He presented them with the special visas signed personally by the viceroy in Canton, and when he showed them the scroll that bore the seal of the Princess An Mien, the visitors became obsequious. Lai-tse lu and Sarah, escorted by their own men at arms, were carried ashore in covered palanquins, and no sailor of the Imperial Navy, no soldier of the Imperial Army caught even a glimpse of them.

They were lodged in a suite in the fort, where the rooms were large, although sparsely furnished. Even at this season the building was so damp that charcoal fires burned day and night in braziers to ward off the clammy dampness.

The governor of the garrison paid the women his respects in a brief, formal visit, but did not have the temerity to ask them for the honor of dining with them. That evening Kai made the necessary arrangements for the resumption of the journey the following morning. Members of the escort were provided with spirited mounts, and two gentle mares, each with a palanquin-like covering above the saddle, were made available for the ladies. Twenty-three mule carts carried the party's belongings and the supplies of food, bedding, and the tents that would be needed on the road. As a final gesture, the governor also provided an escort of fifty of his own cavalrymen who wore the uniforms of lavender and bright red that marked them as members of the Imperial Household Guard. Each of these men, in addition to his curved sword, carried a wicked, razor-sharp ku ming, its double-ended blades honed to perfection.

Thieves frequently attacked commercial travelers on the road from Tientsin to Peking, but none would dare to come near this special group. A dragon pennant carried by the standard bearer at the head of the procession indicated that these riders were under the special protection of the Celestial Emperor, so bandits who hid in the pine forests or concealed themselves behind farm buildings knew they would not only have a fight on their hands but would be beheaded instantly if captured. Obviously, the shrouded women in the center of the convoy were personages of importance.

Lai-tse lu, cut off from all contact with everyone but Sarah and Kai, was bored by her isolation. At least she had the consolation of knowing she would be safe on the last seventy miles of the seemingly interminable journey.

Peking, or "capital of the north," was still regarded as the new center of the government of the Middle Kingdom, even though four hundred years had passed since it had replaced Nanking as the home of the nation's rulers. By the same token, the Manchus who had given their name to a dynasty were sometimes considered interlopers, even though almost two hundred years had passed since they had led their armies into China from Manchuria, circumventing the Great Wall that lay to the west of the city.

No census had been taken for at least two or three generations, so the exact population of Peking was unknown. It had expanded far beyond its original walled areas, however, and now sprawled across the dusty hills whose trees had been removed to provide housing and fuel for an ever-growing community. According to the educated guess of the eunuchs who held most posts of importance in the government bureaucracy, at least two million people now lived in Peking.

Twice in years past Lai-tse lu had visited Peking with her father, so the main thoroughfares, broad and paved, crowded with even more people than she had ever seen in

Canton, were already familiar to her. So were the people of Honan Province, the men tall and broad-shouldered, the women slender and regal, all of them towering over the far shorter people of the south. Her own family had come from Peking, which accounted for their height.

Small houses with pagoda-like roofs stretched in every direction as far as the eye could see, with the region intersected by the high walls of stone that were one of the city's principal characteristics. Public structures here were mammoth, as befitted the capital of the most populous nation on earth, and Lai-tse lu still remembered the awe she had felt when she had first seen the cavernous and magnificent Temple of Heaven, the largest house of worship and contemplation in the Middle Kingdom. She could only hope she would have an opportunity to visit it during her present sojourn here.

The high walls of the Imperial City, white-painted plaster covering the stones, loomed directly ahead now, and Kai rode forward with the commander of the cavalry escort, the procession halting as they conferred with the officer in charge of the sentry detail at the huge gate, guarded by stone lions on pedestals, with an intricately carved pagoda roof curling above it.

The amenities having been observed, the procession moved forward again, and the girl peered out of the folds of gauze-like silk that surrounded her. The Imperial City was the center of the government, and thousands of persons worked in these huge structures of stone under the command of eunuchs who held the top posts. Nearly everyone who worked in the Imperial City lived here, too, and there were endless rows of small but substantial dwellings behind the mammoth office buildings. The overall effect of the Imperial City was gracious and pleasant because of the many gardens and artificial lakes placed at intervals throughout the area. Flower gardens, laid out by experts who had attended special schools for years, were riotous with colors, the pagodas that shielded visitors from the elements and the covered bridges had roofs and walls of wood and stone, metal and plaster, every inch covered with designs that had taken artisans lifetimes to create, all painted three times each year in bright, contrasting colors.

Ordinary citizens other than servants and those who provided for the needs of the inhabitants were not permitted to enter the Imperial City, and everyone who worked and lived here carried a bronze disc on which his name and occupation were carved. Even the vendors who sold dim sum or roasted chestnuts in the streets carried such discs. Soldiers in uniforms ranging from the imperial lavender and red to the drab green of the infantry were everywhere, many of them carrying ku ming. Officers wore sashes of various colors which denoted their rank and without exception were armed with curved, double-edged swords. A few also carried cumbersome pistols that were more ornamental than useful.

Deep inside the Imperial City was another vast, high-walled area, its plaster painted lavender, each of its large, pagoda-roofed gates guarded by stone dragons that stood ten to twenty feet tall, some resting on bases of alabaster or marble. This was the Forbidden City, the home of the Celestial Emperor, his family, and his staff. At the Gate of Six Heavenly Dragons Lai-tse lu and the members of her entourage had an even longer wait, and when they were allowed to enter the members of the cavalry escort from Tientsin had to remain behind.

The girl looked around eagerly, but even though she had been told much about the Forbidden City she was astonished by its size and complexity. Everywhere she looked there were large, handsome buildings, gardens of breathtaking beauty, and still more walls. Here and there she caught glimpses of porcelain jars fifteen feet tall, huge statues of silver and gold, as well as a variety of other works of art so dazzling that her mind reeled.

The core of the Forbidden City consisted of two groups of buildings surrounded by high walls and moats, with three large palaces in each group. But there were so many other structures in view that it was impossible even to count them while riding past. Lai-tse lu knew that the Tao Kuang Emperor kept seventy-two official concubines, each of whom lived in her own palace, surrounded by her personal servants, her relatives, and her attendants. Every government minister had his own palace, as did the highest-ranking generals and admirals. The nine chiefs of the corps

241

of eunuchs lived here, too, each ensconced in a palace of his own.

No commoners were allowed to pass through the gates of the Forbidden City without special documents signed by the imperial chamberlain or one of his three principal assistants. Any commoner who failed to produce an appropriate document when challenged by patrols of lavender-clad soldiers was executed on the spot. Guests who belonged to the top four classes of mandarins were not required to carry identification documents, but the commanders of military patrols were provided with lists of such guests, brought up to date each day by the imperial chamberlain and his staff. Lai-tse lu was given no document, but each member of her party was handed a paper, which had to be carried on one's person day and night.

Kai and the men at arms were allowed to accompany Lai-tse lu and Sarah as far as the entrance gate to a small building and then were taken to a military compound that stood opposite it. Kai was reluctant to part with the young woman whose life he was sworn to protect, but his own military escort, a booted, silver-spurred commander-of-one-thousand, gave him no choice. He looked back over his shoulder at the veiled girl as he was led to the barracks, but he had to accept the inevitable, knowing he would lose his head instantly if he dared to complain.

A middle-aged woman of regal bearing, a dragon embroidered in silver on the back of her flowing robe denoting that she was in the service of the Celestial Emperor, came to the gate. "Welcome to the Forbidden City," she said in Mandarin, addressing herself only to Lai-tse lu and ignoring Sarah. "You and your servant may dismount and come inside."

"This lady," Lai-tse lu replied quickly, "is my esteemed tutor and governess. She is no one's servant!"

The middle-aged woman bowed stiffly to Sarah Applegate, who silently returned the gesture.

A corps of women appeared to carry the luggage into the miniature palace, and Lai-tse lu knew at once she was being housed in a dwelling in which no men were permitted. She followed the woman in charge through a delightful formal garden, and after crossing a covered bridge over a stream, she entered a world that dazed her. The walls in the entrance hall and what appeared to be a living room beyond it were covered with sheets of gleaming, hammered copper. The railing of the staircase that led to an upper floor was crafted of carved ivory; Lai-tse lu thought the scenes depicted on the ivory were taken from the mythology of the ancients, but a later examination revealed that they dealt with episodes, real and imagined, from the lives of the Celestial Emperors.

The walls of Lai-tse lu's bedchamber were made of burnished silver, on which were painted the lacquered figures of great ladies of the past. The furniture was made of silver, too, with deep cushions of embroidered velvet covering each piece. Behind the low bed a waterfall cascaded down a stone wall, and in a pool at its base were scores of tiny silver fish, each with a delicate, fan-like tail.

The girl was enchanted with her surroundings and continued to watch the waterfall after the woman in charge and the servants carrying the lacquered clothing boxes vanished. But there was no respite in this place where efficiency was taken for granted. More women in trousers and dragon-embroidered tunics appeared, emptied the boxes, and took away the contents to be pressed.

They were followed by another group, who brought a tub of marble four and a half feet long into the chamber, its outside carved with figures that Lai-tse lu was certain she recognized as representations of gods and goddesses. Hot, perfumed water was poured into the tub, then two of the women undressed the girl, bathed her, and, after drying her, massaged her with perfumed oil.

They brushed her long blue-black hair, letting it fall free, then dressed her in a loose-fitting, sashed gown of silk as soft and fine-spun as a cobweb. Lai-tse lu felt as though she were living in a dream world that no stories from the mythology of China could equal.

The door of the adjoining room opened, and Sarah, still wearing the gown in which she had traveled, sauntered into the chamber. "Not bad at all," she said in English as she examined the fantastic decor. "They've given me an ordinary bed and chair. At least your father's worry that you'll be executed won't be realized. Whatever the Princess

An Mien's purpose in bringing you here, I'd say you're a favored guest."

Lai-tse lu giggled and nodded.

"Don't let it go to your head, child. You'll be practicing your languages and needlework as soon as we go back home."

There was a tap at the outer door, which slid back, revealing the woman in charge standing on the threshold. "Order what you wish for dinner or allow me to make the selection for you, as you please," she said.

Sarah took charge. "We would like a simple meal of meat or fish and vegetables, plainly cooked, with a thin soup, if that is satisfactory," she said politely but firmly.

The woman nodded and smiled for the first time. "Very sensible after a day of hard travel. You would be surprised how many guests take advantage by ordering rare dishes."

"Soong Lai-tse lu was not reared that way," Sarah said tartly.

Again the woman approved.

The girl interrupted them. "If you please, when will Her Serenity receive me?"

"When it is her wish," the woman replied, her manner becoming prim. "Perhaps she will see you tomorrow, perhaps on a day that follows. All I can tell you is that you must be ready to go to her the moment she summons you."

"What should I wear?"

"I have taken the liberty of examining your wardrobe, and you have many garments that are suitable."

Lai-tse lu had hoped for help and was disappointed.

The woman took pity on her. "It is contrary to the rules of the Princess An Mien for me to give you specific advice. But I can hint. I have read in the dossier compiled on you that the Viceroy Teng Ting-chen has been a guest in the home of your father. Dress as you would if he were paying a visit to your house." The woman stepped out and slid the door into place.

"I wanted to ask her why I've been called here," Lai-tse lu said in English.

"If she wouldn't tell you what to wear, you can be

certain she'd tell you nothing of greater consequence," Sarah replied.

"So I realized." The girl sighed. "My clothes should be returned to me soon, so after we eat you'll have to help me plan what to wear."

Sarah shook her head and laughed. "That won't be necessary. If I know you, your mind is already made up."

"Well," the girl admitted, "I'm thinking of my red and gold cheongsam. With my red, gold-wedged slippers."

"You're vain. No other dress fits you more snugly."

"That's exactly why I want to wear it!" Lai-tse lu retorted.

A short time later they were served a meal of steamed fish and crisp vegetables, followed by a clear soup with chopped scallions and mung bean noodles. No food could have been simpler, but the porcelain bowls and dishes in which it was served were exquisite.

"No man in Canton is wealthier than your father," Sarah said, holding a marvelously thin plate up to the light of an oil lamp. "But not even he could afford dishes like these."

"Or the silver in this room," Lai-tse lu said. "There's as much in the chairs and walls as my father keeps in his strongbox, and this is just one room. Think of the treasures there must be in thousands of others throughout the Forbidden City!" All at once she thought of the countless poor people she had seen the night she had walked through Canton with Kai and Lo Fang, but she knew it would be impolite to mention the contrast when she was a guest here. The ways of the world were strange, but this was not the moment to dwell on the imponderables of justice.

That night Lai-tse lu was so excited she thought she would stay awake for hours, but the sounds of the little waterfall behind her bed soon lulled her to sleep.

The singing of "golden throats," tiny greenish-yellow birds that were perching on the branches of trees in the garden outside her windows, awakened her in the morning.

Sarah soon joined her for a breakfast of spiced beef served with plain boiled rice and tiny, rolled pancakes, each filled with a jam or jelly of a different flavor. The tea was hot and fragrant, but was far weaker than the breakfast tea the two imperial guests brewed for themselves at home.

After the meal Lai-tse lu dressed with great care in her scarlet cheongsam with gold frogs and gold piping on the edge of the mandarin collar and side slits in the skirt. She took her time applying cosmetics, and as a subtle gesture to the princess, she daubed her eyelids with a thin coating of lavender salve. The hair styles of the lacquered figures on the walls were ornate, and a perverse streak in the girl impelled her to let her long hair hang loose. At least she had found one way to express her individuality.

"Now," she said with a sigh, "I may do nothing all day but sit here and wait."

"We're not being compelled to wait indoors, you know," Sarah replied.

Lai-tse lu brightened, and they descended the staircase to the ground floor, then wandered out into the garden and sat on an ivory bench near some flowering jasmine. The sun overhead was bright, but even in this protected place a layer of Peking's dust seemed to hang in the air.

In order to pass the time Sarah questioned the girl at length in Spanish about Cervantes's *Don Quixote*, which she had read recently, and insisted she reply in the same language. The better part of the morning passed, and then the woman in charge of the house appeared.

"Your presence is desired," she said.

Lai-tse lu sprang to her feet.

"Follow that path," the woman said, pointing.

Sarah smiled reassuringly.

The girl walked alone down the gravel path, the sound of her wedge-soled slippers echoing in her ears. It was odd that no escort was accompanying her.

About thirty paces away, at the far end of the garden, a thick mass of flowering bushes stood. Lai-tse lu had paid scant attention to the foliage, but as she drew closer she realized that the bushes concealed a wall of stone. As nearly as she could tell, there was no break anywhere in the vegetation.

As she moved still closer, however, a door slid open noiselessly, and she realized for the first time that the house in which she was lodged stood almost adjacent to a far larger building.

The door slid closed behind her, but the light was undiminished, and she realized the ceiling overhead was pagoda-like, made of clear glass that admitted the daylight. The long corridor was lined with priceless porcelain vases that stood seven feet tall and magnificent cabinets with superbly carved doors. She would have loved to inspect some of these works of art, but this was not a time to dawdle, and she walked briskly down the corridor, seeing no one. The silence was eerie.

At the far end of the corridor another door slid open, and the visitor entered a small, comfortable chamber with a thick rug on the floor, jade carvings on the walls, and, at the far end, three chairs, each carved from a single block of jade, with cushions on the seats and backs. What mattered was that one of the chairs was occupied.

The Princess An Mien, in her late twenties, had the high cheekbones, exaggeratedly slit eyes, and bold features that caused most Chinese to regard Manchurians as ugly. Somewhat overweight, she was attired in a gold-trimmed cheongsam of red silk that was almost identical to the gown Lai-tse lu was wearing.

Not knowing whether to laugh or cry, the girl lowered herself gracefully to the floor. Suddenly it occurred to her that the princess had been told what she was wearing and chose to appear in a similar costume in order to put her at her ease. A feeling of relief flooded Lai-tse lu as she stared carefully at a black dragon in the white rug.

"I have eagerly awaited your arrival, Soong Lai-tse lu," the princess said in a surprisingly musical voice. "Sit beside me, please, and tell me if you prefer rock candy or a slice of citrus fruit in your tea."

Swallowing hard as she rose to her feet, Lai-tse lu struggled to find her voice. She was actually being invited to sit in the princess's presence. "I—I'd like citrus, Your Serenity," she said.

An Mien poured tea into fragile, dragon-decorated cups with large, firm hands. "I admire your taste in earrings," she said. "While you're here I must give you a pair, somewhat longer, that were made for me." She laughed quietly. "I can't wear them. My face is too square, and I'm already homely enough."

Lai-tse lu was about to protest politely, but at that moment a door at the side of the room slid open, and a middle-aged man with strong Manchurian features wandered into the room. He looked vaguely familiar, and the girl was fascinated by the snug cap that covered his entire head. It was completely covered with pearls, hundreds of them.

All at once she knew she had seen that face on silver and bronze coins! She was actually in the presence of Tao Kuang, the Celestial Emperor himself, the living descendant of the gods, a divinity who had absolute powers of life and death over his subjects!

Lai-tse lu started to rise, intending to prostrate herself on the floor at his feet.

"Stay seated, please," An Mien said quietly. "He who joins us chooses to remain invisible."

The emperor nodded amiably, seated himself in the third chair, adjacent to that of the visitor, and calmly accepted a cup of tea from his sister.

Lai-tse lu was giddy. She was so close to the emperor she could touch him. Not in her wildest dreams had she ever imagined being admitted to his august presence, much less sitting beside him in a chair of carved jade.

An Mien continued to chat about earrings to put her guest at ease.

The emperor blew on his tea to cool it.

The familiar gesture steadied Lai-tse lu. The emperor wore his fingernails short, she saw, and his only jewelry, other than his headgear, was an emerald ring the size of a robin's egg. He was attired in a simple gown of black silk, similar to those worn by scholars, and the toes of his gold, dragon-embroidered slippers were slightly scuffed.

The princess became brisk. "You are wondering why I sent to Canton for you. Let me explain. For thousands of years the women of China have been the servants of the men. We have had few rights and no voices in selecting our own destinies. Now, for the first time, there is a change in the air. I sense it. Obviously you sense it, too."

Lai-tse lu felt compelled to speak the truth. "I do,

Your Serenity. In a land such as ours changes take place slowly, but I believe there is a beginning, like the tiny, green shaft of a lily that appears above the surface of the ground."

"Well said!" the princess exclaimed.

The Celestial Emperor's expression remained unchanged, but his faint nod was encouraging.

"I do what little I can to encourage our women to be less faint-hearted," the princess declared. "I am not advocating that we join our soldiers in battle against our enemies, that we try to engage in such ancient and honorable professions as soothsaying or the practice of medicine. I do not even propose that we select our own husbands. I ask only that we become less timid and make our voices heard. For five years I have worked on this campaign. Only recently I learned of a girl, a mandarin of the third class, who did more in one day than I have done in all the five years I have labored."

The emperor forgot he was supposedly invisible and laughed aloud. "Our viceroy in Canton," he said in a husky voice, "sent us a most amusing letter. He told us that the daughter of Soong Chao actually dared to interrupt a meeting in which petitions were being granted or denied. But he failed to tell us one word that the young woman spoke."

Lai-tse lu felt hot color suffuse her face, and she wished the ground would open and swallow her up.

An Mien patted her hand. "There is no need to be embarrassed. What you said to Teng Ting-chen must have been convincing. I have been eager to hear your arguments myself."

"We wish to hear them also," Tao Kuang said, and sighed. "One who sits on the Great Dragon Throne hears what those who approach him think he wishes to hear. Or they fill his ears with causes which they advocate. We rarely know when we are being told the truth." He set his teacup and saucer on the low table, gripped the arms of his chair, and stared hard at the visitor. "For thousands of years the Middle Kingdom was closed to foreigners and prospered. In the time of the corrupt Ming Dynasty, before our ancestors seized the throne and

249

cleansed it, the adventurer Marco Polo came to the Middle Kingdom. Since that time, foreigners beat at our gates. Our ministers and the eunuchs of our council urge us to exclude them. But a girl in Kwang-chou raises her voice and asks that we increase our trade with the Fan Kuei. Why should this be done?"

Lai-tse lu was so miserable that her mind went blank.

"Speak only the truth as you see it!" the emperor commanded in a harsh voice.

An Mien was annoyed. "Kuang," she said, "you're frightening the poor child half to death. You promised you'd allow me to conduct this conversation."

Tao Kuang muttered an apology.

Few people beyond the confines of his immediate family realized he was mortal, and his human gesture steadied Lai-tse lu. "I am no scholar, Your Celestial Divinity," she said, "and I lack the wisdom of your ministers and the council of eunuchs. But I have studied the principles of the yin and the yang, on which our society is based, and I know that the positive and the negative, the male and the female, the light and the dark must be brought into perpetual harmony with each other."

The princess was delighted and nodded encouragement.

Tao Kuang's face was as stiff as the features of the stone dragon on the Great Throne.

"In the Middle Kingdom," Lai-tse lu said, "we revere and worship wisdom above and beyond all else. Only through learning can we reconcile the yin and the yang. For thousands of years we have succeeded more than any other people. Think of the inventions the Fan Kuei have stolen from us. Paper. The art of printing. Gunpowder. I have even been told that after the visit of Marco Polo, the people of his country began to eat our noodles and now think of them as their own."

The emperor relaxed enough to smile.

"We are a wise, great people, but we do not possess all of the world's wisdom," Lai-tse lu said, gradually gaining confidence. "The Fan Kuei stole gunpowder from us, but now they make cannon and rifles and pistols far superior to ours. Their printing presses are more efficient than ours. Their physicians know much of the art of healing that is hidden from us. I have seen copies of their great paintings, which are unlike ours, but as fine in their own way. I have read many of their poems and plays and stories in their own tongues. They are not like ours, but many creative men of genius have lived in their lands. They have mastered the science of making war—"

The emperor couldn't resist the temptation to interrupt. "Have they known conquerors as great as Kublai Khan?" he demanded.

The girl well knew that the Great Khan was Tao Kuang's direct ancestor, so the answer had to be delicately contrived. "Only a few years ago," she said, "there lived in France a great conqueror named Napoleon Bonaparte. Of course, he used the guns and the powder that were first invented in the Middle Kingdom. So I cannot believe he would have defeated Kublai Khan had they lived at the same time and met in battle. Surely no conqueror was as great as the Great Khan."

The emperor looked pleased. "The girl is wise beyond her years," he said to his sister.

"But the Great Khan is not alive now," Lai-tse lu added quickly. "In the lands of the Fan Kuei there are many inferior generals and admirals. But they conquer because they have made tremendous improvements in the machines of war whose existence they first learned from us."

Tao Kuang's smile turned into a frown of deep concentration.

"The Fan Kuei become strong because they learn from each other as well as from us." Lai-tse lu spoke now with genuine conviction. "Just as the yin and the yang must be brought into harmony for man to be happy, so the people of the world must learn from each other. We remain chained to the past while the western world makes progress. And those who stop learning soon atrophy!"

"Would you open the doors of our seaports to the Fan Kuei?" the emperor asked. "Would you allow them to sell their wares wherever they wish in the Middle Kingdom?"

An Mien drew in her breath sharply. The questions

seemed innocent, but they cut to the heart of the most vital issues that China faced in her relations with the outside world.

Lai-tse lu did not hesitate. "No," she said firmly. "It is far too soon for that. The westerners are greedy and would bleed us while we were becoming accustomed to their ways of doing business with us. We must learn from them, just as they must learn from us."

The princess relaxed somewhat. This young woman was as sensible as she was exquisitely beautiful.

"The Fan Kuei must be taught to accept our disciplines," Lai-tse lu continued. "They must stop sending opium into our country and taking the silver of the poor. When they deal honorably with us, then we might consent to open our doors little by little."

Tao Kuang nodded in satisfaction. He had baited a trap, but the girl had avoided it with ease.

"I am ignorant and know very little of the world," Lai-tse lu declared. "But it seems to me there must be a beginning some place. The Fan Kuei have seized property at Canton for their warehouses, and there is no way short of waging a war we cannot win to force them to leave. So I say, let us make a virtue of necessity. Let us open the gates of Canton bit by bit. And while we trade with them, let us study their methods. Let us obtain their advanced cannon and rifles so we may make improved weapons of our own. Let us glean all we can discover about their civilization and put to use that which would be beneficial to us." Afraid she had said too much to the absolute monarch who could destroy her with a nod, she clapped a hand over her mouth.

"You have given us much to ponder," the Celestial Emperor said slowly. "We will need time to digest your words." Gripping the jade arms of his chair, he peered intently at her. "How would you halt the opium traffic?"

Lai-tse lu was on safe ground now. "I would cut off the heads of all who deal in drugs, the sellers and buyers alike, no matter what their nationality," she said. "Any foreigner who brings opium into our waters should be executed, just as any Chinese who buys the drug should die. Let there be no exceptions, and let the law be enforced with vigor. Soon even the greediest will discover that the risks are too great, and no more opium will reach our shores."

Tao Kuang turned to his sister. "You were right," he said. "On occasion a woman can show wisdom greater than can a man." Removing the emerald ring from his finger, he dropped it into Lai-tse lu's hand.

The enormity of the gift overwhelmed her. The gem was worth a vast fortune, even by her family's luxurious standards. "I—I cannot accept this," she stammered. "I have not earned so rich a prize."

The Celestial Emperor silenced her with a sharp gesture. Then he pulled himself to his feet.

The girl would have prostrated herself, but again An Mien intervened. "He who joined us for a time once more has become invisible," she said with a smile as her brother quietly left the room, the door sliding open before him as he approached it.

"You have done well, Soong Lai-tse lu," the princess declared. "In the years to come my brother will listen with care when a woman of intelligence speaks. I cannot pretend to know whether he will accept any of the advice you have given him, but you have done a great service for all women in the Middle Kingdom."

The lavish compliment brought blood to the girl's face.

An Mien clapped her hands sharply, and a serving woman in a lavender tunic and trousers appeared, then prostrated herself in front of the jade chair. The princess addressed a few words to her in a northern dialect the visitor did not understand. The woman rose to her feet and quickly vanished.

"She who has been your tutor and governess must be a remarkable person to have instilled so much wisdom into one who is so young," An Mien said.

"I am very fortunate that my father brought Missy Sarah into our house and put me in her care when I was only an infant," Lai-tse lu replied.

"I wish to speak with this woman and come to know her," the princess declared. "I cannot bring her into this palace because she is a Fan Kuei, and no foreigner has ever set foot in a building where those who carry the blood of the Manchu in their veins reside." She frowned for a moment, then found a solution. "Later in the day I will come to your house incognito to dine with you and this woman. No one will mention my name and rank. On this evening, and for several more days to come, I will assume the guise of a mandarin of the third class. We will speak as equals and by the time you return to Canton we will have become friends."

Before the girl could reply, the serving woman returned and handed the princess a box of carved ebony. An Mien promptly handed it to her guest. "Accept this with my thanks for helping to open the eyes and ears of my brother to the minds of women," she said.

The box contained a pair of superbly carved jade earrings, so long they would fall to Lai-tse lu's shoulders. She made an inadequate attempt to express her gratitude.

The princess smiled. "You owe me no thanks," she said. "Only today my private soothsayer told me I would soon meet one who has won the favors of the gods who rule the heavens and the earth. Now it has happened as she predicted. You enjoy good fortune, Soong Lai-tse lu, and those whose lives touch your life will enjoy it also."

II

Flying Dragon's officers and crew were tired. Following the Twenty-first Parallel westward from the Sandwich Islands, the clipper enjoyed favorable winds that enabled her to maintain her high speeds day and night as she sliced through the waters of the Pacific. Consequently, no one on board enjoyed more than brief periods of rest, but a feeling of growing exhilaration more than compensated for a lack of sleep, or for meals eaten hastily at duty posts.

The ship actually traveled even faster during two severe rain squalls, and no one on board doubted that every conceivable record would be broken. Jonathan's private estimate was that he would cut approximately forty percent from the sailing time from New London to Canton, but superstition prevented him from citing any figures aloud. Others made their own arithmetical calculations, and the entire company shared in the growing sense of excitement.

Plotting a course that carried the vessel north of Luxon in the Philippine chain of islands owned by Spain, Jonathan sailed through Bashi Channel south of Formosa, then slashed through the Straits of Formosa and moved on, timing his arrival so accurately that he reached the Pearl River Delta soon after daybreak. Not wanting to waste time taking on a local pilot, he relied instead on the detailed charts he had obtained from the Rakehell files, and by mid-afternoon he arrived just off Whampoa, where he was at last halted by a gig from the new Royal Navy flagship, H.M.S. *Endurance,* a seventy-four gun ship-of-the-line.

At the polite request of the lieutenant in command of the gig, Jonathan took his manifests and other documents with him, accompanying the officer to the fantail, where Commodore Sir William Alexander sat under a canopy that shielded him from the sultry, early October sun. Ships came and went, but Sir William, it appeared, was being forced to remain in China indefinitely.

The commodore showed less than his customary reserve as he greeted the American ship's master. "You're the captain of the strange vessel that appears to be all sail and very little hull, eh?"

"I am, sir," Jonathan handed him the documents and waited for the explosion he felt certain was inevitable.

He was not disappointed. "Surely your sailing date is in error, Captain Rakehell."

"No, sir. It's accurate, and so is the date I put into Oahu in the Sandwich Islands. I can verify every date on my voyage."

Sir William's calm was shattered. "My God! That means you've sailed here all the way from New England in three and a half months."

"That's correct, Commodore. We've made it in one hundred and seven days."

"Damn my soul! I thought you Yankees were boasting again when I read the outrageous claims for your new clipper ships, but I was mistaken, obviously. When we've completed our formalities I'd very much like to see your ship."

"Join my officers and me for supper, Commodore. Assuming those boats clustered around me are providing us with some fresh food. Our supplies were running a trifle low."

"At the speed you maintained, I'm surprised your eggs and vegetables didn't stay fresh," Sir William replied with a chuckle, then examined the manifest. "You carry an odd cargo, Captain. Very ingenious of you, I must say."

Jonathan happily accepted the compliment.

"I note that your first officer is one Charles Boynton. Is he a member of the English shipping family, by chance?"

"Sir Alan is his father—and my uncle, sir."

"I shall accept your supper invitation with great pleasure, Captain, and I'd like to see your ship now, while we still have light, if I may." The commodore rose, then hesitated. "There's nowhere you could have picked up a cargo of opium, but one never knows when dealing with Boyntons. Are you carrying opium on board?"

"Under no circumstances would I allow as much as an ounce of it on board any ship that I might own or command, sir!"

The vehemence of the response surprised Sir William, but he saw that the rugged young American was sincere in his protestation. "Just asking to prevent possible trouble for you," he said lightly. "Come along. It isn't often that I have a chance to learn something about sailing ships."

The gig carried them to *Flying Dragon,* where casks of fresh water and mounds of fresh vegetables and fish purchased from boatmen by Edmund Barker and the cook were still piled on the aft deck. Jonathan presented his officers to the commodore and was not surprised to learn that Sir William long had been acquainted with Sir Alan. The ice was broken, and the British commodore inspected the clipper with great interest, astonishing his hosts by climbing to the mainmast crosstrees and even plunging into the hold.

"Gentlemen," Sir William said, "this confounded clipper defies every rule of shipbuilding known to civilized man for more than three thousand years. But you've jolly well set a precedent that proves your peculiar notions are effective. I congratulate you!"

Jonathan was sorry he could offer the commodore no drink stronger than the mild sack he carried in his personal supplies.

The weather was so humid they decided to eat in the open, on the after deck. The cook from New London was unfamiliar with such exotic vegetables as Chinese cabbage, snow peas, water chestnuts, and bean sprouts, but he nevertheless prepared an edible meal, and the fish, similar to the sea perch found in the Atlantic, were deftly fried.

"While you're here," Sir William said, "have your cook take lessons from one of the locals. Chinese food,

257

properly prepared, is the finest cuisine in the world. It's one of the few things that makes life here tolerable."

As the meal progressed, he gave other advice freely. A berth was open at the wharves in front of the American factory, he said, and urged that *Flying Dragon* proceed there later in the evening.

"Sir William," Jonathan said, "I was told to deal with a Cantonese merchant named Soong Chao. I wonder if you know anything about him."

"He's my closest friend here. My only friend, really. And I was going to suggest that you see him. I know of no one else in Canton who would appreciate the value of your cargo." The commodore paused. "Unfortunately for you, his daughter has just returned from a visit to Peking, so I think it unlikely that he'll visit his Whampoa factories for the next few days."

"Perhaps I could go to his office in the city," Jonathan said.

The commodore laughed. "My dear boy, this is China! No foreigner is permitted to go beyond the Petition Gate in Whampoa!"

"Then I suppose I'll just have to wait until Soong Chao makes an appearance in Whampoa." Jonathan tried to rid himself of the feeling of impatience that surged up within him. He hadn't broken every known speed record in order to cool his heels indefinitely while waiting for a Chinese merchant to come to his properties in Whampoa.

"Not so fast," Sir William said. "I haven't yet been informed of any details, but I understand that Soong's daughter brought a new imperial directive to the viceroy from Peking. Henceforth, a very few foreigners engaging in legitimate business will be permitted to enter Canton proper. I can give you a letter to Soong that may be of help to you, and I can also direct you to his house through the rabbit warrens they call streets here. You understand that you'll be taking some personal risks by going into the city."

Jonathan shrugged. "Anything is better than sitting around in Whampoa, doing nothing."

Before returning to the *Endurance* the commodore wrote a letter of introduction to Soong Chao for Jonathan, then provided him with a rough sketch that would make it possible for him to find the merchant's estate. Before departing, Sir William had a final word with Charles.

"Young Boynton," he said, "I can't imagine what possessed someone in your position to cast in your lot with a clipper ship. But if this voyage is a fair example of what these ships are capable of doing, you're on the right road. You'll build an enterprise that will make Boynton Shipping seem puny."

Flying Dragon weighed anchor and, maneuvering through the crowded harbor under jibs and topsails, reached the American factory in mid-evening. There, in return for a minimal fee, Jonathan was able to rent a wharf on the understanding that he would be able to use it as long as he wished. Chinese shore guards armed with axes and spears were hired to guard the clipper, and Charles went ashore almost immediately, followed by the members of the crew who went in search of liquor and women after their long, cramped voyage. As they soon discovered, both were easy to find in the dark, cramped lanes between the various warehouses.

Only Jonathan and Edmund Barker remained on board, the latter writing a letter to Ruth that he hoped to dispatch on one of the standard merchantmen, berthed nearby, that might be sailing home in the immediate future. Jonathan went to the forward hold, where he unpacked a single cotton loom, which he brought to his cabin and wrapped neatly. He would take it with him in the morning when he would visit Soong Chao and begin his new career as a Cathay trader.

Lai-tse lu was far too restless to resume her studies of European languages. Still flushed with the success of her visit to Peking, she spent almost two hours after breakfast trying to develop an interest in Voltaire's *Candide*. Giving up the struggle, she wandered out to the hillside garden and gazed at the familiar city below her. She was still thrilled by the knowledge that she had played a direct role in the development of Canton's trade with the outside world. The imperial edicts bearing the personal seal of the Tao Kuang Emperor were relatively minor, it was true, but they undoubtedly would facilitate relations with the West.

Beginning this very day, foreigners who were certified by merchants of the co-hong as legitimate traders would be allowed to pass through the Petition Gate and visit the Canton offices of those with whom they had honorable business. Thanks to her. And the viceroy was authorized to grant trading licenses to such foreigners, who would be permitted to engage in almost unlimited trade, provided it complied with Middle Kingdom law. Again, thanks to her.

She took care to conceal her pride from her father and Missy Sarah, who would be certain to lecture her severely if they should become aware of her feelings. She was taking a risk, of course, by wearing the emperor's superb emerald ring and the long jade earrings that Princess An Mien had given her, but she was willing to admit she was vain. She had earned these treasures, and it was her right to enjoy them, even though common sense told her to put them under lock and key in her jewelry chest.

Musing on her sojourn in Peking, Lai-tse lu looked out at the city below her with unseeing eyes. Gradually, a jarring noise intruded on her consciousness, and she saw an angry, growing mob of men at the base of the hill, about a half-mile away. Armed with spears and heavy sticks, they were menacing a tall figure who stood with his back to the wall of a house.

With a sudden sense of shock Lai-tse lu realized that the man was white-skinned, a Fan Kuei.

Apparently he was one of the foreign traders now permitted to enter Canton, but the people of the city obviously were unaware of the imperial edict. If this stranger should be murdered or severely injured, which seemed likely, all that she had accomplished in Peking would be lost. Foreign governments would become ugly and demand reparations, and then the advisers of the Celestial Emperor who wanted to keep China sealed off from the outside world would find it easy to persuade Tao Kuang to reverse his rulings.

Something had to be done instantly. "Kai!" she called.

The urgency in her voice brought the majordomo on the run.

Pointing to the scene below, the girl explained the situation quickly. "Bring a palanquin for me and an escort of men at arms. At once. We must help the Fan Kuei before those men tear him apart!"

Kai unhesitatingly obeyed her commands.

But Jonathan Rakehell, surrounded by a howling, gesticulating mob at the base of the hill, had no idea that help might be on the way. Never had he found himself in such a precarious situation, and there seemed no way out. All he knew for certain was that the crowd that had him backed against a wall was growing surlier and might attack him at any moment.

Commodore Sir William Alexander had spoken with typical British understatement when he had said there might be some element of personal risk involved in making a simple journey through Canton alone. It was impossible to exaggerate his present danger.

The worst of his situation was that he could not communicate with these Cantonese who obviously hated all foreigners. He wanted to assure them he was here on a mission as beneficial to them as it would be helpful to him, but they couldn't understand a word of English, and he could not speak their language.

"Fan Kuei," they chanted, and newcomers who pushed those in the front rank still closer to the foreigner joined in the cry. "Fan Kuei!"

The bewildered Jonathan had no idea what they meant.

He carried a pistol in his belt, but knew better than to use it. He was a deadly accurate shot, but he realized that if he killed one member of this ugly crowd the others would show him no mercy. Within moments they would come within arm's length, forcing him to draw his sword, but at best he could merely try to ward them off with it. If he killed or wounded one of these Cantonese with his blade, the mob would be certain to inundate him and murder him. Never had he seen so many people simultaneously expressing such violent hatred.

"Fan Kuei!"

Holding the package containing the disassembled

cotton loom under one arm, Jonathan slowly and reluctantly drew his sword.

The men in the front rank involuntarily pressed backward.

He had gained a respite, but he knew it was only momentary. There were hundreds in the mob now, and when those in the rear regained their courage, the men in the front ranks would be compelled to attack him. It was senseless that he should lose his life so meaninglessly after accomplishing so much on his record-breaking voyage.

There was a stir at the rear, and slowly, almost imperceptibly at first, the crowd began to part.

Some moments passed before Jonathan became aware of what was happening. Stalking toward him was a Chinese giant who was using the flat of a large, curved sword to push the mob out of his path. He was followed by a dozen armed men carrying double-ended spears, which they wielded with great dexterity, using the flat of the curved knife blades at one end of their spears to control the throng.

The armed men marched in formation, forming a hollow square, and in the center was a palanquin carried by four uniformed bearers. Curtains of beaded bamboo fell on every side, concealing the rider from the astonished American.

The giant reached the side of the foreigner, and the procession halted.

Then the person inside the sedan chair spoke, and Jonathan could scarcely believe he was hearing the soprano voice of a woman.

"Foolish men!" Lai-tse lu said in Cantonese. "Would you defy the divine will of the Celestial Emperor? Have you not heard that certain Fan Kuei are now permitted inside the walls of Canton? It is so written by the Tao Kuang Emperor himself! Go at once to your homes so you may escape his divine wrath!"

Jonathan blinked and shook his head when he saw the mob quietly beginning to disperse. He had no idea what the woman had said, but her words had worked magic.

The biggest surprise of all was still in store: the unseen woman addressed him in American-accented English.

"Walk beside my chair," she told him, "inside the phalanx of my guards. Then all will be well for you."

Jonathan did as he was bidden and walked up the hill in a daze. Soon they came to the entrance gates of an estate, and it seemed to the young American that this was the place the commodore had described briefly when making his sketch.

The gates opened, and the entire party went inside. The palanquin was placed on the ground, and the men at arms dispersed, with the giant who had led them the last to leave.

Jonathan's throat went dry when the most exquisitely lovely young woman he had ever seen emerged from the sedan chair and stood before him. His pulse sang in his ears, and he couldn't help staring at her.

Lai-tse lu found herself returning his gaze steadily. She read character and intelligence in the face of this ruggedly handsome man, and he fascinated her.

That moment in the formal garden seemed to last for an eternity. Huge chrysanthemums were in full bloom, and for the rest of his life he would associate their scent with this indescribably appealing girl.

"I am Jonathan Rakehell of New England," he said at last, bowing to her. "I am indebted to you for my life. Now I seek the house of Soong Chao."

She pressed her fingertips together and giggled. "I am Soong Lai-tse lu," she said, "and this is the house of my father."

At that instant Jonathan knew that, in some way he could not understand, their destinies were intertwined.

Lai-tse lu knew it, too. The expression in her liquid eyes told him as much.

Suddenly a tiny, gray-haired woman in a Chinese gown bustled out of the house. "Child," she scolded in Mandarin, "have you nothing better to do than stand here flirting with a Fan Kuei?" Then she wheeled on Jonathan. "Land sakes alive! Don't you know better than to get yourself killed by wandering alone through the streets of a Chinese city? You must have been born with better sense than that!"

Jonathan felt certain he was dreaming. Not only was

this miniature virago a white woman, but she spoke with the nasal drawl of New England. "Ma'am," he replied, "I'm just beginning to realize I'm both stupid and lucky. I understand this is the house of Soong Chao, whom I seek." He handed her the commodore's letter.

The communication was unsealed, and Sarah Applegate glanced through it, then sniffed aloud. "Wait here!" she commanded. "And both of you, see if you can stay out of trouble for just a few minutes, if you please." Walking briskly, she disappeared down a winding gravel path.

Jonathan was acutely aware of the beautiful girl's presence.

Lai-tse lu broke the tense silence. "Missy Sarah's bark is—how do you say it?—worse than her bite."

He didn't want to talk about the woman named Missy Sarah. "I don't know how to thank you for saving my life."

Her smile was radiant. "Please don't try. I must admit that it isn't something I do every day."

"Did you recognize me to be an American?"

"Yes, by the way you dress. There are subtle differences in the styles of the Americans, the English, and the other Fan Kuei of Whampoa."

"Fan Kuei. That's what the mob was shouting. What does it mean?"

A gleam of humor appeared in her enormous eyes. "If you must know, it means foreign devil."

Jonathan grinned at her, then followed her example and laughed aloud.

They were still laughing when Sarah Applegate reappeared, and both immediately fell silent, like small children who had been caught misbehaving. "Soong Chao will see you," she said. "Take the path that leads to the right." Giving him no chance to reply, she took the girl's arm and, as they walked away, resumed her scolding in Mandarin.

Jonathan could not move until Lai-tse lu vanished from sight. Only then did he remember his mission and, following instructions, made his way to the rectangular, pagoda-roofed room that Soong Chao used as his office and study.

The merchant rose from his low table, removed his eyeglasses, and bowed. "Captain Rakehell," he said, "I regret the dramatic manner in which you found your way to my home."

Jonathan returned the bow, then extended his hand. "I'm grateful to your daughter for saving me."

"As you should be." Soong Chao sighed. "Only the spirits of my ancestors know what she will do next. Sit, please."

Jonathan seated himself in a low chair that was too short for his long legs.

A serving woman came into the room with tea, which she placed on the desk before backing out.

The ritual of serving tea was long and delicate, and Jonathan was so fascinated by the ivory-handled strainer and other implements that he forgot his natural impatience.

Soong Chao chatted amiably, as though this were a social visit. Only one Rakehell merchantman had ever visited Canton, he said, but he knew the fleet was large. He also indicated he had already learned that a son of Sir Alan Boynton was *Flying Dragon*'s first mate.

"Charles is my cousin," Jonathan said.

The merchant's face became mask-like. "Is your cargo like that of Boynton Shipping?"

The young American grasped his meaning at once. "Charles and I do not deal in opium and never will, sir. We're agreed that the practice is disgusting. I assure you that no Rakehell ship will ever carry a cargo of drugs, and neither will Boynton ships when Charles gains control of his father's company."

A faint smile touched the corners of Chao's lips. "It well may be that we can trade with each other, Captain Rakehell. I am overcome with curiosity about your magical ship, but we will wait until dinner to discuss it so my daughter and her governess also may hear what you have to tell us."

The realization that he would see the incandescent girl again made Jonathan giddy, even though he knew his betrothal to Louise Graves should prevent him, morally or socially, from paying attention to any other woman. Nevertheless, he had to wrench himself back to the business at hand.

"Sir William writes to me that you carry a cargo that is unique," Chao said.

The next few minutes would tell whether Jonathan's major financial gamble would pay off. "Walking here this morning—before that mob assaulted me—I noticed that most Cantonese wear clothing of cotton."

"Even the few who own silks wear cotton most of the time."

"Well, Mr. Soong, I also noticed that the fabric is very coarse." Jonathan opened his package and slowly assembled the small loom, placing it on a corner of the table. "This is an American cotton loom, developed in New England. It creates a far finer fabric than any I've seen here. The shirt I'm wearing right now is New England made."

Chao leaned forward and fingered the material, his eyes shrewd as he continued to listen.

"My entire cargo consists exclusively of such looms," Jonathan said. "I'm prepared to sell more than one thousand of them at a price of two dollars, American, per loom."

"You wish also to buy cargo for your return voyage?"

"Yes, sir. In the days of our War of Independence the people of the United States became accustomed to drinking green tea from Indonesia, and to this day they've never cared much for the taste of Indian tea. Some of your Chinese tea is very similar in taste to what the Indonesians grow. I have space in my hold for five hundred boxes of tea, if I can obtain them."

"That should not be difficult," Chao said with a smile. "What will you pay?"

"Whatever the equitable price of the moment may be."

"I can provide you with five hundred boxes from my own Whampoa factories at two dollars, American, per box."

"Very fair, Mr. Soong!"

"And giving you a clear profit of one thousand dollars. Captain Rakehell, I would like to see this loom of yours in operation, and if it performs as you say it does, I will take the entire consignment myself. I am in a position

266

to deal directly with our manufacturers of cloth, which you are not permitted to do under our law, so I will also show a handsome profit."

"You have a deal, sir." Jonathan held out his hand.

The Chinese merchant bowed to him before extending his own hand. Then he summoned a servant whom he commanded to lift the loom and carry it from the room. He followed the servant, and Jonathan was abruptly left alone.

For more than two hours Jonathan waited in the merchant's study, occasionally pacing or glancing anxiously out of the window. The lovely formal garden outside gave him little solace. He wondered what had become of his loom and the mysterious Chao. At length, the merchant reappeared, a smile playing upon his features.

"You have an excellent loom, Captain Rakehell," Chao said, "for I have just come from having it tested by a master weaver whom I know well. I am satisfied. You did not exaggerate its merits, and my daughter is right."

"Your daughter, sir?"

"She believes that China has much to learn from the West. Now, allow me to show you through the gardens before we dine."

Jonathan knew very little about plants and had never been particularly interested in them, but as he wandered with Soong Chao, it dawned on him that a Chinese garden was very different from those of the Rakehell and Graves families. There was a remarkable sense of balance here, in which flowers and rocks, water and trees and shrubs, miniature bridges and discreetly placed Buddhas, marble phoenixes, lions, and dragons all had their places. Somehow these elements were blended into a harmonious whole, and in spite of his ignorance he was impressed.

When they came to the outer edge of the garden, they paused on a little hillock above a stone wall to admire the city, and here Lai-tse lu quietly joined them. She had changed into a sleek-fitting cheongsam of pale yellow silk that revealed every line of her perfect figure and had applied subtle cosmetics that emphasized her eyes and mouth.

Jonathan caught his breath. He was being disloyal to Louise, but this girl had a magnetic effect on him.

In the presence of her father Lai-tse lu was respectful and subdued, participating in the small talk only when her father invited her comments.

Then Sarah Applegate came into the garden, glaring at the girl because she had changed into more attractive attire. "I should have known you were a Rakehell," she said to Jonathan. "You're the spitting image of your grandfather."

It was strange to hear a reference to his family so far from home. "You knew my grandfather, ma'am?"

"Aye, and your father. My late husband was a mate on Rakehell ships for ten years before we moved to Newport, and he became the master of his own ship, the ship that ultimately took him to the bottom." Sarah shook off her painful memories and turned to Chao. "This young man may not have behaved intelligently when he tried to make his way here alone this morning, but he is a member of an honorable family."

Chao was pleased. "That is good," he said, "because we are doing business together. More business, perhaps, than Captain Rakehell realizes." He did not explain the cryptic comment.

A servant appeared to announce that the meal was ready, and they walked to the dining pavilion, where Jonathan's long legs again interfered with his comfort as he sat on a cushion in front of the low table. But Lai-tse lu was seated opposite him in his direct line of vision, so he didn't care.

The meal began with dim sum, and Jonathan looked hopelessly at the two carved ivory chopsticks beside his place.

Lai-tse lu came to his rescue. "Hold one stationary in the crook of your hand, anchored by your fourth finger," she said, illustrating for him with her own chopsticks. "And manipulate the other with your forefinger and middle finger."

"You make it look easy," the embarrassed Jonathan muttered as he found he could not master the art.

Laughing lightly, Lai-tse lu ignored Missy Sarah's glare and, jumping up from her own place, rearranged the chopsticks in Jonathan's hand.

When she touched him he felt as though a bolt of lightning had struck his hand.

The girl reacted in the same way, and for a long moment both remained motionless, bewilderment in their eyes as they looked at each other.

There was a warning in the sound Sarah Applegate made as she cleared her throat.

Lai-tse lu laughed again and proceeded to supervise the way the visitor handled his chopsticks.

Trying his best to concentrate, Jonathan was conscious only of the girl hovering beside him, her touch feather-soft, the scent of her jasmine perfume filling his nostrils. He was aware of her gleaming hair, her chiseled profile, and, above all, her overpowering appeal. With something of a shock he knew he wanted her, but that wasn't a fair description of his feelings. He couldn't dishonor her by trying to make her his mistress, yet it was insane, when he was already engaged, even to allow the thought that he wanted a permanent relationship with this enchanting young woman to enter his mind.

The obstacles, other than his betrothal to Louise, were virtually insurmountable. Soong Lai-tse lu was an Oriental, while he was a Caucasian. They lived at opposite ends of the earth and, as far as he knew, had nothing in common but their youth and, apparently, a shared sense of humor. And, he had to admit, the chemical reaction to each other that both of them felt. Both would need to exercise care in order to avoid complications they could not handle.

"Now you can manage," Lai-tse lu said, and returned to her own seat.

Her smile melted Jonathan.

Sarah Applegate talked at some length about her life in New England before she had come to the Orient, and Soong Chao discussed the prospects and problems of trade between East and West. Jonathan replied automatically to both, but his eyes remained riveted on Lai-tse lu throughout the meal.

The dishes they were served were strange to him, but he neither knew nor cared what he was eating. After a time he became more adept in the use of his chopsticks, perhaps because he wasn't thinking of what he was doing, but he glowed when Lai-tse lu complimented him.

According to the Chinese custom soup was the final course, and when it was served Chao said, "Now tell us about your magic ship, Captain Rakehell."

Jonathan forced himself to concentrate and explained the principles of building and sailing a clipper.

Lai-tse lu listened intently, her expression indicating that she understood and appreciated what he was saying.

He felt a stab of disloyalty to Louise when he recalled her total lack of interest in his vocation.

"It is true, then," Chao said, "that you sailed from New London to Canton in one hundred and seven days."

"Yes, sir," Jonathan replied with quiet pride.

"Perhaps you enjoyed extraordinary winds and exceptional weather?"

"No, Mr. Soong. Now that my crew and I are expert at working together, I believe I can cut time from that record on my return voyage. I'll do still better with the next clipper I build, and although this may sound insane, I predict that within a relatively few years clippers will make the voyage between the Eastern Seaboard of the United States and China in no more than three months. With about the same time for a voyage between Great Britain and China, although I must admit I know less about that route."

"May we visit your ship?" Lai-tse lu asked, earning a glare from Sarah.

Here was his chance to see her again! "I'll be honored," he said, "if you three will come to *Flying Dragon* tomorrow and join me for dinner. And if you're agreeable, Mr. Soong, perhaps we could arrange then for me to take all of you out for a sail after the cargo has been landed."

"Nothing would give me greater pleasure, Captain Rakehell," Chao declared.

Lai-tse lu and Sarah were surprised by the vehemence of his reply. Apparently he had something in mind that he was telling no one.

Alice Wong's "apartment" was located in an alleyway behind the Danish factory in Whampoa, and the building of gray, plastered brick was drab and unimposing. But the room itself was huge and cheerful, appropriately dominated by an oversized bed that stood inches from the rich rug that covered the floor. Few of Alice's clients realized this was her place of business rather than her real home, and fewer cared.

But Charles Boynton was curious. Lolling in an overstuffed chair of English leather, he found the place as extraordinary as the voluptuous young woman herself was unique. Most of the furnishings were Western, other than a small alabaster Buddha that sat on a shelf, the bamboo blinds that kept out the glare of the south China sun, and the joss stick in an incense burner that removed the stench of the alleyway. The chairs and tables, even the oil lamps were European.

The girl herself was totally Oriental in both manner and appearance, to be sure. Sitting in his shirtsleeves and sipping a cup of warm rice wine, Charles watched her as she moved around the room in her short robe of raw silk, which bore a Chinese inscription on the back. He was slightly surprised to discover that he enjoyed observing her, just as he had relished bedding her. Her favors were expensive, making her available only to foreigners of means, but she was generous beyond measure with her time. He had spent the night with her, and now, at noon, he felt no inclination to leave, but she showed no sign of wanting to be rid of him.

On the contrary, she seemed pleased that he was lingering here and continued to fuss over him, bringing him a plate of bitter-tasting, bite-sized crackers, then offering him a bowl of lichi nuts, which she insisted on peeling for him one by one as she sat at his feet.

"You're spoiling me, you know," he said.

A light of genuine humor appeared in Alice's eyes. "Many men tell Alice that Fan Kuei women not wait on men."

"Indeed they don't."

"Different here," she said, but refrained from telling him the other thoughts going through her mind. She had engaged in relations with this blond-haired Englishman three times since she had brought him here, and she fully intended to go to bed with him again. Most of her customers bored her, forcing her to simulate passion, an art at which she was exceptionally adept, but this man was different. The very first time he had aroused her and given her gratification, something that had never before happened in her experience as a trollop. Then, to her mounting astonishment, he had satisfied her twice more.

The reason, perhaps, was that he was such a gentleman. Her other clients, most of them rough, sought only their own pleasure. But "Charrs," as she called him, unable to pronounce the "l" in his name, was tender and considerate, actively seeking to give her as good as he received. He was almost too good to be true.

He was observant, too. "This isn't really your home," he said.

"Why you think?" she demanded, testing him.

"It's obvious. This place has been deliberately furnished to make a Westerner feel at home."

The girl laughed throatily, her full lips parting. "Is true. Alice live with grandfather and grandmother in Canton. Make plenty much money for family."

He wanted to know more about her. "Where are your parents?"

"Mother die long time ago. Never know father," she added with a shrug.

"Your father," Charles said quietly, "was white."

Alice was startled. She never discussed her paternity, and very few people, outside of her own family, knew she was Eurasian, principally because she took care to emphasize the Oriental aspects of her appearance in her use of liberally applied cosmetics. "How you know?" she asked harshly.

"Why, just by looking at you, of course." He placed a hand on her shoulder. "No offence meant, I assure you. It should be plain to you by now that I like you for yourself."

Alice stared up at him, saw he was sincere, and placed her hand over his. She couldn't recall an occasion when a foreign client had spoken to her in an apologetic tone. "Father was Fan Kuei sailor," she said. "Never see, never know."

"I'm sorry. For him. And for you."

The unexpectedness of his response nonplussed her. "Alice glad," she said.

"I can't blame you. I daresay I'd feel as you do." Charles picked up his watch from the table beside him and glanced at it. "I'm taking up your whole day. I should leave."

"Charrs no go," Alice said, sliding an experienced hand up his thigh.

"You've persuaded me to stay," he said. "But later we'll have to go to my ship, where I keep the bulk of my money. I'll have to pay you another fee."

"Charrs pay plenty much already," she said softly. "No pay more."

Never had he known anyone in her position to refuse additional payment. "Very well, but only on condition that you let me take you to dinner later. There must be a decent tavern or dining place in Whampoa."

Her eyes became large and round. "You would take whore to your ship, then take to nice tavern?" she asked, wonder in her voice.

Charles grasped her by both shoulders. "See here," he said. "I don't know what sort of person you think I am, but if I'm not ashamed to sleep with you, I'm hardly going to be ashamed to be seen in public with you!"

For a moment she was too stunned to reply. Then she murmured, "Other people in Whampoa know Alice is whore."

"To hell with other people," Charles declared. "I know *you*."

She leaned against his knee again and resumed her self-imposed task of peeling the shells of juicy lichi nuts for him. His attitude toward her overwhelmed her, but one major test remained. She steeled herself, then took the plunge. "Charrs could get opium for Alice?" she asked.

He jerked away from her. "You must be mad! My God, don't tell me you smoke that poison!"

"No smoke," she assured him with sincerity. "But others pay plenty much for opium."

"They won't pay me for it, and if you have any sense in that pretty head, you'll have nothing to do with it, either. Once a person starts to use opium he can't stop. He smokes it until it kills him. If I had my way I'd hang every opium dealer I could find. They'll destroy China unless they're stopped, and then they'll go on to destroy the rest of the world!"

"Alice glad Charrs feel that way," she said with a happy sigh.

He stared at her, finding her contradictory stand inexplicable.

She couldn't and wouldn't explain why she had asked him the leading question, but she knew how to stem his curiosity on the subject. Surreptitiously tugging at the belt of raw silk that held her robe closed, she allowed it to fall open slowly.

Charles looked at her, then reached for her.

Later, after they made love again, Alice dressed in one of her more dazzling cheongsams, and Charles insisted on taking her to visit *Flying Dragon*. Jonathan had not yet returned from his visit to the house of Soong Chao, but Edmund Barker was on board, and Charles presented him to the girl, promising to return with her on another occasion when Jonathan would be present.

Then, as good as his word, he took her for dinner to the English-owned Crown and Sceptre, the only tavern in Whampoa where the food was well-cooked and the atmosphere suitable for well-to-do merchants and dignified ships' officers. Most of those in the establishment were men, several of whom knew Alice, and a number of eyebrows were raised.

But Charles carried off the occasion with aplomb. He was considerate and attentive, treating the girl like a lady, and his attitude forced others to accept her, too, no matter what their private thoughts. Alice, paying her first visit to the Crown and Sceptre, was overwhelmed.

Charles felt certain his cousin had returned from Canton by now, so after the meal he parted with Alice, promising he would seek her again the following day. Not content with a vague arrangement, he agreed to meet her at her apartment at noon.

Alice waited in the shadows while he walked off toward the wharves. After he disappeared from sight, she made her way to the Petition Gate, ignoring a newly arrived Swedish sea captain who tried to catch her eye. Entering the city, she hailed a palanquin-for-hire.

Dusk was falling by the time she reached Lo Fang's private quarters in the viceroy's palace.

Her expression informed the majordomo that she had much to tell him, so he invited her to sit.

She came to the point at once. "It is true," she said, "that Charles Boynton of the Yankee clipper ship is a member of the Boynton shipping family whose vessels smuggle opium into the Middle Kingdom. But this man hates opium as much as the Society of Oxen hate it!"

Ordinarily Lo Fang would have found it difficult to believe the girl. But Kai had eavesdropped on Jonathan Rakehell during his visit to the Soong house earlier in the day and had given him a similar report. The clipper carried a legitimate cargo, Soong Chao was already engaging in trade with the captain, and Rakehell, before being escorted back to Whampoa, had spoken passionately of his hatred for the opium trade.

"You are quite sure?" Lo Fang asked quietly.

"Very sure." Unable to meet his steady gaze, Alice looked down at the bare floor.

The viceroy's majordomo studied her for a few moments. "This man Boynton interests you."

"It is true," Alice admitted.

"You have fallen in love with him?"

She shrugged. "It is too soon to speak of love. But I admit it is possible that in time I might learn to love him."

"Then your feelings may color your judgment," he said.

"Never!" she cried. "I have sworn an oath to uphold a sacred cause, and I will be true to that cause."

"Even if it becomes necessary to drive all Fan Kuei from the soil of the Middle Kingdom?"

"Many Fan Kuei are bad," Alice said, "but some are good. And," she added, knowing he was aware of her personal secret, "if they are driven out, I must be sent away, too, because there is Fan Kuei blood in my veins."

"If you were unfaithful to China you would die," the head of the Society of Oxen said.

"I would deserve to die," Alice replied. "But it does not matter how long any one of us lives. The Middle Kingdom has lived forever and will continue to live for all time. I say that Boynton is an honorable Fan Kuei who can be trusted, and you will take my word because you know I would not lie. He and I are not important. Nor are you, Lo Fang. Nothing really matters but the preservation of our land and her ways, and for her sake I would make any sacrifice!"

In spite of his own reservations, Lo Fang was sufficiently satisfied to add the name of Charles Boynton to the list, on which Jonathan Rakehell already appeared, of those foreigners who would be permitted to venture into Canton from Whampoa and, without their knowledge, would be protected while in the city by Society of Oxen members who would follow them wherever they went.

"You have done well," he told Alice. "See that you do not falter in the days ahead."

"You may depend on it," she replied firmly. "What I feel in my heart will never be allowed to interfere with my duty."

Ruth Halliburton Barker found her ways little changed by her marriage to Edmund. Still living under her father's roof, she continued to keep house for him, and she wrote to her husband regularly, even though she had no idea when a bundle of letters might reach him. Not that she had all that much to tell him. She was hooking a rug they would use in their parlor when they had their own home. She continued to see her old friends, although a few of them who were still single had drifted away from her since she had become a married woman.

She added several paragraphs to the letter she was in the midst of writing, dutifully telling Edmund how much she missed him, and then went to work again on her rug, using a large wooden needle. The New England autumn day was chilly, and she added a log to the fire. As she stood again, a tap sounded at the front door, and she was pleased by the interruption; making the rug was a bore.

Louise Graves pulled off her beaver hat as she came into the Halliburton house, her face pale in spite of the biting wind through which she had walked.

Ruth was delighted to see her. Louise was one of the people whose friendship with her had lessened in recent months. "Will you have tea or hot chocolate to warm you, Louise?"

"Either. Anything that's handy," was the listless reply.

Ruth glanced at her but made no comment as they walked into the kitchen. As she brewed tea on the wood stove, Louise remained silent, so Ruth felt the need to make conversation. "By now," she said, "our men-folk must be about two thirds of the way to Cathay. If they're making the good time they expected to make."

"I don't even try to keep count," Louise said dully. "All I know is that they're going to be gone for a long time. Maybe they'll never come back."

"What a way to talk!" Ruth saw she wasn't joking. "Really, Louise, have a little faith in them and in their ship."

"I don't have much faith in anything any more," was the strange reply.

Ruth put on no airs and poured their tea from the kettle. "Let's go into the parlor," she said. "It's more comfortable in there."

Louise seated herself opposite the fire, her cup of tea forgotten as she stared into the flames. "Ruth," she said, "I've got to talk to you."

"Of course." Obviously there was trouble.

Louise had to force out the words. "I'm more than two months pregnant."

Ruth inhaled sharply. "Jonathan?"

Louise nodded.

For a moment Ruth didn't know what to say because she was almost overcome by a feeling of sheer envy. How she would love to be carrying Jonathan Rakehell's baby! The very idea was disloyal to Edmund, she knew, but she couldn't help feeling as she did. Taking great care to hide her reaction, she asked quietly, "Who else knows?"

"No one."

"Including your family?"

Louise nodded.

"You'll have to tell them. You can't hide it from them indefinitely."

"I know. I'm such a coward." Louise took a handkerchief from her sleeve and dabbed at her eyes. "I tried drinking pure vinegar, and then I tried sea water. Both of them made me sick, but nothing else happened. I didn't get rid of the baby. The stories about vinegar and salt water are just old wives' tales."

"Do you want to be rid of it?" Ruth was horrified. If she were the mother of Jonathan's child, she would cherish it as long as she lived.

"What else can I do?" Louise remembered her tea and, trying to gain control of herself, sipped it.

"I've heard of some cures, just as you have, but I don't believe in them, either. Remember that your father is a physician, Louise. He'll be horribly upset if you do any permanent harm to yourself."

"The way things stand," Louise replied with a helpless laugh, "he isn't going to be any too pleased."

"I suppose not." Ruth was silent for a time. "But you've got to face reality. Jonathan is almost half a world away from you and traveling farther every day."

"I suppose," Louise said, her shoulders sagging, "I'll just have to go in hiding somewhere and have the baby. The word is bound to leak out, of course, and I'll be disgraced for life." She began to weep silently. "The worst of it is that our—our relations weren't even worth the results."

Ruth was too embarrassed to comment.

"I realize I'll have to tell Mama and Papa, but I dread it," Louise said.

"They do love you, after all. So they won't shoot you. And they're sure to stand up for you, as I'm sure you must realize. They might even think of some way to prevent a scandal."

Louise shook her head. "I can't imagine how."

"Mr. Rakehell is very smart."

Color drained from Louise Graves's face. "Dear God, are you suggesting that he be told?"

"I don't see how it can be avoided, any more than you can avoid telling your own parents. That's something your mother and father will have to decide. All I can tell you is not to delay. The longer you wait the more difficulties you'll be creating."

"Oh, I know. This is such an awful mess that I'm not sure which of us I hate more, myself or Jonathan."

Ruth stared at her. "There's no place in you for hatred now, Louise. You and Jonathan gave in to a natural feeling, and I see no reason for you to be ashamed. Your family is well able to help you, and so is his family. This isn't the end of the world."

Louise's numbed eyes and dull expression indicated that she didn't agree. But her talk with her friend bolstered her courage, and when she returned home, she forced herself to go to her mother, who was writing the week's menus for the family cook.

Naomi Graves listened in shocked silence to her daughter's few, halting words. Then, fighting a hysteria that threatened to inundate her, Naomi hurried to her husband's office at the far side of the house.

Dr. Graves had just seen his last patient of the day and was writing notes at his desk when his wife came in. He stiffened as he listened to her, then said quietly, "Send Louise to me at once, please."

The girl came to him reluctantly, but he took refuge in his vocation, and while subjecting her to a brief physical examination, he treated her with professional, almost impersonal dignity.

Louise waited for the storm to break.

But no storm materialized. "I suggest you go to your room and rest," Dr. Graves said mildly. "Your mother will have a tray sent to you."

"Papa, I'm so sorry." Her voice trembled.

"We'll waste no time on regrets. Later this evening or tomorrow morning we'll discuss the practical aspects of the matter. Right now I need a little time to organize my own thoughts."

Even in her distress it occurred to Louise that she wasn't the first of her father's patients to be trapped in this predicament. Papa would find some way to help her, and her sense of dread eased slightly.

Carrying his medical bag, Martin Graves went straight to his wife. "Have a light meal sent to Louise in her room," he said, taking two paper packets from his bag. "Mix this powder in a glass of water for her and take the other powder yourself. It will soothe your nerves and help you to sleep."

"Sleep won't solve this dreadful problem, Martin!"

"By the time you wake up in the morning I hope I'll have a better idea of what needs to be done." He patted her on the shoulder and left the house, pausing only to don his beaver hat and a short cloak in the front hall. Then he crossed Pequot Avenue and knocked on the door of his neighbor.

Jeremiah Rakehell had just come home from work. Taking one quick look at his old friend's face, he quickly led the way to his book-lined study before he asked, "What's wrong, Martin?"

"Under other circumstances you and I would be rejoicing today," Dr. Graves replied. "Louise is carrying Jonathan's baby."

Moving with great deliberation, the shipbuilder took two glasses from a tray, removed a cut-glass decanter from a cabinet, and filled the glasses with brandywine.

They sipped in silence, and then Dr. Graves said, "They gave into temptation the night before Jonathan sailed to Cathay."

They sat facing each other, and finally Jeremiah said, "We're old enough to know the young lack self-discipline. I can remember the way I felt, at their age, before going off on a long voyage. Rather than condemn them, I blame you and me, Martin. We should have seem them safely married before Jonathan sailed. We asked too much of them when we set their wedding date a year away."

"If it would do any good, I'd wring their necks," the physician replied. "But their situation isn't unique, and as I think it unlikely that Jonathan will return before his child is born, you and I must make the decisions."

"What are the alternatives?"

"I've had patients who have gone on to other doctors when I've refused to prescribe herbs that supposedly induce a woman to abort. For one thing, I don't believe in the efficacy of such herbs. But even more important, the herbs can cause a violent reaction that makes it impossible for a woman ever to give birth to a child. I'm sure you understand, Jeremiah, that as a physician I can't destroy my own daughter's fertility."

"It wouldn't be fair to her. Or to Jonathan, even though we aren't too terribly inclined to be generous toward him at the moment. What are the alternatives?"

"I've sent a number of patients to a South Carolina plantation that's about an hour's carriage ride outside Charleston. Louise could have her baby there in real privacy. There's certain to be talk, of course, when Jonathan shows up and we send him off to pick up Louise and the baby. But that can't be helped."

"It won't do," Jeremiah Rakehell said bluntly. "Our first goal must be the preservation of Louise's good name. Our second, necessarily, is the protection of our mutual grandchild."

"There is no way to prevent gossip when an unmarried woman has a baby. Louise can't be sent away permanently, and Jonathan's ties to your shipyard can't be broken."

"I'd prefer the scandal," Jeremiah said.

Dr. Graves shrugged. "It's an unsavory dilemma from every point of view."

"More brandywine?"

The physician shook his head negatively. "I need what little ability I have at the moment to think clearly."

Jeremiah stood and paced an imaginary quarterdeck.

Just watching him as he marched rubbed on Dr. Graves's nerves.

"There is a way out, much as I dislike using it," Jeremiah said at last. "I hate chicanery and lies, and I despise the idea of starting our grandchild off on the wrong foot. But I don't believe we have any choice. We move Louise across the street to this house with all her belongings immediately. Tomorrow morning. This becomes her home, and she takes charge at once as the official hostess."

Martin Graves leaned forward in his chair.

"Without making a formal announcement, now or ever, we let it be known at once that Louise and Jonathan were married in private the day before he sailed. And she starts using the Rakehell name."

"But surely people will see through the subterfuge."

"Oh, many of them will talk, to be sure. But they'll have no proof to substantiate their suspicions. And there are other advantages, too. Louise can remain under your care, so there's no need to call in an outside physician. Finally, the very day Jonathan comes home, he and Louise will be married right here, in secret."

"There's an outside chance the scheme might be effective," Dr. Graves said with grudging admiration.

"I see no way it can fail," Jeremiah declared. "You and I are major contributors to the church, and we've all known Reverend Crowell for many years. He baptized and confirmed both Jonathan and Louise. I'm not for a moment suggesting that he falsify the church register when the baby is born. But he's a compassionate man, and I can't imagine him refusing to marry Louise and Jonathan in a very private ceremony."

"Well, no one would be harmed, Jeremiah. I can see that much."

"Everyone directly concerned would gain."

"I can see only one possible cause for concern. I've seen it in young people in the past. Louise may grow to hate Jonathan because she'll feel she's shouldering the entire burden. Other girls in her position have reacted that way. And Jonathan may drift away from her after his travels. I've known young couples in their circumstances who have refused to marry."

"It won't happen in this case," Jeremiah said grimly. "Not only is Louise's reputation at stake, but so is the honor of the Rakehell name. No matter how they may feel a half-year or more from now, Louise and Jonathan will marry!"

III

Jonathan temporarily canceled his crew's shore leave, and the entire company worked feverishly to prepare *Flying Dragon* for the visit of Soong Chao, his daughter, and her governess. The decks were hosed and scrubbed with holystones, brass was polished, and the saloon and galley were cleaned until they became immaculate. In spite of the men's efforts, however, Jonathan was not satisfied and drove them harder.

"This ship must shine from stem to stern," he said.

Charles Boynton winked surreptitiously at Edmund Barker. "We'll grant you that Soong is going to be very important to us in business," he said, "but I'm sure he's seen enough merchantmen not to expect the impossible from us."

"His daughter has never visited a foreign ship. She's admitted it in so many words, and I want us to make a good impression on her."

"Really? I wouldn't have guessed it." Charles grinned broadly.

In no mood for his cousin's humor, Jonathan hurried ashore with the cook, insisting on selecting the food himself at the Whampoa produce market for the small dinner party. "We can't compete with Chinese cooks," he said, "so we'll prepare the best American-style dinner we can put together."

Charles laughed aloud as he watched Jonathan striding toward the market, which stood near the customs building. "Eddie," he said, "I'll wager a gold sovereign to tuppence that Jonnie is infatuated with the Soong girl. He looks as though an inner oil lamp is being lighted every time he mentions her. And he's talked of little else since he's come back from the Soong house."

"I'm afraid you may be right," Edmund replied. "In all the years I've known him I've never seen him react so strongly to any woman. I just hope we're wrong about him."

Charles stared at him. "Why should we be anything other than delighted? I don't believe he's ever had a romance worthy of the name. He's overdue for an attachment that will mean something to him."

"Well," Edmund said, "I'm not forgetting that he's engaged to Louise, and I hope he doesn't forget it, either."

"Louise Graves," Charles replied scornfully, "has the beauty and personality of a wet dish towel. Maybe the Lord will take pity on Jonnie and induce Louise to cancel their betrothal. What you may not realize about our family is that there's a sentimental streak in all of us. Jonnie has been so conscientious he's given his personal life little chance to develop. For years he's thought of nothing but his work, and a romance is just what he needs."

Before Edmund could reply they saw a burly white man coming down the pier toward *Flying Dragon*. His suit of heavy wool and his calf-high boots made no concession to the sultry Canton weather.

Charles saw at a glance that the man's clothes obviously had been tailor-made and were expensive.

"I'll leave you to deal with him," Edmund said. "I want to make sure the wardroom is clean enough for Jonathan's taste."

Charles sauntered to the gangway to greet the visitor. "Captain Rakehell?"

"He's gone ashore," Charles said politely. "My name is Boynton, and I'm first mate. Perhaps I can help you."

Owen Bruce introduced himself.

Charles led him to the aft deck, where several canvas chairs had been placed in the open for Soong Chao's visit later in the day.

"Your accent tells me you're English, and I've also been told you're a member of the Boynton shipping family."

"Your confirmation is correct, sir." Wanting acceptance for himself, Charles didn't elaborate.

"I was also told that you aren't doing your local business here through one of the established foreign factories. There's a rumor abroad to the effect that you're dealing directly with Soong Chao."

"We are." Charles was curt because their business arrangements here were of no concern to outsiders.

"Apparently you aren't aware of the local customs in Whampoa." Bruce smiled, but his eyes remained cold. "Ships operating independently of the big companies never deal directly with the hong merchants. They sell to the factories, and we in turn deal with the hong. If Captain Rakehell chooses not to make an agreement with the American factory, that's his privilege, of course. But the Cantonese merchants are slippery, greedy fellows, and in the long haul you'll do better to make your contracts with one of us. I've come to see if I can be of service."

"Thanks for your interest," Charles said, "but Captain Rakehell—who is my partner—and I are very happy with the arrangement we've already made with Soong Chao."

Bruce frowned. "This is very unorthodox, Mr. Boynton. Perhaps you don't realize that I handle a number of Boynton accounts every year."

"I'm well aware of it, sir." Charles saw no reason to reveal that he himself frequently had recorded the terms of deals that Boynton captains had made with the Bruce factory. "What you may not realize is that Captain Rakehell and I see no reason why a substantial share of our profits should be shared with a middleman when we can work with a reputable hong like Mr. Soong."

"I've been here in Whampoa for many years. I know China, Mr. Boynton, and you young chaps don't. Oh, you may do well enough with a cargo here or a cargo there. But if you're planning to become active in the China trade over a period of years, your profits will be consistently higher. Through me."

"We've already made commitments that satisfy us, sir." Charles began to feel annoyed because the man was pushing too hard.

"You're making a mistake," Owen Bruce said harshly. "When independent shippers store their merchandise in a Chinese merchant's warehouse, they have no recourse when goods are stolen or destroyed."

"Are you saying, sir, that your guards are superior to those of local merchants like Mr. Soong?"

"My warehouse guards are English and Scottish and Irish, every last one of them. I wouldn't hire a conniving Chinaman!"

He was being so contemptuous of the Chinese that Charles actively disliked him.

"There's bad feelings between us and the Chinese, and it gets steadily worse."

"All the more reason, then," Charles said, "to make honest bargains with the Chinese that will satisfy both sides."

"Honest bargains?" Bruce jeered. "The Chinese are cheats by nature, so we squeeze them before they can harm us."

"If Captain Rakehell and I change our minds on our next voyage to the Orient, Mr. Bruce, it may be we'll be in touch with you." He stood and started to walk to the gangway with the visitor.

"I hope for your sakes that you'll be able to make another voyage here," Bruce said. "Independent shippers have been known to lose everything in warehouse accidents." The innuendo in his tone was even more emphatic than his words.

Charles's pale eyes became glacial. "I sincerely hope our merchandise won't be subjected to accidents, Mr. Bruce. We might not be the only ones who would suffer." He did not offer to shake hands again when they parted at the gangway.

Jonathan returned a short time later with the cook, both of them laden with packages.

Charles took his cousin's mind off the meal momentarily by repeating the gist of his conversation with the factory owner.

"It appears to me that he was threatening us," Jonathan said.

"That's what I made of his talk."

"We'll talk to Soong Chao about this," Jonathan said, and hurried off to his cabin to change into his coat with the pewter buttons and his pewter-buckled shoes.

Most members of the crew, other than the cook, were free to leave, but a majority lingered on board, curious to see the guests who had caused such concern in Captain Rakehell.

Soong Chao and the ladies arrived in mid-afternoon. Sarah Applegate had chosen to wear a silk copy of one of her old-fashioned American dresses, and Lai-tse lu's cheongsam, which matched her long jade earrings, caused the seamen to gape at her as Jonathan and his officers escorted the party on a tour of the clipper.

The girl gave no indication that she was even aware of the interest she aroused. Jonathan directed most of his comments to her, and she had eyes and ears for no one else.

But Sarah was irritated, and when the group returned to the deck after an inspection below, she beckoned to Grimshaw. "Sailor," she said tartly, "I want a word with you!"

The boatswain came forward slowly, as stunned by the presence of this white woman in the Chinese party as he was by her command of his kind of English.

"What's your name?" Sarah demanded.

"Grimshaw, ma'am." The boatswain turned to glower at the crew members who stood clustered behind him, grinning at his discomfort.

"Where was your home? And I don't mean New London, which has been your home base."

"I—I come from Rhode Island, ma'am."

"Where in Rhode Island?" she persisted.

"Westerly."

"I thought you looked familiar. You must be related to Hester Grimshaw, as pious and upright a church-goer as ever I knew!"

"She—she was my pa's cousin." The boatswain

wanted to flee, but this tiny woman continued to glare at him, and he felt rooted to the deck.

"What do you think Hester would have said if she'd known that her own nephew was so rude that he just stood around ogling ladies?"

The scarlet Grimshaw didn't know what to reply.

Sarah gathered her skirts around her and went off without a backward glance to join the officers and those of her party.

The boatswain sneaked ashore with other crew members, and none of them dared to look in the beautiful Chinese girl's direction again. Sarah had no way of knowing that she earned a nickname that afternoon, but it would have pleased her had she learned that crew members privately referred to her as "the stone dragon."

Dinner was served on the aft deck, and in spite of all the care that Jonathan had taken in the planning of the meal, he lost all interest in food. It was no accident that he had placed Lai-tse lu opposite him, and throughout the meal he and the girl repeatedly stole glances at each other.

It was plain to Charles, as it was to the perturbed Edmund, that Jonathan was smitten and that the girl returned his interest.

Lai-tse lu surprised her hosts by using a knife, fork, and spoon as gracefully as she managed chopsticks. "Missy Sarah has taught me so much about the West," she told Charles, who complimented her, "that I sometimes feel I have been there."

Jonathan discovered he was jealous whenever she directed a remark to either of his mates. He knew the reaction was absurd, yet he could not control his feelings. She was even lovelier than she had been the previous day, and she totally absorbed him.

He was struck by her genuine, eager interest in *Flying Dragon*. During the tour of the clipper, she had asked several quiet but penetrating questions that indicated an understanding of the sea and the complexities of sailing, and now, as she ate daintily, he saw her look repeatedly at the towering masts.

Soong Chao was equally impressed, and after the

288

meal ended, he strolled to the quarterdeck with Jonathan for a private conversation. "I suppose," he said, "you are anxious to return as soon as possible to your home port in the United States."

"I haven't thought in any other terms," was the candid reply. "I don't know of any alternatives."

"I am about to offer you one," the Chinese merchant said with a smile. "I trade with other nations in this part of the world, and my junks sail regularly to the islands of Indonesia, the province of Taiwan, the kingdom of Siam, and many other places. Because of the speed you can achieve on a voyage in this ship, I could buy and sell various agricultural products in which I can't deal now. My junks are far too slow."

Jonathan knew the prospect of working with the man was appealing, and he realized at the same time that he sparked to the idea because he would see more of Lai-tse lu. His budding relationship with her was irrelevant to business considerations, of course, but the realization nevertheless made him far more willing to listen to a proposal.

"I can earn large sums of money if you will give me your services for six months to a year," Chao said, "and your own rewards will be great. You can earn as much from each voyage you make for me as the profit you will show on your voyage from New London to Canton and return."

"It sounds good," Jonathan admitted.

"Spend a year with me," Chao said, "and I will see to it that your crew earns double their present wages. As for you, Captain Rakehell, I guarantee you a personal profit of ten thousand dollars, American. Depending on the profits I earn, you could make as much as half again more."

Jonathan was stunned by the offer. A clear profit of ten to fifteen thousand dollars in return for a year of work was enormous, far more than he could make sailing *Flying Dragon* elsewhere or building additional clippers at the Rakehell yard.

"You would spend about two-thirds of your time

at sea," Chao said, "and you would make my factories here your headquarters. Naturally I would assume all obligations for expenses and ship repairs."

Spending two-thirds of his time at sea meant that Jonathan would be tied up at Whampoa for one-third of his time and would have ample opportunities to see Lai-tse lu. "As far as I'm concerned, Mr. Soong," he said, "the offer is attractive. But I can't speak for my officers and men. If I may, I'll bring you final word tomorrow."

Chao approved of this young man who wasted no time. "When you are ready," he said, "come to my principal factory, and you'll be provided with a suitable escort to my house. I don't advise you to walk alone through the streets again."

"I learned that lesson," Jonathan replied with a grin. "I don't want to make a habit of being rescued by your daughter."

Charles Boynton unequivocally endorsed the proposed deal with Soong Chao. He would not only earn back his original investment in the clipper but would show a handsome profit as well by the time he returned home.

Edmund Barker hesitated briefly. He disliked the prospect of prolonging his separation from Ruth for many months, but he would be earning so much money that he could not reject the offer. In the next year he would earn at least double what he could make elsewhere in that time.

The following morning Jonathan explained the proposal to the members of his crew, and without exception they agreed to it. Grimshaw spoke for the entire company when he said, "I've had my mouth set on a bowl o' clam chowder, but I'd rather have a fat wallet than a fat stomach. I'm all for it!"

Late in the morning Jonathan went to the Soong warehouse, where a party of eight uniformed men at arms already awaited him. They carried wicked ku ming and, surrounding him as soon as they went through the Petition Gate, they escorted him across Canton to the Soong estate without undue difficulty. A number of men stared at the foreign devil with undiluted hatred in their eyes, but no one tried to halt him or interfere with his progress.

Chao, who received his visitor without delay, was highly pleased by the acceptance of his proposal and again Jonathan was asked to stay for dinner.

Lai-tse lu had been in her own quarters, studying foreign languages in a dressing gown, but when she heard the American was conferring with her father, she dressed and used cosmetics with great care. Her manner was demure when she greeted him at the dinner table.

She didn't fool Missy Sarah, however. The governess saw the expression in the girl's eyes and was privately concerned. It disturbed her that these two young people were so obviously drawn to each other, and knowing China as well as she knew her native New England, she could see insurmountable problems ahead in their relationship. She quietly made up her mind to come between them if such intervention should prove necessary.

Lai-tse lu did not appear to react in any way when her father announced at the dinner table that *Flying Dragon* would be in his employ for the next six to twelve months. She continued to look down at her plate as she ate steadily with her chopsticks.

After the meal, however, she made certain that Missy Sarah had to go off to the kitchen to confer with the cook, and she got rid of her father for a short time, too, by suggesting that he prepare a contract for the unusual arrangement.

Her mask dropped away the moment she and Jonathan were alone. "I am happy that you will stay in Canton to work with my father," she said.

"So am I." Jonathan took a deep breath and steeled himself before he could say, "I would have felt—well, cheated—if I'd had to sail back to the United States before coming to know you better."

"I would have been sad, too." The girl fell silent for a moment. "It is strange. Two days ago we did not know each other, but now we have become friends."

He disagreed silently with her choice of language. What he felt toward her was not friendship. In fact, he had to exercise stern self-discipline to prevent himself from kissing her, and only the realization that such conduct would destroy their relationship held him in check.

291

Ultimately, he reflected, they would grow closer. It was inevitable. Just as it was equally certain that he would be forced to write to Louise Graves and suggest that she break their engagement. Not that Louise would mind. She wasn't in love with him, just as he had formed no permanent attachment to her. He had no idea what might develop between him and Lai-tse lu, but as an honorable man he had to be free and unencumbered for whatever future they might be able to find together.

Flying Dragon's first mission for Soong Chao was a voyage to the island of Taiwan, better known to Westerners as Formosa since the time, almost three hundred years earlier, that it had been given that name by the Portuguese. The clipper's great advantage was that she could reach Taiwan, a backward and long-neglected land that was officially a portion of Fukien province, in a voyage of less than twenty-four hours. Junks from Canton required at least a week to make the same trip.

The clipper's hold was filled with fresh melons, which were in great demand on the island, but as yet were not grown there, and she would return with a cargo of raw camphor, which the Chinese had discovered was effective in killing moths and which could not be obtained in the Middle Kingdom.

Chao sent a member of his staff, Wing T'e, to act as guide and interpreter. The task that faced Jonathan was simple. He would land early in the morning at Chilung, the harbor district for the main city of Taiwan, T'ai-nan. The produce would be unloaded, the cargo for the return voyage would be packed in the hold, and the clipper would be ready to sail back to Canton the following morning.

Seen from the quarterdeck, Taiwan was a land of sharp contrasts. The coastal areas were low-lying, fertile plains, but a range of high, rugged mountains ran up the spine of the island. A number of them soared above ten thousand feet, and although the climate was sub-tropical, there was snow on several of the peaks.

Jonathan knew the performance to expect from his ship, and after rounding the northern tip of Taiwan, he passed a string of fishing sampans putting out to sea. He approached Chi-lung at daybreak, and before the sun rose, he was tied up at a primitive quay alongside an ancient, battered merchant junk.

A local official, carrying a long sword that threatened to trip him when he walked, came on board *Flying Dragon* and was astonished to discover that the master and his crew were white. No foreigners were permitted to land anywhere on Taiwan, which posed something of a problem, but the documents identifying the captain and his men as employees of Soong Chao bore the seal of the imperial viceroy. So the official summoned several colleagues, and after a long discussion, they agreed that the clipper could discharge her melons, take on her new cargo, and depart. But the movements of the strangers were severely restricted.

"It is ordered," Wing T'e said, "that none on board this ship may venture beyond the village of Chi-lung. Any who seek to enter the town of T'ai-nan will lose their heads."

"You heard him, lads," Jonathan said to the crew. "We're the only white men on the island, so you'll stand out if you try to sneak into town. Besides, Mr. Soong told me it's a dismal place, with pigs and sheep wandering down the main streets. When our work is done for the day, take no chances. Stay right here in Chi-lung."

Edmund supervised the unloading of the melons, then began to take on the camphor, which had a smell so sharp and strong that it obliterated the odors of the tiny, provincial port. The task was completed by late afternoon, many hours ahead of schedule, and Jonathan proposed that *Flying Dragon* sail back to Canton immediately.

The bureaucratic complications that caused foreigners to complain in Whampoa were even more restrictive in this remote place. The official who had come on board that morning, apparently the harbor master, again talked at length with a group of subordinates, and together they decided that the clipper could not leave until dawn. Her permit stated that she would depart at that time, so she would be required to remain at the quay until morning.

The frustrated Jonathan granted some of his men

293

leave until midnight, with others on anchor watch, cautioning those who went ashore to remain in Chi-lung, and he intended to go ashore himself with his officers and the interpreter. There was a tavern in the port, the interpreter said, that was notable for the freshness of the food it served.

"Let no man carry firearms ashore," Wing T'e said. "It is forbidden for any man to use gunpowder on Taiwan, so it is better to risk an encounter with bandits than to carry arms. He who dared to fire a single shot would lose his head."

The seamen substituted knives and clubs for their pistols, and Jonathan was amused when he saw Oliver slip a sling into his hip pocket. It was a curious weapon and it was used by twirling it above one's head before letting fly with a stone or some other hard object.

"Do you think that will offer you better protection than a knife, Oliver?" Jonathan asked with a laugh.

The former slave regarded him soberly. "In my land," he said, "a warrior can kill many enemies with such a weapon. I used such a weapon for a long time before traders captured and sold me."

Jonathan was relieved when he saw the entire crew go ashore together. If they remained in a group and no one strayed, it seemed unlikely that they would get into trouble.

The officers carried only their swords when they, too, went ashore. Wing T'e conducted them to the tavern, which was little more than a bare-walled shack with a dirt floor. Patrons sat on woven mats placed on the hard ground and ate at low tables of unpainted wood. In spite of the humble surroundings, however, the meal was delicious. Fish and prawns had been caught within the hour, and all vegetables used in various dishes had been picked that same day.

None of the officers knew precisely what they were eating, but it was enough that the meal was satisfying. They ate heartily, with Charles in particular gorging on dish after dish, and the cost for all four was a small fraction of what a meal for one would have been charged in New London's least expensive inn.

The night was very dark when the quartet emerged

into the open again. A cool breeze was blowing down from the mountain chain and, striking the warm sea air, created a thick fog. "I'm glad we have only a short distance to walk to reach the ship," Edmund said.

"I don't remember a heavier fog in London," Charles said. "It would be easy to walk off a quay into the water without even knowing it."

They strolled slowly and went only a short distance before being surrounded by a party of men dressed in black, all of them carrying thick poles about three or four feet long.

"Bandits!" Wing T'e exclaimed. "Hold them off as best you can, and I will try to summon help." He slipped away in the fog.

It was impossible to tell whether he succeeded in escaping, and the ship's officers were too busy to peer after him in the gloom.

"I'm carrying very little of value other than my watch," Jonathan said as he drew his sword. "But I'll be damned if I'm going to lose it without a fight."

Necessity forced the trio to face in three different directions, standing with their backs to each other as the black-clad men silently surrounded them. It was unnecessary to remind each other that it would be wise to incapacitate rather than kill the villains. Outsiders were not welcome on the island, and the authorities might take a dim view of a death, even if it was a rogue who was killed.

Jonathan quickly discovered, as did his companions, that the bandits were no ordinary villains. The swords of the trio held them at bay for a time, but the robbers handled their wooden sticks with marvelous dexterity, warding off blows and rendering the blades impotent as they pressed closer and closer.

"I can't even wound one of the beggars," Charles muttered in frustration.

"Me, either," Edmund declared angrily. "The best I can do is put a nick into one of their blasted sticks."

It was evident to Jonathan that the bandits had received training in a form of self-defense unknown in the West. The wooden poles were everywhere, protecting the attackers' faces and bodies, and no blade struck home, even though all three of the defenders were accomplished swordsmen.

Jonathan was reminded of the day he had faced the street mob in Canton. Soon he and his companions would be overwhelmed; even now, moment by moment, he was being increasingly restricted in the use of his sword and could no longer thrust or cut at will.

The Chinese facing him was a tall, square-faced man whose smug expression indicated his satisfaction with the progress he and his companions were making. Soon these Fan Kuei, the first any of the robbers had ever seen, would be helpless.

Suddenly, for no discernible reason, the man sank to the ground and sprawled there, lying on his back. He was still breathing, but his eyes were closed and he appeared to have lost consciousness. Jonathan's sword hadn't touched him, and no pistol or rifle had been fired.

The mystery was baffling, and before Jonathan could figure out what had happened, a second bandit crumpled to the ground, moaned, and lay still.

"What's happening?" Charles demanded as he continued to defend himself.

"Blamed if I know," Jonathan said.

A third of the attackers was felled, and the silent, effective assault by an unseen foe was too much for the rest of the band. Concluding that, as they had heard, foreign devils were protected by gods more powerful than any in the Chinese pantheon, the robbers fled.

Jonathan quickly dropped to one knee and examined the first of the bandits to fall. There was an ugly, red welt in the center of the man's forehead, but he bore no other sign of injury.

Turning to another of the unconscious bandits, Jonathan saw a lump on one temple.

The mystery was explained when Oliver came forward, materializing out of the fog. In one hand he carried the sling he had made.

"So you're the one who routed them," Jonathan said.

"Grimshaw want to fight rascals with knives," the grinning Oliver replied. "But this way better. Only bad men get hurt, and soon be well enough to run away and join friends."

"You've saved our watches, and possibly our lives," Jonathan said.

"Better than knife or gun," Oliver replied cheerfully. "Sling kill only if Oliver want it to kill."

The other members of the crew appeared out of the fog, and the entire ship's company went en masse to the quay.

Wing T'e awaited them on board the clipper, explaining that he had been unable to find any local officials because of the fog.

The lesson taught by the incident was plain. "Hereafter," Jonathan said, "we'll know we're obliged to look out for ourselves, no matter where we travel in this part of the world."

Flying Dragon weighed anchor at daybreak and, adhering to her schedule in spite of a squall, reached Whampoa the following day. An hour after the clipper docked, Jonathan, accompanied by the escort from the factory, arrived at Soong Chao's estate to report.

"You have done well," he said, "and I rejoice that no one was hurt when the bandits attacked you. How did they know where to find you?"

"I have no idea, Mr. Soong," Jonathan replied. "I suppose one or more of the band saw us at supper."

"It may be that the attack was prearranged and deliberate," Chao said. "I do not wish to alarm you, but an attempt was made during your absence to destroy the cotton looms you sold to me. I increased the number of guards in my factories after you told me of the threats made by Owen Bruce, so no harm was done. Those who tried to set fire to the factory were driven off."

"Do you think Bruce was responsible, Mr. Soong?"

Chao shrugged. "I do not like to think ill of any merchant," he said slowly.

The subject was raised again, briefly, after Lai-tse lu joined them for dinner. "I do not like or trust this man Bruce," she said gravely, but offered no explanation.

Missy Sarah was not present, sending word that one of her infrequent headaches kept her confined to her bed.

Then a messenger in imperial livery arrived, bringing a message that the viceroy wanted to see Soong Chao immediately.

Jonathan found himself alone at the table with Lai-tse lu and realized he had often daydreamed about just this situation.

Both were so self-conscious there was an awkward silence.

"Why do you mistrust Bruce?" he asked at last.

"I have been told by one who knows that he often deals in opium," the girl replied, unable to tell him that Kai was her source of information. No foreigner, including this man she liked and admired so much, was allowed to learn of the existence of any of the secret societies. Their very existence was restricted to Chinese patriots of unquestionable loyalty.

"I have no use for opium sellers," Jonathan said, "but the fact that he deals in drugs doesn't mean he'd try to burn down a warehouse filled with valuable merchandise."

"He who breaks one law does not hesitate to break other laws," the girl replied. "You have heard of Teng-yo?"

Jonathan shook his head as he continued to drink in her changing expression.

"In our myths he is the god who protects people from injustice. Teng-yo is said to stand more than eight feet tall, and when he speaks it is with the voice of thunder. A statue of Teng-yo stands at the side door of a temple that is only a short distance from here. Yesterday I went to the temple and offered Teng-yo a sacrifice of three live frogs. The frogs made their way down a flight of marble stairs and were not seen again. So it may be the god has changed them into men who will help him study Bruce and determine whether he is guilty. If it was he who tried to burn the looms, Teng-yo will punish him."

For a moment Jonathan didn't know what to make of this confusing legend. "Do you really believe in Teng-yo, and do you think he has the power to change frogs into men?"

Lai-tse lu's merry laugh filled the dining room. "I

want very much to believe in him," she said, "because I admire the cause of justice. It is true that I found three small frogs in our garden and took them to Teng-yo at the temple. It is true also that the frogs hopped away." Still smiling, she managed to sigh simultaneously. "How wonderful it would be if all of our old peasant myths were true. The world would be such a wonderful place."

At the same instant, he reflected, she looked like a wise, sophisticated woman as well as an innocent little child.

"I must answer you honestly," Lai-tse lu said. "I do not believe the myth is really true, but in the Middle Kingdom it is sometimes impossible to distinguish between myths and reality. I offered the sacrifices to Teng-yo because I want so badly to see wicked men like Bruce brought to justice and punished for their transgressions."

Even though he felt close to her, Jonathan realized, the ways of West and East were very different. He and this girl might be close at one moment, but in the next breath their thoughts would be far apart.

"In what do you believe, Jonathan?" It was the first time she had called him by his given name.

"Mostly in myself. And in those like my father and Charles, because I know I can rely on them."

She pondered, then nodded. "I see what you mean. I know I can rely on my father and Missy Sarah. And Kai." She looked hard at him, then asked ingenuously, "Are there no women in whom you believe?"

It would be premature to tell her that he already had unlimited faith in her. "There has been no one since my mother died. My sister is loyal to her husband."

"That is as it should be," Lai-tse lu said primly.

Now was the moment to tell her about Louise. He had to speak while he had the courage. "Before I left home to sail to Canton, my engagement to marry a girl in New London was announced by her parents."

She looked down at her fragile teacup. "You love this girl, Jonathan?"

"I do not, Lai-tse lu," he said firmly, "just as she doesn't love me. Our marriage was arranged—long ago—by her father and my father."

Her face cleared, and she seemed unperturbed. "Often I have thought of what I have read and what Missy Sarah has told me about your country. In many ways the Middle Kingdom and the United States are the same. Here, too, marriages are arranged between parents, and often those who marry do not meet until they see each other for the first time at the wedding."

Jonathan clenched his hands under the low table. "Have such arrangements been made for you?"

"Oh, no. My father has promised that I will have a voice in my marriage."

"That's as it should be," he said, and braced himself. "When another American ship comes to Canton and makes plans to sail home again, I intend to send a letter to the girl. I shall ask her to break our engagement."

"Is it allowed that you do this?"

"I am a man, not a boy, so I am my own master. For a long time I didn't care one way or the other, and I had taken it for granted that I'd be married to her. But now I know I don't wish her to become my wife."

Lai-tse lu knew better than to pursue the subject.

Jonathan looked at her, and their eyes locked. Time seemed to stand still.

The girl broke the tense silence. "Unless you wish more to eat, we will walk together in the garden."

He rose quickly and followed her into the open. Again their tensions mounted, and Jonathan, not wanting to remain silent, asked her about various plants, flowers, and shrubs.

She replied mechanically, knowing they were filling a void by speaking of things that didn't matter.

After a time they came to rows of plants filled with fruit the size of the girl's fist and larger. Many were green, but some were beginning to ripen and were turning red. On the opposite side of the gravel path were miniature versions of the same plant. Lai-tse lu absently picked one of the tiny pieces of fruit.

"Don't eat it!" Jonathan exclaimed in alarm.

"Why not?" she was amused.

"We have plants like that at home. They grow wild

every summer. They're called tomatoes, but most people know them as love apples."

"What a quaint name," she murmured.

"That's because of their color when they ripen. What matters most is that they're poisonous. Eating just one of them could kill you!"

"I prefer them to lichi nuts," Lai-tse lu said, and mischievously popped the miniature tomato into her mouth.

Jonathan looked at her in horror.

Lai-tse lu laughed gleefully, plucked another and, holding it in her palm, extended her hand to him. "Join me," she said with mock solemnity, "and we shall die together."

He hesitated for no more than an instant, then took the little fruit and ate it.

"You are still alive, and so am I," she said.

He was embarrassed. "In America," he said, "everybody believes love apples are very poisonous."

"In the Middle Kingdom," she replied, "everyone knows they are delicious and that they serve many useful purposes. We call them ke-tze." Suddenly she laughed again. "You have already eaten the special sauce of the ke-tze."

"I have?"

"In the supplies my father placed on your ship when you sailed to Taiwan was a barrel of meat packed in the cooked sauce of the ke-tze. It is called ke-tze-up, and it is used because it preserves meat and prevents it from spoiling."

Jonathan grinned sheepishly. He and his men had thoroughly enjoyed the meat packed in ke-tze-up, but he would face a certain mutiny if his men learned they had eaten a sauce made from love apples. "When I go home," he said, "I'll take your custom with me, and I'll try to convince everyone I know that ke-tze aren't really filled with deadly poison."

Lai-tse lu's manner changed abruptly, and she looked down at the ground.

"Have I said something wrong?"

"No, Jonathan, but there is much about the ke-tze you do not know."

"Oh?"

Lai-tse lu turned away from him.

Jonathan felt certain he had unknowingly offended her. "If I've hurt you, it wasn't intentional," he said.

She shook her head, but obviously was reluctant to speak.

Bewildered by the change in her attitude, he could only look at her.

Lai-tse lu faced him again, realizing she owed him an explanation. She was inexplicably shy now, and her self-assurance was drained from her. "There is a myth as old as the Middle Kingdom itself," she said. "The ke-tze is a food of the gods, you see, and when a man and a woman partake of it together, it is believed they will love each other as long as they live."

Jonathan's gaze remained steady. "It well might be," he said with conviction, "that there is much truth in the old myths."

IV

The teeming island of Java was the heart of the Netherlands East Indies, which had been under Dutch rule for more than two hundred years. And the soul of Java was the bustling capital city of Djakarta, as the natives of Malay and Chinese origin called it. The Dutch rulers, to be sure, knew it as Batavia, but referred to it by that name only in their official correspondence.

The port area of Tandjungpriok, which lay east of the city, was protected by a double stone breakwater erected by the Dutch, and the harbor was crowded with the ships of every maritime nation on earth. *Flying Dragon* tied up at the sturdy dock that had been reserved for her, and Jonathan said to his officers, "This must be the busiest seaport in the world, even busier than London."

There was good reason for the commercial activity, as the newly arrived Americans well knew. The Indonesian islands that comprised the sprawling, prosperous colony exported large quantities of coffee and green tea, both in worldwide demand. But the most profitable of the islands' products was black pepper, which was grown nowhere else. Originally known by Westerners as the Spice Islands, the Netherlands East Indies could not meet the demand for its black peppercorns, which earned millions of gold and silver guilders every year. Those who claimed that the wealth of the Netherlands itself rested on a base of pepper did not exaggerate.

Jonathan was fascinated by the prahus that moved

in and out of the harbor. These solidly built fishing boats, which had high, uniquely curved prows, were like no other vessels on earth. Each carried a single, enormous sail, which was dyed according to the whims of the owner. Every color of the rainbow was represented, and it was with difficulty that the young American forced himself to concentrate on the business that had brought him to Java.

He registered his arrival with the officious, sweating Dutch authorities who came on board as soon as he docked, and then he went ashore with Charles. Under one arm he carried a heavy, reinforced box of sandalwood, and he knew it was filled with silver. As Soong Chao had explained to him, anyone who traded in Djakarta had to pay bribes if he expected to receive merchandise of quality; this was the normal way of life in the Netherlands East Indies.

Several carriages were available for hire, but the cousins elected to go into Djakarta in a rickshaw, a curious vehicle unique to the East. It had two large wooden wheels, and a seat above them. The operator, who stood in front of the two seats available to the passengers, pulled the rickshaw in order to propel it. The man Jonathan and Charles hailed to take them into town was a frail-looking Malaysian of indeterminate age, but the man's strength was prodigious, and he showed no physical strain as he moved in and out of heavy traffic, deftly avoiding carriages and countless handcarts, horseback riders and innumerable pedestrians, many of whom balanced large packages on their heads as they walked with easy grace.

Djakarta was an amazing community. Carved out of thick jungle, it was the melting pot of the East. Huge warehouses were filled with pepper, coffee, green tea, and rubber, a product for which the demand in the West was growing. Natives sold bunches of bananas, coconuts, and pineapples at roadside stands, and some offered mangoes and a variety of exotic fruits that neither Jonathan nor Charles recognized.

They rode past churches of stone and wood, rickety shacks with thatched roofs, outside of which naked, brown-skinned children were playing, indifferent to their nudity. Here and there they saw Western-style structures, homes and offices, schools and a large, sprawling hospital that included more than a dozen buildings.

Nothing had prepared the two visitors for the sight that greeted them when they reached the Tjiliwung River, which flowed into the sea at the port. Solid homes of three or four stories with leaded windows, all painted in pastel colors, lined both sides of the placid river, which was filled with barges. The Dutch were utilizing it as a canal, and Jonathan grinned.

"If it weren't for the smell of the tropics and the presence of so many Malaysians, Chinese, and all the other dark-skinned people I can't identify," he said, "I'd swear we were in Amsterdam."

Charles stared at a Dutchman in European attire who was walking beside a young woman wearing a breast-band and an ankle length skirt and shook his head. "You wouldn't see a couple like that in Amsterdam," he replied.

The rickshaw left the street that ran along the bank of the river and turned onto a broad avenue lined with palm trees. Here the houses were larger and more imposing, each surrounded by an immaculate lawn and guarded by pairs of small, wiry men armed with double-edged, wavy-bladed swords. These weapons, Jonathan knew, were the *kris* that had originated in the Philippine Islands, and he looked at the swords with interest, ready to believe that a *kris,* wielded by an expert, could disembowel a man with a single thrust.

The operator came to a halt before a huge house of pink stucco, the windows of its upper floors leaded, those on the first two levels utilizing wooden jalousies that admitted the breezes from the mountains that lay behind the city. Charles paid the driver his small fee, and Jonathan raised the door knocker of heavy, ornamented brass.

The summons was answered by a brown-skinned young woman, wearing a sarong and barefooted, with a large, strongly scented flower in her long, flowing hair. She looked at the visitors with huge, kohl-rimmed eyes, and Charles, attracted to her, studied her intently.

Identifying himself and his cousin, Jonathan said, "We're expected."

The girl led them to an anteroom, bare except for a

woven mat rug of copra and several plain benches. "Please to wait," she replied in a lilting voice, and darted out of the room.

"I'm going to like Djakarta," Charles said.

"You're incorrigible."

"I freely admit I have a weakness for pretty girls, and I have no intention of changing my ways."

"Please to come," the girl called from the entrance, and led the pair down a corridor to an inner garden courtyard. Seated in a wicker chair with a throne-like, peacock back and dressed in an old-fashioned, open-throated shirt and knee breeches of coarse, unbleached linen was the most overweight man Jonathan had ever seen.

Rolls of flesh strained the fabric of his shirt, his breeches bulged, and even his white silk stockings above silver-buckled shoes seemed about to burst. On each of his large, pudgy fingers he wore a ring, and a single hoop of beaten gold dangled from one ear. Even more extraordinary than his bulk was his round face, which looked as though it had been carved out of a block of granite. Eyes of pale, glacial blue peered at the visitors beneath droopy lids, and Jonathan was reminded of an unblinking snake he had discovered as a child in a pile of rocks. The man's eyebrows, bushy and tangled, were steel-gray, and he was totally bald.

Perched on one of his massive shoulders was a multi-colored, unmoving parrot, and four or five other, similar birds sat on perches scattered around the little garden.

Standing behind the heavy man, slightly to one side, was another man, dark-skinned and very slender, in a white shirt, black trousers, and a belt at least four inches high. Protruding from the belt were the hilts of several knives, the blades no more than six or seven inches long and perhaps two inches wide. They appeared to be made of a flexible steel and conformed to the line of the man's body, bending slightly. Like his master, the dark-skinned man was unmoving, staring at the newcomers blandly, his expression indicating neither hostility nor pleasure.

The man in the chair raised a thick hand to his chiseled nose and sniffed a strongly scented handkerchief.

306

"Welcome to the humble house of the Fat Dutchman," he said in a deep, booming voice.

The sarong-clad girl made an obeisance, dipping to the floor, then silently left the garden.

Presumably the man had a name, but in trading circles, as Soong Chao had told Jonathan, he was known only as the Fat Dutchman. It was rumored that the wife of the Governor-General of the Netherlands East Indies was his niece and that one of his cousins was the commander of the Dutch regiments that maintained order in the islands. Whatever his connections, no merchandise was bought or sold here without his express approval.

"Heh-heh-heh." The cough-like sound actually was a dry, humorless laugh, more like a nervous affliction than an expression of merriment.

"Heh-heh." The parrot on his shoulder echoed the sound.

"Mr. Rakehell, Mr. Boynton, I have been looking forward to your arrival. Be seated, won't you?"

The only seats available were several three-legged wicker stools that stood chair-high. Jonathan took one and was surprised to find it comfortable.

"I've heard nothing for weeks but talk of your ship," the Fat Dutchman declared. "Everyone in the industry is curious about it, so I've taken the liberty of ordering a double guard while you're in Djakarta. There are rascals in this city who would steal your sails and the wooden planks of your decks if they had the chance."

"We'd be pleased to have you visit *Flying Dragon* at your convenience," Jonathan said.

"I appreciate the offer, but I rarely leave this house. Never fear, I'll soon receive a half-dozen reports on your clipper from shipping men and sailers whose judgment I trust. Now, shall we get down to business?"

"Get down to business!" the parrot screamed.

The Fat Dutchman remained imperturbable, seemingly unaware of the screeching sound so close to his ear.

Jonathan took a folded document from an inner pocket and handed it to him. "Here's my manifest," he said.

"Heh-heh-heh. A cargo of pure silk shantung. I'll take

all of it. Between the wealthy women of our Chinese community and the wives of Dutch officials who will have their dresses made of nothing else, I can always use as much as I can get."

"Mr. Soong's suggested price is listed on the manifest."

"I'll pay it," the Fat Dutchman said flatly. "I never argue or haggle with Soong over prices. We've never met personally, but we've been friends for too long to quibble." He rubbed his pudgy hands together briskly. "What cargo do you want in return?"

"Black pepper," Jonathan said. "As many bags of it as I can cram into my hold."

"Very well. What quality?"

"First grade only. Mr. Soong is willing to pay the current rate of two and one-half silver yuan per bag."

"That's reasonable." The statement seemed to hang in the air.

"Reasonable," the parrot echoed.

All at once Jonathan knew that something more was expected of him. He had wondered how to handle the bribe that had to be paid as a matter of course, but that problem was solving itself. Without comment he gave the man the sandalwood box.

The Fat Dutchman held the box in the palm of his hand, his eyes remote as he weighed it experimentally.

"You may count the contents if you wish," Charles said.

"Heh-heh. That won't be necessary. Soong has never cheated me, just as I don't cheat him."

Suddenly the silent, motionless Malaysian behind the Fat Dutchman whipped a knife from his belt and threw it with great force.

The blade sang past the startled Jonathan's ear, almost grazing him, and his first thought was that the man was trying to kill him.

For an instant the Fat Dutchman glanced behind his guest, then proceeded calmly. "As I was about to indicate, the terms are satisfactory. You shall have your bags of first grade pepper."

Jonathan looked behind him and saw the blade still quivering. It had imbedded itself in the trunk of a palm, and impaled on it was an ugly, gray spider about an inch and a half in diameter.

"Nasty brutes," the Fat Dutchman said casually. "Their sting is lethal."

"I'm in your debt," Jonathan said to the Malaysian.

The man gave no indication that he heard, much less understood.

"Let me go on to a related matter," the Fat Dutchman said. "I well know that Soong won't deal in opium, but I've yet to meet an American or Englishman who'll turn down the chance to make a fat purse. Indonesian opium isn't in a class with the product the British take out of India, but the American captains who buy our opium have no trouble disposing of it. At their own prices."

"Opium is not for us, thanks," Jonathan said firmly. "No matter what the profit, we're not interested."

"Heh-heh. A pity," the Dutchman said.

"A pity!" the parrot screamed.

"However, it may be we can make yet another business arrangement, Mr. Rakehell. Is it true you built your clipper ship yourself?"

"Yes, at my family's yard in New England."

"Splendid. You plan to build others, I assume?"

"Indeed, sir. As soon as I sail home."

"And when will that be, Mr. Rakehell?"

Jonathan shrugged. "Within the next year."

"Would you be willing to build a clipper for me?"

The two young visitors exchanged pleased smiles. "Certainly, sir!" Jonathan said.

"Good! What would you regard as a reasonable delivery date?"

Jonathan did some rapid mental arithmetic. "I'm certain you could get it in no more than two years from now."

"You've made a deal, Mr. Rakehell. Anyone who does business on behalf of Soong Chao and who refuses to buy and sell opium must be honest, so name your own price. Heh-heh." The Dutchman leaned forward suddenly and handed him the sandalwood box filled with silver. "Consider this a down payment."

"It's too much," Jonathan protested.

"Take it," the Fat Dutchman boomed, then turned to a magnificent peacock and a less resplendent peahen that strutted into the garden. "Ah, my friends never fail me. They're telling me it's time to eat. You'll stay for a simple meal, gentlemen." The invitation was expressed as a command.

Jonathan and Charles accepted with thanks.

The Fat Dutchman heaved himself to his feet and led the way into the house, his step surprisingly light and graceful. The parrot continued to cling to his shoulder, and Charles blinked in astonishment when the peacock and the peahen followed the group quietly.

The whitewashed walls of the dining room were bare, but a superb length of lace covered the table, and three places were set with silver plates, goblets, and utensils that gleamed. The Fat Dutchman took his place at the head of the table, with the silent Malaysian again standing behind him.

As soon as the host was seated, four sarong-clad young women, one of them the girl who had admitted the visitors, appeared with large trays laden with food.

"Have you ever tried *rijstaffel*, gentlemen? No? A blend of the best in Indonesian and Dutch cuisines. Help yourselves to some of everything."

Jonathan did as he was bidden and counted eighteen kinds of dried, smoked, broiled, and raw fish, which he heaped on his plate. Following his host's example, he added raisins, salted peanuts, shredded coconut, almonds, and a mango chutney, along with a number of other substances he could not identify.

Charles was active, too, but found the time and opportunity to flirt with the girl who had struck his fancy. She smiled steadily at him in return.

Some of the fish were fiery, and Jonathan was grateful for the goblets of cool ale served with the meal. He assumed that the various fish dishes comprised the main course and was surprised when the young women cleared away the plates, then brought platters of vegetables and fruits.

"After this," the Fat Dutchman said with relish, "we will come to the meats, and finally to the combinations of foods. A proper *rijstaffel* should consist of no fewer than eighty-seven dishes. I always include some of my own favorites not on the classical list, like shrimp bread, which is actually more of a hard biscuit, so there are a minimum of ninety-eight at my table." He held aloft a wafer-thin sheet of a dark brown substance. "Be sure you try the Bombay duck on the curry dishes," he said, crumbling the sheet by rubbing it briskly between his hands, scattering the shreds onto his plate.

"Bombay duck?" Charles asked, following his example.

"A misnomer applied by your English compatriots, who have a genius for making such mistakes and then refusing to admit they're wrong. Actually it's the skin of a large fish, which has been slowly smoked for a number of days until it becomes brittle. It was first invented by Indonesian fishermen on the island of Sumatra and ultimately found its way to India."

"It doesn't taste like fish," Jonathan said.

"Any more than it tastes like duck," the Fat Dutchman said. "In fact, it tastes like nothing else I've ever eaten, but it is an addictive dish, and I find it indispensable with curries."

Platter after platter came to the table, and eventually Jonathan had to give up. Charles continued to eat for a time, but his appetite could not match that of the host, and he, too, had to stop.

The meal ended with a variety of Dutch cheeses, mugs of strong coffee, and glasses of an Indonesian wine that was simultaneously sweet and tart.

"You may think of this as a simple meal," Jonathan said, "but I call it a banquet."

"Before you return to Canton," the Fat Dutchman said, "I hope to serve you a true banquet." He turned to Charles, who again was flirting with the nubile serving maid. "You like Mirana," he said.

311

Charles nodded, slightly embarrassed but basically unabashed.

The Fat Dutchman said something to the girl in a language neither of the visitors understood.

The girl smiled slyly at Charles.

"She's willing," the Fat Dutchman said. "Just follow her, and she'll take you to one of the guest rooms I keep for the purpose."

Charles and the young woman left the room.

"Heh-heh. What about you, Mr. Rakehell? Does one of my young ladies strike your fancy?"

Jonathan smiled and shook his head.

"I make it a habit to present gifts to friends at the conclusion of a business arrangement, and you and I have struck two separate bargains today. What would you like?"

"Perhaps you can tell me where I might buy two pairs of peacocks. I've never seen such beautiful birds."

"You have good taste, Mr. Rakehell. Heh-heh. The peacocks of Java are the loveliest in all the world. They're unique. Surely you aren't thinking of raising them?"

"No, I'd like to present one pair to the daughter of Soong Chao. And I've learned enough about China to know it would be impolitic for one of the emperor's subjects to have a rare possession the emperor himself doesn't own. So I thought Soong Chao could send the second pair to Peking as a gift for the emperor."

"You're shrewd, Mr. Rakehell, and you shall go far. Very well, you shall have your two pairs of birds."

"Only on condition that I be allowed to pay for them."

"If you insist." The Fat Dutchman uttered his dry laugh, which the parrot, still on his shoulder, promptly imitated. "I must take my siesta, and your friend is—ah—occupied. What may I do for you that will keep you amused for the next hour or so?"

"Well, there is something," Jonathan said, nodding in the direction of the statue-like Malaysian. "I'd be deeply grateful for a set of knives like his, along with instructions in their use."

The Fat Dutchman spoke at length to his retainer.

The Malaysian came to life for the first time, a toothless grin spreading across his face as he said something succinctly.

"A set of knives will be made for you, and you will have them before you sail, Mr. Rakehell. Right now, if you will go into the garden with Ahmed, he will teach you how to use them. You have impressed him, Mr. Rakehell. Many foreigners come to this house, but you are the first who has ever wanted to learn an ancient Indonesian martial art that is unique in all the world."

Flying Dragon tied up at her berth in front of the Soong factories in Whampoa in mid-morning, and the merchant's dockhands immediately began to unload the cargo of precious black pepper.

Jonathan was eager to report on the success of his mission and was pleased when he found that Kai, the majordomo, happened to be on hand at the factories. They communicated in sign language, and Kai agreed to lead the escort that would accompany the American to the Soong estate.

Kai raised an eyebrow when the caged birds were taken ashore, and Jonathan reflected that it was just as well that he couldn't explain to the majordomo why he had brought them. He saw, too, that Kai noted the Indonesian knives he was carrying in his belt, and he grinned amiably. He had spent an hour on board ship each day practicing with them, throwing them at a target he had erected on the aft deck, and although he was showing steady improvement, he wasn't yet ready to demonstrate his skill with them. In a few more weeks he would become proficient, but he thought it unlikely that he would ever be able to challenge Ahmed to a contest.

Lai-tse lu happened to be looking out of a window in her sitting room when the procession arrived at the estate. Her heart pounding when she saw Jonathan, she was overcome by curiosity over the four cages that retainers were carrying. So she checked her appearance quickly, then hurried to her father's workroom.

The four cages had been placed side by side in the

garden, and Jonathan, after greeting the girl with a bow, opened the doors. A peacock of brilliant green and another of a pale, delicate blue emerged, spreading their gorgeous tail feathers, and were followed by a green peahen and a blue peahen, both perfect matches for their mates.

They were so lovely that Lai-tse lu clapped her hands together in delight.

"One pair," Jonathan said, "is a gift for Lai-tse lu. The other pair is for you, Mr. Soong, so you can send them to the emperor in Peking."

The girl was so happy she was rendered speechless.

But her father was puzzled. "I have done business for twenty years with the Fat Dutchman. Never before has he sent me gifts. Why does he do so now?"

"He procured them for me," Jonathan said. "But I paid him for them. They're gifts from me."

Lai-tse lu stared at the American for a moment, then impulsively kissed him on the cheek.

The spot where her lips touched his face seemed to burn.

"You are generous and wise, Jonathan," Chao said. "As you can tell for yourself, no gift could please Lai-tse lu more. I, too, am grateful to you because you give me the opportunity to make a lasting impression on the Tao Kuang Emperor. I shall send the birds to him on one of my junks this very day."

Aware only of the shining expression in the girl's limpid eyes, Jonathan said, "I'd like Lai-tse lu to take her choice. The pair she wants will belong to her, and the other can be sent to Peking."

"Oh, no," she said quickly. "There can be no choice."

Her father nodded gravely. "You are right, my daughter. Your thoughts are sound."

Jonathan was puzzled.

"According to one of our oldest myths," Lai-tse lu explained, "once there lived an Emperor of Heaven, long before the Middle Kingdom was formed. The emperor and his wife loved each other, but they were unhappy because the wife was barren and could bring no children into the world. The gods took pity on her and sent her a peacock and a peahen to distract her. The birds were so beautiful that she soon loved them with all her heart, and that love changed her. One day the peacock and peahen vanished, and that same day the wife of the emperor gave birth to twins, a son and a daughter. In the myth, the peacock and the peahen that brought happiness to the wife of the empress were a lovely, soft blue color. No greater flattery could be offered the Tao Kuang Emperor than to give him a pair of blue birds."

Jonathan realized that fortune was smiling on him. "And will you be satisfied with the green pair?"

"I prefer them," she said, her smile radiant. "They are my favorite shade of jade green." Watching the peacock preen, she laughed aloud.

The gifts were completely successful, but Jonathan momentarily put the girl's joy out of his mind as he went into the workroom with Chao to discuss the business he had conducted in Djakarta.

"You have done well, as always," the merchant said when he finished his report. "My profits from this voyage will be so great that I shall give you a bonus of one thousand dollars, American."

"Thank you. I'll share it with my officers and men."

Chao nodded. "I felt sure you would. Soon I will talk with you about another voyage I will want you to undertake, but first we must speak of another matter." He removed his eyeglasses, polished them slowly and, after returning them to the bridge of his nose, opened a jar of smoked, salted watermelon seeds, which he offered the younger man.

The symbolism of the gesture was not lost on Jonathan. He had spent enough time in China by now to understand that food had to be shared when matters of great importance were discussed.

"For months," Chao said, "I have watched you and my daughter grow closer to each other. I have seen the way you exchange glances, the way each of you looks privately at the other. Both of you are swimming in waters that are too deep for you."

"I can speak only for myself, sir," Jonathan said earnestly. "And the feelings I have been developing for Lai-tse lu are unlike any I have ever felt before."

"I have no doubt of it, just as I know she feels much as you do. You are a man of the West, Jonathan. My daughter, although she knows much about the West and can speak many of its languages, is a woman of the East. I fear for both of you because your thoughts, your cultures, your backgrounds are so different."

"Those differences, if they exist," Jonathan said forthrightly, "haven't shown themselves to either of us."

"Perhaps not, but they are real, and I am afraid neither of you could make the other happy for more than a short time."

Jonathan braced himself. "Are you saying, sir, that you want us to walk separate paths?"

Chao shook his head vigorously, then picked up a small, alabaster Buddha from his table and turned it over in his hands while he weighed his reply. "That would be the worst thing I could do," he said. "How foolish I would be if I forbade you to see more of each other. That would only cause you to yearn more for one another because the young always rebel against the authority of the old and believe they know best. That has been the way of the world since the beginning of time. Lai-tse lu would obey me, of course, for no Chinese girl who has been reared as she has been reared would disobey her father. But she would be certain to convince herself that she loves you. You, too, would obey me because you are a man of principle and honor, but you would come to believe with all your heart that you loved her."

Jonathan had to admit he made good sense.

"Continue to see each other without restrictions," Chao continued. "But be alert to the dangers that face both of you. Know and understand why you are drawn to each other."

"I don't know why, and that's the truth," the young American declared. "All I know is what I feel, and I sense what Lai-tse lu also feels."

Chao smiled, but there was sadness in his wise eyes. "You are far from your home, living and working in a world that is alien to you in every way. My daughter is a great beauty, but she is much more. She is intelligent, but she has more than intelligence. She is a woman of great compassion and warmth. In her there is the essence of all that is feminine. You have been lonely without realizing it, so you have responded to her natural warmth."

"It may be that you're right, sir," Jonathan had to admit.

"I have lived long and I have seen much in the world, so I know I am right." Chao carefully placed the alabaster Buddha on the table again. "Now we must examine the reasons that my daughter is drawn to you. Thanks to the teaching of Missy Sarah, Lai-tse lu has learned not only your language but she has also become familiar with the ways of the West. We have an ancient saying attributed to Confucius. It is said that the best rice is always grown in the fields on the far side of the mountains. Lai-tse lu has come to admire all that is good in the West. That is why she has been so eager to see the Middle Kingdom expand our trade with the Fan Kuei. Just at the time she has been at her most vulnerable to Western thought and styles, you have appeared. You are intelligent, you work hard, and you are honorable, so you possess the qualities she has always admired. You are handsome, just as she is beautiful, so like attracts like, and it is very easy for her to imagine that she is falling in love with you."

"How is it possible to tell the difference between real love and imagining that one is in love?" Jonathan asked.

"Only a fool would dare to answer such a question," Chao declared. "Our wisest philosophers and soothsayers have pondered for thousands of years, but none have been able to distinguish between reality and illusion in matters of the heart. It must suffice that you and Lai-tse lu will be on your guard, particularly in the days that lie ahead in the immediate future."

"Why should the immediate future be so important?"

"It is necessary for me to make a voyage myself, to the court of King Rama of Siam. With your permission I wish to take Lai-tse lu and Missy Sarah with me—on board your ship. Their presence will be helpful in consolidating the agreement I hope to make with the ruler of Siam, and although his country is closed to all foreigners, he cannot refuse you and your crew admission to

Bangkok if you are with me. I choose your clipper because of the impression it will make on the Siamese court, whose members have seen no ships other than junks and sampans."

"I'd be honored to sail you there," Jonathan said.

"I am grateful, but heed my words. You and Lai-tse lu will spend much time together, and the dangers that both of you face will be greatly increased."

Louise was in labor for a full day and night, apparently reluctant, as her father put it, to bring her baby into the world. Two midwives were in constant attendance in the Rakehell house, and Dr. Graves never ventured far from his daughter's bedroom, the same chamber in which Jonathan had been born a quarter of a century earlier.

At last the exhausted young woman gave birth, and her torment came to an end.

"You have a son," Dr. Graves told her as he prepared a dose of laudanum that would ease her distress and enable her to sleep peacefully. "He's a healthy, perfect baby."

"I knew I would have a boy," Louise murmured. "Tell Papa Rakehell that he will have the name of Julian."

Naomi Graves and Judith Walker, who were giving each other moral support in the parlor, were the first to learn the news. A messenger was sent to the Rakehell yard, and a short time later Jeremiah arrived home.

He exchanged congratulations with Martin and Naomi Graves, held his newborn grandson in his arms for a few moments, and asked the physician to remain behind when his wife went across the street to her own house.

They wandered together into the study, where a cheerful fire was burning in the hearth. "Reverend Crowell will announce the baby's arrival from the pulpit on Sunday," Martin Graves said. "He's already agreed to use the name of Rakehell on the parish register, so I'm confident that next month he'll baptize the boy as Julian Rakehell. I see no problems for us in the immediate future."

"We face a far greater problem than you know, old friend," Jeremiah said. "Do you prefer rum or brandywine?

I've just acquired a splendid twenty-year-old rum that one of my captains brought back from the West Indian islands. I suggest we tap the keg."

"By all means." The physician asked no questions and waited patiently while two glasses of the dry, pungent liquor were poured.

"To our grandson," Jeremiah said, raising his glass. "And to the prayer that all will be well when Jonathan returns."

Martin drank, then asked, "Why shouldn't it?"

"I didn't want to upset you or distract you while you were in attendance on Louise," Jeremiah replied. "But just yesterday a schooner put into port from Cathay, and I received our first packet of letters from Jonathan." He opened a drawer in his desk and removed a sheaf of papers.

"Has he encountered difficulties in China, Jeremiah?"

"On the contrary, Martin. He's written to me in detail that he's enjoyed an enormous success. He sold his cargo for a splendid price, and he'll bring home a cargo of fine tea that he obtained for a bargain. But that's just the beginning. He worked out an arrangement with the most prominent merchant in Canton and will stay in the East for an additional six to twelve months, sailing from one port to another on behalf of this Chinese. He obtained first-rate terms, and by the time he comes home he'll have paid for the building of his clipper several times over. He expects to come home with a very tidy sum in his purse."

"That's good news. He'll be well able to afford to support a wife and son, even without his connection with you."

"I'm pleased by his business acumen," Jeremiah said. "And I'm proud of his vocational achievements. Rakehell blood always shows." Jeremiah frowned and stared into the fire.

"What's wrong, then?"

"Included in the packet was a letter Jonathan wrote to Louise. The wax that sealed it was crushed in transit, so the letter was open. Ordinarily I wouldn't read a letter addressed to someone else, but this time I gave in to temptation. And I'm not sorry I did."

Dr. Graves leaned forward in his chair and watched as his friend picked up a letter and unfolded it.

"Jonathan tells Louise briefly about his business success and describes some of what he's seen. He's been impressed by the contrasts between the very rich and the very poor. He devotes several paragraphs to his descriptions of what he calls the 'boat people.' It appears that entire families—by the thousands—spend their entire lives on tiny sampans."

"Incredible," Martin murmured.

Jeremiah picked up his spectacles, donned them, and cleared his throat before he began to read. " 'I have been thinking a great deal about our relationship, Louise. Our enforced separation by many thousands of miles has given me a new perspective, and I've gained a new insight. You and I have done what was expected of us. For years our parents wanted us to marry, and we dutifully agreed. It never occurred to either of us that we might not find happiness together.' "

"My God," the physician muttered.

"The worst is yet to come," Jeremiah said, and resumed his reading of the letter. " 'As both of us know, we don't love each other. If there was to have been love, it would have developed long before now. We enjoy each other's company, but as friends, not as a man and woman who intend to spend their entire lives together. I know you feel as I do. We made an error by giving in to temptation the night before I sailed, and I offer you my deepest apologies for any pangs of conscience you may have suffered. I mention that night now only because I have realized that even then there were no deep feelings binding us together.' "

"Their son lies upstairs at this very moment," the anguished Dr. Graves said.

" 'Certain that you share my views, I suggest that you cancel our betrothal. Our parents will be unhappy for a time, but they'll ultimately come to accept our decision as right. What matters most is that you and I will be spared the boredom and pain of an unsuitable marriage.' "

Martin Graves drew a sharp breath.

"There's still more along the same lines," Jeremiah said, "but I've read enough."

"This is a nightmare."

"Indeed it is, Martin." Jeremiah sipped his rum. "I don't doubt that Jonathan speaks the truth and that neither of them really wanted a marriage. But for such a letter to arrive the day before Louise gave birth to their son is an unbearable irony."

The physician became lost in thought. "If my experience with my patients over a lifetime of medical practice offers any guidelines," he said, "there's more here than meets the eye." He reached for the letter and read it slowly.

There was no sound in the room but the crackling of the burning logs in the fireplace.

"It's my educated guess," Dr. Graves said at last, "that Jonathan has developed a serious interest in some other woman."

"In Cathay?" Jeremiah ran a hand through his gray hair. "That's unlikely."

"I suppose it is, and no matter what we might guess, it doesn't solve our dilemma."

Jeremiah Rakehell, who was positive in all things, hated indecision, and sighed deeply.

"All I know for sure," Martin said, "is that there's no way we can allow Louise to see this letter after she's given birth to a son. She's done well all these months, holding her head high while she's lived the lie that she and Jonathan are already married. This could be a blow that might harm her mental stability."

"I quite agree," Jeremiah said. "It's our obligation to put Louise and her baby first. I must say, in Jonathan's defense, that if he were here, he'd want to do what's honorable and right."

"I'm sure he would, but he's halfway around the face of the globe." Martin threw the letter onto the desk.

Jeremiah spoke slowly. "We're tampering with the lives of our children, but we have a grandson to protect now, so I don't believe we have any choice. I can see only one solution."

Martin hesitated, then nodded firmly.

Jeremiah, looking far older than his years, heaved himself to his feet. Reaching out slowly, he picked up the letter, walked to the hearth, and dropped in onto the burning logs.

The two men stood side by side, watching the paper as it turned to ashes.

The weather was fair, the winds were hot but brisk, and *Flying Dragon* was a perfect lady as she sailed swiftly through the South China Sea into the Gulf of Siam. Her crew was on its best behavior too, thanks to the intimidating presence on board of Sarah Applegate. Not only did the diminutive, tart-tongued woman remind the sailors of their mothers and grandmothers, but she had a sound working knowledge of navigation and sailing procedures, and she was not reluctant to criticize slovenliness and mistakes.

As Charles Boynton remarked, "Never has this crew been so efficient."

Jonathan gave his cabin to Lai-tse lu and Sarah, the mates surrendered their quarters to Soong Chao, and all three officers slept in the wardroom, hastily tidying it at mealtimes. Unable to resist the desire to show off for Lai-tse lu, Jonathan proceeded under full sail on the entire voyage.

The girl was well aware of what he was doing, but nevertheless was impressed by the clipper's grace and by the incredible speeds she was able to attain. It was no accident that, whenever Jonathan had the watch, she found an opportunity to come to the quarterdeck, where she stood at the aft rail, observing him in silent admiration.

At these times he found it difficult to converse with her as much as he wished. Crew members were at work, and he felt it would have been an insult to Lai-tse lu to pay court to her in front of an audience. What he failed to realize was that her feelings and his were obvious to the entire ship's company.

It was enough for him that the girl smiled in appreciation when the clipper wore or tacked, that she clasped her hands in joy when strong winds sent the ship slicing through the clear blue-green waters at speeds faster than man had ever before traveled at sea.

Apparently Chao had held a private conversation with his daughter about the budding romance, because her self-consciousness was as great as Jonathan's. At meals, when others were present, she rarely addressed him and looked in his direction only when she thought no one was watching her.

These moments were enough to satisfy Jonathan. For as long as he lived he would remember how she looked when she stood on deck, with the wind blowing through her long hair and flattening the silk of her dress against her incomparable body. *Flying Dragon,* he thought repeatedly, would be haunted forever by Lai-tse lu's presence.

Only when he took advantage of off-duty hours each day to practice his knife-throwing on the aft deck did she absent herself. Sarah, who openly approved of what he was doing, sometimes came to watch him, as did Soong Chao. But Lai-tse lu, hating violence, elected to spend that hour each day reading in the cabin.

The voyage was far too short for Jonathan's taste, lasting only a few days. His only satisfaction was that he reached his destination in a fraction of the time that a junk would have required.

The clipper entered the broad estuary of the Maneam Chao Phraya, then threaded her way through heavy river traffic for twenty-five miles. There, on the east bank, lay the crowded metropolis of Krungthep, which, with its environs, was known as Bangkok.

Three other major rivers and many minor streams also met here and formed the city's only roads, other than in the area known as the royal dominion, where the extensive palace of King Rama III stood. Even Jonathan, Charles, and Grimshaw, who had visited Venice, had never seen a place like Bangkok.

Houses stood on stilts at both sides of every waterway, and wherever there was higher ground, a Buddhist temple had been built. Innumerable barges brought the produce of the countryside to the city, and uncounted tens of thousands of Bangkok's residents were boat people who were born, lived, and died on cramped sampans. Business offices and shops of all kinds were located on board junks, as were brothels and the community's schools and two hospitals. Bangkok was literally a city that lived on water.

Officials in loose-fitting shirts and baggy pantaloons of a gauze-like material came on board *Flying Dragon*, and Soong Chao took charge of the formalities. To Jonathan's surprise the officials spoke Mandarin, and the American learned that approximately half of the city's people were of Chinese origin. The clipper was allowed to cast anchor, and Chao went off with the officials in a boat rowed by ten tiny sailors of the Siamese navy.

None of the whites, including Sarah, were permitted to leave the ship, and there was no place that Lai-tse lu wanted to go alone. Everyone on board sweltered in the tropical heat, and the disadvantages of life in Bangkok soon became obvious. The boats of peddlers soon crowded around the clipper, offering the visitors food and furniture and clothing, cheap trinkets and fresh fish and girls. The stench of the canals, in which garbage and human refuse floated, was overpowering.

Whenever Lai-tse lu and Sarah came onto the deck they held scented handkerchiefs to their noses. The malevolent odors sent them below again, but the heat was so intense they were forced to return to the deck.

Jonathan refused to buy any produce and was reluctant to purchase casks of supposedly fresh water. He would wait until Soong Chao returned to advise him, he decided, and that wait dragged on for thirty-six hours. By the time the merchant was rowed back to the clipper, tempers were fraying.

But Soong was cheerful. He had sold the cargo of finished silk for an exceptionally good price and had arranged to buy a cargo of long-grained Siamese rice, much in demand in Kwantung. Even more important, he had been negotiating with ministers of the Siamese government and would be received early that evening by King Rama III to conclude a long-term trade agreement. His daughter was invited, and permission had been granted for Sarah and the owner-master of *Flying Dragon* to accompany them.

Lai-tse lu knew what was expected of her and, dressing in a cheongsam of paper-thin yellow silk, she looked ravishing. As a special touch she wore a huge, white gardenia in her hair.

Sarah also wore a cheongsam, and Chao was resplendent in a gown on which lions and phoenixes were embroidered in silver thread. In spite of the heat Jonathan wore his coat with pewter buttons and promptly regretted the gesture.

A Siamese barge arrived for the party, but Chao halted Jonathan before they left the ship. "Leave your sword and knives behind," he said. "Anyone who carries arms in the presence of His Most August Personage is beheaded instantly."

With great reluctance Jonathan divested himself of his weapons.

The aft section of the barge, which was rowed by sailors, was filled with lounges on which cushions of silk were piled, and the guests were invited to loll there. Lai-tse lu and Chao accepted the invitation quickly, and even Sarah appeared at ease. But Jonathan could only hope he didn't look as ludicrously uncomfortable as he felt.

Bare-breasted young women, attired only in ankle-length skirts, brought the guests cups of solid gold filled with a sticky drink in which rose petals were floating. As nearly as Jonathan could determine, the contents consisted of a strong honey liquor. For the sake of politeness he took one swallow.

The barge swept around a bend in the river, and directly ahead, behind a high stone wall that stretched as far as one could see in any direction, lay a complex of buildings that stood higher than the largest temples in the city. This was the royal compound, the nerve center of an absolute monarchy. Short soldiers in white tunics and scarlet pantaloons, some armed with double-headed axes and others carrying long bows and quivers of arrows, were on hand to greet the party, and two officials escorted them to a handsome, European-style carriage pulled by a team of spirited, matched horses.

They rode through seemingly endless gardens, past building after building, and what Jonathan noted above all else was that the air here was pure and clean. At last he could breathe deeply. The carriage drew to a halt before a pavilion of marble, its roof held up by mammoth double rows of columns. This building, surrounded by what appeared to be a regiment of soldiers, was open on all sides and was lighted by clusters of blazing torches.

Mounds of cushions were piled on the perimeters of the pavilion, and reclining on them were middle-aged men, short and stocky, all wearing loose-fitting shirts and pantaloons. They were drinking from cups of gold and silver brought to them by girls who were naked to the waist, and it seemed strange to Jonathan that none of the men paid any attention to the young women.

Lai-tse lu divined his thoughts. "The girls are the king's concubines," she whispered. "Any man who touches one of them would be killed."

At the far end of the long pavilion was a dais, on which the mound of cushions was higher than anywhere else, and as the visitors approached it they were watched by a gray-haired man, somewhat taller and stockier than the others, who was being attended by a number of the scantily clad young women. A huge ring blazed on the forefinger of his left hand, and in his belt he carried a curved, jewel-hilted knife.

The fact that he was armed told Jonathan that this was His Most August Personage, King Rama III, the grandson of the ruler who had extended Siam's borders and made the nation the most powerful in Southeast Asia. The set of the monarch's mouth was cruel, but his dark eyes were lively and quick.

At the foot of the dais was a rug, and Chao and Lai-tse lu immediately prostrated themselves before King Rama. Sarah Applegate hesitated for an instant, then followed their example, her expression indicating her distaste for the gesture.

Jonathan bowed low, but nothing could persuade him to make a total obeisance.

Suddenly everyone in the pavilion was staring at the American. Men sat up on cushions, the girls serving

326

wine and drink to the king gaped, and Rama himself sat upright.

As Chao rose to his feet he looked deeply concerned.

Lai-tse lu gasped, then held her breath.

A squad of soldiers began to move forward unobtrusively.

Several of the men on the cushions closest to the dais muttered to each other in angry, low undertones.

"Tell His Most August Personage," Jonathan said to Chao in a clear, resonant baritone, "that I mean him no disrespect. In fact, I admire him for his leadership and the prosperity he has brought to his subjects. But I will kowtow to no one, not even my own President, Andrew Jackson, whom I believe to be the greatest man on earth."

Chao translated quickly into Siamese, his tone deferential.

King Rama sat unmoving, his glittering eyes so narrowed they looked like slits.

Jonathan knew he might be in serious trouble, but his principles were more important to him. Had he known what might develop, he would have found some excuse to remain on board his ship.

The squad of soldiers edged still closer.

King Rama exploded in laughter. He had granted audiences to few foreigners since his accession to the throne, only a handful of them white men, and this totally unexpected act of defiance amused him. He laughed until tears appeared in his eyes, and one of the concubines wiped his cheeks with a square of multi-colored silk.

The tension was broken, and the soldiers retreated.

Rama gestured, indicating that the visitors were being directed to sit on the cushions nearest the dais.

"You frightened me badly," Lai-tse lu murmured as she lowered herself to the mound.

"I wasn't any too comfortable myself," Jonathan replied.

Concubines brought the guests cups of honey liquor and platters heaped with spicy meat patties rolled in delicate crusts of baked bread. The chopped meat was so peppery he promptly choked on it.

"Land sakes, boy," Sarah whispered sharply, "stop calling attention to yourself."

Jonathan swallowed part of his drink, which burned his throat, but at least his cough subsided.

Rama launched into a long discussion with Soong Chao. Everyone else in the pavilion was ignored, and the two men, negotiating their trade agreement, might have been the only people present.

Ultimately, however, the king turned to one of the men nearby, and he contributed a few remarks. Later Jonathan would learn that he was the minister with whom Chao had opened negotiations.

Bored by the talk in a tongue he could not understand, Jonathan noted that Rama's gaze returned repeatedly to Lai-tse lu. The monarch eyed her closely, and he made no secret of his admiration for her.

Suddenly Rama pointed to her and made a speech in which the words poured out.

Chao waited until the tempest subsided and replied blandly.

The king spoke again even more vehemently and at greater length.

Again Chao replied in a mild voice.

Jonathan saw that Lai-tse lu was outwardly demure but that her shoulders were shaking with silent laughter.

Rama turned away from her, and the interminable business discussion was resumed.

At last an agreement was reached, and the king said something to several of his concubines, who promptly disappeared.

The girls returned a few moments later, bringing gifts to each of the guests. Soong Chao received a quill pen made of gold and studded with gems. Lai-tse lu was given a small jade object that Jonathan couldn't quite identify, but it was apparent that she was elated. And Sarah was handed a small statue of marble.

To the American's surprise he was given a gift, too, a length of pure, shimmering cloth of gold, as soft as it was pliant.

The audience had come to an end, and Chao, Lai-tse lu, and Sarah again prostrated themselves on the floor.

Again Jonathan bowed, which caused another royal burst of laughter.

"Don't try the king's patience too far," Lai-tse lu whispered to him as she stood. "We must continue to face him as we back out."

Jonathan felt foolish, but obeyed the injunction.

Not until they were on board the barge that would return them to their ship did Jonathan learn what had happened at the pavilion. King Rama had suggested, in the midst of his negotiations with Chao, that the merchant sell him Lai-tse lu as a concubine in return for a fortune in gold and gems. When Chao had refused, the monarch had countered with an offer to make her one of his wives.

"But my father told him that my marriage has been arranged to one of the ministers of the Tao Kuang Emperor," Lai-tse lu said. "Even Rama fears the wrath of the ruler of the Middle Kingdom, so the king said nothing more."

"But our strategy was effective, just as we had planned," Chao said happily.

Jonathan looked at him blankly, then turned to Lai-tse lu for an explanation.

"Rama is known everywhere in the East for his fondness for pretty young women. They are sent to him from many lands, and he pays very high prices for them. My father brought me on this journey because he knew Rama would want me and would be influenced in his negotiations."

"It is true," Chao said, "that the terms are more favorable than they otherwise would have been."

"Weren't you taking a great gamble, sir?" Jonathan asked. "Suppose the king had insisted?"

"There was no risk," Chao replied calmly. "I knew in advance what I would say."

Sarah laughed dryly. "Young man, you still have much to learn about the way business is done in the East!"

What mattered right now was that Soong Chao's business in Bangkok had been concluded. After they reached *Flying Dragon*, Jonathan learned from the merchant which of the water sellers might provide them with a supply of pure water. Casks were taken on board quickly, and the crew cheered when Jonathan gave the order to weigh anchor. Everyone on board was eager to put the heat and stench of Bangkok behind him.

Charles took the watch, and river traffic having subsided after dark, the clipper sailed swiftly toward the Gulf of Siam.

Chao retired, as did Sarah, but Lai-tse lu lingered behind, and a pleased Jonathan joined her on the aft deck.

"I was hoping we might have a few minutes to ourselves," he said. "What was King Rama's gift to you?"

She handed him an exquisitely carved, round medallion of magnificent jade.

Recognizing the expert craftsmanship, he saw a tree from which three branches protruded, the tiny leaves on the branches so well done they looked real.

"Do you know this symbol?" Lai-tse lu asked.

He shook his head.

"No symbol in all of the Middle Kingdom is greater," she explained. "The tree is the tree of life. The branch on the left signifies health. The big branch in the center stands for wisdom. The branch on the right signifies honor. He who has wisdom, health, and honor has his roots firmly planted in life itself." Her eyes shone in the moonlight as she studied the medallion.

A sudden thought leaped into Jonathan's mind. "Near the waterfront in Whampoa," he said, "I have seen the shop of a wood-carver whose work is very clever. He is a man of talent. If you wouldn't object, I would like to have him carve a large copy of this medallion."

"I wouldn't object, naturally. But why would you do this?"

"In my country," Jonathan said, "it is a custom for every ship to carry a figurehead—an ornament on her prow. Ever since I built *Flying Dragon,* I haven't been able to decide on an ornament that I wanted, an ornament that would be appropriate. Now I know. I want the tree of life. Because it will remind me of the way you looked just now, with the moon shining on your face."

She became shy, then recovered her poise. "I am honored," she murmured.

330

"There's something else." He reached behind him for the bolt of cloth of gold. "I'd like you to have this."

"I cannot take it. It is too valuable a gift. The peacock and peahen were more than enough!"

"I have no use for this cloth myself," he said. "My mother is dead, and I have no wife. It is appropriate that you—and only you—have it. It will give me great happiness if you will accept."

"Then you give me no choice," Lai-tse lu said simply. "For the sake of your happiness I must take it, Jonathan." She placed the bolt on a coil of heavy line and turned back to him, intending to thank him.

But their eyes met, and neither could speak. Their feelings, which they had suppressed for so long, overwhelmed them. With one accord they moved together into each other's arms, and their lips met in a lingering kiss, passionate yet tender, that obliterated all else from their world.

They were so lost in each other that neither heard Sarah Applegate come onto the deck.

Restless and unable to sleep, Sarah had decided she needed more fresh air to remove the memory of Bangkok's stench from her nostrils. She stopped short when she saw the couple in their tight, loving embrace, and for a moment she stood very still, gentle concern in her eyes.

They wanted each other so badly, and they were so young, so vulnerable that her heart ached for them. Creeping back to the cabin, she knew something had to be done, but this was not the moment to make plans. It was enough, for the moment, that she had been warned.

Book
IV

I

The trouble began shortly after Captain Frederick Flint sailed up the Pearl River Delta and docked his schooner at Owen Bruce's wharf in Whampoa. According to his manifest, which was false, Flint was carrying a cargo of woolen goods from England, and, as usual, Commodore Sir William Alexander ordered no inspection of the merchantman's hold. Normal procedures were observed as dockworkers in Bruce's employ began to carry the cargo, loaded in boxes that weighed approximately fifty pounds each, into the warehouse.

A simple accident sparked the difficulties. A young Cantonese worker, recently hired, piled too many boxes onto his cart, and when the top container fell to the ground it broke, spilling some of its contents on the ground. The worker was startled to find that the box contained raw opium, and in spite of the efforts of the English foreman to silence him, he made no secret of his discovery.

What happened next was unclear, and several stories, some of them conflicting, were told. It was established as a fact that the unfortunate dockworker was dragged into the warehouse, and that night persons unknown deposited his lifeless body on one of the unoccupied islands in the Delta.

The small vessel that carried him—some said it was a sampan, while others claimed it was a Western rowboat—was seen by the occupants of a fishing boat that happened to be returning late to its mooring. The crew investigated and found the worker's body, subsequently stating that the man had been bludgeoned to death.

Rumors began to fly, and the following day most of the Chinese in Bruce's employ refused to appear for work. Owen Bruce discharged the men on the spot and hired others. Canton's poor always clamored for work in the Whampoa warehouses of the foreigners. The incident appeared to be closed.

Two nights later, however, as Captain Flint was returning to his ship after spending the evening drinking in a Whampoa tavern, three unidentified assailants, all of them allegedly Chinese, attacked him as he was about to emerge from the dark alleyway near the tavern's entrance. There were no sounds of a fight, and the following morning an English foreman found Flint's body. The master of the schooner had been knifed repeatedly.

All hell promptly broke loose. The commodore paid a formal call on Soong Chao and requested him to convey a demand to the imperial viceroy that Flint's murderers be apprehended and handed over to the British for the administration of justice. Teng Ting-chen ignored the request.

The murder of an English sea captain was an act of violence that deeply disturbed the entire foreign community in Whampoa. No one was safe, they said, and at sundown that evening they sent all of their Chinese employees through the Petition Gate, instructing them not to return until morning. It was obvious that the crisis would grow worse.

Sir William Alexander had no personal sympathy for the late Captain Flint, but a British subject had been killed, and the commodore's duty was clear. In the morning four warships of the Royal Navy took up positions close to the shore and their gunports were lowered. Again Sir William called on Soong Chao, and this time he delivered an ultimatum. Unless the murderers were given into his custody within twenty-four hours, he would be obliged to shell Canton and would maintain the artillery barrage until his demands were met.

Some Cantonese panicked and fled into the hills, but most residents of the city appeared phlegmatic.

The viceroy conferred with members of his staff, then summoned Soong. "Do you think the British will actually make good their barbaric threat?" he asked.

"In my mind there is no question of it," the unhappy merchant replied. "Sir William is a civilized man, but he will be recalled to London in disgrace if he fails to act. The British believe their national honor has been sullied."

"Is honorable to kill thousands of innocent people?" Teng Ting-chen asked angrily.

"Certainly not, but that is the British way. They know our defenses are weak and that our war junks cannot drive off their great ships. I am certain that Alexander will do as he has threatened."

The viceroy thought of loading unmanned junks with explosives, casting them adrift in the vicinity of the British squadron, and sending them crashing into the warships. But the scheme was not realistic, so the mortified viceroy felt compelled to bow to the ultimatum.

It was impossible to discover the identity of Captain Flint's killers, so—as the British commanders later learned —imperial troops seized three citizens of Canton at random, and a scant hour before the deadline these bewildered innocents were taken in chains to Whampoa and handed over to the Royal Navy. White men were shocked by this extraordinary Chinese concept of justice, and their belief that they were dealing with a nation of untutored savages was confirmed.

Later that same morning *Flying Dragon* returned from a voyage to Djakarta, laden with pepper and other spices. She tied up at one of Soong Chao's wharves, and while dockworkers began to unload her cargo, Jonathan Rakehell went off with his customary escort to report to Soong Chao at his house. He knew nothing of the crisis, but noted that the people of Canton were more openly hostile to him than they had been. Many screamed, "Fan Kuei," and the members of his escort had to form a tight cordon around him in order to take him to his destination in safety.

Soon thereafter the three substitutes for Flint's murderers were taken on board the British flagship and in the presence of Commodore Sir William Alexander were hanged from the yardarm with due ceremony.

The Chinese employees of the foreign factories promptly deserted their duty posts and left Whampoa. News of the executions spread quickly, and armed mobs began to roam through the streets of Canton, searching for foreigners. No one blamed the imperial viceroy for the tragedy, and the people were unanimous in their agreement that the British alone were responsible for the deaths of three innocent men.

Kai brought news of the latest developments to Soong Chao as Jonathan was concluding his report.

The merchant ordered his majordomo to strengthen the guard detail on duty around the estate, then told the young American what had been happening.

"This is insane," Jonathan said. "I wasn't acquainted with Flint, but it was common knowledge that he was smuggling opium into Whampoa."

"Just as everyone has long known that Bruce hides it in his warehouse," Chao agreed with a sigh.

"What will happen now?"

"Who is to say? When men lose their ability to reason they behave like animals."

Jonathan's first concern was the safety of his crew and ship. "It seems to me that as fast as my cargo is unloaded, which should be some time this afternoon, I should put out to sea and stay there until the situation becomes calm again."

"I agree that it would be wise for *Flying Dragon* to leave Whampoa for the present," Chao replied. "But it will be necessary for Charles Boynton to take command. You will be obliged to remain here indefinitely as my guest."

"But—"

"The moment you leave this property you will be attacked. You won't live more than a few minutes, and it wouldn't surprise me if my own guards turned on you. Walk out of my gate, and you'll go to your certain death. You will stay here until tranquility is restored, and I urge you not to show yourself near the outer wall. So many hundreds and even thousands of our people would pour into the estate to tear you apart that an entire regiment of imperial troops could not give you adequate protection."

"But I'd feel like such a coward hiding here," Jonathan said.

"Surely you are mature enough to know the difference between cowardice and wisdom." Chao's tone was chiding. "Men have taken leave of their senses. The English who killed the dockworker were brutes, and so were the Chinese who murdered Flint. The opium issue is at the heart of this trouble, but that is a problem neither Sir William nor the viceroy can solve. The Celestial Emperor must find ways to enforce his edict against traffic in the drug and must compel the greedy British traders to obey his laws. Your death will solve nothing and will bring the end of the crisis no closer. All it will accomplish will be to cause hard feelings between the Middle Kingdom and the United States. What good will be done if the Americans also send warships here and threaten to bombard Canton?"

"I'm afraid you're right, sir," Jonathan said, his common sense overcoming his own wishes. "I'll stay. It seems I have no real choice."

Chao gave him paper, ink, and a brush, and Jonathan wrote a note to Charles, instructing him to put out to sea and stay there until peace was restored. A member of the guard detail immediately took the communication to Whampoa.

At dinner a short time later Lai-tse lu obviously was pleased that Jonathan would be an involuntary guest under her father's roof, but she made no comment. A disapproving Sarah Applegate assigned the visitor quarters in a small building that happened to be located across an inner courtyard from Lai-tse lu's living room and bedchamber.

"Kai is approximately your size," Chao said. "I shall see to it that he provides you with some shirts and trousers. And I shall give you a razor and some aromatic twigs for the brushing of your teeth."

Lai-tse lu remained silent until the soup that would end the meal was served. "It has bothered me for a long time that you speak no Chinese, Jonathan," she said.

"Now is the time for you to learn both Mandarin and Cantonese, and I shall be your teacher. We'll spend two hours every morning at your studies, and another two hours every afternoon, too."

He grinned at her as it dawned on him that his "imprisonment" would be less onerous than he had believed. The compensations more than outweighed the disadvantages.

Sarah frowned, but kept her thoughts to herself.

After the meal Jonathan accompanied Lai-tse lu to her sitting room, and his lessons began. He and the girl were so absorbed in each other and in what they were doing that the time flew.

Sarah found reasons to drop in on them frequently, but did not interrupt the lessons.

That evening the young couple adjourned to Chao's library and spent the evening reading. Chao went off to a conference at the viceroy's palace, and Sarah stationed herself on the terrace of her own quarters, where she could see the young people in the library. To her relief they behaved decorously, but when they rose to go off to their separate bedchambers for the night they embraced at length just inside the library entrance. Their proximity would create an explosive situation, the governess knew, but there seemed to be nothing she could do to halt the inevitable. Circumstances were conspiring against what she believed right.

In the morning Jonathan was served a breakfast of broiled fish, rice, cheese, and tea in his own quarters. Then, as he was going out into the garden to practice throwing his Indonesian knives, he encountered his host.

"Affairs are still very bad," Chao said. "Troops have been stationed at the Petition Gate and along the length of the Whampoa wall to prevent mobs from burning and looting the foreign factories. I have closed my own warehouses and posted strong guard details there until the trouble ends."

"Did Charles receive my message?"

"Yes, and he went out to sea as soon as he took on water and enough supplies to last for at least a month."

"Do you think the turmoil will last that long?" Jonathan was dismayed.

Chao shrugged. "Tempers are so high it is useless to predict. Two other American ships have followed the example of *Flying Dragon* and have gone off to sea, too. But a number of foreign ships are still at the wharves, and they make a tempting target for the mobs. Much will depend on the ability of the viceroy to persuade or force the people not to attack more foreigners. I intend to visit Sir William Alexander myself later today to see if he will cooperate with us in preventing new outrages. Right now no man can say what will happen from one day to the next."

Relieved because *Flying Dragon* and her crew were out of danger, Jonathan went on to a wall-enclosed garden. There he set up an old latticework of bamboo as a target and began to throw his knives at it.

Someone approached behind him and, unobserved, watched him. Kai was depressed because, like most members of the Society of Oxen, he believed the time was ripe to rid Canton permanently of all foreigners. But Lo Fang had insisted that the will of the imperial viceroy had to be obeyed. Teng Ting-chen was afraid that excesses would lead to violent Fan Kuei reprisals, so the Society of Oxen and the city's other secret societies were acting as a moderating force, holding the citizens in check.

Perhaps, Kai reflected, the viceroy was right. This young American who was throwing knives with surprising, deadly accuracy was in his master's employ and served him faithfully and honestly. Society of Oxen members checked *Flying Dragon*'s cargo every time she returned to Whampoa, and her manifests were precise and correct. What was even more important, she had never brought as much as an ounce of opium to Canton. The majordomo had seen for himself that this foreigner and Lai-tse lu were falling in love with each other, and at first he had been outraged, but he had to admit he was changing his mind. Here was a man who showed as much respect for Chinese as he did for his own people. So it was at least possible that Lai-tse lu was right.

Kai was willing to give this Fan Kuei the benefit of the doubt, but wanted to make up his own mind about him. For that purpose he would need to know the American better, so he deliberately moved forward.

Jonathan practiced his few words of newly acquired Cantonese. "Good morning," he said, then pointed to the borrowed shirt and trousers he was wearing. "Thank you."

Kai smiled slightly and bowed, then indicated with a gesture that the guest should go on with his knife-throwing.

"Would you care to join me?" Jonathan asked in English, then indicated in pantomine what he meant.

The majordomo promptly took several knives, threw them, and had to laugh when he discovered that none hit the target.

Jonathan showed him the proper way to balance, take aim, and release a knife.

Kai tried again, then again, and showed some improvement. Suddenly he seemed to lose interest in what he was doing, however, and left the garden.

Surprised by his abrupt departure, Jonathan resumed his practice.

A short time later Kai reappeared, carrying two padded jackets, one of which he gave to the American.

Jonathan was puzzled. Lai-tse lu came into the garden and took charge. After bidding Jonathan good morning, she said, "You have honored Kai by giving him a lesson in throwing of Indonesian knives. Now he wishes to honor you in return by teaching you the ancient martial arts of the Middle Kingdom. He wants you to wear the jacket."

Jonathan donned it, not knowing what would happen next.

Kai handed him a bamboo rod, about a foot long, that had been filled with lead.

"Now," Lai-tse lu said, "he wants you to strike him with the club. He wants you to try as hard as you can to beat him with it."

Jonathan took the club and looked uncertainly at the burly man. Kai turned to the girl. "It is not seemly that a woman should be present," he said in Cantonese.

Lai-tse lu wanted to protest, but knew he was right. "I am being sent away," she told Jonathan. "Later you

will have your next lesson in Mandarin and Cantonese."
She smiled and darted away.

Kai indicated in pantomime that he wanted the Fan
Kuei to strike him.

Jonathan half-heartedly cut at him.

The majordomo was obviously annoyed and urged
him to show greater vigor.

This time Jonathan slashed in earnest.

But Kai raised a hand and lashed out with a sharp
yet harmless blow that struck his opponent's forearm
deflecting the strike.

Now Jonathan understood and entered the game
with enthusiasm, wielding the club as he would a sword,
sometimes feinting, sometimes slashing. But no matter
how great his efforts, the Chinese remained unscathed.
The man's footwork was magnificent, and he seemed to
possess a sixth sense that would tell him where the next
blow would be aimed.

Then Kai took the club, placing the American on
the defensive, and showed him in slow motion how to
protect himself.

They worked for an hour, with Kai demonstrating
basic positions, then forcing his opponent to defend himself. Occasionally he slipped past the American's guard,
and the club thumped against Jonathan's chest or shoulders, but the heavily padded jacket protected him. By the
time Kai called a halt both were sweating heavily.

A grinning Kai led Jonathan to a pool surrounded
by a high brick fence, and there they stripped off their
clothes and plunged into the cool water. When they
emerged Kai indicated in pantomime that the following
day they would throw Indonesian knives together and
would have another session in the martial arts.

Clad in clean clothes, Jonathan went off for his lessons with Lai-tse lu in Mandarin and Cantonese. At least
he wasn't wasting his time on his unplanned and un-
wanted holiday, he thought. His most immediate problem
was that of concentrating on language when all he wanted
to do was watch the movement of Lai-tse lu's lips.

He would have been less complacent had he known
that he was a subject for discussion between Soong Chao

343

and Sir William Alexander on board the commodore's flagship in the Whampoa harbor.

"I've been told by Owen Bruce," Sir William said, "that Captain Rakehell is staying at your house."

"Indeed he is," the merchant replied. "As you no doubt know, he and his crew have been working for me under contract, in various trading voyages. The least I can do for him is to offer him the protection of my house. The temper of our people is such that he wouldn't reach Whampoa alive."

"Speaking personally," the commodore said, "I must applaud your generosity. But I'll be placed in an awkward position if Bruce makes a formal protest to me."

"What protest could he make?"

"As you must realize, he doesn't care for Rakehell and young Boynton. They've taken such a strong position against carrying opium that they've irritated him. Bruce has already intimated to me that Rakehell—already your employee, mind you—is actively conniving against the white merchants and traders."

"I urge Bruce to mind his own affairs," Soong Chao declared.

"That's what I've already told him. Remember, it was his staff who created the initial problem here by killing the dockworker, and I'm sure he wants to draw attention away from himself."

"We have more important matters that concern us than a guest in my home," Chao said. "The viceroy and I are afraid that another spark will cause troubles no one can curb."

"I've written a report to London that will satisfy the Admiralty and the House of Commons," the commodore replied. "Every foreigner here knows better than to wander into Canton. If the Chinese on the staffs of the factories will return to work, we should have a gradual return to normality. In the meantime no ships can be unloaded, and our people are complaining because they must cook their own meals and make their own beds."

"Not even Teng Ting-chen would dare to order the Cantonese who work in Whampoa to return to their posts," Chao said. "The foreigners will continue to suffer inconveniences for a time. And the port will remain closed until tempers cool. I see no alternative."

"Neither do I, really," Sir William said. "I regret everything that's happened, as I'm sure you do. I hate to see shipowners and merchants suffering losses, but I'm afraid that only the passage of time will heal the wounds that have opened in the past few days."

"No one's losses are greater than mine," Chao said. "Six of my junks sit idly at anchor, and *Flying Dragon* will remain at sea until trade can be resumed. But I far prefer to be earning no money than to see the blood of Chinese and foreigners being spilled needlessly."

Sir William nodded gravely.

"Eventually, I am certain all will be well again," Chao said. "But the seeds sown in this unpleasantness will take root and grow. Foreigners must learn patience in the opening of the Middle Kingdom to their trade, just as Peking must learn that we cannot remain isolated forever from the West. I pray that even uglier incidents won't occur in the years ahead."

"When they do," the commodore said, "I hope I'll have retired and will be spending my time growing roses in my garden back home."

"When they take place," Chao said with a wry smile, "I shall be right here. Canton is my home, and no nastiness will drive me elsewhere."

Jonathan's routines were well established by the time he had spent a week in the house of Soong Chao. Every morning he and Kai worked first on knife throwing, then practiced the ancient martial arts of the Middle Kingdom. After he bathed he spent the rest of the morning taking language lessons from Lai-tse lu, and they resumed their sessions again immediately after dinner. Neither quite realized what was happening, but they took such delight in each other's company that the lessons grew longer and longer.

Every evening they went together to the library to read, and it was here that the tensions building between them became increasingly evident. No longer content with a single goodnight kiss, they lingered inside the entrance,

345

embracing and kissing repeatedly, their mutual desire mounting.

No one was more aware of the situation and its dangers than Sarah Applegate. One night, after the young couple spent more than a quarter of an hour kissing, she knew she could remain silent no longer, and as soon as they parted she made her way to Chao's workroom, where he was making an estimate of the losses he had been suffering.

Lai-tse lu, knowing her governess as well as Sarah knew her, caught a glimpse of her as she marched down the path. On sudden impulse the girl doubled back, left the path, and made her way through the connecting gardens to the far side of her father's workroom. The windows were open, and by standing close to the pagoda outside the window directly behind her father's table, she could hear the conversation clearly.

The discussion was already in progress. "I suppose I should have come to you at once when I saw them kissing on board *Flying Dragon*," Sarah said. "But I couldn't help sympathizing with them. Now I'm afraid for them. They spend more and more time kissing in the library before they part for the night, and it's just a matter of time before they lose control. How much longer will Jonathan be obliged to stay here?"

"Many days," Chao said.

"By then it will be too late," Sarah said in dismay.

Lai-tse lu was astonished to hear her father chuckle.

"I am not surprised by what you tell me, Sarah," he said. "I have seen the way they look at each other when we sit at the table. But the problem is not nearly as serious as you would make it."

"For an intelligent man," the governess replied tartly, "you're being incredibly short-sighted."

"You fail to understand the nature of the male," he said. "And the solution is far simpler than you appear to realize."

"How so?" Sarah demanded, challenging him.

"Jonathan is young, and like any healthy man of his age he is hot-blooded. He needs a woman, to put it to you bluntly. Once he has been satisfied, his ardor for Lai-tse lu will lessen."

A chill ran up the girl's spine. She hadn't dreamed her father could be so matter-of-fact about a matter of such overwhelming importance to her.

"I will arrange for him to be visited by a woman who will satisfy his desires," Chao said. "He will give in to his natural inclinations, and then he will look at my daughter with indifference. She will become aware of the change in his attitude, and because she has great pride, she will draw back, too."

The girl clenched her fists.

"The thought has been in my mind ever since he was forced to stay here," Chao continued, "and now I shall act upon it. I shall have Kai make the necessary arrangements."

"But what makes you think Jonathan will be agreeable?"

"Nature will take its course," he said confidently. "Lai-tse lu and Jonathan spend about two hours together in the library after the evening meal, is it not so?"

"Well, yes."

The girl held her breath, edging still closer to the window.

"Tomorrow night," Chao said, "Kai will hide the woman in his own quarters. When my daughter and Jonathan leave the library, I will call him here, and I will delay him with talk for about a half-hour. At the end of that time Lai-tse lu will have gone to bed. When Jonathan returns to his rooms, the woman will be waiting for him."

Tears of indignation came to the girl's eyes, but she blinked them away furiously.

"The scheme might be effective," Sarah said dubiously. "I would disapprove of such immorality under ordinary circumstances, but this situation calls for drastic means. It seems to me that everything will depend upon Jonathan's willingness to have—ah—relations with just any woman."

"We must leave that to the woman," Chao replied serenely. "Kai will procure the services of one who is wise

347

in the ways and desires of men. I think we can rely on her talents."

Lai-tse lu had heard enough and silently made her way back to her own building. Her mind was seething, and at that moment she hated her father and Sarah, even though she realized they were acting in what they regarded as her best interests.

Surely there had to be some way to prevent them from carrying out their plan! She knew for certain now that the feelings building up within her over recent months were genuine: she loved Jonathan Rakehell with all her heart.

She intended to allow no other woman to come between them. If she warned Jonathan, or if she told her father she knew of his plan, the scheme would be altered in some way. Her father was far too subtle to admit defeat quickly, and she had to find some other way to thwart him. Making no attempt to sleep, she lay motionless on her bed for hours.

At last a solution came to mind, and she fell into a deep, satisfying sleep. She did not awaken until late the following morning, so late that she had to hurry in order to meet Jonathan in time for his language lesson.

She was at peace with herself, outwardly demure, inwardly serene. She gave no indication to her father or Sarah that she was aware of what was afoot. Jonathan noted that she seemed quietly pleased with herself, but he had no idea of what was in store, and the day passed like those that had preceded it.

That evening, after reading together in the library, the young couple moved together toward the entrance, as they always did. But Lai-tse lu did not linger. Instead, she allowed Jonathan to kiss her only briefly, her quick smile indicating to him that she was not upset or displeased with him in any way.

When they emerged into the open, Kai was on hand to tell Jonathan that Soong Chao wanted to confer with him in the workroom.

"Good night," Jonathan said to Lai-tse lu. "I look forward to my lesson tomorrow morning."

"So do I," she said, and hurried off to her own quarters.

She saw at a glance that oil lamps were burning in Jonathan's sitting room on the far side of the court. She was pressed for time, and now that the moment had come to act she was filled with doubts and reservations, but she couldn't afford to hesitate. Her heart hammering, she crossed the courtyard quickly and entered the sitting room without knocking.

A young woman clad only in a flimsy, short dressing gown, her face heavily made up, rose to her feet, and Lai-tse lu noted uneasily that she was exceptionally attractive.

Alice Wong was startled by the unexpected appearance of this beautiful girl, whose youth and loveliness she instantly envied.

"I am Soong Lai-tse lu. You are she who has been summoned here to give pleasure to the Fan Kuei from the clipper ship."

Alice nodded, trying to hide her own surprise. When Lo Fang and Kai had approached her with this offer, for which Soong Chao was paying generously, they hadn't mentioned that the foreigner with whom she was to make love was a member of *Flying Dragon*'s company. This was an unfortunate complication. She saw Charles Boynton regularly and freely admitted to herself that her involvement with him was becoming deeper. How he would react when and if he learned that she was granting her favors to one of his associates she didn't know, and her uncertainty made her apprehensive.

In any event, she couldn't imagine why the daughter of Soong Chao was interfering in a matter that was of no concern to a lady, so she merely stared at the younger girl.

"I—I want to ask a great boon of you," Lai-tse lu said, "and whatever the fee my father has paid to you, I will double it."

In spite of herself Alice was interested.

"Let me substitute for you," Lai-tse lu said earnestly. "I will make certain the bedroom is very dark, and the Fan Kuei will not know the identity of the woman with whom he lies."

Alice was so startled she made no reply.

"I beg you to do this," Lai-tse lu said. "And we must act quickly, before he arrives."

Alice studied her, still stunned by the whole idea. "Why do you wish to do this?" she asked, finding it difficult to believe that a wealthy member of a high mandarin class, a woman who enjoyed every advantage, would willingly demean herself.

Lai-tse lu found it difficult to meet the other's steady gaze. "I cannot tolerate the thought that he will lie with someone else," she said.

Alice understood, and smiled. "You love him, then."

"As I have not loved and never could love any other man," Lai-tse lu said.

The mystery was solved. Alice had been careful to conceal the depth and intensity of her own feelings for Charles from him and from everyone else, including her grandparents, so she could sympathize with the reaction of this lovely, intense girl. "How would you substitute for me?"

Hope flared within Lai-tse lu. "My dwelling is there, on the far side of the courtyard," she said. "We will change clothes, and you will go to my quarters. Sleep in my bed, if you wish, and before daybreak I will return. Then we will change places again, and no one else in all the world will ever know the secret that you and I will share."

The plan was so ingenious that Alice laughed. "I will agree to do this for you, but on one condition. I have already been paid many silver yuan for services I will not perform. I cannot accept more money from you."

"I insist."

"No," Alice said. "Only one who has come to love a Fan Kuei herself would know how you feel. I do this for you. I make you a gift, from one woman to another."

Lai-tse lu was overwhelmed. But time was pressing and she could not tarry, so she removed her cheongsam and silk underclothes, and while Alice dressed in them she donned the short, flimsy dressing gown.

Alice paused at the door. "May you attain your heart's desire," she said softly, then went out into the night and crossed the courtyard to the dwelling on the far side.

Lai-tse lu watched her until she disappeared inside, then raced into the bedchamber and made certain that the bamboo blinds were closed. Taking no chances, she also drew the heavy drapes of silk at the sides of the windows, leaving them open just enough to admit air from the outside. The chamber was so dark now that she could no longer see any of the furniture, so she was satisfied.

Then it occurred to her, belatedly, that Jonathan would not leave the room in darkness. Certainly he would pick up one of the oil lamps in his sitting room and carry it with him. This was a contingency for which she hadn't planned, and a sense of panic assailed her.

Fighting for self-control, she knew of only one place she could conceal herself. Groping in the dark, she made her way to the high, ornately carved chest of drawers that stood at the far side of the chamber. It was placed about a foot from the wall, and she had to use all of her strength to move it slightly, just enough so she could squeeze behind it.

That task accomplished, there was nothing to do but wait, her heart pounding, her blood singing in her ears.

An eternity passed before the outer door opened and Jonathan entered the sitting room. He stayed there for what seemed like a long time, and the girl in the bedchamber had no idea what he might be doing.

At last he came into the bedroom, carrying an oil lamp. He placed it on top of the chest of drawers, only inches above her head.

She tried to crouch even lower behind the chest, scarcely daring to breathe.

Jonathan undressed swiftly, methodically, then walked to the windows.

For a moment Lai-tse lu was afraid he intended to open the drapes and blinds.

Instead, he left the drapes slightly ajar, and parting two of the blinds with his fingers, he peered out into the night.

It occurred to the girl that he was staring in the direction of her bedchamber, and she was overjoyed. For an instant she hoped that the lady of pleasure wouldn't be standing near the windows, but it occurred to her that the woman was too sensible to reveal her identity to anyone who might be wandering around the compound. It was in her own interest to remain securely hidden.

All at once it dawned on Lai-tse lu that Jonathan was nude. The enormity of what she was doing caused her knees to shake, but at the same time she couldn't help admiring his rugged physique.

At last he turned away from the windows and extinguished the oil lamp.

As he walked a few steps to the bed the girl squirmed out of her hiding place. He was a dark blur in front of her, and she reached up quickly, silently, and curled her arms around his neck.

The startled Jonathan muttered under his breath as he involuntarily took a backward step. Then he became aware of the girl's naked body beneath her open robe. "What in the devil—"

She silenced him with a kiss. The darkness made her bold, the daring of the escapade caused her to cast aside the inhibitions she had shown when they had kissed in the library, and she no longer tried to hide the overwhelming urgency of her own desire.

The body pressing against his was slender and well-formed, and the woman's passion made it impossible for him to resist her. Precisely as Soong Chao had predicted, his own desire came alive.

Lai-tse lu pressed still closer to him, reveling in their intimacy.

Unable to resist this woman whose jasmine scent filled his nostrils, Jonathan picked her up and carried her to the bed. He peered at her, trying to see her more clearly in the dark, but she caught hold of him by the waist and pulled him down beside her, her body demanding exploration.

There was no doubt in Jonathan's mind that he wanted this wench, who was simultaneously brazen and gentle, and he put aside the question of her identity as he began to make love to her in earnest.

Her hands and mouth, body and tongue were as

active as his in their explorations. All that she had dreamed was coming true.

Her eagerness to be loved swept away the last of Jonathan's reservations, and he took her, so passionately that he did not perceive that she was a virgin. Their mutual desire thundered to a climax, and never had he known such lovemaking with any woman. Nothing mattered except their wild, shared yearning.

Their universe seemed to explode, and then they caressed quietly as their passion ebbed.

They rested for a time, and then Jonathan asked, "Who are you?"

She made no reply.

Aware that he had spoken in English, he repeated the question in Mandarin, then in Cantonese.

Lai-tse lu had to curb an almost uncontrollable desire to giggle. Her pupil was proving himself adept in both Chinese tongues.

Jonathan sat up, intending to light the oil lamp.

She guessed what he wanted to do, and reaching for him, she took the initiative of fresh lovemaking.

They dallied longer, and there was a sweet quality in the woman that surprised Jonathan. He assumed she was a trollop, of course, but at times she seemed uniquely shy until, encouraged by his own ministrations, she became bolder again. Ultimately, when they soared to another crescendo, all else was blotted from their minds.

They rested sleepily, side by side, and to Lai-tse lu's sudden horror she realized that Jonathan was fingering the Tree of Life medallion King Rama of Siam had given her. Because Jonathan had so admired it she wore it day and night suspended from a gold chain around her neck, and in her haste when she had changed clothes with the lady of pleasure she had forgotten to remove it.

Given enough time, he might identify it, so she moved close to him again, nestling against him, and the medallion was forgotten. Soon the girl feigned sleep, and she could feel the man beside her becoming drowsier.

Not until his deep, even breathing told her that he was sound asleep did she free herself from his embrace, don the flimsy robe, and creep out of the building.

Terrified that someone might see her, she raced barefooted across the gravel walk to her own dwelling.

Alice Wong had found a bottle of rice wine and was sipping from a glass when the younger girl entered. There was no need to ask any questions: the expression of bliss in Lai-tse lu's eyes expressed her sentiments.

There was no need for conversation between these two whose paths, in all likelihood, would not cross again. Alice retrieved her robe, and on sudden impulse she embraced Lai-tse lu lightly before going off to the house of the waiting Kai.

The majordomo looked up as she entered.

Alice waited until she was attired in her own cheongsam and they were walking toward the palanquin bearers awaiting her inside the main gate before she spoke. "You may give your master a message," she said. "Tell him that never has the Fan Kuei known such ecstasy. He will remember this night to the end of his life."

Early morning daylight that entered the bedchamber through the small opening in the drapes awakened Jonathan. His memory of the previous night inundated him in a sudden rush, and he reached for the woman, but she had gone. Only a scent of jasmine and the indentation in the pillow beside his told him that she had truly been present, that they really had made love.

He threw the drapes open, then searched both rooms of the dwelling thoroughly, but she had left nothing behind, vanishing as mysteriously as she had appeared.

As he ate the breakfast that a servant brought to his quarters, he pondered on the strange experience, unable to understand why he had been selected as the partner of the silent woman who had given herself to him so unstintingly. Certainly she had not been able to enter and leave the closely guarded estate unnoticed, which meant that someone in a position of authority had known of her presence.

When he went off for his session of Indonesian knife throwing and martial arts practice with Kai, however, the majordomo was bland, nothing in his manner indicating an awareness that anything out of the ordinary had taken place.

What Kai actually noted was that Jonathan's aim with the knives was unerring, that there was a greater spring and resilience in his body when they came to blows in the martial arts. Apparently Alice Wong had been telling the truth when she had said that he had enjoyed himself. Soong Chao would be pleased to hear it.

When Jonathan appeared at Lai-tse lu's dwelling for his lessons in Mandarin and Cantonese, he noted instantly that the girl was more radiant than he had ever seen her. In fact, she seemed to be lighted by an inextinguishable inner glow.

At the same time, however, she was inexplicably shy, unable to meet his gaze for more than an instant at a time before averting her face.

He had reached a stage in his lessons where he was composing entire sentences, with Lai-tse lu adding words to his vocabulary, and as they worked a familiar scent struck his nostrils. As always, she was wearing a jasmine perfume, and all at once he realized that the odor was identical to that worn by the woman with whom he had made love. Surely it hadn't been Lai-tse lu who had come to him.

Stunned by the possibility, he faltered in his composition of a sentence. "I'm sorry," he said. "I seem to find it difficult to concentrate this morning."

A tiny, secret smile briefly touched the corners of her mouth.

He peered at her even more intently, and then his eyes became riveted on the jade Tree of Life medallion hanging below the mandarin collar of her solid-colored silk cheongsam. All at once he recalled having fleetingly felt the jewelry that the unseen woman had been wearing. It had been a carved medallion, he was certain of that much. Now that he thought about it, he recalled having felt the main trunk and the branches of the tree, although he hadn't recognized them at the time.

His doubts vanished, and he felt a positive conviction that it had been Lai-tse lu who had come to him and who had given herself to him so unstintingly!

Of course. That explained her unique blend of shyness and boldness.

Now he could understand the entire incident. She had wanted him as much as he had wanted her, but their complicated situation had made it impossible for her to come to him openly. She was a lady of high standing who, according to an ancient, strict tradition, could sleep only with her husband. Certainly her father, if he knew what had happened, would banish her without hesitation to their country house located somewhere in the interior of the province.

She had fulfilled her own desire—and Jonathan's—by coming to him in secret, by making sure that even he would not be able to identify her positively.

Jonathan had to accept her chosen method of handling their relationship, at least for the immediate future. Only if he obtained her father's permission to marry her, an agreement that would not be granted as yet, if ever, would he be able to reveal to her that he knew it was she with whom he had made love.

Yet he had to let her know what he thought of her. He couldn't allow her to believe he had been content to bed a trollop and that the incident had lacked meaning for him.

Jonathan reached out and gently placed his hand on Lai-tse lu's. Then he spoke slowly, in halting but distinct Mandarin. "There is something I want you to know," he said huskily. "Of all the women who live in this world, you are unique."

She made no reply and her head was lowered.

But he felt sure he saw tears of happiness gleam in her eyes. A resolve hardened within him. The obstacles that stood in the way of their permanent union were great, but he would have to overcome them. The differences in their races and backgrounds meant nothing to him, and obviously she was indifferent to them, too. One way or another her father and Sarah Applegate had to be persuaded that he was the right husband for her, that he would take care of her and cherish her as long as they lived.

The late afternoon had become a very special time of day in Jeremiah Rakehell's New London house. By the time he came home from the shipyard, his grandson had awakened from his afternoon nap and was ready for a romp. More often than not they were joined by Dr. Graves, who thoroughly enjoyed the sessions, too. The grandfathers took turns holding the baby, bouncing him on their knees. Little Julian babbled with pleasure, and the two old men laughed out loud.

As Louise confided privately to her mother, the din they made was deafening, and she believed they spoiled the baby outrageously, giving him so many toys. All the same, she was reluctant to curtail these late afternoon sessions because they were the only men of consequence in Julian's life. Lacking a father, he needed substitutes.

It wasn't easy for Louise to sit through these sessions, but she forced herself to be present, even on days like this when she suffered from one of the headaches that made her feel as though a hatchet had smashed into the back of her skull. She no longer mentioned her headaches because the medication her father had given her for them gave her no relief, and she was tired of listening to his lectures to the effect that she would find herself cured when Jonathan came home.

In her private opinion, Jonathan would never return.

"Julian," Jeremiah said, "if Grandpa Graves will be kind enough to hold you on my back, I'll give you a ride on a bucking bronco."

Another gurgle of pleasure from the baby inspired loud laughter in both grandfathers.

Louise decided she had to curb their enthusiasm. Pressing both hands to her temples for a moment, she said, "You're going to excite him too much."

"Nonsense," Dr. Graves said. "I've never known a little excitement to hurt a healthy baby."

"Perhaps not," Louise replied, "but it certainly is upsetting his mother."

Jeremiah and Martin exchanged quick glances.

"Louise," her father said, "I want to give you some advice, professional advice. You need to go away for a little holiday."

"I've offered to take her on a shopping trip to New York or Boston, but she won't hear of it," Jeremiah said.

"I have no need for any new clothes," Louise replied listlessly. "I never go out anywhere, and there's no place I really want to go."

"I'm sure your mother would be delighted to go off to a resort with you," Martin said.

"Thank you, Papa, but I'd be bored."

Julian reached for the watch chain of heavy gold links and stuffed a portion into his mouth.

"He's teething already," Dr. Graves said with satisfaction.

Louise's lingering sigh seemed to hang in the air.

Again the two men looked at each other, and Dr. Graves cleared his throat. "Young woman," he said, "you've got to do what no one else can possibly do for you. Pull yourself together."

"That's so easy to say, Papa. I'm in a delicate, compromised position, and there's no way it can be changed."

"We've discussed this many times," Jeremiah said. "Jonathan will marry you—he'll want to marry you—the very moment he comes home."

"If he comes home," she said.

"I can imagine no reason he won't," Jeremiah declared.

"Every family in this town is related to someone whose ship has been lost at sea. I don't see why it should be so unusual for me to assume that something terrible has happened to *Flying Dragon*."

"It's very unlikely," Jeremiah said.

"I don't see why. Just because he's a Rakehell doesn't make him immune to the sea. And no one knows what one of these new clippers might or might not do in a bad storm."

"You've become very morbid, and it isn't like you," her father said severely.

"After all this time," she said, "you'd think someone might have heard from him."

The two men carefully averted their gazes, burdened by their guilts. Never could they reveal to Louise that they

358

had destroyed the letter in which Jonathan had asked her to cancel their betrothal.

"Only a handful of ships from the United States visit the Orient," Jeremiah said at last. "Some that do go there stay for long periods, as Jonathan appears to be doing. The profits can be very high, you know."

"That sounds reasonable to me." Dr. Graves tried not to sound glib. "Besides, I believe I'm right when I say that most American ships engaged in the Eastern trade have their home ports in New York or Charleston these days."

"That's correct," Jeremiah said.

"There you are, Louise. The masters of such ships well might be reluctant to carry mail for New Englanders. They'd not only be obliged to keep the letters safe on a long voyage, but they'd have to post them after they returned here. I urge you to be more patient."

"It isn't easy to be patient for month after month after month!" the harried young woman retorted.

"Well, I know Jonathan is alive and well," Jeremiah said forcefully.

Louise just looked at him.

Afraid he had spoken out of turn, he had to cover his tracks. "Ships' officers have their own methods of communication," he said. "They pass along news to each other when they meet in various ports, and word has come back to me from some of our own captains that Jonathan has been seen in Canton and is thriving there."

"All I care about," Louise said, "is that he comes back here long enough to make Julian legitimate. Then, as far as I'm concerned, he can sail his beloved clipper off to the far ends of the earth again!"

The realization dawned on the two men that, regardless of what she might have felt before Jonathan had gone off to Cathay, Louise was no more in love with him than he was with her. Perhaps his letter urging her to break their engagement was an accurate appraisal of the way both of them felt.

Well, their feelings didn't matter. Julian was already a very real person, and his grandfathers would not rest until he legally became a Rakehell.

came rather close to Soong, Lai-tec in which, you were
forced to stay at her father's house. What about Louise?"

I wrote to her many months ago, suggesting that she

II

After cruising aimlessly in the South China Sea for two and a half weeks, Charles Boynton grew tired of doing nothing. Putting into Hong Kong Island and dropping anchor in the magnificent natural harbor which lay between the mainland of China and the uninhabited island, he found several other foreign merchantmen already berthed there. Going ashore with his crew for water, he learned from colleagues that the situation in Canton appeared to be quiet.

Charles discussed the problem with Edmund Barker, and they decided to take the risk of returning to Whampoa. If it proved necessary, they agreed, they would go to sea again. So *Flying Dragon* weighed anchor, sailed slowly up the Pearl River Delta, and docked at one of Soong Chao's wharves the following morning.

The clipper's company was not alone in hoping that normal activities soon would be resumed. A British schooner was docked in front of Owen Bruce's factory, and a French sloop and a Swedish barque also had put into port. *Flying Dragon* was followed by a merchantman flying the flag of the Netherlands that had a mixed Dutch and Indonesian crew.

Charles went ashore immediately to assess the situation for himself and quickly discovered that only guards were on duty at Soong's warehouse. A strong detail of Chinese soldiers was still stationed at the Petition Gate, prohibiting all foreigners from entering the city, but there were signs that the tempers of the Cantonese were cooling and that the crisis soon would ease.

The most hopeful indication was the gradual return of Chinese employees to their positions on the staffs of the foreigners. No dockworkers had shown up as yet, but cooks and gardeners, along with other household help, were drifting back to Whampoa singly or in pairs. Even more significant was the mysterious appearance of fresh vegetables, fish, meat, and eggs. These supplies apparently had not been carried through the Petition Gate, but the whites who had been living on dried and pickled foods for almost three weeks were grateful and asked no embarrassing questions at the market.

Hoping to obtain further information and, perhaps, learn how Jonathan was faring, Charles went to the tavern frequented by officers. Although it was only noon the establishment was already doing a thriving business, and Charles, unable to find a seat at a table, stood at the bar and sipped a mug of ale.

He was alone for only a short time before someone came up beside him. "I saw you docking, Boynton," Owen Bruce said.

Charles felt intense dislike for the factory owner, but nevertheless was civil. "Our inactivity made us impatient. From the little I've been able to glean, it would seem that the worst is over."

Bruce grimaced. "This long delay was unnecessary. You're English, so I'm sure you'll agree with the view that the crisis could have been ended in a day if the Royal Navy had bombarded the city. The Chinamen would have buckled fast enough!"

Charles stared at him. "A bombardment," he said, "would have been an act of war."

"It's the only language these illiterate peasants understand." Bruce inched closer to him. "Boynton," he said, lowering his voice, "I wonder if you've considered the possibility that you may be taking permanent command of your clipper."

"It hadn't occurred to me," Charles replied. "Captain Rakehell is still the principal owner and master."

"Your Captain Rakehell is in serious trouble," the

factory owner declared. "He's openly sided with the Chinamen, and he's spent this entire siege in Canton. My God! My blood boils when I think that he's the only white man in the town."

Charles looked at him coldly. "Captain Rakehell happened to be in the city on business when the trouble started. There was no way he could return to his ship, and he's been very fortunate that he's been given shelter by his host."

"Oh, that's his story, I'm sure," Bruce said with a sneer. "But he won't get away with it. I've collected signatures for a formal protest to Commodore Alexander, and even though Sir William may be a weakling, he'll be forced to take action." He paused, caught hold of his listener's lapel, and murmured, "See me when you take command of the clipper. I'll guarantee you an income many times larger than what you've been making from Soong Chao. There's no real money to be earned by dealing with the co-hong."

"I suppose," Charles said, "that you'd want me to sail to India for opium and bring it here."

Bruce winked. "We won't go into details until you're in charge. Just believe me, Boynton, you won't regret it."

"Sir," Charles said quietly, "I can imagine no developments that would deprive Captain Rakehell of his command. In any event, his views and mine are identical. Opium was directly responsible for the present crisis, as you know even better than I, and far worse will happen if unscrupulous people continue to smuggle it into China and break the laws of the emperor. No matter how great the profits, *Flying Dragon* will never engage in the opium trade!"

Giving the startled merchant no time to reply, Charles turned and stalked out, so angry that he failed to see the malice in the Scotsman's eyes.

He started down the alleyway toward the waterfront, but halted abruptly when a hand reached out of a dark entranceway and touched him.

"I hear you come back today," Alice Wong said. "So I come to Whampoa, too."

His annoyance forgotten, Charles grinned at the

363

handsome young woman. It was useless to ask her how she had learned so quickly of *Flying Dragon*'s return; it was enough to know that news of everything that happened in Whampoa passed swiftly through the city. "You have no idea how glad I am to see you," he said, and needed no urging to walk with her to the quarters she had not used in weeks.

They made love at once, and Alice was as eager, as insatiable in her demands as Charles.

Later she brewed tea, apologizing to him because she had no food in the apartment, and as they drank the hot, fragrant beverage she sat on a cushion at his feet, happily leaning against him.

"Some Fan Kuei very special," she said with a laugh.

"Oh?" He couldn't help feeling a stab of jealousy, even though he had no right to expect her to confine her favors to him alone. "You've been busy entertaining other foreigners since I've been at sea, have you?"

Alice shook her head. "No. This first time I come to Whampoa since trouble start."

She was being cryptic, so he decided not to pursue the matter.

"You have friend," she said. "He make Chinese girl plenty happy, too."

"You've seen Jonathan in Canton?"

"Alice not see, not talk, not go to bed with other Fan Kuei," she said. "But friend of Charrs happy man, too."

Apparently she knew more about Jonathan than she was telling him. "He's well and staying out of trouble?"

She smiled slyly. "Alice think that tall Fan Kuei want to stay in Canton for whole life!" Unable to contain herself any longer, she giggled.

All Charles could glean was that Jonathan was enjoying himself, and he was relieved. From the young woman's hints he guessed that his cousin also had taken a Chinese mistress, and he wondered briefly about her identity, but it was possible he would never be told. Jonathan was too much aware of his betrothal to the pallid Louise Graves to discuss his amorous exploits. Charles could only hope he knew what he was doing as the only outsider— other than Sarah Applegate—at present in the city.

Their conversation was interrupted by loud shouts at the end of the alleyway beyond the open windows. Charles peered out and was able to catch a glimpse of a crowd gathering, so he and Alice dressed quickly and went out to the street to learn the cause of the excitement.

Men from a number of factories were gathered, talking in several European languages and gesticulating.

Charles found someone who spoke English and asked him what was happening.

"Two Dutch sailors from the Netherlands merchantman that docked this morning climbed over the Whampoa wall, the damned fools!" the man exclaimed. "A mob of Cantonese attacked them, and soldiers just delivered them on pallets at the Petition Gate. One is dead, and the other will be far better off if he dies quickly!"

Charles's heart sank. Instead of abating, the crisis would flare up anew as a result of this fresh, unfortunate incident. Luckily, the merchantman on which the impetuous pair had served was independently owned. Had she belonged to the powerful Dutch East Indies fleet, a naval squadron from Djakarta would have been certain to sail to Canton, and Sir William Alexander's threat to bombard the city would have been repeated by the Dutch admiral.

There was no way of guessing what might happen now. But, at the very least, tempers on both sides had been aroused again, and a resumption of normal relations between the Chinese and the foreigners would be postponed. The Dutch sailors had paid a heavy price for their stupid escapade, but now the Chinese trade itself would suffer for a longer time, too.

Charles turned to speak to Alice Wong, but she no longer was standing beside him. Gauging the temper of this crowd of badly upset white men, she had wisely vanished and by now was undoubtedly making her way back to Canton. Her disappearance was a symbol of the widening gulf that separated Orientals from the few Occidentals earning a living on the rim of their vast realm. Charles could only hope that the far more serious-minded Jonathan, who so rarely enjoyed himself strictly for pleasure's sake, was not becoming too deeply involved with any Chinese woman.

Bradford Walker withdrew into a shell for several days, and even at home he was uncommunicative with Judith, seemingly indifferent to the activities of his children. He sensed that a major turning point was at hand, provided he played his cards right, and he composed the words he intended to speak to his father-in-law with great care, then rehearsed and revised until he was satisfied that his proposal was foolproof.

When he was ready he went to Jeremiah Rakehell, and closing the door of the private office behind him, he said, "If you have the time, I want to bring up some matters of considerable importance."

Jeremiah silently waved him to a seat. His attitude toward his son-in-law had soured since he had learned of Brad's plot to discredit Jonathan, but the man was competent and conscientious—provided his authority was kept within reasonable bounds.

"I'd like you to glance at these letters from old and new customers," Brad said.

There were seven letters, all from shipowners in New York, Connecticut, and Massachusetts, all inquiring about the possibility of having clipper ships built for their fleets.

"I've put them off for the present by telling them our clippers are still in the planning stage, and I've promised to let them know as soon as we're prepared to go into production."

"Very wise," Jeremiah said, and waited.

His son-in-law adopted the air of humility. "You'll recall that I was opposed to the building of any clipper when Jonathan first proposed the idea."

"It would be difficult to forget it," the older man said. "So was I. That's why *Flying Dragon* is Jonathan and Charles Boynton's personal ship rather than the company's."

"Well, I was mistaken," Brad said. "I still have no faith in clippers, you understand. But there's a new trend underway, a fad for such ships, and I believe we ought to cash in on it. I propose that we turn one of our drydocks over to the exclusive construction of such ships."

"What's the rush?" Jeremiah asked mildly.

Bradford Walker was fully prepared for the question.

"I've heard rather solid rumors that a builder in Boston, one in Marblehead, and another in New York are seriously contemplating the building of clippers."

Jeremiah remained unruffled. "I wish them good luck."

"I hate to see someone else get a head start on us. Isaac McKim is having another clipper built, a sister ship to the *Ann McKim*, but it's for his own use. No one else has entered the field actively as yet, but the company that is first will get the lion's share of the construction business."

"That doesn't necessarily follow, Brad. The critical question at stake is one of expertise. Clippers require a delicate balance, as I daresay you've discovered, so one of them costs about double the price of an ordinary brig to build. Fleet owners will expect to get their money's worth. All we need to do is turn out one poorly constructed clipper, and customers will desert us in droves. I prefer to hold off a little longer and do the job right when we finally do it."

So far the conversation was going as Brad had known it would, and his confidence increased. "Aside from Kennard and Williamson in Baltimore, the only clipper builder is Jonathan, and only the Lord knows when he'll stop gallivanting around the Orient, if that's indeed where he is."

"I'm quite certain in my own mind that he and Charles are working out of Canton." Under no circumstances could Jeremiah reveal to his unreliable son-in-law that he had heard in detail from Jonathan about his current sailing ventures. Not even Judith had been told about Jonathan's letter suggesting to Louise that their betrothal be canceled. In fact, Judith, like everyone else, believed that Louise was already her sister-in-law.

"I can see certain advantages in waiting until he comes home and giving him charge of clipper construction. But I'm afraid if we wait too long we'll suffer for it. So I've made something of a private investigation."

Jeremiah raised an eyebrow.

"Kennard and Williamson's senior man, a fellow named John O'Connor, is highly ambitious. I've been in correspondence with him, and last week, when I was calling on our clients in New York, O'Connor came up from Baltimore to meet me. He's amenable to a change."

"I see."

"I'll admit he's expensive, but he'd be worth every penny to us."

"What does he want?" There was a hint of brusqueness in Jeremiah's manner.

"A base salary of thirty-five hundred dollars a year, plus a bonus of two hundred and fifty dollars for each clipper he builds."

Jeremiah whistled softly.

Brad came to the crux of the matter and spoke almost casually. "He takes it for granted, naturally, that he would be the head of the clipper construction department. I'm quite sure he wouldn't accept a lesser position."

"Where does that leave Jonathan?" Jeremiah asked.

Brad had carefully rehearsed his slight shrug. "Obviously, there will always be a place at Rakehell Building and Shipping for Jonathan Rakehell," he said.

Jeremiah seethed, but did not allow his feelings to show. "As you well know," he said, "Jonathan and Charles set an astonishing record by sailing *Flying Dragon* from New London to Canton in one hundred and seven days. We have every reason to anticipate that they'll also do well on their return voyage."

"So much the better, sir. The demand for Rakehell clippers will increase overnight."

"While Jonathan himself takes second place to an outsider. Or his pride forces him to go into competition with us, build more clippers for himself, and form his own fleet."

"I hope and believe he'd remain loyal to us, but I think his possible defection is a risk we're compelled to take. The demand for clippers makes it necessary that we enter the market without delay, and this fellow O'Connor is the answer to our needs. If we don't take him, another company will."

Jeremiah immediately saw the trap that Brad Walker had prepared. He was trying to create a situation that would compel Jonathan to leave the company that, in the normal course of events, ultimately would belong to him. If Jonathan came home to find that Isaac McKim's former assistant, one of the few men in the United States familiar with clippers, had been hired to head a new department that would construct clippers, he would assume he had been superseded. That assumption would be correct, and he would be forced to go into business for himself, no matter how painful the parting with his father might be.

Jeremiah had no intention of allowing that rift to take place. "It strikes me we'd be placing too great a burden on Jonathan's loyalty. After what he's accomplished with *Flying Dragon,* we'd be expecting the impossible from him. Even if he lacked the funds to start his own company, and I don't believe he will, every builder on the Eastern Seaboard would bid for his services."

"Then he'd be short-sighted. I'm thinking of Jonathan in all this. And of his son, too."

Jeremiah sat back in his chair, peering hard at his son-in-law, and when he spoke again his voice was deceptively soft. "I don't think you are. In my opinion you're looking out only for the welfare of Bradford Walker. You want to get rid of Jonathan so you can succeed me as the principal owner of this company."

Brad tried to protest.

"I happen to know why Jonathan did so poorly on the mail competition voyage to England in *Flying Dragon,*" Jeremiah said. "I've heard the whole story. In detail."

His son-in-law turned white.

"It's a story I've never told anyone. Including Judith, because I haven't wanted to do irreparable damage to your marriage. I've hoped I wouldn't have to mention the matter to you. From now on, Brad, just know that I have my eye on you, and don't play any more of your tricks."

The younger man was tongue-tied.

"You've come a long way since you married Judith. To be sure, you've earned your promotions, and you hold a position of great responsibility. With far more than adequate remuneration, and the prospect of making even greater sums in the years ahead. Be satisfied, Brad. Don't reach too high."

His scheme collapsed around him, Brad could only nod.

"A final word of warning. Don't try to come between me and my son again. In spite of Judith and the children you'd force me to take decisive action."

"I—I understand, sir." Brad hauled himself painfully to his feet.

Jeremiah's attitude changed, and he said cheerfully, "I'm sure you've heard that the Boyntons arrived late last night from London. Alan and Jessica are making a tour of the yard right now. I've already sent word to Judith that the Walkers are expected at a family gathering this afternoon, so come straight to the house when you're finished with work."

Brad mumbled his thanks and escaped.

Alone again, Jeremiah was too upset to concentrate on any of the work piled on his desk, so he went in search of his sister and brother-in-law.

He found them completing their unescorted tour, Jessica having insisted that she needed no one to guide her around the Rakehell yard.

"Your people certainly keep busy," Sir Alan said. "There's a brig under construction in every drydock."

"What I want to know," Jessica said stridently, "is where you're going to build clippers. After Charles and Jonathan return, the clamor for ships like *Flying Dragon* will become positively deafening."

"That's one of the number of matters I want to discuss with you two," Jeremiah said. "In fact, I'm cutting my work day short in your honor, so we'll go along home for a private talk. Shall I order a carriage, Jessica?"

"Really." His sister bridled. "I have no intention of riding until I grow too old to walk. There's nothing wrong with my legs, thank you!"

Sir Alan, long accustomed to her ways, chuckled indulgently.

Jeremiah shook his head, but made no comment, and they left the yard, heading for the house on Pequot Avenue.

As they walked, they confined themselves to inconsequentials, and Jessica commented on changes that she noted. "The Plummers have put on a new side porch since I was last here," she said. "If the Coopers grow any more fruit trees they'll soon have no more lawn."

When they reached the Rakehell house they saw Elizabeth Boynton sitting on a log that had washed up onto the beach. She was staring at the water, her blond hair blowing in the breeze off Long Island Sound, and Sir Alan hailed her.

She stood and slowly came toward them.

"Elizabeth is growing up," Jeremiah said. "She's lovely, and she's developing an adult figure."

"Oh, she's very adult these days," Jessica said. "Do you remember when Judith was about to go into her teens? I love Elizabeth as much as I would if I'd given birth to her, but some days I could cheerfully murder her. I find it very difficult to wait until she's two years older and becomes human again."

Jeremiah laughed indulgently. "The problems boys create are longer lasting."

"I daresay you're right," Sir Alan said thoughtfully.

"I thought you'd be playing with the baby or chatting with Louise," Jessica called.

"Julian is asleep in the nursery," Elizabeth replied, "with his nanny popping in regularly to make sure he's alive and well. As for Louise, she's gone somewhere. I daresay she's across the road, visiting her mother. As nearly as I can gather, that's the only place she goes."

"Don't be rude," Jessica said automatically.

Jeremiah concluded that his young niece-by-adoption was already a shrewd observer of human behavior. Certainly it was true that Louise never took any initiatives and rarely left the house except to talk with her mother. "You looked very pensive sitting on that log just now, Elizabeth," he said. "A penny for your thoughts."

"I'm afraid they're worth ten gold guineas, Uncle Jeremiah, but even then you wouldn't want to hear them."

He chuckled as they walked together to the house.

It would be impossible, Elizabeth knew, to confide her black thoughts to anyone. She had been told, to be sure, that Jonathan had married Louise before sailing to Cathay and that she now had a baby cousin. Well, she really couldn't resent Julian. Not only was he sweet, but he bore a startling resemblance to Jonathan, and for that reason Elizabeth's heart had already gone out to him.

But Louise! She couldn't even allow herself to think of the dreary woman as Louise Rakehell. In her private opinion Louise resembled a watercolor portrait that had been exposed to a rainstorm.

Actually, she had been wondering whether to administer poison to Louise so that Jonathan would become a widower. With great reluctance she had abandoned the notion. For two reasons. First, she had no idea where or how to obtain lethal poison. Equally important, she herself was still so young that Jonathan—damn him!—would be such a good catch that some conniving woman would snare him as a husband before she herself grew old enough for him to take note of her.

Never mind. Fickleness was not one of Elizabeth's faults. She remained convinced that she loved Jonathan, and somehow, when she came of age, she would contrive to marry him. The drab Louise would provide no competition, and perhaps she and Jonathan, acting together, could find some way to be rid of her. Ah! That would be a marvelous topic for a daydream the very next time she had some time to herself.

"This afternoon," Jessica said, "you can go hunting for seashells with Braddy and Judy."

"Yes, Mama."

Jeremiah had more immediate plans. "Elizabeth," he said, "we won't be eating for several hours, but I left instructions this morning that a blueberry pie should be baked, just for you, and I daresay it must be cooling by now."

The girl's attention was promptly diverted. "May I have it with ice cream, Uncle Jeremiah?"

"As much as you like," he assured her.

"Oh, I do love America," Elizabeth said, and broke into a run as she hurried to the kitchen.

Jeremiah led his sister and brother-in-law to his study. "First, tell me what you've heard from Charles."

"He's not the most verbose of correspondents," Sir Alan said. "We've had only one short letter from him.

372

He's informed us that he and Jonathan are prospering through a connection they've made with a prominent Cantonese merchant, but he's told us no details."

"We do glean, however, that he hasn't been gaming or drinking to excess," Lady Boynton added dryly. "And if there are any wenches in his life he's been prudent enough not to mention them."

Jeremiah laughed, then went to his safe, and after opening it he removed the bulky letter he had received from Jonathan. "I want you to see something that no one else has read," he said. "However, for purely personal reasons which I prefer not to discuss, I must ask you not to mention even the existence of this communication to anyone. That includes Louise." Suddenly realizing that the request sounded a trifle odd, he added, "Or Brad or Judith or anyone else."

His sister looked at him for a moment, then shrugged. She trusted him without reservation. "We'll abide by your condition, naturally."

Jeremiah handed them the letter.

Alan and Jessica sat side by side on the overstuffed leather sofa and read it together.

"This is bully!" Sir Alan declared.

"Hurrah for our lads," Jessica said. "They're doing splendidly, far better than I dared to hope from the little that Charles wrote."

"They're making a real mark," Jeremiah said soberly. "Not only have they accomplished sailing miracles, but they're proving the real worth of trade with Cathay. We can be proud of them."

"Jonathan has been mature for quite some time," Jessica said. "You have no idea how relieved I am that Charles is growing up, too."

"If my rough guess is correct," Sir Alan said, "they should be returning here in six to eight months."

"That's my estimate," Jeremiah said. "And I'm making my plans accordingly. I intend to start work soon on erecting four new ways that will be used exclusively for the construction of clippers."

"Four!" His brother-in-law was startled.

Jeremiah nodded. "I'm sure you noted Jonathan's

comments about modifications and changes in design he intends to incorporate into the next clippers he builds. I want to have everything here in readiness for him so he can go into large-scale production without any delays."

"That's sensible," Sir Alan said. "If the demand for clipper ships here is only a fraction of what it is in Britain, you'll be inundated. Especially if the lads show good sailing time on their return voyage. Just remember that I want a minimum of a clipper per year. More, if you can give them to me."

"I haven't forgotten," Jeremiah said.

His brother-in-law sighed. "In some ways I don't envy you, old boy. Your original outlay for four new drydocks will be enormous."

"Oh, it will eat into the company's capital, no question about that," Jeremiah said. "But if Jonathan can build two clippers on each of the ways within twelve months by doubling his work crews, which I hope is reasonable, I'll recover the expenditures in a year and will start showing a profit."

"I don't see how you can fail," Jessica said.

"Neither do I," her brother replied. "Now, Charles is directly concerned in all of this, and I know Jonathan will want him to share in our expansion, just as I want it. And that brings up something fundamental. Alan, over the years you and I have talked, on and off, about consolidating our enterprises into one company. The reason I asked you to pay me this visit is because I'm wondering if this may not be the right time for us to merge."

"I'm all in favor of it," Sir Alan said promptly.

Jessica Rakehell Boynton smiled. "That's been my own dream for many years."

"There are complications of which you may or may not approve," Jeremiah said. "For one thing, I intend to offer Jonathan a full partnership as soon as he comes home. His construction of clippers will earn more than the building of brigs, and the clippers we add to our fleet, if they're properly utilized—on long hauls, carrying nonbulky cargo—should make huge profits. So I believe it will be only fair to make Jonathan an equal partner right now rather than ask him to wait until I retire to take over the company."

Sir Alan chewed on the stem of his unlighted pipe. "An equal partnership is a bit much for me to offer Charles, I must admit. But I'd be willing to offer him a junior partnership."

"I must leave it to you and Charles to work out your own arrangement. I think it's important, since Charles has invested in *Flying Dragon* and is giving the better part of two years of his life to this voyage, that he should have a voice in management and a share in the profits."

"I'm less willing than you to have another hand on the reins," his brother-in-law said, "but I anticipate no problem in coming to a mutually satisfactory agreement with Charles."

"So far so good," Jeremiah said. "There's one serious obstacle to a merger, and I'm afraid you won't like this, Alan. But I know I speak for my son as well as for myself when I say we can pool our efforts only if you'll give up your opium trade with Cathay."

"How Charles will applaud that," Jessica said.

Jeremiah picked up his son's letter and searched for a passage. "Ah, here we are. *'The opium traffic is even more vicious and harmful than we ever imagined it. One of these years, and I believe it will happen soon, the pot will boil over and Westerners as well as Chinese will be scalded.'* I see no reason why any of us should be burned by taking part in an enterprise that's unethical and immoral as well as illegal."

"I could argue legality with you," Sir Alan said, "but I'll confine myself to fact. In the past four years one Boynton schooner has carried a cargo of opium to Cathay each year. That single voyage has earned as large a profit as all of my other operations for the year combined."

"A fleet of clippers, intelligently handled and directed," Jeremiah said, "should bring both the English and American branches of the new company, functioning independently of each other, a far higher profit margin than a fleet of standard merchantmen. At the risk of being stubborn and adamant, Alan, not only is a partnership contingent on your agreement to give up the drug traffic,

375

but I'll go a step farther. No Rakehell clipper will ever be sold—knowingly—to anyone who intends to carry opium in it."

"You confounded Yankee!" Sir Alan exclaimed. "You're holding a gun to my head."

"So I am," Jeremiah admitted cheerfully.

Jessica wisely refrained from making any comment.

"Not only would you force me to get my clippers elsewhere, which could mean a wait of several years," her husband declared, "but Charles would leave Boynton Shipping and take a permanent post with Rakehell."

"I daresay he might," Jeremiah conceded.

Sir Alan scowled at him. "I wonder," he said, "if there happens to be any good Scottish whiskey in this benighted household. I refuse to drink the poison made from corn that you colonials insist on calling bourbon whiskey."

"Knowing you were coming," Jeremiah said, "I took the precaution of having one of my brigs bring me some whiskey from Edinburgh." He walked to a table across the room and prepared a glass of whiskey and water.

Sir Alan sniffed it suspiciously, but was satisfied and raised his glass. "May God help us all," he said. "Here's to the new partnership, long may it flourish."

Owen Bruce was worried. The beating of the Dutch sailors and the death of one of them was delaying the resumption of normal relations. But that was the least of his concerns. Too many people, foreigners and Chinese alike, were making too much money from their trade for the present situation to remain unchanged indefinitely. In another week, a fortnight at the most, the present unpleasantness would become history and the cash would flow again.

What upset Bruce was the advantage that *Flying Dragon* had attained. Not only had her swift voyages been enormously profitable for her owners and for Soong Chao, but she was establishing precedents that conventional merchantmen could not equal. The burly Scotsman was jealous, and knew it.

Even more unpalatable was the lofty attitude toward

opium dealing that the American master and English first mate of the clipper ship had taken. There were others who felt as they did, to be sure, but these captains remained quiet, engaged in legitimate trade, and minded their own business. Rakehell and Boynton were so vocal in their opposition to the carrying and selling of opium that they actively encouraged other ships to follow their example, and that was dangerous.

Bruce was making a fortune from the importation of opium, and he had no intention of losing those profits. Therefore, he had to neutralize the efforts of the idealistic young pair.

The present crisis gave him his opportunity. He had already complained to Sir William Alexander, but the commodore had paid scant attention to him. That made it necessary for Bruce to act more forcibly. He wrote a petition, then took it to each of the other English factory owners and managers in Whampoa.

"Captain Rakehell of *Flying Dragon* is undermining all of us and acting against our best interests. Not only has he been working for Soong Chao, taking money out of our pockets and bread out of our mouths, but during this difficult period he's become intolerable." He argued with great sincerity. "We sit here in Whampoa, losing money every day until trade is resumed. But Rakehell sits in Canton—the only white man in the city—making his plans with Soong Chao. Unless we take a firm stand, together, Rakehell will corner the market on Eastern trade. His blasted ship is so fast that he can do it, too, make no mistake about that!"

He was so persuasive that all six of the other English factory representatives, including the local manager of the powerful East India Company, signed the petition demanding that Sir William Alexander curb him.

Bruce went to the American warehouse, too, but the two New Englanders in charge there would not listen to him. "The Rakehell Company is one of the most distinguished in the United States," they said. "And if Jonathan Rakehell is smart enough to win the complete confidence of a man as influential as Soong Chao, more power to him."

Rebuffed but in no way discouraged, Owen Bruce went back to the commodore. "Sir William," he said, "the British here have taken a united, solid stand. It's an outrage, when all of us are suffering, that the master of *Flying Dragon* should be able to take advantage of our plight. He's been spending this entire embargo time as the guest of Soong Chao, and it isn't right. We're sending copies of our petition to the Admiralty in London, it's only fair to tell you."

"Naturally," the commodore said dryly, well realizing that he was being maneuvered into a position that would compel him to take action. Their Lordships of the Admiralty were totally ignorant of what was happening in the Orient, and their only concern was that he keep the warehouse owners and shippers happy while maintaining the peace.

"I'm sure, Sir William," Bruce said, "that you'll want to rap young Rakehell so hard across the knuckles that he'll realize it's essential for all white men in China to form a solid front at all times."

"Quite so." Sir William concealed his contempt for the greedy Scotsman.

Later, when he was alone, the commodore faced the problem squarely. If he failed to go through the motions of administering a reprimand of some strength to Jonathan Rakehell he would be in trouble at home. After weighing the matter, he wrote a deftly worded letter to the imperial viceroy. Teng Ting-chen was a subtle man, well able to read between the lines, and would act accordingly in dealing with the American who had won the confidence of Soong Chao, the viceroy's principal lieutenant for international trade.

His duty done, Sir William sent his letter to the viceroy's palace, giving it to a trusted Chinese messenger for the purpose. Then he relaxed. He continued to hope he would be transferred back to England, and at the worst he would remain here for only a few more years before he would be able to retire. When he closed his eyes he could see his rose garden so clearly.

No one in Soong Chao's compound knew what was brewing, and Jonathan, had he been informed, would have laughed at Bruce's machinations. He and Lai-tse lu were totally immersed in each other, and he so relished every moment of her company that, in spite of his eagerness to return to work, he was almost sorry the present situation could not last forever. He and Lai-tse lu were suspended in time, and never had he known such happiness.

Sarah Applegate took a different view of the romance, however, and late one afternoon she went to Soong Chao, deeply troubled. "I'm afraid," she said, "that the visit of the woman who slept with Jonathan didn't achieve the effect we wanted."

Polishing his eyeglasses, as he always did when he was worried, Chao sighed.

"Jonathan and Lai-tse lu have become inseparable," Sarah said. "And that's the least of it. They are falling more and more deeply into their infatuation every day. They look at each other constantly. Their hands are always touching—"

"I know," Chao interrupted. "I am not blind, Sarah."

"Then you've got to do something."

"I cannot forbid them to have more to do with each other. That would make it certain they will come together."

"I realize it is very difficult."

"It may be," he said thoughtfully, "that the first woman I sent to Jonathan failed to satisfy him. That leaves me no alternative but to arrange for another one to visit. Perhaps it isn't the best solution of the problem, but I cannot think of anything else."

Lai-tse lu was unaware of her father's scheme, but she was preoccupied with her own dilemma. There was no doubt in her mind that Jonathan knew she had been his secret nocturnal visitor. Certainly he had sensed from her response, too, that she knew he was not mystified. Therefore, she reasoned, they were playing a foolish game, maintaining a useless facade.

Now, as she said good night to him after they had embraced and kissed in the library, she realized anew that he yearned for her, that he wanted her again as much as she wanted him. He could not take the initiative, however, because he was an honorable man living in her father's house. Only she could break this new impasse.

Returning with great reluctance to her own dwelling, she knew that she alone could end the deadlock. It would be such a simple matter to cross the courtyard, open Jonathan's door, and walk into his arms. Yet the most simple, direct acts could be the most complicated. The scheme her father and Missy Sarah had devised had given her the perfect excuse to substitute herself for the other woman. But she was still a lady, and she was afraid Jonathan might think less of her if she came to him openly, boldly.

Torn between desire and the upbringing that caused her to hesitate, she looked out of her windows across the courtyard. The blinds in his sitting room were open, and she watched him as he paced up and down. It was plain to her that he was agitated, and she guessed he was going through the same inner struggle that was creating such torment for her. She could feel her resolve weakening.

Suddenly Lai-tse lu froze. A young woman with cosmetics thick on her face, wearing a skin-tight cheong-sam, its skirt slit thigh-high on both sides, was walking toward Jonathan's dwelling with a mincing, confident gait!

Too late the girl realized what was happening. Her father and Missy Sarah, not satisfied with their previous efforts, were sending another woman for Jonathan!

Lai-tse lu wanted to race across the courtyard, tear out the wench's hair, and send her screaming into the night. Almost simultaneously her instinct told her it would be too dangerous to create a scene. By showing too great an awareness of what her father and Missy Sarah were doing, by intervening and spoiling their plan she might reveal too much. Under no circumstances did she want them to figure out that she had gone to him in place of the first woman they sent.

While she hesitated, the brazen young woman entered Jonathan's sitting room, closed the door behind her, and struck a provocative pose.

Watching in an agony of jealousy and anger, Lai-tse lu could not hear what the woman was saying, but it was apparent that she was offering herself to Jonathan.

380

In the light cast by the oil lamps Lai-tse lu could see his startled expression, and to her dismay he laughed. Wanting to leave the window, the girl nevertheless continued to watch.

The lovely visitor reached for the frog at the top of her dress, intending to unbutton it.

Jonathan said something emphatically.

One button was open, then another.

Suddenly Jonathan acted. He went to the woman and, placing his hands on her shoulders, turned her around and propelled her out of the door.

Lai-tse lu's spirits soared. He would have nothing to do with any other than Lai-tse lu. It was true that only one woman in all the world interested him, and she was scarcely aware of the rejected wench stalking haughtily in the direction of Kai's dwelling.

Her father's latest scheme had failed, thanks exclusively to Jonathan's loyalty, and Lai-tse lu rejoiced.

She could not go to him tonight, when her father, Missy Sarah, and Kai would be awake after the collapse of their latest plot, but the die was cast. This latest perfidy relieved her of any obligation to abstain from being intimate with Jonathan. Hereafter she would go to him openly, her conscience clear.

Never one to act hastily, Teng Ting-chen waited a day and a night after he received the letter from Commodore Sir William Alexander. The intent of the British commander's communication was plain to him, and he agreed with the sentiments. The only question in the viceroy's mind was how to carry out his part of an unspoken bargain.

At last he summoned his majordomo, and the towering Lo Fang came to his private sanctum.

"I trust you have passed the word to the right places. Tomorrow our people who work for the Fan Kuei in Whampoa will return to their positions there."

"It is your will, Excellency, and your orders will be obeyed." Lo Fang spoke sullenly.

Teng Ting-chen smiled. "I know you do not approve.

If you sat on my throne, the Fan Kuei would be driven from the Middle Kingdom."

"It is so," the majordomo replied.

"What you forget is that the Tao Kuang Emperor shares in the profits earned by trade with the foreigners. I also share. And the Tao Kuang Emperor wishes to learn many of the inventions of the Fan Kuei. So the problem is like that of the devil from the nether regions in the ancient myth. He offended the gods, and when he cut off the head of the great serpent that was about to attack him, twelve other heads appeared in its place."

Lo Fang appreciated and understood the meaning of what his master was saying. It was his place to carry out imperial policies, not to make them.

"You know of the American Fan Kuei who has been forced to live at the home of Soong Chao in this bad time?" the viceroy asked.

Surprised by the question, the majordomo nodded. "It is said that he is not like other Fan Kuei. He is faithful in his service to Soong Chao, who is loyal to the Middle Kingdom in all things. It has been said," he added, preferring not to mention that Kai had been his informant, "that the American has a Chinese sense of honor. He refused to deal in opium. He does not try to cheat Soong Chao or any other man."

"I also have heard only good about him," Teng Tingchen said. "So it has been inevitable that he should have made enemies among the other Fan Kuei. They have demanded that he be punished because he has spent this bad time at the house of Soong Chao. The English commodore has sent this request to me, but he, too, likes the American and does not wish him hurt badly."

"Why can the request not be forgotten?" Lo Fang asked.

"The ways of the Fan Kuei are strange. The English who make money here in opium and other trade have powerful friends at the court of their king in England. If they think the commodore is too lenient he will be replaced by an officer who will cause much trouble for us. So it is in our interest to see that the request is heeded."

"What do you wish done, Excellency?"

"The American must be attacked. But he must not be killed or made to suffer permanent injury."

"There are few who could carry out such a contradictory order, Excellency."

"I know of only one. He is expert in the martial arts, but he is wise enough to know when his strength should be subdued and his skill should be muted."

Lo Fang bowed low. "I will attend the matter myself, Excellency," he said, and as soon as he returned to his own quarters he sent a message to Kai.

Soong Chao resigned himself to the inevitable when his own majordomo came to him. The command of the imperial viceroy could not be disobeyed or ignored, so immediately after the evening meal he insisted that Lai-tse lu and Sarah, riding in palanquins, accompany him to a special fireworks show that would be held in the gardens of the viceroy's palace. The more sophisticated, particularly those of high mandarin classes, rarely bothered to attend such spectacles, and Lai-tse lu protested because she had secretly been intending to visit Jonathan in his quarters after they followed their usual evening routines.

Her father was adamant, however, so she and Sarah had no choice. One of Kai's assistants took charge of the party's protection, and neither woman took particular notice; had either thought about it, she would have regarded it as strange that the majordomo did not go with them himself.

Jonathan was left to his own devices, and bringing a book to his sitting room, he settled down to spend an evening of reading alone.

A short time later a tall, husky man, dressed in black, was admitted to the compound by Kai through a side gate.

Jonathan was startled when his door opened and a totally bald, black-clad giant stood in the entrance.

Knowing that the American's mastery of Cantonese was limited, Lo Fang spoke slowly and distinctly. "Fan Kuei," he said, "prepare to defend yourself."

Noting at once that the man did not appear to be armed, Jonathan put aside his book. "Would you rob me?" he demanded.

"No, I shall teach you respect."

For a moment Jonathan thought the giant was joking, but he had spoken solemnly and there was no humor in his eyes. This intrusion made no sense. He had understood the purpose of the visit of the woman he had sent away, but he could imagine no reason why Soong Chao might have had a hand in this stranger's unexpected appearance.

He could not remain seated when he was being threatened, no matter what the man's motive, so he rose to his feet and braced himself, sensing that he would be rushed.

Lo Fang advanced toward him and, launching a classical martial arts attack, tried to strike the American on the head with the edge of his hand.

Kai had practiced this blow many times, and Jonathan easily deflected it with his elbow.

Lo Fang was astonished, realizing instantly that this foreigner was familiar with at least the rudiments of the ancient martial arts of the Middle Kingdom. Very well. The giant aimed a kick at his opponent's groin.

Jonathan sidestepped neatly, then drove his extended, stiff fingers, which he held together, into the pit of the giant's stomach.

Lo Fang gasped for breath, his eyes narrowing. The Fan Kuei had actually dared to counterattack, using a Chinese method of fighting. This was no longer as simple a matter as the head of the Society of Oxen had assumed; his own self-respect was at stake, and he made up his mind to end the fight quickly and decisively.

Conscious of the change in his foe's attitude, Jonathan defended himself vigorously, trying to remember all that Kai had taught him in their daily lessons. It soon became obvious to him that he was not in this giant's class. The man fought smoothly as they circled each other, his timing and rhythm perfect. It would be just a matter of time, Jonathan knew, before he would be knocked unconscious or maimed.

Consequently, he had to resort to his own method of fighting as soon as he could create the opportunity. If he was going down to defeat in this battle without a cause, at least he would not disgrace himself.

He feinted with his left hand, knowing that the Chinese would recognize the blow before it landed and would move to his right.

Lo Fang reacted precisely as his opponent had thought he would.

Striking with all of his strength and putting his entire body behind his fist, Jonathan launched a Western-style punch that caught the Chinese on the cheekbone with such explosive force that it dazed him.

The American followed with a series of punishing lefts and rights to the body, then connected with an uppercut that sent the giant crashing into the far wall.

Thoroughly aroused now, Lo Fang bounded back into the center of the room, arms flailing and legs kicking.

Jonathan employed what he knew of Chinese fighting to keep out of harm's way. Convinced that he would be destroyed if he utilized the same approach, however, he awaited another opportunity. A short right jab to the giant's stomach did little damage, but a left hook to the jaw sent him sprawling.

As Lo Fang went down, however, he managed to kick his opponent's legs from beneath him, and Jonathan dropped, too.

Neither had the chance to regain his feet. They grappled on the floor, rolling over and over as each sought to gain an advantage. Lo Fang utilized the techniques of the martial arts, and the aroused Jonathan instinctively wrestled in the free-for-all style of his New England boyhood.

Both were powerful, endowed with great resilience, and neither could gain a decisive advantage. Their endurance ebbed as they continued to fight, and even after both were exhausted they continued to struggle.

Only when someone stood above them shouting, "Enough!" did they pause.

A laughing Kai held a painted jug in one hand. "You will kill each other if you don't stop," he said.

The antagonists parted, so weary they could scarcely drag themselves to their feet.

"Jonathan," Kai said, "permit me to present my good friend, Lo Fang. Fang, I present Jonathan."

"We've already met," Jonathan said, gasping for breath.

Kai gave them the jug, and each of them drank.

Jonathan knew the moment he tasted the potent liquor that it was mao tai, but it gave him enough energy to stagger to a divan heaped with cushions.

Lo Fang collapsed beside him.

"Never have I seen a better fight," the beaming Kai said.

The weary Jonathan held his head in his hands and, looking around the sitting room, realized it had been reduced to a shambles. A table had been knocked over, two delicate chairs were broken, and bric-a-brac, which Kai was picking up, examining, and replacing on shelves, was everywhere.

"Would someone mind telling me what this is all about?" he demanded, unconsciously speaking in his own tongue.

The two Chinese looked at him blankly.

He repeated the question as best he could in the Cantonese dialect.

Lo Fang, fingertips exploring the swollen bruise on his cheek, tried to explain.

Jonathan was bewildered. "Then the English commodore is my enemy?"

"No!" Lo Fang was emphatic. "He must do the will of the factory owners who have powerful friends at the court of the English King."

"Then who would want me reprimanded for staying here—when the crisis made it impossible for me to leave?"

"One who is jealous of you," Lo Fang said solemnly. "One who hates you because you will not bring opium to the Middle Kingdom."

Jonathan was too tired to think clearly.

"The Fan Kuei who is called Bruce is your enemy," Lo Fang said, drinking more mao tai and passing him the jug.

Jonathan took a swallow, then wiped his mouth with the back of his hand, noting for the first time that his knuckles had bled. "I'm not a vindictive man," he said, "but I give you my word that, before I leave China, I shall repay my debt to Owen Bruce."

Kai capped the jug and, before escorting Lo Fang to the gate, suggested that Jonathan go to sleep.

The two men who had fought until both had become exhausted shook hands in the Western style and bowed to each other in the Chinese manner.

Perhaps the evening had not been spent in vain, Jonathan thought as he dragged himself to his bedchamber. Lo Fang, who had spoken only vaguely of his own position but apparently was a member of the viceroy's staff, had become his friend. And Kai had treated him with greater cordiality, too. Although he couldn't explain his feeling to himself, his instinct told him that the bonds he had forged with them would be important to him for a long time to come.

After a long night's sleep Jonathan awakened to discover that his body was still sore, so he decided to abstain, for the first time, from practicing his knife-throwing and taking a martial arts lesson. His fight with Lo Fang had been enough for the present.

Emerging into his sitting room, he was astonished to see the broken furniture had been replaced and that there were no signs of damage in the room.

Another surprise awaited him when a servant appeared to tell him that, instead of breakfast being served to him here, Soong Chao would appreciate his company in the dining room.

Lai-tse lu and Sarah were present, too, and the girl studied him anxiously, but was reassured when she saw he had suffered no broken bones.

"I offer you my congratulations," Chao said as he took his seat on a cushion-covered stool. "Lo Fang is a powerful man, and it delights me that you did so well."

"If I had known what would happen," Lai-tse lu said indignantly, "I would have insisted on staying home last night, and I would have forbidden a fight."

"That is precisely the reason I took you elsewhere," her father replied, then abruptly changed the subject. "Jonathan, the crisis has ended. At this moment, those who are employed at the factories are returning to their work. *Flying Dragon* is tied up at my wharves, and by midday her hold will be filled with cargo, and supplies of food and water will be delivered. By midday, too, word of the new peace will have spread throughout the city, and it will be safe to have you escorted to Whampoa. If you wish, you will be able to sail to Formosa for me on the afternoon tide."

"The Lord be praised!" Jonathan said, and did not allow himself to look at Lai-tse lu as he continued. "I've lost more than three weeks of work time, Mr. Soong. Not that I begrudge a moment that I've spent here."

The girl's eyes were limpid as she looked across the table at him.

"I agreed to stay with you for a year, and in another six weeks that year will end. My duty to my family—to my father and our company—will make it necessary for me to return to America at the end of that six weeks."

Sarah Applegate's sigh of relief was inaudible.

"In that time," Jonathan said, "I want to make as many voyages for you as I can."

Even Lai-tse lu had to applaud his dedication and industry, but she could not conceal her sadness as, instead of going to her sitting room for a language lesson, she and Jonathan strolled together in the garden after breakfast. "I shall make myself a Western calendar," she said, "and each day for six weeks I shall make another mark on it. How I dread the day you will sail away."

Jonathan put a hand on her arm and halted her. "You know I must go home. But I swear in the name of the love I have in my heart for you—a love I've never admitted aloud until this moment—that I'll come back to you."

She searched his face, and although tears came to her eyes, her smile was luminous.

"Your father is wealthy, as is mine," Jonathan said. "I have earned substantial sums in the East, but I must make certain I can provide a secure future for you after I return home. It won't take long. Then, if you will have me, I want to marry you."

"There is nothing on all this earth I want as much," Lai-tse lu said.

Even though they were in the open they kissed, finally drawing apart with great reluctance.

"Before I sail to New London," Jonathan said, "I will speak with your father about our future."

A mischievous gleam appeared in Lai-tse lu's eyes. "It is best that you wait until the last before you go to him," she said. "Because I shall insist that when you are in port between voyages, you will live here, as you have done during the crisis."

Jonathan understood her meaning instantly and wanted her too much to protest.

III

The wood-carver who had made the replica of the Tree of Life jade pendant had been busy during the crisis and delivered the figurehead soon after Jonathan and his crew were reunited. Jonathan was so pleased that he immediately commissioned a seamstress to make a new pennant for his ship that bore the same symbol.

It quickly became apparent that there was a bright side to the long layoff. Trade orders had piled up during the hiatus, and there was more business than even the swift clipper could handle. With her men working feverishly, she sailed without further delay to Formosa. Officers and crew knew better than to venture far from the ship on the island where robbers preyed on visitors, and no untoward incidents marred the brief stay there.

As *Flying Dragon* sailed through the always busy Formosa Strait on her return to Canton the lookout reported that a schooner sailing in the same direction was flying the American flag, so Jonathan backed his topsails and brought to as he came up alongside the cumbersome vessel. Then he identified his ship.

"*Sally Ann,* five and a half-months out of Charleston," the captain of the other vessel replied.

"What's new back home?" Jonathan asked.

"Martin Van Buren has been elected to succeed Old Hickory as President."

"Great! How are business conditions?"

"Not so good. Banks have been in trouble, so they're

cracking down on their customers. A lot of factories are closing, and in some places farmers are losing their land."

Jonathan felt a sharp twinge of conscience and knew the time was indeed at hand when he should return to the United States. If the country was suffering financial setbacks he knew that international trade would be reduced, too, so his help would be needed at Rakehell Building and Shipping. "How is American shipping holding up?" he called through his megaphone.

"It's fair. European trade is still solid, but a great many ships on the Caribbean and coastal runs have gone into drydock," the other ship's master replied.

"Where are you bound?"

"Canton."

"We'll see you there," Jonathan said, and, ordering sail increased, soon outdistanced the lumbering merchantman.

Charles, who had heard the exchange, joined him on the quarterdeck. "No matter what happens in our part of the world," he said, "trade with the East will hold up for years and years to come."

"There's no doubt of that," Jonathan said. "That's one reason I'm eager to build more clippers."

His cousin nodded. "Even on the Caribbean and European runs, we can save so much time that clippers will be far more economical than standard ships."

"That's why I'm anxious to test my theories about altering the shape of a clipper's hull. We've got to find ways to increase cargo space."

"You take care of that end," Charles said, "and I'll see to it that we get orders from merchants."

Jonathan nodded and grinned. Their business relationship was as solid as their personal friendship, and he felt certain that Papa and Uncle Alan would be pleased.

Charles hesitated for a moment. "This is none of my business, Jonnie," he said as he gazed out across the swells of the green-blue sea, "but it appears to me that you became rather close to Soong Lai-tse lu while you were forced to stay at her father's house. What about Louise?"

"I wrote to her many months ago, suggesting that she

392

break our engagement. We've never loved each other, Charles. We were just accommodating our families."

"You love Lai-tse lu, then?"

"If her father will give his permission, I'll marry her on my next voyage to the Middle Kingdom. I hope to spend no more than six months getting new clippers built at the yard, and then I'll come back out here."

"She's beautiful and charming," Charles said, "but if you'll forgive me for asking, are you really prepared to take an Oriental wife to New England? London is far more cosmopolitan, but the social barriers there would be insurmountable."

"Anybody bigoted enough not to accept Lai-tse lu can go to the devil," Jonathan growled. "She's the only woman with whom I've ever wanted to spend my whole life. If her father won't agree, we'll find ways to overcome his objections. She feels as I do, and we intend to let nothing stand in the way of our marriage."

He was so firm that Charles dropped the subject, admiring his courage while at the same time fearing that his cousin and the lovely Chinese girl would be creating more difficulties for themselves than they could handle. He himself had grown fond of Alice Wong, but he couldn't imagine taking her back to England as his wife. Even if she weren't a trollop. A prolonged stay in the East obviously had changed Jonathan's perspective, and he was ignoring the problems that he and Lai-tse lu would face. Well, whatever might happen, they would have his full support.

Flying Dragon reached Whampoa at daybreak after her short voyage, and Soong Chao, determined to utilize the clipper's services to the maximum extent possible in the short period she would remain in the East, had the cargo unloaded at once and replaced with a cargo for the Dutch East Indies. Supplies and water were on hand, too, and *Flying Dragon* set sail again that same day for Djakarta.

Jonathan had wanted to show Lai-tse lu the new figurehead and was disappointed that there was no opportunity for her to visit the ship during his few hours in Whampoa. But he, like Chao, knew that every day was important now, and business considerations had to be placed ahead of personal desires. On the run to Java the clipper passed eleven other Western ships as well as many junks, according to Edmund Barker's count. Word of *Flying Dragon's* achievements undoubtedly had spread far in shipping circles, and he was confident there would be a clamor for clippers from many customers when he returned home. The future looked bright indeed.

In Djakarta he and Charles paid their usual call on the Fat Dutchman, who continued to do business in his garden, surrounded by his parrots. At his request Jonathan demonstrated his prowess with the throwing knives, and the Fat Dutchman was pleased.

"Now," he said as they sat down to a *rijstaffel* feast, "you will always have reason to remember this country. So you will not forget that you will build a clipper ship for me."

"I have your silver to remind me," Jonathan replied. "What's more, you have my promise. Before we sail back to Whampoa I wish you'd draw up a contract for a clipper."

The man waved his pudgy hand. "Contracts," he said, "are pieces of paper used by men who do not trust each other. A contract can be torn into shreds or burned. You have become my friend, so there is no need for a written agreement between us. I prefer to do business with you that way."

Flattered by the Fat Dutchman's faith in him, Jonathan knew, too, that the man was being shrewd. By refusing to write a formal contract he was placing the American under obligation to him to provide him with one of the first clippers built at the Rakehell yard.

When *Flying Dragon* returned to Whampoa her crew was given a shore leave of only three days before she would sail again on her next voyage. Jonathan spent his days at the vessel, supervising the loading of silks, but he lived at Soong Chao's estate, returning there with his escort at sundown every evening.

He and Lai-tse lu greeted each other decorously because of the presence of Sarah Applegate, who stayed with them until the evening meal was served. After they ate there was no opportunity for them to go off to the library together, either, because Chao wanted to discuss a number of business matters.

By the time Jonathan returned to his own dwelling there were no lamps or candles burning in Lai-tse lu's sitting room or bedchamber, and he assumed she had retired.

Soon after he closed his own door behind him, however, she came to him, and he knew she had been watching for him.

Lai-tse lu gave herself openly, passionately, and without shame to the man she loved.

There was no need for Jonathan to see her in the dark. His own desire was greater than any emotion he had ever known, its intensity leaving him shaken. She was his woman for all time, just as he was her man, and so complete, so deeply gratifying was their union that both believed it had to have been foreordained.

The following morning Kai saw to it that he was in charge of the escort that took Jonathan from the estate to Whampoa, and as they drew near the Petition Gate he revealed, indirectly, his awareness of their affair.

"You will be good, always, to the daughter of Soong," he said, making a flat statement.

Jonathan halted and looked him in the eye. "It is my prayer to my God," he said, "that the daughter of Soong will become my wife. I will take no other woman, and I will kill any man who tries to come between us."

Kai's slow smile of relief was his only answer. The young American had satisfied his doubts.

For three nights Jonathan and Lai-tse lu slept together, and on the day of his departure she came to the wharves with her father to see his figurehead and the Tree of Life ensign flying from the clipper's yardarm.

This voyage, which was unique, created a stir in the foreign factories. It was taken for granted that British colonies and nations dominated by Great Britain were out of trade bounds for all but the British East India Company, Boynton Shipping, and other English-owned ships. But Soong had obtained permission from Commodore Sir William Alexander to send *Flying Dragon* on a special mission to the island of Singapore, which lay at the base of the Malay Peninsula.

A decade earlier the British had established a colony there, and in recent years, thanks to its strategic location between India to the west and China and Indonesia to the east, the sleepy village had grown into a booming town. A year and a half earlier the wives of British administrators, military officers, and those who were establishing rubber plantations on the Malaysian mainland had started to join them, and Singapore now boasted a population of almost ten thousand.

When Edmund took the watch after the clipper reached the open waters of the South China Sea en route to the tropical island, Charles joined Jonathan in his cabin. "As I understand it, we're taking a cargo of silk to Singapore, where the English ladies will pay Soong Chao's trading partner there almost any price he wants."

"Right," Jonathan said. "They can buy cottons from India, but they want dresses made of silk."

"Fair enough, but what on earth is the cargo of cinchona bark we'll be bringing back to Canton?"

"Soong Chao says the cinchona is a tree that grows only in tropical climates. Chinese physicians have discovered that the bark has medicinal properties, so there's apparently a great demand for it. Chao is sure the physicians in the Forbidden City of Peking will take the entire cargo."

Charles smiled and shook his head. Like so many foreigners who came to the Orient he found the medical practices of the Middle Kingdom quaint, and he thought it as absurd to attribute medical value to a tree bark as it was to ascribe properties as an aphrodisiac to the harmless root of the ginseng plant.

In this instance, however, he was badly mistaken. Another three quarters of a century would pass before Western doctors would learn what their Chinese counterparts already knew, that the cinchona bark, made into a drug they would call quinine, would cure patients of the disease known as malaria.

The sea was turbulent, thanks to increasingly violent storms that indicated the monsoon season was approaching, but *Flying Dragon* reached Singapore without delay. Jonathan and his crew soon discovered it was a dreary place, with a thick tropical jungle occupying the better part of the main island and spreading to the mainland behind it.

But Charles's standing as a Boynton proved useful, and the cousins received more dinner invitations from members of the socially starved British community than they could accept. It was just as well they were kept busy because the cinchona bark that would comprise their cargo on their return voyage to Canton had not yet appeared from the mainland, and they had to wait almost two weeks for it.

That fortnight was not pleasant for the crew. The companies of British merchantmen resented their presence, and so did the British shore supervisors and their Malaysian dockworkers. Grimshaw became involved in a brawl in a waterfront tavern, and the seamen from a Royal Navy sloop-of-war tried to goad Oliver into a fight by telling him he was on the wrong continent and should return to Africa. Thereafter, the members of the clipper's crew always banded together when they went ashore.

The intense humidity and blistering heat were enervating, far worse than the Americans had encountered elsewhere, and the entire company was relieved when the cargo finally appeared from the jungle. But a final indignity had to be suffered. The British dock supervisors, still treating Yankees with disdain, forced them to linger for an additional thirty-six hours before the Malaysian workers finally loaded the cinchona bark into the hold.

A brilliant, early morning sun was shining as Jonathan finally gave order to cast off. The breeze was so slight it was almost nonexistent, but all sails were hoisted and *Flying Dragon* crept out through Singapore's magnificent deep-water harbor. Soon after she reached the open sea, thick gray clouds rolled in overhead, the sea became choppy, and a strong headwind began to blow in irregular, unpredictable gusts.

The clipper creaked in protest as the weather began to worsen, and the winds were so strong that *Flying Dragon* had little room to maneuver and tack in the traffic-infested waters of the Straits of Malacca, where junks and sampans appeared to be everywhere.

Flying Dragon was rolling and tossing under full sail, lurching and groaning whenever a powerful wave struck her hull, and Jonathan went to the quarterdeck, where Charles had the watch.

The first mate was concerned. "We've known better weather," he said.

Jonathan looked up at the black, fast-moving clouds and, bracing himself as the quarterdeck rose and fell, felt the surges of searing wind.

These were monsoon winds, as Jonathan well knew, the monsoon season having begun. A very fine rain had been falling continuously, and he had been told that a "typhoon rain" often heralded the approach of a storm. Taking no unnecessary risks, he gave orders to put a couple of reefs in his mainsail and take in his royals and moonsails.

They would soon find out whether they were in for a real blow.

"It seems to me," Charles said, "that we should either put back to Singapore or make a run for Djakarta."

"I'm none too sure we'll have time to do either," Jonathan replied, scanning the horizon with his glass and paying particular attention to a small island that lay about two miles off the starboard bow. "I'm going aloft while I still can to have a better look at that island yonder."

Removing his boots and stockings, he joined the lookout at the masthead, which seemed to sway perilously as the clipper climbed to the peak of a wave, then swooped to the trough of the next. Water was racing across her deck now. It wouldn't be long before the storm became much stronger.

He studied the island with great care and saw that it was covered with thick jungle foliage that extended to the shoreline. After the clipper fought through the increasingly angry seas for some moments, he saw what appeared to be a cut in the foliage, and he immediately climbed down again and hurried to the quarterdeck.

"Set course for the island," he told Charles. "There's

a channel of some sort there, and with luck we can steer into it."

Flying Dragon tacked and sailed toward the island.

The channel was more than fifty feet wide, more than broad enough to admit the ship, but the spreading branches of mammoth tropical trees extended far above the waterway on both sides, threatening to cut the sails to ribbons.

Jonathan took the watch.

There were numerous reefs in the area, so he took the precaution of stationing a man in the chains to take continuous soundings. Sailing only under jibs and topsails, the clipper moved carefully, with Charles relaying Jonathan's almost unending stream of orders to the helmsman. The wind howled through the rigging, making it necessary for commands to be shouted, and the rain fell in torrents.

After what seemed like an eternity the ship entered a tiny lagoon, its waters as yet barely ruffled by the mounting storm. This sheltered harbor was uninhabited, surrounded on all sides by huge tropical trees that cut off all views of the outside world.

"We're going to be all right," Jonathan said. "The Lord is watching over us."

There was still a great deal of work to be done. In the sudden quiet of the lagoon Jonathan heard Edmund murmur the suggestion to Charles that they tie the clipper to some of the bigger trees, but the master demurred.

"Typhoons are so violent," he said, "that they frequently uproot trees, just as ships that drag their anchors can be driven ashore." He attended to his anchoring with meticulous care, putting out two anchors in order to keep *Flying Dragon* safely head to wind.

The wind was so strong now that occasional gusts caused the men on deck to stagger. Driving rain half-blinded them, and even the waters of the lagoon had become choppy. There was no longer any doubt in Jonathan's mind that the storm was a vicious typhoon, and he was grateful to have found a safe anchorage. The worst danger came from trees that the wind might topple, but as nearly as he could judge, none would crash down on the ship if it were felled. No tree was taller than about one hundred feet, and *Flying Dragon* was at rest in the center of the lagoon, at least two hundred feet from any shore.

There was nothing to do now but go below and await the full fury of the storm.

The typhoon raged for eighteen hours, the winds shrieking, the deluging rain sounding like rifle fire as it struck the deck overhead. Occasionally the men on board the clipper heard a sharp, cracking sound as a tree trunk snapped, and everyone winced, waiting for the worst to happen, but the fallen trees thudded onto the ground or fell short of the ship in the water.

The galley fire was dampened down as a precaution, so the men ate cold rations, and no one slept. *Flying Dragon*'s hull was as tight as man could make it, but water nevertheless found several places to seep in, which was natural under the circumstances. Repairs would have to wait until the storm ended.

When the eye of the typhoon was directly overhead the rain and wind abated, and the sun came out in what sailors long had called "the false miracle."

Jonathan and Charles went on deck briefly, and paying no attention to the shambles ashore, they made a thorough inspection of the ship's exterior. So far the clipper was intact.

Jonathan took full advantage of the respite. The upper yards were undamaged as yet, but he ordered them sent down lest they be carried away by the force of the wind when the storm worsened again. The men who went aloft worked swiftly, often glancing at the miraculously blue sky.

The carpenter went to sound the bell again, as he had been doing periodically and would continue to do until the typhoon abated.

The anchors, the master and mate were relieved to see, were holding.

They went below again as the sky grew darker, and then the typhoon returned. The water level was rising, but the hull was sound; the lines were still in place, preventing the wind from driving the ship up onto the shore, and Jonathan had every reason to hope *Flying Dragon* would not be transformed into kindling.

"We're all right so far," he said.

Charles nodded, "I daresay we could have ridden out this storm at sea," he said. "But we're safer and more comfortable here, although this isn't my notion of comfort."

Ultimately the storm subsided, the winds abated, and the tropical sun reappeared in a cloudless sky. There was debris everywhere, with broken branches floating in the water and felled trees resting partly in the lagoon, partly on land. So violent had been the storm that the astonished Americans saw that several mammoth trees had been literally uprooted.

Flying Dragon had suffered very little damage, although her decks were littered with small branches and leaves. The debris was cleared away, essential repairs were made, the anchors were weighed, and the jibs and topsails were hoisted. With a seaman again taking soundings in the chains, the clipper once again moved out to sea.

Only then did the entire company feel relieved.

Flying Dragon dipped her Tree of Life ensign in salute as she inched past the anchored Royal Navy flagship off Whampoa, but the gesture was not returned, which was unusual.

Edmund, who had become expert at navigating in the Pearl River Delta, saw that something out of the ordinary was happening on shore and called to Grimshaw, "My compliments to Captain Rakehell. Ask him to join me at once!"

A few moments later Jonathan hurried to the quarterdeck.

"Look yonder," Edmund said.

A large crowd was congregated on the base of the pier at which the clipper would be berthed. Any large-scale greeting was out of the ordinary, but what made this occasion especially different was the presence of more than one hundred uniformed Chinese soldiers, some carrying ancient breech-loading muskets, while others were armed with long, double-bladed spears.

Several Chinese customs officers stood in front of the troops, and near them was Lo Fang in full uniform, his yellow and purple sash indicating that he was acting in an official capacity as the representative of the imperial viceroy.

Soong Chao was present, too, marking the first time he had ever come in person to greet the clipper after a voyage, and beside him stood Kai. The thought flicked through Jonathan's mind that both appeared concerned.

Off to one side, at the base of the adjoining slip, Owen Bruce was standing with several English factory managers and the proprietor of the Danish warehouse. It was plain that they were keeping their distance from the soldiers.

Edmund steered *Flying Dragon* gently into her berth, and as the lines thrown ashore were made secure the soldiers moved into position, blocking anyone from leaving the ship.

Soong Chao came on board immediately, followed by Lo Fang, Kai, and the two senior customs officials. The merchant bowed gravely, shook hands Western-style with Jonathan, who met him at the gangway, and then spoke in Cantonese for the benefit of the Chinese accompanying him.

"You are charged," he said, "with trying to bring opium into Whampoa."

Jonathan was stunned, but the accusation was so absurd that he laughed. "Whoever has made such a charge is mistaken," he said firmly. "Surely my hatred of the opium trade is well known." He translated the charge for Charles and Edmund, who stood behind him, and they were also incredulous.

"I have faith that you are completely innocent," Soong Chao declared.

Lo Fang cleared his throat. "His Excellency, Teng Ting-chen, knows of the services you have performed for Soong Chao and is aware also of your feeling of friendship for the people of the Middle Kingdom. Nevertheless, a charge has been made, so your ship must be searched."

"Certainly," Jonathan said. "Mr. Boynton, please conduct these gentlemen on a tour of *Flying Dragon*."

The customs officials wanted to be taken first to the hold, so Charles went below with them, while several members of the ship's crew followed.

"How could such a ridiculous charge be made?" Jonathan demanded.

"The imperial viceroy received an anonymous letter calling your supposed breaking of the law to his personal attention. Teng Ting-chen is required by law to make an investigation."

"I can't imagine who would make such an accusation, or what reason he'd have to make it."

Kai spoke very softly. "Does Jonathan forget that he has enemies in Kwantung?"

Lo Fang nodded. "The memory of the American Fan Kuei is short," he said, and grinned at the only man who had ever managed to fight him to a draw in personal combat.

Jonathan found himself looking toward the shore, and for a moment his gaze met that of Owen Bruce. Of course! Not only was Bruce jealous of his success, but his stand against opium was influencing other ships' captains, and if the rumors were to be believed, the man regularly received opium and smuggled it into Canton.

The Scotsman looked away, said something to the others with whom he was standing, and then sauntered off toward his own warehouse, his self-confident walk indicating a lack of concern for what was taking place.

The wait on deck under the heat of the late afternoon sun was interminable.

At last Charles reappeared, white beneath his suntan. "I can't believe it!" he shouted. "Someone is deliberately trying to hurt us!"

The customs officers and three seamen followed him, each of them carrying a large, square case, its markings indicating that it came from India. The cases were piled on the deck.

"These boxes," the older customs official said, "contain the finest grade of raw Indian opium. Each of them would bring a price of at least one thousand imperial silver yuan in the smugglers' market!"

Jonathan stood still, staring at the cases.

"This is outrageous!" Charles declared. "The boxes

were placed just inside the entrance to the main hold, where it would be impossible for anyone conducting an investigation to miss them!"

The startled Soong Chao translated his remarks into Cantonese.

Lo Fang nodded, his eyes shrewd. "Jonathan," he said, "is not a stupid peasant. If he had tried to smuggle boxes of opium into the Middle Kingdom he could have hidden them with ease. He would not have left them where they would be discovered so quickly."

Soong Chao became angry. "I am very certain in my own mind," he said, "that Jonathan is not guilty. The man who sent the anonymous letter to Teng Ting-chen must have had these boxes of the drug placed in the hold of this ship."

Lo Fang stared at him. "What makes you so positive?"

"Remember," the merchant said, "that the American ship did not sail to India. Captain Rakehell went only to Singapore!"

"We can prove the length of our stay in Singapore by the receipts we carry for the wharf space we occupied there," Charles said. "For two days we had to seek shelter from the typhoon that struck us off Singapore Island, and I assure you that not even a clipper could sail to India and back in that length of time."

When Soong Chao translated for Lo Fang, the imperial viceroy's majordomo nodded. "The English Fan Kuei speaks sense."

A rage had been building within the silent Jonathan, and suddenly his temper exploded. Picking up one of the cases, he threw it overboard into the filthy water of the harbor.

Everyone present knew that immersion in water ruined opium and made it unfit for human consumption.

One by one the cases went overboard. "So much for the opium," Jonathan said in a low voice. "Now all I want is to find the man responsible for this crime!"

"No harm has been done," Lo Fang said. "I will place the seal of the imperial viceroy on the documents in the office of Soong Chao, so all the world will know of your innocence. And I will tell Teng Ting-chen of all that was said here. This attempt to harm your good name was so crude it failed."

Everyone on the deck of the clipper watched in grim silence as the floating boxes sank, one by one, into the slimy waters of the harbor.

"That opium will never be smoked," Charles said.

Lo Fang called a command, and the officer in charge of the soldiers immediately marched his men off toward the Petition Gate. The group watching from the inner end of the adjoining pier drifted away, the men returning to their own factories, and the dramatic confrontation came to an end.

Soong Chao escorted Lo Fang to the office he maintained but seldom used in his Whampoa complex, and the customs officials, their duty performed, went ashore, too.

Kai lingered behind for a moment before joining Soong Chao and his comrade. "I knew from the very beginning that you would not bring drugs into the Middle Kingdom," he told Jonathan. "Lo Fang knew it, too. It was plain that someone was trying to cause trouble for you, but your reputation has not been harmed."

Jonathan nodded absently, his mind still seething, but he made no reply.

Within a short time the dock area returned to normal. A crew of Soong Chao's workers was waiting and soon began to unload the legitimate cargo of cinchona bark under the supervision of Charles and Edmund.

Jonathan knew he was expected at Soong Chao's office for the walk to the merchant's house under guard. He was eager to see Lai-tse lu, but there was unfinished business in Whampoa that had to be attended first. Had Lo Fang chosen to believe the charge against him, he could have been placed under arrest, jailed in a bamboo cage in a public square for days or weeks, and then executed. Chinese justice in no way resembled that of the West, and he would have had no right of appeal, no opportunity to plead his innocence. At the very least he could have been expelled from Canton and forbidden to engage in trade with China for the rest of his life. The knowledge that Rakehell ships would have been denied the privilege of coming to Whampoa was as aggravating as the thought of the personal fate he had escaped only because Soong Chao and Lo Fang knew and trusted him.

Slow to anger in spite of his occasional impulsiveness, Jonathan realized he would never be satisfied until he obtained retribution. The man or men who had tried to trick and ruin him had to be repaid.

The finger of guilt pointed to one person, and only one. During the many months he had been sailing to and from Whampoa he had come to know most of the factory owners and managers, but his acquaintanceship with them had been casual. Most would have had no reason to plant incriminating, expensive evidence on board his ship. He had met the Chinese merchants who owned warehouses, too, but until recently, when he had started to gain some command of Mandarin and Cantonese, he had been unable to converse with them. Furthermore, having dealt exclusively with Soong Chao, he had never had any reason to speak with the other members of the co-hong.

That left Owen Bruce, who had made no secret of his dislike for the American.

Jonathan made up his mind to confront the Scotsman and force an admission of guilt from him. He owed himself that much, even though he had no idea what he would do if Bruce agreed that he had been responsible.

Saying nothing to either of his mates, he went ashore quietly, his knives in his belt and a pistol hanging at his side.

Only Oliver saw him depart, and the boatswain's mate watched him with concern as he walked with a rapid, firm stride toward the factory owned by Bruce.

The sun was dropping lower, Jonathan noted, so he walked more rapidly. He didn't want to keep Soong Chao waiting when the merchant was ready to return home.

A wizened English foreman sat at a desk in the shabby office, which was located in the center section of the U-shaped warehouse. He was making notations in a ledger and looked up, his face expressionless, when the visitor entered.

"Where can I find Bruce?" Jonathan spoke brusquely.

The foreman gestured. "He's off in the east wing, last I knew," he replied in a thick English Midlands accent.

"How do I get there?"

'Go through the receiving area to your right and keep walking."

Barely nodding his thanks, Jonathan followed the directions and headed into the east wing. The light coming in through the small, unwashed windows was growing dimmer, but he could still see well enough to distinguish cases of tea, bolts of cloth, and other merchandise.

Ultimately he heard a noise somewhere ahead of him, then caught a glimpse of a lighted oil lamp standing on top of a pile of packing cases. Beyond the lamp, scribbling notations on a sheet of paper, stood the burly Owen Bruce. He turned when he heard the footsteps on the hard-packed dirt floor, and the expression in his eyes was one of outright hostility when he recognized his visitor.

"You may be surprised to see me, Bruce," Jonathan said in a hard, flat voice. "I imagine you suspected that by now the Chinese would have arrested me and squeezed me into one of their bamboo cages for criminals."

"You're of no interest to me," the Scotsman replied, "and I don't give a hang what becomes of you."

"Really? That didn't seem to be the case after I docked, and the representative of the viceroy came on board with the customs officers. You were craning your neck and talking—obviously about me."

"What do you want with me, Rakehell?" Bruce was gruff.

"The question is what you want of me. I hold you responsible for planting five cartons of Indian opium on board my ship when I was in Singapore."

There was a long silence before the Scotsman demanded, "That's a strong charge. Can you prove it?"

"We're not in a court of law right now," Jonathan said. "I'm making a flat accusation, and I call on you either to affirm or deny it, sir."

"The devil take you," Bruce said.

"I know of no one else in all of the East who had reason to cause me harm!"

Bruce's slow smile was more like a leer. "Suppose I tell you that I did arrange for opium to be found on your stinking ship, Rakehell. Suppose I tell you plain that the

407

holy-holy-holy attitude you've had ever since you first came to Whampoa makes me sick to my stomach. Suppose I freely admit—with just the two of us here and no witnesses within earshot—that I'd do anything and everything I could to see Whampoa rid of you for all time. What are you going to do about it?"

For an instant flashes of red inflamed Jonathan. Then his rage became cold, deliberate, and he took several steps forward. "This is what I'll do," he said, and drove his fist into the Scotman's broad face.

The punch sent Bruce crashing against the outer wall, near an open window. His initial reaction of stunned surprise gave way to an anger as deep as that of the young American. He shook off the blow and gathered himself for a counterattack.

Jonathan noted that the man carried no arms, which was just as well. If he used his pistol or knives he well might kill the Scotsman, but that would be an act of murder, and he wasn't prepared to go that far. His one desire was to beat the man to a pulp.

Bruce propelled himself from the wall, both fists raised, but when he came within arm's reach he suddenly kicked his opponent in the groin.

The shock and pain numbed Jonathan for a moment, and the realization that he had been struck an unfair blow caused him to lose his temper again. All at once he realized that Bruce was trying to tug his pistol from its holster. Even though the American was reluctant to use firearms, the warehouse owner suffered from no similar inhibitions. On the contrary, he could kill with impunity and subsequently claim that he had acted in self-defense when an attempt had been made to rob him. The foreigners in Whampoa were subject to the laws of no nation in their dealings with each other.

Jonathan sent the man reeling with a short, sharp punch. The pistol was half out of the holster, and the young American shoved it back into place.

Bruce cursed, then came forward again.

By now Jonathan was wary, realizing the man would use any tactics, fair or unfair, to win the fight.

Again Bruce aimed a kick at his opponent's groin.

This time Jonathan was ready for him and, side-stepping, moved forward with both fists flailing. Blows rained on the Scotsman's face and torso.

The product of Glasgow's slums, Owen Bruce knew how to absorb punishment. He waited for his opportunity, then drove his own right fist into the pit of his opponent's stomach.

Jonathan gasped and, during the instant he was incapacitated, felt Bruce again trying to snatch his pistol. Recovering quickly, the American regained the initiative, splitting Bruce's lower lip with a short left, then hitting him so hard with a right to the cheekbone that the man rocked on his feet.

Responding to the inner urge that demanded he knock the man unconscious, Jonathan delivered blow after blow.

But Bruce would not collapse, and using all of his remaining strength, he grappled with the intruder, then deliberately tripped him.

They crashed to the dirt floor together, rolling over and over, their fists flying.

Neither of the antagonists knew it, but they were not alone. Oliver had followed Jonathan to the warehouse and, hearing the sounds of the vicious fight, had found them. He crouched outside the window now, appalled by the spectacle of what he was witnessing. Common sense told him to summon Kai or Lo Fang, but he was afraid that by the time he located them and brought them here, Jonathan would be dead.

It was obvious to Oliver that Bruce intended to gain possession of one of his foe's flexible knives. He reached repeatedly for one of the supple blades, and only because of the need to trade punches did he fail. Sooner or later he would manage to get his hand on the hilt of a knife, however, and Jonathan would not survive.

Oliver had only one course of action left to him. Aware that he was no match for either of these strong giants, he realized he would accomplish nothing by entering the fight on Jonathan's side.

Instead, he crawled through the window into the warehouse and, unnoticed by either of the men struggling to attain the upper hand on the floor, he picked up the oil lamp. Quickly turning up the wick and removing the glass shield, he set fire to the packing case that rested at the bottom of a pile.

Some moments passed before the raw pine of the case caught on fire. The pair on the floor came within inches of Oliver, then rolled in the opposite direction again, both of them taking and giving punishment so severe that the boatswain's mate winced. Only white men, he thought, could fight in such a brutal manner.

The packing case began to flame, and then the fire spread quickly to the contents of the case. The other cases in the pile were smoldering, and when they became enveloped in flames the fire spread quickly.

His emergency mission accomplished, Oliver climbed into the open again.

Jonathan began to cough and all at once realized that the contents of the warehouse were on fire. The smoke was growing so thick it was becoming difficult to breathe.

The glare was intense, seeming even greater than it actually was because night had just fallen.

Owen Bruce screamed in anguish and broke off contact with his foe.

Jonathan saw that boxes and cases that were burning fiercely blocked his exit by the way he had entered the warehouse wing. The only route to safety was by way of the open window, and he hauled himself to his feet, then staggered toward it.

Venomous to the last, Bruce tried to shove him past the window in order to insure that he would be trapped inside the burning building.

But the Scotsman no longer had the strength to accomplish that end, and instead he succeeded only in pushing his foe closer to the window.

The smoke was so thick that Oliver's eyes were streaming, but he reached inside as far as he could, his hands groping until he made contact with Jonathan. His grip tightened, and he drew his employer and friend toward the window.

Still unable to see clearly, Jonathan scrambled into the open and lay on the ground, panting and drawing clean air into his lungs.

Men were appearing from every direction as the fire spread through the east wing of the warehouse. This section of the building was about one hundred yards from the neighboring factory, but if the early evening wind picked up strength, as it sometimes did, the danger that the fire might spread was great. Dock hands, sailors from the merchant ships, and employees of the factories were forming bucket lines, and soon water from the filthy harbor was being thrown onto the flames.

Jonathan recovered quickly and looked up to see Oliver kneeling beside him. Grimshaw and two other members of *Flying Dragon*'s crew, attracted by Oliver's presence so close to the building, were standing only a few feet away.

"Where's Bruce?" Jonathan demanded, his voice hoarse. "Did he get out?"

Oliver shook his head. "Still inside," he said.

"I've got to get him!"

"No go back," the slender man insisted.

Jonathan ignored the protest. "Fetch me a line," he said, "and step lively!"

One of his crew members, long accustomed to taking orders from him, hurried away, returning quickly with a length of rope.

Jonathan made one end secure around his middle, then handed the loose end to Grimshaw. "It's blame near impossible to see in that inferno," he said, "but I have a pretty fair notion of where to locate Bruce. When I tug twice on the line, that will be a signal. Haul on your end—not too hard, because I may have to carry Bruce. The idea is that you'll guide me back to the window."

"Cap'n," the veteran boatswain declared, "I'd much rather we sail into the teeth of another typhoon."

"No go!" Oliver was adamant.

But Jonathan paid no attention to either of them. He was directly responsible for Owen Bruce's weakened condition, and his conscience would not allow the Scotsman to die in the burning building. He had to do what he could to help the man.

Taking a large bandanna from his hip pocket, he dipped it into a bucket of harbor water that was being passed from hand to hand. Tying the sopping cloth over his nose and mouth, he climbed back inside, not listening to the shouted warnings of a dozen men.

The heat was searing, stifling, and the air was so thick that it was virtually impossible to breathe. Jonathan instantly dropped to the floor, and by keeping his face only a few inches from the ground he was barely able to draw in enough air.

He began to crawl in circles, blinking tears from his eyes, and gradually widened the circles. After what felt like a very long time he felt something directly in front of him and was able to open his eyes long enough to make out the body of a man.

Owen Bruce was still breathing.

Jonathan knew instantly that he would not be able to stand and carry the Scotsman. The smoke in the upper portion of the chamber was so thick he himself would collapse. So, he decided, he would be compelled to drag the man.

He caught hold of Bruce by his scorched shirt with one hand, then tugged twice on the rope with the other. To his horror a loose, burned end only a few feet long soon rested on the floor in front of him. The fire had eaten away the better part of the line, destroying his ability to send a signal to those who were outside.

Instinct urged him to save himself at any cost, but he had to make the effort to take Bruce to safety, too. Grasping the man's seared clothing with both hands, Jonathan started to crawl backward. Then he halted, realizing he had no idea where he was going. He had to find the window.

Rising to his hands and knees, he opened his eyes for a second or two at a time, peering intently in one direction, then in another. Tears streamed down his face into his bandanna, moistening it slightly, and at last he saw what he was seeking: the smoke appeared to be drifting in one direction. He took note of the place as best he could, estimating that he would have to travel about ten feet.

That ten feet proved to be the longest distance he had ever negotiated. Hauling and tugging Bruce, Jonathan was able to move about a foot at a time before he was forced to pause and lower his face to the ground. Coughing and gasping, he retched twice, and an inner voice told him he was being stupid to risk his life for a man who first had tried to get him into trouble with the Chinese authorities, then had tried to kill him.

But his stubborn Rakehell streak was stronger than the inner voice. It would be too hard to live with himself if he allowed Bruce to die.

Discovering that one of his own sleeves had caught fire, he beat out the flames with his other hand.

Realizing he could not survive much longer in this blazing inferno, he called on his remaining strength, and gradually the smoke became a trifle lighter, then lighter still.

The window was only inches from him now. He hoisted Bruce to the sill, then pushed and shoved until the man's limp body toppled onto the ground outside.

Utilizing his last reserves of energy, Jonathan clawed his way up to the sill and finally managed to work his head and shoulders into the open. But that effort drained him, and he could move no farther. A group of men had retreated a short distance with the unconscious Bruce, but Oliver was standing by the window. He hauled the exhausted Jonathan to safety moments before the roof over that section of the warehouse collapsed with a crash.

Time seemed to stand still, and Jonathan was only vaguely aware of the commotion around him. Then competent hands were inspecting his face and body, and a soothing ointment was spread on his burns. He heard from afar the voice of the Welsh physician who was in charge of the little foreign concession hospital.

"These two have the constitutions of bulls," the doctor said. "Both of them will survive."

Jonathan tried to struggle to a sitting position and to his surprise found Soong Chao and Kai on one side of him, while Charles and Oliver were close on the other.

"The fire soon will be under control," Charles said. "No more than a portion of this wing is lost. I wonder what was inside."

Kai laughed savagely and replied in Cantonese, so neither Charles nor Oliver knew what he was saying.

But Jonathan, in spite of his own condition, understood every word.

"Fan Kuei who are honorable do not know the peculiar odor. He who has smelled it but once will never forget it."

Jonathan managed to sniff, and now that the alien odor had been called to his attention, he realized it was sickly sweet, faintly reminiscent of tea, but stronger and heavier.

"The Fan Kuei Bruce tried to destroy Jonathan by claiming he was smuggling opium," Kai said. "But it is Bruce himself who once again is guilty. There are cases of opium in the warehouse that are being turned to harmless ashes." He refrained from adding that it would not be necessary for the Society of Oxen to conduct another clandestine raid on the place.

Jonathan smiled as he was lifted onto a stretcher-like palanquin in which he would be carried to the estate of Soong Chao. A quantity of the potent drug was being rendered useless by the fire, so he had not fought Owen Bruce in vain.

Now he would see Lai-tse lu again, and she would nurse him back to health, so he was content.

IV

For the first week after the fire Lai-tse lu and Sarah Applegate took turns looking after Jonathan. One or the other was always at his bedside, spreading sweet-smelling, soothing ointment on his burns, feeding him, and talking with him during his lucid moments. Gradually his pains became less intense, he remained awake and in his right mind for longer periods, and by the early part of the second week he was able to sit up in bed.

"You are fortunate you did not die," Lai-tse lu told him, then scolded him. "It was madness to save the life of the wicked man who tried to harm you."

"He didn't succeed, and I have no regrets. I spend hours with you every day."

"You are fortunate also," she concluded, ignoring his remark, "that His Excellency, Teng Ting-chen, sent his own physician to attend you. The Fan Kuei doctor said it would take months for you to become completely recovered—"

"Months!"

"—but His Excellency's physician prescribed the oil of a plant that grows near the edge of the desert on the far side of Chungking. It is very strong, as we know from the ancient myth of the god who descended to the nether regions because he was so curious and was almost consumed by the flames there. The principal gods took pity on him and anointed him with this same balm, and soon he was made whole again."

"That's all well and good," Jonathan said, "but I can't afford to spend weeks recuperating. It's essential that I go to sea again."

"You are well enough now for my father to discuss business matters with you. I will fetch him."

She stood, smoothing the skirt of her cheongsam.

"Wait!"

The girl stood beside his bed and smiled down at him.

"You've been wonderful to me, taking care of me and looking after my needs. There's no way I can thank you enough."

"I want no thanks."

"I love you," he said simply.

Lai-tse lu giggled. "I know it, and so does everyone else in the household. When you were out of your mind you bellowed it at the top of your voice, and you have a very loud voice when you wish to be heard."

"Then your father and Sarah know."

"You told Missy Sarah yourself," she said. "Often." Seeing his sudden concern, she bent down and kissed him gently on the lips.

"All will be well, as you shall see," she told him. "For the present you are not permitted to worry. About anything." Her heels clicked on the tile floor as she left the building.

Before Jonathan had a chance to compose himself Soong Chao entered the bedchamber, bowed, and seated himself on a deep cushion near the convalescing American. "Your nurses have been very strict," he said, "so I have not been allowed to see you until now."

"I'm very glad you're here, sir," Jonathan replied. "Women simply don't understand business obligations. I appreciate everything the ladies have been doing for me, but I've got to live up to my word to you. I've got to take my clipper to sea!"

A faint smile appeared on the merchant's lips. "If *Flying Dragon* is adhering to her schedule," he said, "she is in Manila today. As soon as she returns here with a cargo of hemp, she will be on her way to Djakarta again."

Jonathan was startled.

"Charles Boynton and I had a long talk," Chao said,

"and we agreed it would be wise for him to take command of your ship until you are recovered. This way no time is lost and no harm is done."

"That's true, sir. But I feel very foolish."

"That is wrong. You performed a great service for the Middle Kingdom. The imperial viceroy is grateful to you and has sent a letter to the Tao Kuang Emperor so the entire court in Peking will know that all Fan Kuei are not our enemies. As nearly as we can estimate, several hundred cases of raw Indian opium were destroyed in the fire at the warehouse of Owen Bruce."

"How did the fire start?" Jonathan asked.

The merchant shrugged. "No one knows. But you returned to the warehouse and saved Bruce after fighting with him, so you are being given complete credit for the destruction of the drugs. Everyone in authority here, including the viceroy, is delighted. It would have been impossible to conduct a formal raid on the warehouse without causing the British Navy to intervene. The evidence has disappeared in smoke, of course, so it will be difficult to order Bruce to leave China. But it will take him a long time to recover his losses, even longer than will be required for him to become healthy again."

"I can't feel sorry for him," Jonathan said.

"It is for the best that you will return to America before he leaves the hospital. Kai, who has ways of learning everything that happens here, has told me that Bruce hates you more than ever and swears he will obtain vengeance."

"I'm not afraid of him, I assure you."

"You've already proved that, Jonathan. But the problem becomes academic. There is no harm he can do you in the United States."

"I intend to return to China, sir." Jonathan braced himself. "Mr. Soong, I gather I did a great deal of talking when I was delirious, so it will come as no surprise to you when I tell you that I love Lai-tse lu."

"I had no need of your ravings to inform me of what I have recognized for a long time. I know also that my daughter loves you."

"With permission, sir, I want to marry her when I

return here. I'd ask for her hand immediately, before I leave, but I feel the need to establish a firmer financial position for myself first."

Chao nodded, but did not reply immediately. "You would take her to America?"

"Yes, sir."

"She would be accepted there?"

"The people who matter to me—and to her—will accept her. Others will do so in time."

"My daughter's happiness is very important to me, Jonathan. I would not want her to be hurt."

"Nor would I, Mr. Soong."

"My daughter tells me you are—or were—betrothed to a young woman in the United States."

"That's correct, sir, and it's another reason I feel it would be wrong to be married before I leave. I wrote to Louise many months ago, asking her to cancel our understanding. I want her to release me before I marry the only woman for whom I have ever cared."

"Missy Sarah tells me the Rakehell family is old and honorable as well as wealthy." Chao paused for a moment. "You know, of course, that when I go to join my ancestors, Lai-tse lu will inherit a large fortune, perhaps as large as that of your own family in America."

"I do know it, sir, and I assure you that her inheritance is irrelevant to my feelings."

"I have never thought otherwise. But I must obtain a pledge from you before I give my permission for you and my daughter to marry. If the gods smile on you, Lai-tse lu will bear children. My grandchildren. I wish them to be trained in the ways of commerce."

"Rakehells know no other ways, Mr. Soong."

"Hear me out. When those children are old enough to manage their own affairs, it is my wish that they come to the East and take charge of the business I have founded. When I die, I want it to be in the knowledge that my direct descendants will direct the house of Soong."

"I accept your conditions with my whole heart, Mr. Soong," Jonathan said firmly, "and I give you my solemn pledge that Lai-tse lu and I will do as you direct."

"You may want time to ponder this matter," the

merchant said. "Make no promise lightly. I would think you would want your sons to become active in the business of the Rakehells."

"I've been thinking about all this for some time," Jonathan said, "and even without making a pledge to you I had already made up my own mind. I can see no reason why the sons Lai-tse lu will bear shouldn't be active in America and in the East. Trade between my country and the Middle Kingdom is sure to expand greatly in the years ahead. My sons will enjoy a natural advantage over their competitors if their feet are planted firmly in both the Middle Kingdom and the United States!"

Soong smiled at him, his eyes bright. "It makes me happy to know I will have a son-in-law whose mind functions like my own. The union of a Soong and a Rakehell will cause both dynasties to flourish." He stood, shook Jonathan's hand, and left the building.

The interview had gone so well that Jonathan was astonished. The last hurdle had been overcome, and he rejoiced.

A short time later a radiant Lai-tse lu returned. "All has happened as I knew it would," she said.

He challenged her. "How did you know?"

"Two days ago I had a long talk with my father. I told him I would never willingly marry anyone else, even though he has the right to command me to marry anyone he chooses. My future means much to him, so he agreed, but I had to promise him I would say nothing to you, particularly about the pledge he wished you to make. Your reply has delighted him." She leaned down to kiss him again.

Jonathan reached for her.

Lai-tse lu backed away hastily. "Not yet," she said. "We must wait until you are stronger and your burns are better healed."

He grinned at her. "I'll be sensible because you give me no choice. All the same, this is a day of celebration. I can't offer you a ring to compete with the emerald the Tao Kuang Emperor gave you, although some day I'll match it. Right now I want you to have my most precious possession." He reached for the gold watch and fob that rested on the table beside him.

"This watch belonged to my grandfather, and to his grandfather before him," Jonathan continued. "Accept it as a symbol of my love for you."

"I cannot," the girl replied, shaking her head. "It is too valuable. No one knows better than a Chinese the sentiments that one attaches to the belongings of one's ancestors."

"I insist that you take it," Jonathan said. "If you wish, give it to our first son when you think the time is appropriate."

There were tears in her eyes as she took the watch. Suddenly she removed the Tree of Life medallion that had been the gift of King Rama of Siam and placed it around Jonathan's neck. "Now you, too, have a symbol of the love we bear each other," she said.

This was a golden moment, a high point in his life that he would always treasure. He leaned toward her, ignoring the pains in his side and shoulders, and their kiss was a token of the love they would share as long as they lived.

Edmund Barker and the crew of *Flying Dragon* happily accepted Charles Boynton—who fortuitously had his master's ticket—as their acting captain, and harmony on board was maintained on voyage after voyage. "Rakehells," Edmund Barker said, "have sea water in their blood. Sailing a ship is as natural to them as breathing."

The clipper was on the move constantly, weather permitting, seldom spending more than a day or two in port as she made trip after trip to Formosa, the Philippines, and the Dutch East Indies. Charles thoroughly enjoyed his visits to Djakarta, where he was the guest of the Fat Dutchman, and the pair had a natural affinity, both of them enjoying good food, fine wines, and the company of attractive young women.

During his brief stays in Whampoa between voyages Charles invariably spent his nights with Alice Wong, and on one occasion he was surprised to find himself having a serious talk with her.

"Soon you go to England," she said, "and Alice not see Charrs again."

"You're wrong," he said. "I'll be back here—often."

The young woman shook her head. "All Fan Kuei go and never come back."

"Here's one Fan Kuei who will. I intend to spend the rest of my life trading with the East."

"Alice happy," she said dubiously.

"I want to do something for you while I'm gone," Charles said impulsively, and opening the leather purse in which he carried his money, he spilled the contents onto the table beside him. A stream of silver coins descended, some of them falling onto the floor.

Alice immediately gathered the coins and placed them in neat piles. "Too much here," she protested. "More than five hundred silver yuan."

"So much the better," he replied. "I've been earning far more than I ever expected to make here, and I won't miss this money. I want you to have it."

No man had ever shown her such generosity, and she stared at him.

"You need a sense of independence so you can tell men like Owen Bruce to go to blazes," he explained.

"Alice no want any man except Charrs!"

Charles became distinctly uncomfortable. Alice was a more than satisfying part-time mistress, but he had no permanent place for her in his long-range plans. Under no circumstances could he take a part-Chinese trollop to England, where he would inherit his father's baronetcy, and he couldn't see himself providing for her total support in Canton, either. He began to regret his impulsive gesture, but he didn't want to hurt her feelings. "Whenever I come here," he said, "I'll sleep only with you."

To his surprise the reply contented her. She gave herself to him unstintingly, but she expected little in return.

Alice was still on his mind when Kai and an escort conducted him to Soong Chao's estate so he could pay a visit to the convalescing Jonathan. This was the first time Charles had traveled into Canton, and he was fascinated by the sights, sounds, and smells of the bustling city. The industrious, hard-working Chinese, he concluded, were infinitely more subtle than Westerners ever realized.

Jonathan, clad in an open-necked Chinese shirt and trousers, was practicing throwing his Indonesian knives in the garden when his cousin arrived. He had lost weight, but was still tanned and looked fit.

"You don't appear very sick to me," Charles said.

"I'm not," Jonathan replied, leading him to his sitting room. "The viceroy's physician, who comes to see me almost every day, says I'm nearly recovered, but he won't let me go back to work for another two weeks. We'll have spent more than a year in the East, but it can't be helped."

Looking out of the window, Charles saw Lai-tse lu leaving her own dwelling on the opposite side of the courtyard. "There are compensations," he said with a grin.

An unsmiling Jonathan gravely agreed. "All the same, as soon as he gives his approval, I want to sail for home. Soong Chao is making a drydock available to us whenever we want it, so *Flying Dragon* could have the barnacles scraped off her bottom, and she'll have to be painted. Then there's the matter of supplies for our return voyage—"

"Leave all that to me," Charles said, and gave him a detailed account of his stewardship, telling him about each voyage the clipper had made and how great the profits had been.

"You've been busy," Jonathan said.

The young Englishman stared at the jade medallion that was revealed beneath the open collar of his cousin's shirt. "So have you."

Jonathan touched the Tree of Life jade piece with his fingertips. "I'm going to marry Lai-tse lu on my return to Canton," he said. "Soong Chao has given his consent."

"She's a lovely girl and exceptionally bright. Accept my congratulations."

"Thank you."

Charles hesitated for a moment. "I hope you know what you're doing. You're asking for problems."

"We'll overcome them," Jonathan said firmly.

"Suppose, when you arrive in New London, that Louise Graves refuses to break your engagement."

"That's impossible." Jonathan spoke with confidence.

"Louise is no more in love with me than I am with her."

Charles was far less certain that the outcome would be clean-cut. His cousin was naive in his relations with women and failed to realize that Louise well might balk if she didn't have another acceptable suitor to whom she could turn.

Soong Chao invited the young Englishman to stay for dinner, and Charles became even more troubled. He sensed a change in the relationship of Jonathan and Lai-tse lu. Not only were they openly in love, but he felt certain they were sleeping together. He admired Jonathan's courage, but at the same time couldn't help wondering whether possible complications might await him in New England. On the other hand, a man who intended to bring an Oriental wife to the most conservative, tradition-bound section of the United States undoubtedly could find ways to create his own destiny.

Jeremiah Rakehell insisted that a small family party be held on Louise's birthday. Louise showed no enthusiasm for the idea, but agreed to it when her parents concurred.

The baby, who was crawling now and talked a language of his own, was the center of attention, with his grandfathers happily competing with each other as they spoiled him. After everyone had eaten, Julian was taken off to bed for his nap, the restless Walker children were allowed to go outdoors to play, and the conversation of the adults naturally turned to Jonathan.

"I keep wondering when he's coming home," Naomi Graves said. "He should have been here long before now."

Perhaps something untoward had happened to him in the Orient, Bradford Walker hoped, but he kept his thoughts to himself. Nothing would please him more than the total disappearance of his brother-in-law. Brad had been careful of everything he said and did since the day that Jeremiah Rakehell had rebuked him, but, like everyone else, he could only wait. His own claim to the directorship of the company would be strengthened immeasurably if Jonathan conveniently vanished from the face of the earth, and now that Rakehell and Boynton had merged, he was more eager than ever to assume control of the American operations.

Louise said nothing, allowing the conversation to swirl around her. She waited until her parents and the Walkers had gone home, and then she brought up the subject anew with Jeremiah. "Papa Rakehell, it's possible, isn't it, that we'll never see Jonathan again?"

"I consider it unlikely, but anything is possible when a man goes to sea," he replied.

"Well, I can't help worrying," she said defensively.

Her pessimism irritated Jeremiah, but he tried to be kind to her. "That's only natural."

"Oh, I'm not concerned for myself," Louise said, and failed to notice that his eyes widened because of her open expression of indifference. "I'm thinking of Julian. If anything has happened to Jonathan, our son will never become legitimate."

"In that event, we shall have to see to it that no one ever learns the truth." Jeremiah was emphatic. "What's far more important is that he is a Rakehell, and he'll grow up to take his place in the company. He's a healthy baby, he's quick, and I don't for a moment doubt that he'll prove to be a great asset to Rakehell and Boynton."

The company, the company! Jeremiah was as obsessed with it as was his son. They thought in terms of business day and night, and their only concern was their precious dynasty. The fact that she would be marked for life as an unmarried mother didn't bother Jeremiah in the least. She wanted sympathy, but was given it only by her own mother, who regularly commiserated with her.

Louise felt as though she was carrying the weight of the world on her shoulders and sighed plaintively.

In spite of himself, Jeremiah became even more annoyed. The sudden thought occurred to him that Louise didn't really belong in the tradition of Rakehell women, all of them self-reliant and resilient. Having had this girl under his roof for so many months he could understand why Jonathan had wanted to break his engagement to her.

But it was too late for that now. Julian, the representative of the next generation, had to be protected at all costs and in every way possible.

It was easy enough to assure Louise that steps would be taken to make certain no one ever found she and Jonathan had not married, but Jeremiah was privately concerned. Certainly his son should have come home by this time. And if he failed to appear there was no way that an honorable man could forge a marriage certificate or persuade an equally honorable clergyman to certify it as genuine. Like everyone else, Jeremiah knew he had to exercise patience.

But there was no reason he had to linger in the presence of this lugubrious young woman. "I'll see you at supper time," he said. "I have some important work to attend to at the office."

Not until he had walked almost all the way to the shipyard did it cross his mind that he was actually avoiding Louise's company. He felt sorry for his son, who would be saddled with her for the rest of his life, but it was too late now to bemoan that unfortunate circumstance. Julian represented the Rakehell future, and his welfare had to be placed ahead of everything else.

Sir Alan Boynton almost always went to his club for his midday meal, and it was fortunate that so many of his fellow members were his more important customers because it was easy for him to combine business and pleasure. He came home at noon only on rare occasions, but when he appeared unexpectedly one day, Lady Boynton was able to cope, demonstrating her customary formidable efficiency.

A quick conference with the cook promised to produce a meal of ox-tail and barley soup, mutton chops with potatoes and two vegetables, a raspberry trifle, and a savory of grilled sardines on toast. Having guaranteed that her husband would not starve when he ate what he regarded as his lightest meal of the day, Jessica joined him in the small sitting room of their bedroom suite.

Clenching an unlighted pipe between his teeth, Sir Alan looked distressed.

His wife was not one to mince words when unpleasantness threatened. "What's wrong?" she demanded as she came into the room.

"I could commit murder. Quite cheerfully."

"Do you have any particular victims in mind, Alan?"

"Our beloved son and our revered nephew."

"Oh, dear." Jessica temporized, and would make up her own mind after she learned about their supposed sins.

"While they're having a high time in the East, doing God alone knows what—although I have a few suspicions of my own—they've placed me in a most embarrassing position. I've had a deuce of a morning."

She saw that he was not exaggerating and was genuinely upset, but she continued to reserve judgment.

"First off," Alan said, "two of our directors pounded on me, and then I had a visit from Lord Vincent."

"Dudley Vincent," Jessica said succinctly, "is a pompous ass."

"Granted. But he happens to be Britain's largest independent tea importer. And the purpose of his call today was to impress upon me the fact that the demand for Chinese tea—as opposed to Indian—is growing at an astronomical rate in this country."

"I'm pleased to hear it," she said. "Why should the increased demand for Chinese tea make you want to annihilate Charles and Jonathan?"

"Because," the exasperated Alan declared, "they're staying on and on in Cathay when they should be taking advantage of the revolution their own exploits started!"

Jessica poured whiskey and water into a glass and handed it to him. "So far I can't follow you, so I hope you'll explain."

He made an effort to curb his anger. "As you know, *Flying Dragon* created a sensation when she reached Cathay in such a short time. Now there are rumors in the coffeehouses that she's been setting other records sailing between Canton and such places as Djakarta and Formosa. The details are vague, but the exploits are authentic."

"I can speak only for myself," Jessica said, "but I'm enormously proud of Charles and Jonathan."

"Confound it, so am I, but that has nothing to do with the matter. The clamor for clippers and more clippers is unbelievable. Every shipper in the industry wants them for his fleet. American builders intend to fill that demand. They'd be bloody fools if they didn't. A number are already under construction in the United States. Our builders are being cautious, as usual, so they have no prints on their drawing boards as yet. If Charles and Jonathan would return to civilization—where they belong —they could corner the market."

His wife was unperturbed, but didn't dare smile. "I see no cause for alarm. You can be sure that, even with Jeremiah's ambitious building plans, Jonathan will get more orders for clippers than he can possibly fill."

"He's going to face stiff competition. Lord Vincent made it painfully clear to me that he's willing to give Rakehell and Boynton an exclusive contract for Chinese tea only on condition that I give him a specific date for the start of our own clipper fleet's operations. Well, we have no fleet, and we'll have none until Jonathan builds the ships and Charles trains the crews. Why, I'm ashamed to admit that *Flying Dragon* is the lads' personal property and doesn't even belong to our fleet."

Jessica watched him as he sipped his drink. "How long will it take these companies in America to build their first clippers?"

Alan shrugged. "They're still working on their designs, so it will be at least a year before they launch any clippers. To be on the safe side, call it eighteen months."

"There you are!" his wife declared. "When we were in New London you heard Jeremiah say—again and again —that he's confident Jonathan can produce eight clippers every year."

"Oh, I don't doubt his capabilities, not after what he's done with *Flying Dragon*." Alan struggled with his temper again and won the battle. "But there's nothing to prevent him and Charles from staying on indefinitely in Cathay and hiring themselves out to Chinese merchants."

Jessica shook her head. "You read Jonathan's letter to his father. He said they might stay in Cathay for as long as a year, but no longer. They'll be home sooner than you think."

"I hope you're right," her husband said, "but I can't count on them, and I certainly can't afford to take unnecessary risks. I'm being compelled, against my will, to

427

order at least two clippers from other American builders."

She looked hard at him, and her eyes gleamed. "You shall do no such thing. After forming a partnership with my brother you cannot order ships built anywhere other than in his yard! You'd become the laughingstock of the industry."

"I think not. Every shipper knows that business is business. Jonathan and Charles changed my mind when I had no faith in clipper ships, but that doesn't mean I must allow my competitors to surge ahead of me."

"As a stockholder in both the English and American branches of Rakehell and Boynton," Jessica said, "I could demand a meeting of the master company's board before you make such a drastic move. It would take too long to arrange a meeting, of course, so I'll make you a sporting offer. My dear, I'll wager you that Jonathan will be the first builder to put new clippers into the water, and Charles will be the first to operate them out of England. If I lose, I shall turn my stock in both branches over to you, with no strings attached."

"And if you win?"

Jessica thought for a moment. "Ah, I have it. My dear, I shall want the first year's profits from the first two clippers that Jonathan builds and Charles puts into operation for you. With no strings attached. I shall want to spend, squander, save, or invest those funds in any way I see fit."

Her husband grinned at her, his anger rapidly dissipating. "And how long must I wait for the lads to come back from Cathay and buckle down to work?"

"Another four months. No longer."

"My dear," Alan said, "I accept the wager." He rose and kissed her lightly on the cheek. "Shall we go downstairs to eat?"

"Sit down again for a minute or two. Since you've come home, there's another problem I want to discuss with you."

He looked at his watch, then moved back to his chair.

"This morning, while Bridget was cleaning Elizabeth's bedchamber, she asked me to come in. She found a letter under the pillows."

428

"Oh?"

"A long, long letter Elizabeth was writing. A love letter."

Alan bristled. "To whom?"

"Jonathan."

"I hope to God she has better sense than to mail it," he said with a chuckle.

Jessica was not amused. "Oh, she won't mail it. I did a bit of snooping, which is a mother's right when dealing with a child not yet in her teens, and I found a whole pack of similar letters. Written over a period of several years."

"I see no cause for alarm. Elizabeth is indulging in a little girl's daydream."

"A daydream, certainly," Jessica said, "but she isn't a little girl any longer. She's maturing rapidly."

Alan laughed. "Jonathan is safe from our siren, protected by a wife and a child of his own."

"That isn't my concern. Elizabeth is being consistent, far too consistent. To the best of my knowledge she's had this romantic obsession for at least four years."

"Jonathan," Alan said, "is fifteen years older than Elizabeth. I'm quite certain he thinks of her only as his baby cousin, if he thinks of her at all."

"You and I know that, but she doesn't. She makes quite a point in her letter—which I freely admit to you I read in full—to emphasize that they aren't blood relatives."

"My dear," Alan said, "you're worrying needlessly. In another year or two young gallants will begin to squire Elizabeth, and as she develops a natural interest in them she'll forget this obsession, as you call it."

"I hope you're right," Jessica said. "It isn't healthy for a girl to give in so completely to a wild dream, and for so long a period of time."

Flying Dragon was scraped and painted, her spare suit of sails was unpacked, and she began to take on supplies for her return to the United States. In the days immediately prior to her sailing, Jonathan came to the wharves in Whampoa from the Soong house every morning, and he allowed no one else to supervise the loading of the cargo, cases of green tea that had been part of his original deal

429

with Soong Chao. Every evening he went back to the estate at the far side of Canton, and every night he and Lai-tse lu managed to sleep with each other.

One afternoon, as he came ashore from the clipper, he saw Owen Bruce approaching him. A livid scar marked one side of the Scotsman's face, and he walked now with a decided limp, using a gold-headed cane. Jonathan had no desire to speak with him, but didn't want the man to think he was afraid of him and therefore halted and waited.

Bruce wasted no breath on civilities. "Rakehell," he said, "you and I have unfinished business to attend."

"You're mistaken, sir," was the calm reply. "I have no business with you."

The Scotsman ignored the comment. "I should be grateful to you," he said, "for saving my life. But I feel no gratitude. There would have been no fire if you hadn't come uninvited to my warehouse."

"I wouldn't have gone there in the first place," Jonathan said, "if you hadn't arranged for opium to be found on board my ship. But this talk leads nowhere."

"Do you know how the fire that cost me an entire wing started, Rakehell?"

"I have no idea."

"Well, I have my suspicions about that, but we'll let it pass for the present. I have noted that your ship is being prepared for a long voyage, so I assume you're going back to America."

"Your assumption is correct, sir." Jonathan started to move past him.

"One moment." Bruce raised the walking stick to detain him. "I want to give you a last word of advice, Rakehell. When you get back to America, stay there. You'll come to Canton again at your peril."

They exchanged steady, hostile stares, and Jonathan knew this man would be his mortal enemy as long as they lived. "I shall sail wherever I please on the high seas," he said, "and you may depend upon it that I shall return to Canton."

He walked away quickly, not looking back.

Their paths did not cross again.

The last days in the Middle Kingdom passed quickly

for the clipper's entire company. The crew members, their purses swollen by the past year's profits, in which they shared, went on buying sprees for their relatives. Even Grimshaw bought a teapot and a set of cups and saucers for the sister he claimed he despised.

Edmund Barker purchased a length of embroidered cloth for Ruth, then splurged on a pair of jade earrings for her. Charles bought a number of gifts for his parents and Elizabeth, and Lai-tse lu, acting on Jonathan's behalf, purchased many items for his father, his sister, and her family. She also presented him with an exquisite porcelain vase.

"This," she told him, "is for the girl to whom you were engaged. Even though you will not marry, she will understand that you are still her friend."

Charles spent the last night on shore with Alice Wong, to whom he gave a necklace of intricately worked silver as a farewell present.

"When Charrs come back to Canton," she told him, "Alice have very special gift for you." She refused to elaborate.

Sarah Applegate was waiting for Jonathan when he arrived for his last night at the Soong estate, and she approached him as soon as he and his escort came through the front gate. "I want a word with you, young man," she said.

Even though he towered over her by more than a foot, she intimidated him. "Yes, ma'am," he said meekly.

Sarah led him to a secluded corner of the formal gardens. "You and Lai-tse lu may think I'm deaf, dumb, and blind, but I'm not," she said with her usual asperity. "I know what goes on under my nose." She sniffed audibly as if to prove it.

He knew what she meant, of course, but had no reply other than, "Yes, ma'am."

"You're a grown man and she's a grown woman," the New England widow said, "so I won't waste my breath delivering sermons on morality. Besides, times have changed, and what was wrong in my day doesn't seem wrong to the young any more. But that's not my point. It's the future I have on my mind."

"Missy Sarah," Jonathan said, "you well know that I love Lai-tse lu. You also know I'm coming back here as soon as business arrangements permit and that I intend to marry Lai-tse lu as soon as I land."

"See to it that you do," she snapped. "I brought up that girl as I would my own, and if you disappoint or hurt her, Jonathan Rakehell, I swear to goodness I'll find a way to come to New London myself and give you the thrashing you deserve."

"I believe you would," he said with a chuckle, "but I'll save you the bother. A Rakehell doesn't break his word." Suddenly he picked her up, held her at eye level for a moment, and kissed her.

Sarah gasped. "Land sakes!" was all she could say when he deposited her on the ground.

Ordinarily, Soong Chao avoided discussions of business affairs at meals, but this was a special occasion. He told his future son-in-law in detail about the land he had recently purchased near the Petition Gate inside the city walls. There, he said, he intended to build yet another warehouse. An adjoining building would be devoted to other purposes: he was going to branch out and, buying loose tea in bulk, would pack it for shipping in his own plant.

"Before you return," he said, "try to find looms that will weave a cloth even finer than those you sold to me when you first came here. If you can obtain them, we will start still another new business and will make our own silk cloth."

"I think I know where I can have such looms built to order, sir," Jonathan said.

The merchant smiled. "I will give you several samples of cloth to take with you. If the looms make a cloth of similar texture, do not hesitate to order them."

Lai-tse lu, who had been listening intently to the conversation, entered it for the first time. "It would appear, my father, that you believe trade between the Middle Kingdom and the West will continue to increase."

"If we think in terms of decades, there can be no doubt that it will grow larger," Chao said. "Our people want the merchandise that is made by the advanced machines of the West, and the people of the West are hungry for what we produce." He looked at his daughter, then at Jonathan, and smiled. "It is a perfect marriage."

Sarah Applegate's slight frown indicated that she didn't necessarily agree with him.

"I am less optimistic about the years immediately ahead, however," Chao continued. "Many Fan Kuei, particularly the English, are growing more arrogant month by month. Unscrupulous factory owners like Owen Bruce and immoral shipowners and captains are smuggling ever larger quantities of opium into the Middle Kingdom. This cannot and will not be permitted to continue indefinitely. The Tao Kuang Emperor has been very patient because our army and navy are weak, but the time will come when he can tolerate no more. Then he will be obliged to show the West that the Middle Kingdom is not a paper tiger, that our claws and teeth are real and draw blood."

"Surely the West will learn to obey the laws of the emperor," Lai-tse lu said.

Jonathan and Chao exchanged a long look, and the former said, "I'm afraid not. The laws will be ignored, not because they are Westerners, but because they are men. Just as there are many in China who will continue to disobey the emperor. The greedy will take great risks because the profits from the drug trade are so huge."

"That is why I say that sooner or later there will be a nasty explosion," Chao said. "Soldiers and sailors of both East and West will die."

"You don't think war can be avoided?" Jonathan wanted to know.

The wise merchant shrugged. "Not unless the West changes its policies, which seems unlikely at present. The Middle Kingdom is far from nations like England, and our problems are of no concern to foreign governments. Only if the emperor bows his head and cravenly allows the Fan Kuei to send as much opium here as they wish will there be no war. But the Tao Kuang Emperor is a man of great courage, and the time will come when he cries, 'Enough.' "

"I don't see how any Western power, even Great Britain with her powerful Royal Navy, could successfully

433

invade China," Jonathan said. "Your territory is too vast, and you have too many millions of people!"

"I am a trader, not a soothsayer," Chao replied with a sigh. "I know only that when silver flows in a stream as mighty as the waters of the Yangtze Kiang, the greatest of our rivers, the minds of men become irrational. I am relieved when I think that my daughter will be safe in America when the time of trouble comes. But enough! This should be a joyous occasion!"

The subject was dropped instantly.

When the meal ended, Chao presented Jonathan with a pair of delicately carved, ivory chopsticks. "Use these in the home of your father," he said. "They will remind you of this house and will speed your return."

"I'll use them," Jonathan said.

Sarah laughed. "I'd love to see the faces of New Englanders when you do," she said, and continued to laugh as she left the table.

She and Soong Chao pretended not to notice that Lai-tse lu and Jonathan paid only a token visit to the library that evening, and they secluded themselves in their own quarters so they would not see Jonathan cross the courtyard to the girl's dwelling a short time later.

That night the young couple made love repeatedly, fired by a sense of urgency. Then, before they drifted off to sleep for a short time, Jonathan presented Lai-tse lu with a ring of plain, solid gold that had been made in accordance with his instructions by a Whampoa jeweler.

"Wear this on the fourth finger of your right hand," he told her. "When we are married I will transfer it to the fourth finger of your left hand. In my land that is a symbol to indicate we will be husband and wife for all time." He slipped the ring onto her finger, then kissed her hand.

They slept fitfully, the knowledge that they would be parted for well over a year weighing on their minds. Jonathan was tempted to put off his sailing long enough to marry Lai-tse lu immediately, but he could not allow himself to give in to his own desires. He could not take her as his wife until he had acquired greater wealth in his own right, not merely as a Rakehell heir. And as an honorable man he had to obtain Louise's release from the formal pledge he had made to her.

He would have gone off alone to the Whampoa wharf, but Lai-tse lu had insisted for days that she intended to see him off. So she and Sarah climbed into their palanquins at dawn, and Kai led the entourage across the awakening city, with Jonathan and Soong Chao walking beside the women's bearers.

The clipper's crew was already at work, making last minute preparations. A load of vegetables, fruit, and eggs was being taken on board, and Lai-tse lu presented Jonathan with a case of tangerines as a last farewell gift. In mid-morning Edmund came to the ship's master to report that all was in readiness.

Jonathan escorted his visitors to the gangplank. "Take care of the daughter of Soong and see that no harm befalls her," he told Kai, speaking in Cantonese.

The majordomo touched the hilt of his double-edged sword with his fingertips. "I will defend her life with my own," he replied.

Tears appeared in Sarah Applegate's eyes as Jonathan bent down to kiss her. "See that you behave yourself, young man," was all she could say as she went ashore.

Soong Chao and his future son-in-law faced each other in silence for a moment. In the thirteen months of their association they had achieved a remarkable degree of mutual trust, understanding, and affection, and there was little need for words. They exchanged bows in Oriental fashion, shook hands in Western style, and then the merchant went ashore.

Lai-tse lu moved to the gangplank, and when she turned to the man she loved her gaze was steady. "Every day," she said, "I shall pray to my gods and to your God that you will return safely to me."

"I'll pray, too," he said, "and you can depend on it that I'll come back for you."

Their lips touched for an instant, and the girl walked down the gangplank and stood, dry-eyed, between her father and Missy Sarah.

Jonathan walked briskly to his quarterdeck. "Mr. Boynton," he said, "you may cast off and make sail."

"Very good, sir." Charles was deeply touched by his cousin's farewell and was relieved that the time for action had come.

Flying Dragon edged slowly out of her berth, her sails cracking in the morning breeze as they were unfurled, and began to make her way through the crowded harbor of Whampoa.

Jonathan turned for a last glimpse of Lai-tse lu. She stood unmoving, and when their eyes met both of them renewed their promise to each other. Neither raised a hand in farewell.

Sailing at a lively clip, *Flying Dragon* moved east and north of Australia and Fiji into the vast reaches of the Pacific Ocean. The sky was overcast and the whitecaps frothed on the waves of the dull, gray sea. The wind was all that seamen who had encountered it previously had claimed. Blowing steadily, unrelentingly with gale force, it filled the clipper's great sails and propelled her forward at a speed never before achieved.

With the entire crew at duty stations, Jonathan and Charles stood on the quarterdeck and marveled. Even the rhythmic creaking of the ship's hull seemed to be in harmony with the elements as *Flying Dragon,* pitching and rolling predictably, sailed faster, then still faster.

"Good Lord!" the awed Charles murmured. "We must be doing twenty-two knots!"

"More like twenty-five," Jonathan replied. "By adding still more sail and reducing stress lines on my next clippers, I wouldn't be surprised if we can come close to thirty knots."

"No one who doesn't make this voyage himself would ever believe our speed," Edmund Barker said as he joined the other officers. "I'm right here, and I can scarcely believe it."

The company took full advantage of the remarkable, unvarying winds, and for day after day the clipper maintained her extraordinary speed. Men slept in snatches, ate at their duty posts, and rejoiced in silence. The superstitions of the sea prevented anyone from mentioning the obvious: if they continued to enjoy reasonably favorable weather they would break every existing record by the time they reached home.

Jonathan had intended to put into either Valparaiso or Concepción in the young republic of Chile for water and fresh food, but the winds remained steady, so he headed straight for Cape Horn.

There his good fortune seemingly deserted him, and he was forcibly reminded that all sailing ships had to depend on the vagaries of the weather.

A howling gale, with winds of more than fifty knots, blew up in the Straits of Magellan, and it was impossible for *Flying Dragon* to navigate in such a narrow channel. She might be torn apart if her master rashly decided to tempt the fates.

Instead, Jonathan put into the fairly calm waters of a Pacific fjord. He put out two anchors, stripped his masts, and tried to curb his natural Rakehell impatience as he rode out the storm.

The gale raged for three days and nights. Jonathan, seeing a new speed record eluding him, was in a foul mood, but Charles and Edmund resigned themselves to the inevitable.

Then, suddenly, the storm abated several hours before dawn. Jonathan had been sleeping lightly, and when he heard the winds subside he raced to the quarterdeck, bawling an order to Grimshaw to summon all hands. In less than a half-hour *Flying Dragon* was under way again.

Jonathan was worried. Summoning his officers to the quarterdeck for a conference as he sailed northward into the South Atlantic, he presented them with a problem.

"We have two choices," he said. "The first is that we put into the Falkland Islands for water and supplies. If we do, we'll have to put in for provisions again after we reach the West Indies. The second choice is to push on to Montevideo, in Uruguay, and then try to stretch our run all the way home."

"Can we last until we reach Montevideo?" Charles asked.

"I think so," Edmund replied, "although we'll be low on both water and food if we run into any prolonged bad weather."

"Let's give the ships that come after us a real record to beat," Charles said. "I'm in favor of running the risk, so I cast my vote for Montevideo."

"So do I," Edmund said without hesitation, and suggested that water be rationed.

Jonathan grinned at them. "I'm glad we're in unanimous agreement," he told them. "The second choice is what I wanted, but I'd have given in if either of you had been overly cautious."

He was still learning, he reflected, and vowed that his next clippers would provide greater space for both water and food. He was committing himself to a serious modification of a clipper's lines by giving his new ships bottoms that bore less resemblance to the sharp under-fins of barracuda. But he was convinced the alteration would not hamper a clipper's speed, provided she remained slender and carried enough sail.

It did not occur to him that he had become the world's leading expert on the design and performance of clippers. He had proved that these new vessels would revolutionize world commerce, and his dreams for the future were based on demonstrable fact. No designer, no fleet owner, no ship's master could ask for more.

Flying Dragon reached Montevideo early in the morning, and when Jonathan saw dilapidated warships flying the flags of Argentina and Brazil in the harbor, he decided not to go ashore. Uruguay was one of the world's newest republics, having established herself as an independent nation less than a decade earlier, but true independence had not yet been secured. Argentina and Brazil were competing for supremacy there, with both nations eager to annex little Uruguay, so political conditions were unsettled.

"Any man who dares to go ashore takes his life in his hands," the pilot who came on board to guide the clipper into the harbor declared. "There are no neutrals in Montevideo. Everyone must stand for independence or he is a tool of our enemies."

Jonathan had no desire to become embroiled in a South American dispute. All that mattered to him was the speed record he wanted to achieve, so he bought water and food from harbor boats, and by early afternoon he put to sea again, gradually sailing eastward so he could clear Brazil without hugging the shore.

The clipper happily fought through rain squalls when she reached the sub-tropics, where trade winds remained favorable. Now a great deal depended on whether there would be breezes near the Equator. Wind velocity dropped sharply, but at no time did the air become stagnant in the dreaded Doldrums. The experienced seamen knew how to coax something extra out of even the gentlest puffs of breeze, and *Flying Dragon* continued in motion, even though her speed was reduced to a stately crawl of no more than five or six knots before she edged into the Caribbean and picked up the far more active trade winds.

Each day Jonathan posted the ship's position on a chart as *Flying Dragon* sailed closer and closer to her home port, and the crew's excitement mounted accordingly. The hope that the America to Cathay record would be broken was a reality easily within grasp. Proud of themselves, their ship, and what they were accomplishing, the sailors had come to know the clipper so well they were able to anticipate orders, and their work was unfaltering. They were indifferent to sleep and hot meals, and the fever of conquest gripped everyone on board.

A storm that blew up in the Atlantic east of St. Croix threatened for a day to spoil the crew's hopes, but the gale proved to be a blessing in disguise. Taking the familiar course of even stronger hurricanes, it provided *Flying Dragon* with a wind that sent her slicing madly through the waters off the coasts of Florida, Georgia, and the Carolinas. Soon after the clipper swept past Cape Hatteras, the gale veered sharply eastward into the Atlantic, her task accomplished.

Winds remained brisk, however, and when Jonathan sighted the golden beaches of New Jersey through his glass, the outcome was no longer in doubt. "We'll smash the record, lads," Jonathan told his men.

No one quite dared to ask by how much the sailing time would be reduced.

He knew what was in their minds, and his confidence in himself, his crew, and his ship was sufficiently great for

439

him to cast superstition aside. "Barring the unexpected," he said, "it begins to look as though we'll cut at least a week off our old record."

Flying Dragon continued to behave like a thoroughbred. When she heeled sharply as she rounded Montauk Point at the eastern tip of Long Island for her final run, she sighted the U.S.S. *Constellation,* the magnificent old frigate that was still the flagship of the United States Navy's Atlantic fleet. Shouted information was exchanged between the quarterdecks, and the frigate dipped her ensign, a rare tribute for a warship to pay a merchantman.

The warship's signal guns were fired in succession, roaring a salute to the gallant clipper that was accomplishing what no other vessel in history had ever achieved.

A cutter of the United States Coast Guard heard the sound of the shots rolling toward the mainland and herself raced to New London to give advance word of the welcome news.

Only now, when Jonathan stood on his quarterdeck looking at the familiar sights on both banks at the mouth of the Thames River, did he realize how happy he was to be coming home. He missed Lai-tse lu desperately and would continue to miss her every moment until they were reunited, but he was looking forward to sharing his triumph with his father. Only a Rakehell could truly appreciate his feelings at this moment.

The thought that he would see Louise again in the immediate future did not enter his mind.

Book
V

I

Precisely at noon on the one hundredth day of her voyage from Canton, *Flying Dragon* swept up the Thames Estuary, took in sail, and eased toward an empty berth at the docks that lined the waterfront at the Rakehell yard. She had broken the previous record of a crossing from Cathay, held by a schooner from Marblehead, by thirty-seven and one-half days. The clipper's astonishing speed would be news in every nation of the Western world, and overnight would double and treble the demands of shipowners for similar "miracle-makers."

Thanks to the warning shots fired by the Coast Guard cutter's small guns, a large crowd was hastily assembling at the foot of the wharf. Jeremiah Rakehell had to walk only a short distance from his office, and nearby, wishing himself elsewhere, was his son-in-law. Had Bradford Walker known what would happen today he would have arranged a business meeting in Norwich or Groton that would have made it possible for him to avoid Jonathan's triumphant homecoming. Instead, when his wife and children arrived from their house, he was forced to stand beside them, pretending to be overjoyed.

Ruth Barker, who hadn't had time to change out of her house dress of linsey-woolsey, had thrown a long cape over her drab attire. Other wives and mothers of crew members had done the same, but their appearance didn't matter. Their loved ones were coming home after an absence of almost two years.

Louise was one of the last to arrive at the yard, bringing little Julian with her. Judith Walker had stopped off long enough to tell her the meaning of the Coast Guard cutter's shots and to offer her a ride in the Walker coach. Instead, Louise had changed hurriedly into a silk dress, but even though she was more presentable she was filled with a sense of dread.

Left to her own devices she would have awaited Jonathan at the Rakehell house, but the delicate situation demanded her presence and that of her son at the docks. Many people would be watching Jonathan greet his son and heir for the first time, and to deny them that pleasure would cause gossip.

So Louise had to participate in the public welcome and pretend to be the wife of the man who would come ashore from his ship. Never close to Jonathan in all the years she had known him, Louise had come to feel even more alien to him since she had moved into his father's house and started using the Rakehell name. She had no idea how Jonathan might react to her—and to the baby, and she prayed for the strength to see her through the ordeal that awaited her.

On board *Flying Dragon* the seamen were grinning broadly as they took in sail, and when they saw their wives or other family members, they shouted their greetings.

Edmund Barker, standing on the quarterdeck with the other officers, raised his bicorne and waved it over his head when he caught sight of Ruth in the throng. His quiet smile told its own story of his feeling.

Jonathan and Charles saw Jeremiah Rakehell at the same moment, and they saluted him together. Then Charles took note of the pale Louise a few paces away, but he made no comment. Vividly recalling Jonathan's warm and tender farewell to Lai-tse lu, he thought it wise not to interfere in a delicate and difficult relationship.

As the ship maneuvered into her berth little Julian could not be seen by those on board for the simple reason that he was hidden by the crowd. Louise had held him in her arms for some minutes, but the child had become restless. Now that he could walk he disliked being held and had insisted on standing on his own feet.

The moment the clipper was made secure the seamen were permitted to go ashore to greet their families. Then they would return to dry the sails and perform other essential tasks before beginning their well-earned furlough of three weeks.

Tradition demanded that the officers display greater dignity. Dockworkers would attend to their sea chests in due time, so Edmund Barker was unencumbered as he walked ashore to the applause of the crowd and went straight to his wife, whom he held in a long embrace.

The cheers became louder as Charles Boynton walked down the gangplank, greeted his uncle, and hugged Judith Walker.

Jeremiah Rakehell walked alone down the wharf in order to be the first to see his son.

The applause mounted to a crescendo as Jonathan, settling his bicorne firmly on his head, began to descend the gangplank. He grinned at his father, then glanced toward the base of the wharf. At that instant he felt as though he had been immersed in ice water, and his smile froze on his lips.

Standing apart from other family members was Louise, who was holding the hand of a boy who appeared to be just under a year old.

One look was enough to tell Jonathan that the child was his son. The boy's features and hair, eyes and coloring marked him indelibly as a Rakehell.

At that moment Jonathan's world collapsed around him.

"Welcome home, son," Jeremiah said in a voice loud enough for others to hear. "Accept my congratulations on your achievement."

"Thank you, sir," Jonathan replied, knowing he had to observe the amenities of the occasion. "I'll be obliged if you'll sign my arrival time on my sailing certificate." His hand trembled slightly as he handed the document to his father.

As Jeremiah filled in the necessary information on the certificate he spoke in a low tone. "I had to see you alone for a moment, Jonnie. Louise has never seen the letter you sent her in which you asked her to break your

445

engagement. The letter arrived a day before your son was born. So Louise has no idea you ever wrote such a letter." He spoke with quiet compassion.

"I—I'm grateful to you for this warning, Papa," Jonathan said, trying in vain to hide his anguish.

Then, squaring his shoulders, he started to walk down the pier at his father's side. It was the longest walk of his life.

Jeremiah knew the tension had to be broken. "Julian," he called, "come and see your father!"

The little boy squirmed out of Louise's grasp and began to run down the pier as rapidly as his short legs could carry him.

For a second a feeling of blind rage and frustration engulfed Jonathan. This child was depriving him of a lifetime of happiness with the only woman he had ever loved or would love.

Then his self-discipline asserted itself, and he told himself not to be stupid. The destruction of the glorious future he and Lai-tse lu had envisioned was hardly the fault of this small child, who had not asked to come into the world.

Julian toddled toward the grandfather he knew and loved, ignoring the tall stranger.

Jonathan reached out for the boy, scooped him up, and held him at arm's length. "Here, now, none of that," he said. "You don't know me yet, any more than I knew you even existed, but I reckon we'll have to get acquainted in a hurry. I'm your papa."

"Papa," Julian said dubiously.

Jonathan hugged him, and his resentment of the child faded away, never to return. This was his son, the first of his generation in the direct Rakehell line, and the boy already filled his proper niche in the dynasty.

Louise stood alone at the base of the dock, trying to overcome the terror that overwhelmed her.

Aware that scores of people were watching them, Jonathan continued to hold his son in one arm as he bent to kiss Louise. His lips were as cold as her lips.

"I'm so sorry for all this," she murmured, her voice

inaudible to any adult other than Jonathan. "I wrote you twice, but I—I guess you never got my letters."

"No, I didn't," he replied, his mind still reeling. "But there's no need to feel guilty. I'll accept the full blame."

"What's done is done," she whispered.

At this moment Julian began to squirm, indicating that he wanted to get down—and providing a welcome diversion.

Jonathan turned away to greet his sister and her family, accepting the dry congratulations of Brad Walker with an equally dry smile. Brad hadn't entered his thoughts for a long time, but it was plain that his brother-in-law disliked him. However, his mind was too full of other matters for him to be concerned.

Charles Boynton grasped his arm for a moment.

Jonathan appreciated the gesture. There was one person present who could understand his bewilderment and the aching void that, he knew, would grow deeper and become all-pervading.

Several of the carpenters who had worked on *Flying Dragon* were present, and Jonathan knew his duty. He spoke to each of them, thanking them for their part in the establishment of the clipper's dazzling record.

Jeremiah watched him and knew his son had not changed. He was still a Rakehell, placing his duty to the dynasty above everything else.

Dockworkers brought the officers' gear ashore, and while Charles drifted toward Ruth and Edmund, Jonathan made arrangements with a yard foreman to have his valuable cargo of tea stored under guard in one of the company warehouses.

Several carriages were waiting, and Jonathan rode with his father, Louise, and Julian, who suddenly became shy and clung to his mother.

"Later in the day," Jeremiah said, "I want to bring you and Charles up to date on some major developments in the business. We'll attend to all that before the family assembles for a welcoming dinner. But first there's something even more important to attend to. Everyone here believes you and Louise were married secretly before you sailed to Cathay. Under the circumstances we had to lie, but now we're going to rectify the situation. As fast as possible. I've already sent a messenger to Reverend Crowell, and I'm sure he'll be joining us at home very shortly."

Louise stared straight ahead, her dry lips parted. Obviously she was suffused with shame because of the need for a marriage ceremony to be performed under such circumstances.

Jonathan couldn't help feeling sorry for her, even though he yearned for Lai-tse lu, who was now beyond his reach. "I want Charles to stand up with me," he heard himself say.

"No one except Louise's parents, Reverend Crowell, Judith, and I know the truth, and I asked Judith not to tell Charles. Julian has already been baptized as a Rakehell, and I see no reason for anyone else to learn anything more."

"Charles and I have no secrets from each other," Jonathan said stubbornly. His real reason for demanding that his cousin be present, he knew, was that Charles was his only link now with Lai-tse lu, whose love he was being forced to betray.

His father couldn't understand his adamant stand, but gave in to him. "Very well," he said, and was at least relieved that the future American and English directors of the new company were still so close.

Soon after they reached the Rakehell house and the Walkers dropped Charles there, Louise's parents crossed the street. They greeted Jonathan cordially enough, but there was reserve in their attitude for which he could not blame them. After all, he had seduced their daughter and forced her to struggle alone in an untenable position for many months.

"You'll want to change into a prettier, more appropriate dress, dear," Naomi Graves said to her daughter when she learned that the clergyman would arrive momentarily.

Jonathan was startled when Louise spoke harshly to her mother.

"Really, Mama!" she exclaimed. "This isn't the usual

wedding, and I want to make as little of it as possible. We're taking a necessary legal step for reasons that are very clear to everyone concerned, and it would be absurd to make a fuss!"

Naomi promptly subsided, her lips compressed.

Jeremiah handed his son a gold band. "I had this made months ago," he said. "Louise has been wearing another, but she'll appreciate a genuine wedding ring in place of a mockery."

Jonathan thought of the gold band he had given to Lai-tse lu on their last night together. The true mockery was far worse than his father knew, and his anger began to mount again.

Charles quietly led him to one of the auxiliary parlors and handed him a small glass of whiskey. "Drink this before you explode, old boy," he said.

Jonathan gulped the contents of the glass.

"Think you can go through with it?" his cousin asked, watching him closely.

"I have no real choice," Jonathan said bitterly. "My God! You've seen my son. I knew the instant I set eyes on him that he's a Rakehell."

"Tough luck," Charles said.

"No, I believe we get what we deserve in this world. Louise and I made a mistake, and now we'll pay for it. For the rest of our lives. But why should Lai-tse lu be forced to suffer, too? All this is so damned unfair to her. I know my duty, and I won't evade it. Because I couldn't live with myself. How I'll manage to live with Louise I can't imagine. But that doesn't much matter. I'd give anything or do anything to prevent Lai-tse lu from being hurt. I'm tempted to reassemble the crew, sail back to Canton, and stay there. But I can't. Because I'd be living an even bigger lie."

"Steady," Charles said. "The padre has just arrived."

They walked together to the principal parlor, where the Reverend Crowell offered Jonathan his felicitations on his magnificent sailing feat.

That achievement already had lost its savor, and Jonathan replied automatically.

The parlor doors were closed, and the ceremony

began without further ado. Jonathan and Louise did not look at each other.

When the time came for him to place the gold band on her finger his hands were numb and hers were icy.

At the end of the ceremony their lips brushed in a token kiss, a gesture as hollow as the feeling in the pit of the bridegroom's stomach.

Reverend Crowell, refusing an invitation to stay for dinner, had a parting word for the couple. "I'm quite sure you'll make your way through life together, and the unhappiness you've known will strengthen rather than weaken the bonds that unite you. I have known others who have been married under—ah—similar circumstances, and their marriages have been stronger because of it."

Louise looked glassy-eyed and remained silent.

Jonathan tried to thank the clergyman, but the words stuck in his throat.

Only Naomi looked pleased and relieved.

But Dr. Graves was aware of the tensions in the air and announced that he and his wife would return home, coming back in time for the family dinner.

Louise felt an even more urgent need to escape. "It's time for Julian to be fed," she said. "I—I always like to be present when he eats." She fled quickly from the room.

Never had Jonathan felt so low, so miserable.

"Come along to my study, boys," Jeremiah said to his son and nephew. "We'll have a glass of sack and exchange our news."

Jonathan was silent, so Charles had to take the initiative and tell his uncle about the huge profits *Flying Dragon* had earned during the thirteen months she had been in Soong Chao's service.

"That's splendid," a beaming Jeremiah said. "Now, I trust, both of you are prepared to return to the fold in earnest." He told them in detail about the merger of the Rakehell and Boynton companies.

Jonathan sat with his fists clenched, forcing himself to listen. His own life was a shambles and he had condemned Lai-tse lu to an unhappy existence for the rest of her days, but at least he could work. That was his only salvation.

"Jonnie," his father said, "I'm giving you enough of my stock to make you an equal partner immediately. You'll also be a partner, Charles, but I think it will be more appropriate if your own father explains the details of that arrangement to you."

"Of course, sir," Charles murmured, even in his excitement over the business changes keeping a wary eye on his cousin.

"As you may guess," Jeremiah said, "we've had more requests for clipper ships than any one company can possibly handle. I've had four new ways built for you, Jonnie, so you can construct four at a time, if that suits you."

Jonathan looked grim. "Give me enough competent carpenters," he said flatly, "and I'll turn out eight clippers every year. I've already made my sketches for a new design, and I'll be ready to go into production when the yard opens tomorrow morning. If you'll give me the men and have enough seasoned timber on hand."

"Certainly," his father replied. "I've scoured all of New England for lumber, anticipating your return. But there's no need for you to pitch in all that fast. Take a holiday with Louise for a couple of weeks, why don't you? Take Julian with you or leave him here, as you and Louise see fit."

"I want to get to work as soon as I can," Jonathan said, his voice grating.

Charles shifted the emphasis of the conversation before his uncle began to guess what was amiss. "Are any others building clippers?"

"There are several companies here that are fairly far advanced in their plans," Jeremiah said, "but we'll be the first."

"That's as it should be," Jonathan said, showing grim satisfaction.

"For the next year or two, at the least," Jeremiah said, "I'll want a minimum of two clippers for my fleet, and Alan will want two for his."

"Fair enough, Papa," Jonathan said, "but the very first will have to go to the Fat Dutchman in Djakarta. I reckon," he added bleakly, turning to his cousin, "that you'll want to sail her to the Dutch East Indies." He had

451

planned to make that voyage himself en route to his reunion with Lai-tse lu, a reunion that could never take place now.

"Of course," Charles said quickly.

"That should work out well," Jeremiah said, unaware of the cross-currents. "Your father and I have seen you taking charge of operations in the East for both branches of the company, if that's to your liking."

"There's nothing I'd enjoy more," Charles said, and avoided looking at Jonathan.

"What about you, Jonnie?" Jeremiah asked. "Have you put your wanderlust out of your system after your long stay in Cathay?"

"A part of me will remain in the Middle Kingdom as long as I live," Jonathan replied. "But, to answer your question, I'm prepared to spend my full time building clippers. And working with Charles—from this end. Both of us have acquired a sound understanding of markets in the East, and by continuing to work together I believe we can teach even the biggest of our competitors a few tricks."

Charles agreed, but was concerned because Jonathan took no pleasure in the prospects. He was coldly determined to do his part, but he was totally lacking in buoyancy.

They concluded the session with an agreement that Charles would return to England after the clipper was refitted and her crew returned from furlough. Thereafter, in accordance with Jonathan's wishes, Edmund Barker would become her master.

As they rose to their feet Jonathan asked suddenly, "Papa, have you and Uncle Alan designed a new house flag for the Rakehell-Boynton fleet?"

"No, we've been so busy that's one detail we haven't yet worked out."

"Then I propose that we adopt the Tree of Life design that flies from my masthead," Jonathan said. "I want every ship in our combined fleet to carry that pennant." He knew he was making a forlorn gesture on Lai-tse lu's behalf, but it was all he could offer.

As the three men emerged from the study, Louise came downstairs with Julian, and before the child was put to bed for his afternoon nap, Jonathan began the process of becoming acquainted with him. The man was clumsy and self-conscious, the boy was shy and leery, but they managed to break the ice and soon were laughing together as they romped. Then Jonathan opened one of the packages of gifts he had brought from China and presented his son with a jade dragon. Julian was fascinated by it.

Remembering the magnificent porcelain vase that Lai-tse lu had given him to present to Louise, Jonathan interrupted his play with the baby long enough to hand it to the woman who had so unexpectedly become his wife.

Louise smiled for the first time since his return. "You didn't forget me, after all," she murmured.

Her reaction jarred him. Perhaps she wasn't as indifferent to him as she appeared, and that possibility made him realize that their relationship was certain to be complex. Nothing could dilute or destroy his love for Lai-tse lu, but Louise had a right to demand his loyalty, and no matter what might develop he was trapped.

He had little opportunity to dwell on his impossible situation. Judith and her family soon arrived, Dr. and Mrs. Graves returned, and the gifts that Jonathan and Charles had brought from China were distributed. Jeremiah was particularly pleased with a carved pipe fashioned of rare wood.

"The American market for products like this is almost unlimited," he said.

Louise glanced at him briefly, then silently shook her head. Rakehells, it seemed, always thought in terms of commerce.

Jonathan had been looking forward to his first American meal in almost two years, but he was so heartsick he had little appetite for the clam chowder, broiled sole, beef roast with trimmings, or the blueberry pie that had long been one of his favorite dishes.

Charles amused the company by demonstrating his facility with chopsticks. Judith urged her brother to show that he, too, could eat with them, but Jonathan refused. The ivory chopsticks that Lai-tse lu's father had given him were precious souvenirs, and he wanted no one to see

453

them. They belonged to a part of his life that had come to an abrupt end.

At the close of the meal Jeremiah made an announcement. "You'll be pleased to hear," he said, "that I'm transferring enough of my stock in Rakehell and Boynton to make Jonathan a full partner. He's going to devote all of his time to the building of new clipper ships and working with Charles on the development of our trade in the East."

Judith was delighted, as were Dr. and Mrs. Graves, and Louise smiled vaguely. Bradford Walker looked as though he had been struck a sharp blow. Color drained from his face, and Charles, who sat opposite him, saw that he was badly upset.

Jeremiah was not unaware of his son-in-law's reaction, and after the meal he took him aside for a private word. "In reorganizing our operations, Brad," he said, "I've decided to put you in charge of the brigs and schooners. How does that strike you?"

"It's fine with me, sir." Brad forced a smile, but seethed inwardly. Clippers were the ships of the future, and he was being saddled with responsibility for constructing and operating the old-fashioned vessels whose days were numbered. His new post might appear to the outside world to be a promotion, but he knew that he would advance no farther. His worst fears had been realized, and there seemed to be nothing he could do to curb the archrival who had passed him in the race.

But he could not and would not admit permanent defeat. He had to find some way to regain the lead. Jonathan had been lucky, but like all people he had to be vulnerable in some way. Brad promised himself he would find and exploit that weakness.

Everyone adjourned to the parlor, and Charles, conscious of Jonathan's silence, enlivened the party with stories about life in the East. He talked at length about the Fat Dutchman in Djakarta, forcing Jonathan to admit quietly that he had become expert in the art of Indonesian knife-throwing. Charles took care, however, to make no mention of Lai-tse lu when he talked about life in Cathay.

Jeremiah's questions were penetrating, dealing principally with trade and its potentials. Jonathan was drawn into the conversation, and he and Charles talked at length about commercial matters. Dr. and Mrs. Graves were bored, and soon after they departed the Walkers went home, too. Louise went up to the nursery to give Julian his supper, and the discussion of Eastern trade went on.

"You boys are indebted to Soong Chao," Jeremiah said. "Thanks to the voyages you made on his behalf, you've gained an understanding of every major market in the Orient."

"We're more in his debt than I can ever explain," Jonathan said. "I lived in his home for weeks at a time, and he treated me like a son." Circumstances were making it impossible for him to return to Canton, and the realization crushed him.

When Jeremiah began to yawn Charles excused himself, saying he needed a breath of air. Knowing his cousin's ways, Jonathan was certain he would visit a tavern, then go on to one of the town's bordellos. What he failed to realize was that Charles, sensitive to Jonathan's cruel predicament, had to escape for a time.

Not until Jeremiah retired did Jonathan face the full force of his dilemma. Louise had not come downstairs again, but he lingered in the parlor as long as he could. This was his wedding night, and never had there been a more reluctant bridegroom. Ultimately, however, he was compelled to mount the stairs, dreading the scene that awaited him.

For a long time he stood in the corridor outside the chamber he had occupied as a bachelor. Too upset to think clearly, he knew he could not spend the whole night in the hallway, so he raised the latch and went in.

Oil lamps were burning on tables at both sides of the four-poster bed, where Louise was propped up against the pillows, dressed in a nightgown and a high-necked negligee. She had unpinned her hair, and as Jonathan came into the room she put aside the book she was reading and tried to speak casually.

"I didn't come back downstairs," she said, "because you and Charles were talking business with Papa Rakehell, and I didn't want to disturb you."

"We wouldn't have minded," he replied politely. "You're always welcome to join us, you know, even when we get involved in business matters."

"I don't believe a Rakehell ever talks about anything else," she said, her tone matter-of-fact.

Jonathan excused himself and, going to the adjoining dressing room, changed into the silk Chinese pajamas he had learned to wear at night. Conscious of the Tree of Life jade pendant that he had not removed since Lai-tse lu had given it to him, he made an effort not to think about it. Again he hesitated, but there seemed to be no way to avoid the inevitable, and he went back into the bedchamber.

Louise was obviously flustered and embarrassed, and averted her gaze.

Taking a deep breath, Jonathan climbed into the four-poster beside her. "Forgive me for finding this unexpected," he said.

"I know. It can't be easy for you."

"For either of us. Just as you must have had a difficult life the whole time I was away. When did you learn you were carrying Julian?"

"About two months after you left."

"I'm sorry," Jonathan said. "That night was my own fault."

"No, I've got to share the blame with you. Anyway, now we're facing the consequences."

"We have no choice," he said.

Louise stared off into space for a time. "It would be so much simpler if we loved each other," she murmured. Still not looking at him, she asked in a small voice, "You don't love me, do you, Jonnie?"

He wished there were some way he could reply diplomatically without hurting her, yet at the same time he knew she deserved the truth. "I wish I did," he said. "And could."

She nodded. "I've told my mother how we feel, and she keeps telling me not to worry about it. She says she wasn't in love with my father when they were first married. But people become accustomed to each other, and that helps."

"I suppose it does." He knew he was expected to take a physical initiative, but his love for Lai-tse lu was overwhelming him, rendering him immobile. "You know I'll always do my best for you. And for Julian," he said lamely.

Louise nodded. "I know." His code of honor was so firm and unyielding it had never crossed her mind that he might refuse to live up to his obligations to her.

They could not spend the whole night talking in circles. "Shall we put out the lights?"

"I guess so." She extinguished the lamp beside her.

Jonathan did the same. Steeling himself, he moved closer to her, then tentatively reached for her.

The chain that encircled his neck snapped, and the jade medallion fell to the bed between Jonathan and Louise.

He broke into a cold sweat. At that instant he felt that Lai-tse lu herself was present, telling him forcibly that even though circumstances he had been unable to control had compelled him to marry Louise, his love would be denigrated and mocked if he made advances to anyone else, even to this woman who had become his wife.

Closing his eyes for a moment, he could see Lai-tse lu looking at him, her lovely face unsmiling, her eyes grave.

She was right.

He picked up the medallion, vowing to repair it early in the morning. Still clutching it, he wrenched himself out of bed and went to a chair at the far side of the room.

Louise sat up. "Shall I light the lamp?"

"If you wish."

"I—I'd rather we talk in the dark," she said.

Jonathan turned the jade medallion over in his hand. "I tried just now," he said, "but I can't live a lie. Or force you to live one with me."

"Thank you, Jonnie."

He was surprised to hear relief in her voice, and he knew that she had been dreading his lovemaking.

"I'll sleep on the sofa in our sitting room," he said. "And tomorrow I'll have a bed brought in there for me."

"Yes," Louise said faintly, "it will be best that way."

"Papa asked me tonight if we want to move to a house of our own. What do you think?"

"It's very comfortable here," she said, "and I know very little about hiring servants and running a house. I—I just wonder if Papa Rakehell will think it strange that we're using separate bedrooms."

"Never," he said, "would my father interfere or even comment on our private lives."

"Then," she replied with a sigh, "I'd rather stay here, if that's agreeable with you."

"Indeed it is." The familiar surroundings he had known since earliest childhood would make Jonathan's strange new existence easier to bear.

Taking a pillow and blanket, he went to the adjoining sitting room. He supposed, as he drifted off into an uneasy sleep, that in time he would learn to accept the fact that he had a wife and a son. For the rest of the night he dreamed of Lai-tse lu, and in his dream she wore the gleaming Tree of Life jade medallion.

"The real secret of a clipper ship's success," Jonathan told his father, "lies in the efficiency of her crew. I'm leaving my old company intact when Charles and Edmund sail *Flying Dragon* to England because they'll be breaking in two new mates. Then, after she comes home under Edmund's command, he'll have to get himself a new bo's'n and bo's'n's mate, preferably by promoting a couple of the present crew members who are easily eligible. I'm detaching Grimshaw and Oliver for special duty."

"Can you be more specific, Jonnie?"

"Certainly, sir." Jonathan was crisp. "We've already built the mock deck, masts, and shrouds of a clipper. Grimshaw and Oliver will put the crews of our new clippers through a rigorous training course. Charles and I have already laid out a detailed schedule."

"You'll start training your new crews several months before they go to sea?" Jeremiah was surprised. "That will be expensive."

"Damned expensive, Papa. But it will pay rich dividends in the long run. If there's one thing I've learned, no clipper is better than her crew. A new company, unfamiliar with the peculiarities of a clipper, would take three weeks to reach England. But mark my words. Charles will break the west to east transatlantic record with our seasoned hands."

Charles Boynton proved to be as good as his cousin's word. *Flying Dragon* created a new sensation and made newspaper headlines throughout the Western world when she made the crossing in the remarkable time of fifteen days.

The Boynton family gave Charles a warm but decorous welcome, celebrating his return home with a banquet that included all of his favorite dishes. He presented his mother with an exquisite, lacquered tea tray as well as a dozen almost transparent porcelain cups and saucers. Sir Alan was the recipient of a handsome replica of *Flying Dragon,* carved in jade by a Canton artist.

Elizabeth's principal gift had a mixed reception. She went off to her room to change into the cheongsam of silk, embroidered with imperial dragons, and when she returned to the drawing room in it, her parents and brother instantly realized that her figure was no longer that of a child. Her breasts were developing, her waist was small, and her legs were long.

"I was afraid the dress would be too large for you," Charles said. "But when I described you in detail to the—ah—lady who made it, she swore it would fit a tall English girl of thirteen, and she was right." He refrained from explaining that the seamstress had been Alice Wong, and he had no intention of mentioning his own relationship with her.

Elizabeth preened as she walked up and down the room beyond the borders of the thick Ottoman rug, her first pair of high heels clicking on the hardwood floor. "It fits like a glove," she said proudly.

Jessica was dubious. "A bit too much like a glove, if you ask me. Those slits in the sides of the skirt show so much of your legs that the dress is positively indecent."

"That's the way they're worn in the Middle Kingdom," Charles said.

"This is England, not Cathay," Jessica declared. "Perhaps you may wear it to a costume party, Elizabeth, but nowhere else."

"Please, Mama, let me wear it to the Dutch Minister's reception tomorrow," the girl begged. "Last year there were several ladies from Indonesia wearing clothes like this."

"It can do no harm," Alan said, entering the conversa-

459

tion for the first time. "She isn't a grown woman yet, you know, so I can't see the harm."

Jessica made it a principle never to enter into a dispute with her husband concerning the children in their presence. "Very well."

"Thank you," Elizabeth said, glowing. "Oh, how I wish Jonathan could be there to see me!"

"In case you've forgotten it," Jessica said sternly, "Jonathan has a wife and child."

Far more important than that, Charles thought, his cousin had left the love of his life in Canton, and a man of his character never again would be interested in any other woman.

The following morning Charles marked his return to work by going off to the family shipyard in Southwark to recruit the crew for the first English clipper. "Those who sign up," he told a large group of assembled seamen, "will go to America when *Flying Dragon* returns there in a few days. Those of you who accept the assignment will go on full sea pay the day you leave. In America you'll be given a special training course until your ship goes to sea."

So great was the lure of the highly publicized, romantic clipper ships that seamen clamored for the right to sign, and there were more than enough volunteers to make up two crews, those who were postponed until the second clipper came off the ways understanding that they would not travel to the United States for another half-year.

Charles had expected the task to last the better part of the day, but he reached the office in time to discuss the Eastern trade situation with his father before lunch. Then they walked together down streets lined with elms to St. James's. The whole district was located in the vicinity of the palace now occupied by the young Queen Victoria when she was in London, and everywhere men in top hats, carrying walking sticks, were strolling to their own clubs. More than a dozen of these institutions, several of them two hundred years old, were located within a stone's throw of each other, their membership composed exclusively of blue-blooded noblemen and gentlemen of means from the rapidly expanding middle class.

Sir Alan's club was one of the most distinguished. Not

even the oldest living members could recall the reasons for some of the organization's peculiar rules. Smoking of pipes and *cigarros* was permitted in some rooms but forbidden in others; the lighting of coal fires was allowed in some chambers but prohibited in others. The only rule that made sense, Charles long had thought, was that which forbade talking in the library.

In the cavernous, high-ceilinged dining room the members ate at so-called "common tables," each with a dozen places. Diners sat where they pleased, and it was an unwritten but strictly observed regulation that no member could be denied a seat at any table. Sir Alan and Charles, who were among the latecomers, took the last two places at a table where a banker, the proprietor of a coal mine, two factory owners who had new plants in the Midlands, and a marquess and several earls were already seated. The most conspicuous man at the table, because of the dress uniform which he had worn to the launching of a warship that morning, was Vice Admiral Sir Nigel Howe, the second sea lord. He had received his knighthood in the Order of the Bath for winning a battle as a frigate captain off Guadeloupe in the West Indies during the interminable sea war between England and France that had been waged, almost without pause, from 1793 to 1814.

Charles ordered raw oysters and a steak and kidney pie. Everyone at the table was interested in his exploits as first mate of *Flying Dragon* on her record-breaking voyage to China and, as the clipper's master, the just-completed voyage from the United States. While he sipped a pre-meal pint of ale he was bombarded with questions about clipper ships.

The admiral appeared not to be listening to the various queries. "Would you recommend clippers as warships, Mr. Boynton?" one gentleman wanted to know.

"Only to carry messages and dispatches, and that wouldn't be practical."

The admiral unbent sufficiently to ask, "Would you utilize them as troop carriers?"

"Not in their present form, Sir Nigel. Jonathan Rakehell is currently building several clippers twice the size of *Flying Dragon,* but the deck, cabin, and cargo space would

461

have to be enlarged still more to make them practical for that purpose. Perhaps that will be done some day, although I doubt it. A clipper of four thousand or five thousand tons displacement would be too cumbersome and would reduce the great speed that is a clipper's greatest primary asset."

The banker and the two industrialists inquired about trade prospects in the East.

"The Middle Kingdom, because of her size and population, is our best potential market," Charles said. "If we behave ourselves I believe the Chinese gradually will ease their restrictions on trade with us. The Dutch East Indies also will become a valuable market, especially now that the Netherlands government is allowing freer trade there. The Philippines are developing very slowly under Spanish rule. Siam is so isolated that even if King Rama granted trade permits, which is unlikely, I have no idea what we might buy or sell there. And Formosa is so primitive that I don't think it will be of major interest to us for many decades to come."

The admiral raised a shaggy eyebrow. "What did you mean, Mr. Boynton, when you made that remark, 'if we behave ourselves' in Cathay? Surely you didn't mean it literally."

Charles sipped his ale thoughtfully before he replied. "I became fairly well acquainted with Commodore Sir William Alexander at Whampoa, Sir Nigel. I like him as a person. He's a fine fellow. But his policies in dealing with the Chinese are harsh."

"I've known Billy Alexander since he was a midshipman," the second sea lord declared, "and I agree with your personal assessment. As a representative of the Crown, however, he's sometimes a trifle too lenient in his dealings with the Chinese."

"Lenient, Sir Nigel?" Charles had to keep his temper under control. "He threatens the Chinese with his cannon and makes it impossible for their authorities to control the smuggling of opium into the Middle Kingdom!"

Sir Alan tried to warn his son with a glance.

But Charles was too incensed to pay any attention to his father. "Surely the Royal Navy wouldn't send warships to New York or Cherbourg and force the Americans or the French to allow our merchant ships to bring opium into those countries!"

The admiral became distinctly chilly. "China, Mr. Boynton, is neither the United States nor the Kingdom of France. The Chinese are a primitive, barbarian people."

Charles was shocked to hear a senior official in Queen Victoria's government display such profound ignorance. The Chinese were the most cultured people he himself had ever encountered.

Sir Alan kicked him under the table to keep him silent.

"Only a backward people would develop a taste for opium," the admiral declared. "You don't see people here smoking the filthy stuff."

"There are whites in the Orient who have become addicted to it," Charles said carefully. "I've seen several of them in Djakarta and Manila. Opium doesn't respect race, Sir Nigel, and once the craving spreads to the British Isles, I think you'll find our government will take steps fast enough to halt the traffic."

"I think it unlikely that day will ever come, Mr. Boynton," the second sea lord said stiffly. "For the present we have every right under international custom to demand that the emperor of China open his doors to our trade. And the trade of other Western nations. No nation can hide behind walls in an enlightened age."

Charles well knew the admiral was expressing a view commonly held in official circles and was appalled by the man's arrogance. "As someone who earns his living in trade," he replied, "I'm eager to see every nation open her doors to us, Sir Nigel. The Chinese have been isolated for several thousand years, but they're beginning to see the benefits of exchanging products with us, and I believe that if we proceed gently the doors will be opened wider and wider to us."

"Are you implying that we shouldn't force them open?"

Charles realized there was nothing to be gained by arguing with someone who would not change his views. "When our clipper ship had the good fortune to visit Siam," he said, "we were permitted to anchor at Bangkok because the Chinese gentleman who had us under hire was on board. He took our captain on shore with him, but the rest of us were required to remain on board."

"That was outrageous!" the second sea lord declared.

Charles vividly recalled the sewer-like odors of Bangkok, and smiled. "Frankly, Sir Nigel, I wanted to weigh anchor as rapidly as possible and leave the town."

"The day will soon come," the admiral thundered, "when the Royal Navy will blast open the gates of nations like Siam, too!"

Charles merely nodded and devoted his attention to his raw oysters. Unless Britain changed her insolent attitude she would be piling up problems for herself and other Western nations in the East. But he didn't know how to convince men who had never visited the Orient, had predetermined ideas about that part of the world, and insisted on their own superiority. Unless they adopted new policies blood was certain to flow, the blood of Westerners as well as that of the men, women, and children of the East.

The eunuchs who ruled the bureaucracy of the imperial government in Peking intensely disliked Lin Tse-hsü, an aristocratic mandarin of the second class, because he was independent, had no use for subtleties, and was fearless both in his actions and his opinions. Tall and distinguished, Lin could have led the life of a scholar, but instead he had chosen a career as an administrator. He won the confidence of the Tao Kuang Emperor when he eliminated corruption in two provinces, where he served as governor.

Now, consulting no one, the emperor appointed Lin as the new Imperial Viceroy of Kwantung. Teng Ting-chen, who had served faithfully, would be moved to another post after talks with his successor. The eunuchs of the court were furious, but lacked the courage to persuade the emperor to change his mind.

Lin Tse-hsü demonstrated that he was a man of simple tastes by arriving in Canton on board an ordinary junk. He came ashore with a retinue of only ten persons, and like his subordinates, he wore a gown of inexpensive cotton similar to the attire of scholars at the institutes of higher learning. To the astonishment of local officials he was accompanied neither by a wife nor the usual concubines of the highest-ranking officials.

Surprising the members of the foreign community at Whampoa, he spoke a fluent English, and displaying a great interest in the compound, he insisted on inspecting the factories before proceeding through the Petition Gate, accompanied only by the members of his staff and escorted by a sub-company of only twenty soldiers.

He arrived at the palace without fanfare, and the astonished officer in charge of the guard, who failed to recognize him, was so abashed that he killed himself. Lin's first act was to order a pension paid to the unfortunate officer's widow.

For three days and nights Lin and his predecessor conferred in private behind closed doors. The first person summoned by them was Lo Fang, who was reconfirmed in his post of viceregal majordomo.

Teng Ting-chen departed with a company of more than one hundred, including eleven concubines, and he and the members of his entourage paraded through the city to Whampoa, surrounded by three thousand imperial troops. Three large junks were provided for the party's comfort, and when they sailed off to Tientsin, fireworks were lighted, gongs boomed, and cymbals crashed.

Meanwhile Lin settled into the palace and went to work, holding private sessions with each of his principal subordinates, then summoning prominent citizens for individual conferences. The first of these was Soong Chao.

The new viceroy received him in a small, comfortably furnished chamber, and after Soong made his obeisances the representative of the Divine Emperor made him feel at home by offering him tea, mints, and a bowl of lightly salted nuts.

"You are known in the Forbidden City as an honest and honorable man who is totally opposed to the traffic of opium. That view has been reconfirmed by my predecessor, who assures me I can rely on you in all things."

Soong Chao bowed modestly.

"The Tao Kuang Emperor has sent me here for a special purpose," the new viceroy declared. "Until such time as I am ready to act, that purpose must be concealed from all Fan Kuei."

"You may count on my discretion, Excellency," Chao said.

"I hope I may also count on your active cooperation," Lin declared. "I have come to Canton to rid the Middle Kingdom of the vile trade in drugs."

Chao was delighted and showed his pleasure.

"The patience of the emperor has been exhausted. Thousands of his subjects have been enslaved by the smoking of opium. Our physicians know of no cure for them, and their only release will be death. In the meantime our silver pours into the hands of criminal dealers and of the Fan Kuei who have no regard for our laws." The viceroy's voice became firmer. "I have been given the powers to take any steps—any steps, mind you—that I regard as necessary and appropriate to end this traffic for all time. Whether I shall succeed remains to be seen in the years ahead, but if I fail it will not be due to cowardice or lack of effort."

"What may I do to help in this enterprise, Excellency?" Chao asked.

Lin smiled. "My heart becomes lighter when I hear you volunteer your services," he said. "Heed my words. I intend to tread quietly for a time. I intend to make my preparations with great care, and then I shall strike boldly. For your private information, I have already ordered my majordomo, Lo Fang, to learn the identities of all Chinese who are engaged in the drug trade. All of them, without exception. I will make no move until I know every name and the man's place of residence. Then my agents, wearing the dress of ordinary citizens, will arrest every one of these criminals at the same hour. They will be paraded through the streets in chains, and then they will be executed in public, one by one. The streets will run with their blood."

Chao's reading had given him an understanding of the equities of Western concepts of justice, and he asked, "You will not place them on trial, Excellency?"

"They are guilty of murder, so there will be no need for them to be tried," the new viceroy said firmly. "If we are to rid ourselves of the drug trade, I can afford to show mercy to no one."

It was possible that innocent men falsely accused might suffer along with the real malefactors, but no one, not even Soong Chao, could question the decision of the Celestial Emperor's representative.

"I intend to move with equal force in the Pearl River Delta and Whampoa," Lin Tse-hsü declared. "My war junks—and I shall have many of them, heavily armed— will intercept those who board the vessels of the foreigners. I shall raid every warehouse in Whampoa that hides opium, and I shall hold the governments of the Fan Kuei responsible for the acts of their citizens."

Chao was stunned, knowing that the Western governments would react violently to such treatment of their people. And he knew enough of Western ways to realize that no Fan Kuei government would accept the blame for deeds performed by its individual citizens. This difference in the principle of justice was the most serious potential cause of misunderstanding and contention between the Middle Kingdom and the nations of the West.

"The Chinese who work on the docks and in the warehouses of Whampoa," Lin continued, "are known to you and your foremen. Let these workers keep their eyes opened wide in the months ahead. I want you to have them questioned, regularly and privately. Find out which of the warehouse owners and managers are defying our laws by hiding opium. Find out the exact location of that opium. Then, when my agents raid the warehouses, they will know exactly where to look for the drugs. The Fan Kuei will have no chance to destroy or remove the boxes before I seize them." The viceroy looked grimly triumphant.

"I will do as Your Excellency commands," Chao murmured.

Lin studied him for a moment. "I detect a lack of enthusiasm in your voice, Soong."

"It is so," Chao admitted. "I have come to know the foreigners well. I believe I am better acquainted with them than anyone else in all of the Middle Kingdom. And I am afraid their governments will not tolerate such acts on our part."

"Their wishes do not matter to me," Lin said. "They are guests on our soil, and they must act accordingly."

"Excellency, you are unfamiliar with their arrogant ways. Some are decent, honorable men who obey our laws." Chao thought of Jonathan, who would become his son-in-law. "Others have no regard for what we believe is right. Commodore Sir William Alexander, the commander of the British squadron in our waters, is my friend. He is a gentleman, and he feels great sympathy for us. But he is an officer in the service of his queen, so he must obey his own superiors."

"If British citizens break our laws, I will instruct this commodore to inform his queen that she is responsible," the viceroy said emphatically. "She will be required to offer her apologies to the Tao Kuang Emperor and to deliver British criminals into his hands. She will be commanded, too, to offer reparations to the divine ruler of the Middle Kingdom, before whom all potentates on earth must bow their heads."

Chao was appalled by his inability to understand the foreign mentality. No self-respecting foreigner would abase himself by kowtowing to any high-ranking imperial representative—or to the emperor himself. "It may be," he said delicately, "that the British commodore and others who command the soldiers and sailors of the West will refuse our demands."

"If they do, our war junks will send their ships to the bottom of the sea, and our soldiers will cut off the heads of their troops." Lin was defiantly adamant.

The merchant's heart sank. "Their guns," he said, "are more powerful and more accurate than our cannon. Their soldiers are better trained, and they carry weapons far more modern than our ancient rifles and spears."

"Perhaps Chinese blood also will be spilled," the viceroy conceded. "But for each of our war junks the Fan Kuei sink, two others will appear in its place. I am determined to end the traffic in opium, no matter how great the cost!"

As Soong Chao returned to his own estate he knew the cost to China would be very high.

Lai-tse lu came to her father's workroom almost as soon as he returned home.

"There is dread in my heart," he told her, and repeated his conversation with the viceroy.

She immediately grasped the principles of what was at stake. "There will be war between the Middle Kingdom and the nations of the West."

"I share that fear," her father replied. "I believe the traffic in opium will be ended only when we negotiate with the West rationally, and this we can do by demonstrating to their governments that the opium trade is evil."

"The British, who have more factories in Whampoa than any other nation and whose warships stay in our waters, will be the first to go to war with us," Lai-tse lu said.

Chao nodded. "The new viceroy appears to be convinced that their queen must accept the Celestial Emperor as her overlord, and in his ignorance he cannot understand that this will never take place."

"I shall go to the Temple of Serenity and Peace this very day," Lai-tse lu declared, "and I will light joss sticks in honor of the gods. I will pray that they will prevent a war between the Middle Kingdom and the United States."

"May your prayers be answered," her father said.

She stood erect, her luminous eyes blazing. "Even if the gods are deaf to my pleas," she said, "I will let nothing stand between me and Jonathan. Even if our nations should go to war with each other, our love for each other is so great that we shall be married."

II

The panic of 1837 engulfed the United States, and President Martin Van Buren was powerless to halt the deepening economic depression. Banks failed, factories in the Eastern Seaboard states closed, and farmers everywhere lost their homes. Former President Andrew Jackson added his voice to those who were asking the people of America to remain calm, saying in a statement that the growing nation was strong and that the turning of the financial tide depended on a change in public attitude. But the panic continued to spread.

Few industries were spared, but shipbuilding actually enjoyed a boom. There was a widening recognition of the need for increased international trade, and clipper ships promised a glittering salvation because they could carry American products to any part of the globe far more rapidly than any other vessels. The demand for clippers was insatiable, and the yards in New York and Boston, Marblehead and Newport began to construct them.

But no company enjoyed the prosperity of Rakehell and Boynton, whose *Flying Dragon* had set the pace and demonstrated the worth of these sleek, new ships. The first of the new clippers were launched on schedule, and the keels were laid for their successors the following day, with work crews given no respite. Jonathan Rakehell was eager to add facilities that would enable him to build five clippers simultaneously, but his father, who was reluctant to expand too rapidly, dissuaded him.

The first of the new clippers was sent off to England with a British crew trained at the Rakehell and Boynton yard in New London. Charles Boynton had hoped to come to America in order to command the vessel on her maiden voyage, but he was too busy at home and postponed his assumption of the command until her arrival, when he had her fitted for the long voyage to the Dutch East Indies. Nothing, he wrote to his cousin, would deprive him of the pleasure of delivering the clipper personally to the Fat Dutchman in Djakarta.

"All Rakehells are demons for work," Ruth Barker's father told her and Edmund, who was home on a brief leave before resuming command of *Flying Dragon,* now in trans-Atlantic service. "Mr. Jeremiah keeps his nose close to the grindstone, just like his pa before him. But that Jonathan is a maniac! Work, work, work! I swear, the man don't think of anything else!"

The master carpenter spoke the truth. Jonathan went off to the yard with his father every morning, returning long enough at noon for a quick meal and a romp with his small son, but he rarely returned with Jeremiah at the end of the day, staying at the yard so late that the family's schedules had to be changed. Supper now was served an hour later than previously in order to accommodate him.

The carpenters and shipwrights working at the four separate ways never knew when he would appear next, and he seemingly performed the impossible feat of showing up simultaneously in four different places. Critical and demanding, he supervised every phase of each clipper's construction, and he left nothing to chance. He drove his men hard, but he was loyal to them, and when Bradford Walker suggested that wages be cut because the national Panic was making so many carpenters available, Jonathan responded by giving his men increases in pay. They replied to his devotion by working that much harder for him.

The yard was open six days each week, and Jonathan would have ordered Sunday shifts, too, had public opinion in the New England town not demanded that the Sabbath be observed. He was prepared to do what others could not, however, and each Sunday, after dinner, he went to the yard. With increasing frequency he took his son with him, and

Julian, to Louise's horror, enjoyed pretending to trim sail. Twice, when new clippers went to sea on their trial runs, Julian accompanied Jonathan.

More often than not Jonathan brought work home with him at night. Changing one of the parlors into an office, he used this time to supervise the voyages of his own growing fleet, and he corresponded regularly with merchants in the Caribbean and Europe. In these efforts, as in his other activities, he was meticulous, and no detail was too small to capture his complete attention.

His appetite dwindled, hollows appeared beneath his eyes, and he began to look gaunt, with flecks of gray hair starting to show at his temples. Yet he drove himself unsparingly, unmercifully, his work devouring him.

Jeremiah grew increasingly concerned and spoke privately to Louise. "I'm worried about Jonnie," he said. "Can't you persuade him to slow down?"

The young woman sighed. "I have no influence over him, Papa Rakehell," she said. "Besides, his work makes him happy, so I don't think I should interfere."

Knowing that his son and daughter-in-law slept apart and that their relationship, as nearly as he could judge, was remote and politely impersonal, he made no further attempt to persuade Louise to intervene.

Instead, as father and son walked to the yard one morning, Jeremiah said, "Come into my office for a few minutes. I'll try not to disrupt your day's schedule for too long."

The irony seemed lost on Jonathan.

"Jonnie," Jeremiah said as he settled himself behind his desk, "I'm wondering if the time hasn't come for us to hire you an assistant."

"Thanks for the thought, Papa, but I couldn't expect an assistant to take responsibility for things I've got to do myself."

"You're trying to do too much!"

Jonathan shrugged and smiled without humor. "My father always taught me there's only one way to tackle a job. Roll up your sleeves and pitch in."

"Well, your father is telling you right now that you're eating more work than you can digest. You've lost too much weight, and I sometimes hear you wandering around the house at all hours of the night."

"Oh, that." Jonathan had a logical explanation. "I've been working on a still newer design for our next generation of clippers, and I believe I've finally solved the problems. I plan to elongate the stem by another two feet, and I'll add some more stun's'ls for the sake of additional power and speed. By making my stem sharper-raked than she already is, I'll be reducing the hull's contact with the water, and that will enable me to build a still flatter bottom. According to my calculations I'll be increasing the cargo space in the holds by one to two tons. Without the sacrifice of even one knot of true clipper speeds."

The achievement was noteworthy, and Jeremiah had to praise it. "Congratulations. You're staying several leagues ahead of our competition. We now have enough orders to keep us busy for the next three years."

"The new design is sure to increase the demand again, Papa. That's why I think the time has come to expand our facilities."

"So you can push yourself still harder—and drive yourself into an early grave? I won't even consider an expansion until you reorganize your work time so you can enjoy some of life's pleasures, Jonnie. Why, last Sunday you were in such an all-fired hurry to come down to the yard that you wouldn't stay at Judith's clambake long enough for a slice of raisin pie. And I can remember the day when you'd eat an entire raisin pie by yourself."

"I guess food isn't as important as it used to be," Jonathan replied lamely. Then he added, grinning weakly, "In another half-year I'll start pestering you seriously about adding more facilities."

His father became facetious. "Why are you doing me the favor of not annoying me for another six months?"

"As soon as I go into production on the revamped design," Jonathan said, "I intend to indulge myself."

"By going off on a holiday with Louise and Julian, I hope."

"No, sir. By building a special clipper. It will be one of a kind, unlike any other on the high seas."

Jeremiah saw him truly smiling now, but his eyes were strangely wistful, and it was impossible to guess what he might be thinking.

"After she's built," Jonathan said, "I'll burn all my design prints, and there will never be another like her. She's going to be unique."

"What's the purpose of this unusual ship?"

"I want to build her." His son suddenly became harsh. "I must build her." Rising abruptly, he went off to inspect the ships currently on the ways.

Jeremiah realized that he had failed to achieve the desired results, and it was obvious, too, that Jonathan had no intention of discussing the "special" clipper or his reasons for building her. Charles Boynton, to whom his cousin might have listened, was at sea, sailing the clipper owed to the Fat Dutchman to Djakarta. So the only other person to whom Jeremiah could turn was his daughter.

"I don't know that Jonnie will listen to me, Papa. I've had no authority over him since we were children. But I'll certainly try. I realize he's been a changed person since he's come home from the East, but he doesn't appear to have lost the common sense that the Lord has been good enough to give all Rakehells, so it may be that I'll get through to him. Invite us for dinner this Sunday, and I'll take him aside for a private talk if I'm forced to tie him down!"

The invitation was issued, and the Walkers came to the Rakehell house after church services. The meal was enlivened by the presence of Julian, whose father had decreed that he was old enough to join the family on Sundays. It seemed to Judith that her brother truly enjoyed himself only in his relationship with little Julian.

When everyone rose from the table, Jonathan reacted as anticipated by announcing that he intended to go to the yard for a time.

"I'm coming with you," his sister told him.

He raised an eyebrow.

"I need the exercise," she said, and picked up her cloak, giving him no opportunity to deny her the right to accompany him.

Both were silent until they reached the street, and then Judith said, "Instead of going to the yard, let's stroll down the beach."

"The weather won't be warm enough for another month or more," he said. "Besides—"

"Besides, I want to have some words with you, obviously. And having lived in this climate for more than thirty years, I won't freeze."

He shrugged and walked at her side as she headed for the deserted beach. Then he started to increase his pace, and she found it difficult to keep up with him.

"That's unusual seaweed," Judith said, pointing to clump on the hard sand.

Jonathan paused to examine it.

She touched his arm. "We're not having a foot race, you know. Let's sit on the rocks."

He knew he was being maneuvered, but nevertheless followed her. "Jonnie," she said, "I was the first person in the family other than Mama to see you. Papa and Grandpa were on their way home from the yard when you came into the world, and I came running into the room no more than five minutes later. So it's fair to say that I've known you all of your life."

"Very fair."

"That gives me the right," Judith said, "to ask you a very personal question. What's wrong?"

"What makes you think something is wrong?" he countered.

"You're being evasive, little brother," she said, looking up at him. "You work day and night—"

"There's work to be done."

"But not all at once, Jonnie! The only time you smile is when you play with Julian. You and Louise act like strangers who have just been introduced to each other. You haven't taken as much as one full day of rest since you came home from Cathay. You talk business constantly with Papa and with Brad, whenever we're all together. You have no interest in anything else. You've lost your capacity for enjoyment, and lately you've been looking twice your age. You no longer swim or hike, and as far as I know your only form of exercise is your throwing of those horrid Indonesian knives. So you can't tell me that nothing is the matter."

Jonathan made no reply and stared out beyond the mouth of the Thames Estuary at the expanse of salt water sparkling in the early spring sunshine.

"If you force me to guess," Judith said, "your marriage has turned sour."

"No, that's not really true. Louise and I have never had a real marriage."

His sister remained silent, hoping he would continue.

Jonathan fought a grim, inner battle. Many months had passed since he had last seen Charles, and he couldn't really discuss his personal situation with Edmund Barker, who probably had formed his own ideas but didn't know for certain. In all this time Jonathan had bottled his hopeless love for Lai-tse lu within himself, and sometimes he had thought he was losing his reason. Sundays were the worst because he couldn't keep fully occupied.

"I reckon I've got to confide in someone," he said, "and I'm afraid Papa wouldn't understand. You've elected yourself, Judy, so I'll cast my vote for you, too."

He was trying to speak lightly, but Judith was conscious only of the haunted expression in his eyes. "I won't let you down, Jonnie," she said quietly.

"I know." He found himself telling her the whole story of his romance with Lai-tse lu, omitting only any mention of their actual affair. When he was done he opened his shirt and showed her the Tree of Life jade medallion that he wore around his neck.

"I've wondered why all of your Rakehell-Boynton clippers carry pennants with that design," she said, putting her hand on his arm. "What a horrid mess. I'm so sorry, Jonnie."

"I've written a thousand letters to Lai-tse lu, but I've torn every one of them to shreds. I know I'm being unfair to her, that I've got to tell her the truth, but I keep postponing really writing to her because I know I'll break her heart. God knows she'll have good cause to hate me. I'll be just another unreliable, disreputable Fan Kuei. A no-good foreign devil."

"Would it be easier for both of you if you go back to Canton and tell her in person? At least she'd know you were telling the truth," Judith said.

"I know, and I'm tempted every single day. But I can't. I know myself too well, Judy. The very instant that I saw Lai-tse lu again, my soul would cry out for her so loudly that I'd give up everything for her. My honor and what's left of my good name. The company and its future. Even Julian. I'd never leave her side again, even though I'd have to stay in exile until I died."

"Then you leave yourself no choice."

"I know. She doesn't expect me to return for another six months to a year, so I'm planning to send her my letter of explanation with a special gift. A clipper—unlike any other that has been built or will ever be built. I'm going to name it for her, and all I can do is hope she'll understand."

"If she's the kind of woman you say she is, I'm sure she'll understand," Judith said, and was silent for a time. "That's just part of what needs to be done, Jonnie. Sooner or later you've got to mend your relations with—Julian's mother."

"Louise and I knew each other too long without any love between us, Judy. We shouldn't have listened to our families, but we were too young and too naive to know any better. Not that I'm offering any valid excuses for what's happened."

"There can be no excuses," Judith said. "Louise Rakehell is your wife."

"I never forget it, I can't. But I'm sure there are other loveless marriages in this world, tens of thousands of them." He spoke savagely.

"Are you so certain your marriage is loveless?" Judith asked in a low tone.

"Of course! Haven't you been listening to me?" He sounded tortured.

"I was thinking just now of the way Louise feels. You've made your own position very clear."

"Louise is no more in love with me than I am with her, and never has been," Jonathan said. "We became engaged because it was expected of us, and one night we all

478

owed the animal desires of the young to get the better of us. Our relationship is that simple."

"I believe you're mistaken," his sister said.

He stared at her, his eyes widening.

"I've known Louise all her life, too," Judith said. "She's terribly shy and withdrawn because she's always been dominated by her mother. An observer hasn't had to be a genius to see that much, Jonnie. But I've watched her when she's looked at you—especially at times when you haven't known she's been looking. I'm a woman, too, so I have intuition as well as the Rakehell brain that the good Lord gave me. And I'm willing to swear on a whole stack of Bibles that Louise Rakehell loves her husband."

He shook his head in wonder and bewilderment.

"I'll grant you that she may not realize it herself, Jonnie. Your courtship, if it can be called that, was very rigid. She went through hell while she was pregnant, and she suffered agonies that I can't even imagine until you came home, married her, and made your son legitimate. Louise has been repressing her emotions all of her life, and I'm sure she's continued to repress them in the light of your present relationship. If I'm any judge of another woman's nature, though, I'm dead certain she loves you."

"I can't begin to cope with that possibility until Lai-tse lu releases me—with or without her rancor and lifetime hatred. And even then I'll continue to love her—and no one else."

"Oh, I know all that, Jonnie. We Rakehells aren't fickle. I know I could never love any man except Brad. But you're strong and you're honest and you have the courage to persist. So I believe you should know the whole truth. Because, some day, you'll have to deal with it."

Captain Charles Boynton happily showed the world that more than one ship designed and built by Jonathan Rakehell could smash records. Commanding a crew trained by his cousin, Charles sailed the ship known for the moment only as *Rakehell-Boynton II* from England to Djakarta in one hundred and two days. The Dutch customs officers who met the ship required more than the usual proof of his departure date from England because he had smashed the previous record by forty full days.

The Fat Dutchman, surrounded as always by his parrots and nubile serving girls, gave Charles a hearty welcome. "Heh-heh," he chuckled, his dry laugh echoing across his tropical garden. "My judgment of men is never mistaken. I knew all along that you and Rakehell would keep your word to me."

Without further ado he sent for his strongbox, then presented the young Englishman with the final payment for his ship.

"This is too much," Charles protested.

"I know no one else who would have been honest and fair with me, except of course for Soong Chao, who is always straight in his dealings," the Fat Dutchman declared, as one of the girls mopped sweat from his forehead and face with a linen cloth that had been soaked in cool water. "Consider the extra three hundred gold guilders a bonus that you and Rakehell have earned."

"We can't accept it, sir," was the prompt, firm reply. "We made you a fair price that gives us a reasonable profit, and neither Jonathan nor I can take more."

"Heh-heh. You've got to allow me some way to show my gratitude, Captain Boynton."

"We hope to trade with you for many years to come, sir," Charles said.

"So you shall, m'lad, but that doesn't seem adequate to me." The Fat Dutchman led him to the dining room, where the customary gargantuan feast awaited them.

As they were eating Charles asked, "What will you name your clipper?"

"I'm not quite certain." The Fat Dutchman eyed the girl, clad only in a wrapped skirt with a flower print, who was waiting on them. She came from Bali, one of the hundreds of Indonesian islands, so she was much fairer and taller than the Malayans of Java, being of Polynesian extraction. "I'm thinking of promoting Molinda and making her my number one concubine, so perhaps I'll name the clipper for her."

The girl smiled, her dark eyes dancing, and dimples appeared in her cheeks.

"What do you think of Molinda?" the host asked.

"She's a raving beauty, sir, as you well know," Charles said earnestly, and did not add that she was as lovely, in her own way, as Lai-tse lu.

"You like her, eh?"

"She's incomparable," Charles said, and the girl preened as he gazed at her admiringly.

"Molinda," the Fat Dutchman said, "is also very bright. She speaks Dutch and Malay as well as her own Polynesian, and I've been teaching her English. She's understood every bloody word we've been saying."

Molinda giggled.

Charles was entranced.

"Take her for this afternoon, Captain Boynton."

"That's kind of you, sir."

"On second thought, let me give her to you."

Charles was alarmed and gulped his drink of mild Dutch gin. He was looking forward to his reunion in Canton with Alice Wong, and he had no idea what disposition he could make of a Balinese slave girl. God knows he couldn't take her back to England with him! "The afternoon," he said, "will be a great boon. More than that would be too much."

The Fat Dutchman emptied a mug of ale, and one of the girls hastened to refill it. "You make it very hard for me to reward you, Captain Boynton," he said, and his chuckle was even raspier than usual.

"There is one favor you could do for me, sir," Charles said as they began their next course. "Sail me and my crew on the *Molinda,* or whatever you choose to call your new ship, to Whampoa. Another of our new clippers will arrive there shortly, and I'll sail her back to England with a double crew on board. The voyage would enable my men and me to teach your crew the rudiments of clipper sailing."

"I'll be delighted to oblige you, naturally. But let me hasten to point out to you that by training my crew you'll be doing me the favor. Heh-heh. No matter. Sooner or later I'll find a way to show my regard for you."

Molinda was charming and wise beyond her years as well as sexually provocative, and Charles relished the afternoons he spent with her in the next few days. But he retreated rapidly when the Fat Dutchman again offered her to him as a "gift." A successful young English businessman and ship's captain who some day would inherit a baronetcy simply could not return to London with a slave girl in tow.

Putting thoughts of Molinda behind him, Charles sailed from Djakarta on the familiar run to Canton. As he made his way up the Pearl River Delta he quickly became conscious of a change in the atmosphere. There were more British warships lying at anchor than he had ever seen in these waters, although most of them were small. Gun crews for their deck guns were standing by, as were a number of Royal Marines, all of them armed with muskets.

A new flagship, H.M.S. *Repulse,* a seventy-four-gun ship-of-the-line, lay off Whampoa, and Charles went on board to pay his respects to the commander of the flotilla. Somewhat to his surprise he found that officer was still Sir William Alexander, now promoted to the rank of rear admiral.

"I very much doubt that you're carrying opium on your clipper," Sir William said, "but I must ask you about it as a matter of course."

"My position on that matter hasn't changed," Charles replied.

"Well, I thank the Almighty there's one Englishman who won't give me more gray hairs."

"What's happening here, sir? Your ships seem to be braced for trouble."

"So they are," the admiral said, shaking his head, "although I can't yet pinpoint what the trouble will be or when a crisis will develop. The Chinese emperor has appointed a new viceroy for Kwantung, and Lin Tse-hsü is a difficult and secretive man. I've met him four or five times, and I've tried to settle into a pleasant relationship with him, but he positively bristles with hostility. I have the feeling that he despises all foreigners and is seeking some way to send us packing."

"That's unfortunate," Charles said.

"It's far worse than that. We hear rumors that Lin is planning some major move against the Western factories

482

in Whampoa. The stories keep changing, but the meat of them is always the same."

"And you can't find out what's actually behind them?"

Sir William shook his head. "Not even the best of our Chinese friends will even discuss the subject. I've tried talking about it with Soong Chao, but his face becomes totally blank and I can't pry a word out of him."

"That isn't like Soong," Charles said with a frown. "Do you suppose he knows whether this new viceroy really is planning some move against us?"

"I'd be willing to wager a year's pay that he does," the admiral declared. "You Rakehell and Boynton people have been closer to him than any of the rest of us, so it's possible that he may tell you what he won't say to me. If he should, I'll be obliged for any information you can pass along to me."

"You know I will, sir."

"All of us here have the feeling that we're sitting on a powder keg and that a fuse is burning toward it. I don't know how much powder is in the keg, and I can't even guess the length of the fuse, but I'm deucedly uncomfortable."

"So I can imagine." One aspect of the situation was Charles's principal concern. "Do you believe our legitimate trade with the Middle Kingdom is threatened?"

"I've informed the admiralty in a dispatch I wrote recently that I think it is, although I can't prove it as yet."

Charles's sense of pleasure over his return to China began to diminish.

"Never fear," Sir William said. "Britain is a nation that depends on commerce to survive, and I have no intention of allowing our lifeline here to be cut. I've asked London for another squadron of ships, and I'm making no secret of my request for a minimum of ten thousand of our best troops, to be held in reserve for me in India. If Lin Tse-hsü wants a fight, he shall have it!"

The change in the atmosphere was even more drastic than Charles had thought.

"By the way, Boynton," Sir William said in the casual drawl that upper-class English reserved for pressing matters, "keep your eyes open in Whampoa, and tell your men to do the same. They'll be wise to roam around the concession in fairly large groups, particularly at night."

"What's the problem, sir?"

"Foreigners, especially Englishmen, are being beaten for no apparent reason. They're not being robbed, mind you, simply subjected to a severe drubbing. I've complained repeatedly to Lin, and when a British subject was stabbed to death last month he turned two Chinese over to me. I'm certain they weren't guilty of the crime, but you know the Chinese system. They snatch a couple of innocents off the street rather than try to find the actual criminals. I had to execute the wretches, of course, and I felt badly about it, but I had no choice. It was Lin, not I, who sentenced them to death."

Thankful for the warning, Charles communicated it to his officers and crew. "Remember this is the Orient," he said. "Their way of thinking and acting is far different from ours. Stay out of brawls, and don't wander alone down any alleyways, no matter how much you want a drink."

Immediately after docking he went ashore, and as he headed toward Soong Chao's compound, he caught a glimpse of Owen Bruce about fifty feet away. The Scotsman glared at him briefly, then turned away, and Charles knew that the man hated him, just as he hated Jonathan, because of their growing trade in the East and their implacable opposition to the opium trade.

A runner was sent to Soong Chao's house to tell him of the young Englishman's arrival, and little more than an hour later Kai arrived in Whampoa with an escort. Having learned only a smattering of Chinese, Charles found it difficult to communicate with the majordomo, but as they made their way through the teeming city to the Soong estate he could sense a change in the attitude of the people who looked at the Westerner.

Previously one person in four or five stared at foreigners with hatred and contempt, but now the entire population bristled. Small boys shouted, "Fan Kuei," and had to be kept at a distance by Kai's guards. Many men shook their fists at Charles, and any number of women spat on the ground before turning their backs to him. The experience was far from pleasant, and he felt uncomfortable.

The contrast with the welcome he received from Soong Chao was startling. Beaming and genuinely delighted to see the visitor, the Chinese merchant met him at the front gate and took his arm as they walked through the gardens toward the cluster of buildings.

Sarah Applegate was the next to appear and was so pleased to see him that, for an instant, he thought she intended to kiss him.

Then Lai-tse lu hurried out of her dwelling and was even more ravishingly lovely than Charles remembered her. "Welcome," she said warmly, and extended both hands to him in a totally Western gesture.

His heart ached for her and for Jonathan.

The cook had been instructed to prepare a special meal in honor of the guest, and while the kitchen staff worked feverishly, Charles was escorted to the principal drawing room. He was offered a Western-style chair that had been placed there only recently, but instead he deliberately elected to sit on a low, cushioned stool, even though he could not stretch his long legs.

Dispensing with the customary formalities that opened conversations in the Middle Kingdom, Charles said, "I know you want to hear about Jonathan." On the voyage from London to Djakarta he had pondered at length what he would say and had actually rehearsed his speech on his quarterdeck.

He spoke at length about Jonathan's activity at the shipyard, describing in detail the new clippers that he was building. "He devotes all of his time to his work," he said truthfully. "Even on our Sabbath day he goes to his office after he attends church. He walks to the yard early every morning with his father, and he does not come home to eat until late at night."

"He is well and happy?" Lai-tse lu asked.

"He is well," Charles said bluntly, "but he will never be happy unless you are at his side." That, too, was the truth. Under no circumstances, he had decided, could he breathe even a hint of his cousin's tragic personal situation or mention that he had a son. Only Jonathan himself could break the news to Lai-tse lu.

As he talked the girl twisted the gold band that she wore on the fourth finger of her right hand, turning it constantly.

Charles became aware of the gesture and realized anew that he needed to be alert every moment of his stay here. If Lai-tse lu knew the truth about Jonathan's situation she would be devastated, but he alone was responsible for enlightening her.

The meal was one of the most delicious Charles had ever eaten. He could identify few of the many dishes, but it hadn't occurred to him until now how much he had missed Chinese cuisine. In spite of his apprehensions he ate heartily.

What he dreaded most was a question about the girl to whom Jonathan had been betrothed, and he had no idea what he would reply. He couldn't say that the birth of a son and Rakehell heir had made it necessary for Jonathan to marry her, but at the same time he was reluctant to tell an outright lie. Certainly Lai-tse lu had to be curious about Louise, but he felt somewhat relieved when it finally dawned on him that her sense of delicacy forbade her to make inquiries of anyone other than Jonathan himself.

Soong Chao looked older and very tired, the fatigue lines at the corners of his eyes and mouth indicating that he had been undergoing a severe strain. Missy Sarah was unchanged; perhaps her hair had grown a trifle grayer, but she was as indomitable and as crusty as ever, speaking her mind sharply whenever she wished. Lai-tse lu, whose questions made it evident that she was deeply in love with Jonathan, was suffused with an inner glow because of that love and was even more radiant, more beautiful than she had ever been. There was no explanation for the cruelties that life sometimes inflicted on the unsuspecting.

Having discussed Jonathan's work and daily routines at length, Charles finally turned to the subject that Sir William Alexander had raised. "I understand there has been a strong growth of anti-foreign feeling here."

"I'm sad to say that is correct," Chao admitted. "It has spread to people in all walks of life, including educated mandarins who should know better."

"To what do you attribute it, sir?"

The Chinese merchant's shrug was noncommittal.

Lai-tse lu looked down at her plate, her chopsticks clicking as she withdrew in silence.

But Sarah Applegate refused to be diplomatic. "It's that Lin Tse-hsü," she said vehemently. "The new viceroy, in case you hadn't heard, young man. Chao and his friends keep telling me he's a fine administrator and a man of high principles, but there's no doubt he's directly responsible for the feeling. Whenever he makes an address of any kind he invariably makes nasty comments about Fan Kuei, so he fans the prejudices that already exist here."

"In my opinion, as I've indicated to you, Sarah," Chao said, "His Excellency is not opposed to all Westerners or what he regards as good in their civilization."

"Then why does he go out of his way to attack us?" she demanded tartly.

Chao hesitated for a moment, then shrugged again.

"Will this attitude cause serious problems?" Charles wanted to know.

"That depends on how much worse the feelings become and how the governments of the Western nations react," the merchant declared.

Charles realized the reply was meaningless. "Do you suppose our mutually beneficial commerce will suffer?"

Chao's attitude changed, and he became firm. "I assure you I am doing and shall continue to do everything to make certain our foreign trade is neither interrupted nor diminished. On the contrary, it must continue to grow. The stopping of the exchanges of products and merchandise would be a blow to the West and a catastrophe for us."

"All I know," Sarah said, "is that a war would place me in an impossible position here. Even now I don't dare leave the house without closing the bamboo curtains of my palanquin, and I don't like it. I just hope and pray that Jonathan comes back to marry Lai-tse lu before the fighting starts. Jonathan may not know it, but he's taking me back to New England, too."

Charles was tongue-tied, unable to tell her that her plan never could be fulfilled. "If you wish," he said, "I'll have a cabin prepared for you on the *Elizabeth* when she arrives here in the next few days?"

"The *Elizabeth?*" Lai-tse lu asked.

"The newest clipper that Jonathan built for me. I named it for my little adopted sister."

"You're generous," Sarah said, "but I wouldn't leave Lai-tse lu, no matter how bad things become here. I'd rather die than desert her!"

When the meal ended Charles accompanied Chao to his workroom for a discussion of cargoes.

"I wonder if you'd consider making a change in your sailing routes when you leave Canton," the merchant said. "I've just acquired a stock of superb green tea that is superior to any other grown here or in Indonesia. I'm certain Jonathan could dispose of it in America for a very high price."

"There's no doubt of that, Mr. Soong!"

"Perhaps, then, you would be willing to return to England by way of New London."

Charles made some rapid calculations. "Rakehell and Boynton will earn a far greater profit than we would if I took a load of silks and porcelains back to England. I'll do it, Mr. Soong. I have no choice."

A short time later, when he said good-bye to Lai-tse lu and Missy Sarah, he accepted their invitation to return for another dinner before he left Canton. He couldn't help regretting his change of plans because he knew that now Jonathan would examine him in detail about Lai-tse lu and insist he repeat every word she said.

When he returned to Whampoa he had nothing to occupy him, the Indonesian crew having taken full possession of the *Molinda*. Quarters had been found for his officers at a nearby inn, and his crew had been placed in lodgings at the concession's only hostel for foreign seamen. He had plans of his own, however, and hoping they would materialize, he walked down the familiar alleyway to the building where Alice Wong maintained an apartment.

Precisely as he had anticipated, Alice had learned of his return to Canton through her own private means of communication and was waiting for him. She was somewhat thinner than she had been when he had last seen her, but she was still exceptionally attractive and was so delighted to see him that emotion threatened to overcome her.

Their lovemaking was so explosive that Charles forgot Molinda and all of the others he had bedded since he and Alice had parted.

That evening, after she had prepared a light meal for them, he told her, "I expect to be here for at least a week, perhaps twice that long. A clipper from England is coming here, and after I load cargo for America I'll be taking her there. How would you like to have me here as a paying guest until I sail?"

"Charrs stay," she said. "Alice not let him stay any other place. But no pay!"

"Indeed I shall, as well as for your time," he said firmly. "And that reminds me of something." He crossed the room to his suit coat and, taking a small box from a pocket, presented it to her.

Alice gasped when she saw the contents. Lying on a lining of satin was a brooch and chain, with a small diamond in the center of the ornament.

Charles had purchased the gift for her in London, and although it had not been cheap, he had not paid an extravagant price for it, either. "You can wear it either around your neck or as a pin, on a dress," he said.

The young woman continued to stare at the brooch, then looked at the name of the London jeweler on the box. "You bring this to Alice from England," she said in wonder. "You think of Alice even when you far away in London."

Her awe made him uncomfortable. "It's just a token," he said. "I'd have bought you something fancier, but I'd rather give you a substantial sum in cash when I leave."

Alice did not appear to hear him. She sank gracefully to the floor in a cross-legged position, the Chinese version of a deep curtsy, then bent her back and lowered her head. When she looked up again there were tears glistening in her eyes.

"Here, now, we'll have none of that." The embarrassed Charles went to her and lifted her to her feet.

She embraced him, and moments later they were making love again, more wildly than ever before.

For several days they spent all of their time in the apartment, and when Alice went out to purchase food she refused to allow Charles to accompany her. "Not good now for people to see Fan Kuei man with Chinese woman on street," she said. "Fan Kuei no like, Chinese no like. Maybe Charrs be hurt."

"I can look after myself," he said, but for her sake he stayed behind.

Later that same day he felt the need for exercise and wanted to take a walk, but Alice, to his irritation, protested vehemently. "Bad for Charrs to walk with no place to go," she said. "Charrs no have ship here yet, no have work in factory, so many men wonder what you do. These men become afraid of Charrs, and maybe use gun or knife."

The statement seemed so outlandish that he laughed.

"Whampoa much different now," she said somberly.

Charles insisted on taking his walk and discovered that Alice had not exaggerated. Chinese dockworkers, warehouse employees, and street peddlers glowered at him when he wandered aimlessly through the streets of the foreign concession, and a number of white men, some of them English, stared at him with narrowed eyes. He returned to the apartment in a chastened mood, agreeing to remain there until the clipper from London arrived.

That night he and Alice fell into an exhausted sleep after prolonged and repeated lovemaking, both of them still completely unclothed. He had no idea how long he slept, but all at once he was wide awake. Either he had heard a slight noise or sensed an alien presence.

Looking up, he saw that an intruder had entered the room through a window he had opened wide. He was dressed from head to foot in black and wore a hood over his head, with slits cut in it for his eyes and mouth. It was impossible to determine whether he was Chinese or white.

What mattered most was that he carried a long, pointed knife in one hand as he crept toward the bed.

Charles realized at once that his sword and pistol were lying on a chair located on the far side of the chamber and that he would have to pass the man in order to reach them. He started to rise, bracing himself for the only alternative, a hand-to-hand battle. He was taller and huskier than the slender intruder, but the man was armed, and that might make the difference.

At that instant Alice awakened, too, and tried to scream, but she was so terrified she could make no sound.

Charles tried to move her out of his way so he could stand.

She would not cooperate, however, and instead covered his body with hers.

Before Charles could shove her aside, the intruder struck, burying his knife to the hilt in Alice's body.

Charles finally was able to stand.

By that time, however, the masked man had removed the knife and, still carrying it, returned to the window and leaped to the ground one floor below. The night was so dark that the black-clad intruder melted into it and vanished.

Charles stood at the window and shouted for help as loudly as he could, but there was no response. Whampoa was asleep, and its residents had learned to attend strictly to their own business late at night.

Racing back to Alice, Charles realized she was still alive, her breathing shallow. He lighted an oil lamp, and in its soft glare he saw that the blade had penetrated her left side below her ribs. She was losing very little blood, which he recognized as a bad sign.

He wrapped her nude body in a blanket, then cradled her in his arms.

Alice opened her eyes. "Charrs," she said, her voice barely audible as she struggled for breath, "is only man Alice ever love."

Charles read death in her eyes and willingly lied to her. "I love you, too," he said, and bent his head to kiss her.

Alice Wong's life slipped from her body with Charles's lips on hers.

Shocked and angry, he continued to hold her for a

long time, unconscious of the passage of time. Then, gently placing her body on the bed, he dressed hastily. He was uncertain how to proceed and had no idea what to do first in this alien place, but he was determined that her murderer be found and punished. Nothing in the apartment was missing; his own money and watch were intact, and Alice's jewelry, other than the diamond brooch she had not removed from her neck since he had given it to her, was still piled on her dressing table.

A light tap sounded at the door. Charles drew his pistol and unlocked it.

He was astonished to see Kai, Soong Chao's majordomo, who was closely followed by an even taller and burlier man. Behind them were four smaller men carrying a bamboo stretcher.

Lo Fang looked down at Alice, grief and pity in his eyes, and suddenly he barked an order.

The four bearers placed the girl's body, still nude except for the diamond brooch, on the stretcher. Covering her with the blanket, they departed in silence, with Lo Fang following close behind them.

"She was killed in cold blood," Charles said to Kai.

The majordomo's nod indicated that he understood, and that he had already gleaned this information through an informant.

"Something must be done!"

"Kai and friends do," the Chinese replied harshly, and started to leave.

Charles detained him. "I—I want to come to her funeral," he said.

Kai gave no indication that he even heard the request and was gone.

Looking around the silent apartment, Charles's fury mounted swiftly. Alice's death had been such a waste that he was maddened by the brutality. Other Englishmen had remarked in his hearing that life was lightly regarded in the East, but this was one murder that would not be unavenged. Surprised to see that daylight had come, he hurried to the waterfront and hired a sampan to row him out to H.M.S. *Repulse*.

Rear Admiral Sir William Alexander was eating

breakfast alone in his spacious great cabin when a Royal Marine sentry conducted the insistent Charles into his presence.

"Forgive this interruption, sir, but I've just seen a woman murdered, and I demand justice on her behalf!"

"Dear me," Sir William murmured, brushing his mouth with a napkin of heavy linen. "Do sit down, Boynton, and have a cup of tea."

Charles sat on the edge of a chair and poured out the story of what had happened.

The admiral listened in silence, and only when Charles was finished did he ask, "Who was the intended victim, you or this woman?"

Charles was startled. "I—I don't know, sir."

"If you had been stabbed to death by an unknown assailant in Whampoa," Sir William said, "I'd have raised a terrible row and would have been prepared to bombard the viceroy's palace unless reparations had been paid promptly. But, if I may say so, there's a difference between a prominent English shipping man and son of a baronet— and a Whampoa strumpet."

"I can't imagine why anyone would have wanted to kill Alice," Charles cried. "She was gentle and sweet and loyal—a good person."

"I'm in no position to deny that the lady possessed those qualities," Sir William said. "But if you'll forgive the observation, my dear Boynton, there could have been hundreds of reasons why someone would want to kill a waterfront harlot. Please eat some breakfast. I commend the marmalade. Lady Alexander makes it herself at our country place and keeps me supplied with it."

Charles forced himself to drink a cup of tea and became a trifle calmer.

The admiral refilled his cup. "Was this person a British subject?"

"No, sir. She lived somewhere in Canton. I knew her when I was here previously and almost always spent my nights in port with her."

"I'm afraid," Sir William said, "that I'm in no position to protest the death of a Chinese. I'd be told, and quite

493

properly, not to stick my nose into the internal affairs of the Middle Kingdom."

"But she was Eurasian, Admiral."

"That makes no difference. She was a subject of the Tao Kuang Emperor, not Her Majesty. Allow me to give you a bit of advice, Boynton. Be grateful to your guardian angel that you escaped without a scratch, and don't muddy the local waters. Chinese officials are in no mood to hear the complaints of foreigners these days."

The admiral's gig took the frustrated Charles back to Whampoa.

He was astonished to see Kai waiting for him on the waterfront, and he followed quickly when the majordomo beckoned. They walked in silence to the largest of the Soong warehouses, and as Charles was conducted to the office he was surprised to see his sea chest, which he had left at Alice's apartment, in the corridor. He was given no opportunity to ask any questions and found Soong Chao seated behind the desk.

"I came to Whampoa as soon as I heard the news," Chao said, pouring tea. "A most unfortunate incident."

"A damned outrage," Charles said.

"Kai and Lo Fang, the viceroy's majordomo, are conducting an exhaustive private investigation. They set it in motion the moment they learned of the young woman's death and went to retrieve her body."

"Private, Mr. Soong?"

The merchant sighed. "Oh, the constabulary were notified, but they will do little more than add another scroll to their endless records. There are many blood feuds in a city the size of Canton, and there are too few constables here to catch most murderers. If the killer is to be found, rest assured that Kai and Lo Fang will find him—and punish him in their own way."

"It seems to me this is a casual way of handling a tragedy, Mr. Soong!" Charles said bitterly.

"You are mistaken. I happen to have a rather strong suspicion, which I take pains not to confirm, that Kai and Lo Fang are prominent members of one of our very powerful secret societies. Kai has already told me something of interest."

Charles inched forward in his chair.

"He and Lo Fang are quite certain the man with the knife wanted to kill you, not the young woman, and that he ran away in panic when he put his knife into her by mistake."

"It was no mistake, Mr. Soong. She threw her body over mine to protect me as the man struck—while I was trying to stand."

"I shall inform Kai of that fact. It appears to confirm his theory."

"Who here would want to kill me, Mr. Soong?" Charles asked slowly.

The merchant shrugged and smiled sourly. "These are trying times, Captain Boynton. Perhaps the murderer was hired by Chinese opium dealers who know you are opposed to the drug traffic and feel that, as a prominent and prosperous Englishman, you are setting your fellow-countrymen a bad example."

"That was the problem Jonathan had with Owen Bruce."

"Precisely, Captain Boynton. He who hates Jonathan might be your enemy, also, and for the same reasons." Chao poured more cups of the endless tea. "There are so many mysteries these days that not all of them are solved. Perhaps Kai and Lo Fang will learn more and act accordingly. Or it may be they will discover nothing. You and I will never know."

"Why not?"

"When a secret society takes a matter into its hands, the wise man asks no questions."

Charles was completely bewildered by the Chinese approach to life.

"In any event, we must attend to other matters. The young woman's belongings have already been delivered to her relatives. Her grandmother, I believe. And now we must look after you. Until your clipper arrives, discharges her cargo, and loads the green tea for America, you will dwell at my house. If someone wants you killed, he might try again. So I insist you accept my protection."

"That's kind of you," the bewildered young Englishman said. Too much was happening too fast.

"Your chest will be brought to my house, and you will be taken there after you accompany Lo Fang on an errand. He is waiting for you now."

"What sort of an errand, Mr. Soong?"

The merchant was gently reproachful. "I was not told. And as I have already informed you, Captain Boynton, one does not question those who may be active in our secret societies."

Charles was escorted to the door, where Lo Fang, armed with a razor-sharp ku ming, stood impassively.

The giant Chinese beckoned, and unable to communicate because neither spoke the other's language, they walked in silence to the Petition Gate. As soon as they passed through it, with the soldiers on duty there making no attempt to halt the young Englishman, they were surrounded by a guard of other ku ming bearers, all attired in drab padded cotton tunics and trousers.

The group walked rapidly, and Charles, who had no idea where they were taking him or why he had been asked to accompany them, soon lost his sense of direction as the men conducted him down one street after another, turning frequently and sometimes making short cuts through narrow alleyways.

Almost without exception the many people they passed stared with open hostility at the foreigner, and there was little doubt in Charles's mind that, had he been unescorted, a mob would have attacked him immediately. But he knew he was safe and paid scant attention to the residents of Canton.

His mind was too full. The death of Alice still stunned him, as did the knowledge that she had deliberately sacrificed her life in order to save him. He knew of no way he could repay such a debt; she was gone, and there was no way he could even thank her. She had been so ebullient, so filled with the joy of living, so concerned for his happiness and welfare that it was almost impossible for him to realize she was gone.

After a long walk the guards came to a small house, which they promptly surrounded. The building of stone and wood, with a tiled roof, looked exactly like countless others that Charles had seen. Obviously it was an ordinary dwelling, and nothing in its appearance set it apart.

Lo Fang motioned Charles inside, and together they squeezed through the entrance.

The house consisted of two simple rooms, separated only by an arched opening. The farther chamber appeared to be used for sleeping, and several mats were scattered on the floor. The room in which the pair found themselves was almost bare, and its only furniture was a table and a few rickety stools, with items of clothing hanging from hooks on the walls.

Seated cross-legged on the floor was an old woman who was weaving a rug or mat of bamboo, demonstrating remarkable patience as her gnarled fingers slowly plaited the reeds. She glanced up for no more than an instant, then resumed her labors.

At the far side of the room was a little boy, about one year old, who was sitting on the hard-packed ground, playing with a wooden toy beneath a window. Watching him without interest was a plain, scrawny girl in her teens, who was simply dressed.

Unable to understand why he had been brought to this place, Charles reflected as he looked around that he could find nothing to commend it other than the fact that it was scrupulously, surprisingly clean.

Lo Fang jabbed a finger in the direction of the child.

Charles looked at him more closely, and gradually the realization dawned on him that the baby looked only remotely Oriental. His skin was as fair as that of a Caucasian, his hair was a light brown, and his eyes, which were as round as those of a white person, were pale.

Lo Fang again pointed to the baby, then jabbed a finger in the direction of the young Englishman.

Charles was so startled he could only gape as comprehension flooded him. This baby was Alice's son. His son.

Suddenly he recalled that, before he had sailed for home after his year-long sojourn in the East, Alice had told him she would have a gift for him when he returned. He hadn't taken the remark seriously, but now he knew what she had meant.

Recovering from his initial shock, Charles peered more intently at the little boy. Totally absorbed in his play, his expression was like that of Alice when she had concentrated. His forehead, nose, and chin clearly revealed his Rakehell heritage, and his eyes—good Lord!—unmistakably marked him as a Boynton. He was only one-quarter Chinese, and his eyes alone confirmed Charles's conviction that this was his son.

Lo Fang waited patiently, giving the young Englishman ample time to become adjusted to what he had just discovered.

The teen-aged girl was looking at the stranger covertly now, while pretending to show no interest in him. The old woman continued to devote her full attention to her weaving.

Charles's legs felt weak as he made his way uncertainly across the room, leaned down, and picked up the child.

The little boy looked at him, and Charles had the strange sensation that he was seeing his own eyes in a mirror.

All at once the boy grinned broadly, then began to babble in a language of his own.

That settled the matter. Charles made up his mind on the spot. In spite of the potential problems and complications that made him reel, he could not leave his child to grow up in the poverty and ignorance of this Canton hovel. No matter what might happen, he had to take the child with him.

Trying to communicate his decision to Lo Fang, he gestured broadly.

For the first time since they had left Whampoa the viceroy's majordomo smiled, then said something to the teen-aged girl.

She immediately took the baby from Charles, went to the entrance, and waited.

Charles looked down at the impassive old woman. He had intended to give Alice a substantial sum of money before leaving China, and now, on sudden impulse, he reached into his purse, took out a handful of gold sovereigns, and handed them to the woman.

A clawlike hand snatched the money from him. After dropping it into a worn, mended sack on the floor beside her, the old woman resumed her weaving.

In the street there were odors of garlic, frying vegetable oil, and garbage, but Charles nevertheless breathed more easily.

The guard formed around him, the girl, and the baby, and the walk through the city's streets was resumed. It was useless for Charles to ask where he was being taken with his child and this silent young nursemaid, so he contented himself with trying to catch the baby's eye. Twice he suceeded, and the little boy, behaving beautifully, grinned amiably.

To Charles's infinite relief they came at last to Soong Chao's estate, and the realization dawned on him that the merchant had been aware of what was happening and had arranged for father and son to be escorted here.

Lai-tse lu and Sarah Applegate took charge at once, whisking away the baby and the young girl while Charles went to his own sitting room and waited with as much patience as he could muster.

After a time Lai-tse lu joined him. "Lo Fang tells me you already know the boy is your son," she said.

He nodded. "I realized it the instant I looked at him."

"Alice Wong," she said, "intended to show him to you before you sailed."

He swallowed painfully. "I have no choice now. I can't leave my own flesh and blood in—that place. I've got to take him with me."

"The old woman you saw was Alice's grandmother," Lai-tse lu said. "She never approved of Alice's way of life, even though she took money from her, and she had no use for the baby because he's more Western than Chinese. Will you take Wu-ling with you, too?"

Charles had the feeling he was being backed farther and farther into a corner, but he saw no escape. "That's the young girl?"

She nodded. "She is Alice's half-sister, and she was paid to look after the baby."

"I'll gladly pay her far larger wages, and if you'll attend to the details, I'll pay for a suitable wardrobe for her, too. I'll have my hands full at sea, and I won't have time to take care of a little child myself. Besides, I—I wouldn't know what to do."

"Wu-ling is very competent," she said, her smile indicating that his impromptu arrangements pleased her. Then she looked solemn again and said, "Wu-ling has told me the baby's name. He is known as David."

Charles was startled anew.

"Because of you, Alice Wong was trying to learn to read English," she said. "A missionary gave her a Bible printed in English, and she was so fascinated by the Psalms of David that she wouldn't even consider giving her son a Chinese name."

"David." He said the name aloud and it sounded right to him. "David Boynton."

"There is much to be done before you leave," Lai-tse lu said. "The baby will need clothes and special food, and Wu-ling must be fitted for her new clothes, too. But don't worry. Missy Sarah and I will look after everything for you."

"Thank the Lord." His mind still spinning, it was a comfort to know he was being relieved of details with which he couldn't cope. His most serious problem would be that of confronting his father.

It wasn't difficult to predict how Sir Alan would react when he learned his first grandchild was illegitimate, and son of a Eurasian courtesan.

No matter how upset he became, however, Charles had set his course and would not alter it. He owed it to little David to give him the advantages to which he was entitled. Here, too, was his opportunity to repay Alice for the instinctive, unselfish gesture that had taken her life.

III

Judith Rakehell Walker made it a practice, as her mother had done before her, to join her husband at breakfast before he went to the shipyard. The children, who would not go to school for another hour, were just stirring, so she and Brad could speak in private. It was a time of day she cherished, and she enjoyed sitting opposite him at the dining table, sipping a cup of tea while he ate the hearty meal with which he began his day.

This morning, however, Judith was preoccupied and answered absently whenever her husband addressed her.

Brad finished his broiled fish, then studied his wife as he waited for the serving maid to bring his steak and eggs. "What's wrong?" he asked.

"Nothing, really." Judith forced a smile.

"You have hollows under your eyes again, so I assume you didn't sleep well."

"Not too well."

"You've never had trouble sleeping. You ought to see Dr. Graves. At the least he can give you some powders that will make your nights more comfortable."

"There's no need for me to see the doctor. I know why I'm not sleeping." She had said more than she had intended and tried to draw back.

Brad looked at her, raised an eyebrow, and waited.

"I've been worrying about Jonathan," she said reluctantly.

He laughed without humor. "I can't imagine why. He

has everything in the world that a man could want. A full partnership in the business. A worldwide reputation as a builder, with more orders for clipper ships than he can possibly produce, even though he's been spending more time than he can afford on his special clipper, which—in my opinion—isn't practical."

Judith loved her husband and consequently trusted him implicitly. She was unaware of his jealous hatred for his brother-in-law, and thanks to her father's discretion she had learned nothing of his attempts to harm and discredit Jonathan.

She had been carrying the burden of her brother's secret for a long time, and she felt an urge to share it with the one person she knew would never betray her. "Brad," she said tentatively, "I want to tell you something—but it must go no farther."

He became taut and tried to conceal his reaction. "Something about Jonathan?"

She nodded. "Jonnie confided in me months ago. He must never know I've repeated as much as a word to you, and it goes without saying that no one else must ever know, either."

"Naturally," Brad said, his manner soothing. "I've never let you down in all the years we've been married, but if you think it's necessary for me to take an oath—"

"Hardly." This man was her husband, the father of her children, and she was wrong to have hesitated. Without further ado Judith told him in detail about her private talk with her brother.

"He's still in love with this Chinese woman?" Brad asked when she had finished.

"Yes, and I know him well enough to realize he'll never get over it."

"Where does that leave Louise?"

"That's his problem. Jonnie believes that she doesn't love him any more than he does her. I happen to think he's wrong, that Louise cares a great deal for him. He's formed a wonderful relationship with Julian, but he and Louise will never be close."

"Never is a long time." In spite of the ferment seething within him, Brad managed to speak dryly.

"My brother has given his heart to Soong Lai-tse lu, just as I gave mine to you, Brad. Rakehells make commitments for life."

"I don't see what you can do for him."

"Nor do I, except to listen sympathetically. He's building that gorgeous new clipper for her, you see, and when he sends it to her as a gift, as a sign of his love, he'll write to her in full and explain why he and Louise had to be married the very day he came home from Cathay."

So Jonathan and Louise hadn't actually married until that day! The last piece of the puzzle fell into place, and Brad was privately elated. Hurriedly finishing his breakfast, he rose, went to his wife, and kissed her. "Don't lose any more sleep over all this," he said. "No matter what romantic authors have been writing for hundreds of years, I seriously doubt that anyone has ever died of a broken heart."

Stopping in the front hall for his greatcoat, high hat of beaver fur, and a portfolio of papers he had brought home from the office the preceding night, Brad went out to his waiting carriage. Unlike his Rakehell in-laws, he enjoyed riding to the office in style.

His mind continued to work rapidly as he digested what his wife had told him, and instead of being driven direct to his office he told the coachman to let him out at the entrance to the shipyard. His reason wasn't clear in his own mind until, making his way past the stocks where the new clippers were being built, he caught sight of the clipper on which Jonathan was lavishing so much time and care.

As much as he hated to admit it, Brad was forced to concede that she was one of the most impressive vessels he had ever seen, even in her incomplete state. Approximately twice the size of any previously constructed clipper, she would be of almost two thousand tons burthen. Her holds were far larger than those of other clippers, too, thanks to the revolutionary rounded bottom that was one of her more outstanding features, and according to Jonathan's estimates she could carry two-thirds of the cargo that would be normal in a schooner of the same tonnage.

But that was only the beginning. On her main deck were eight cabins for passengers, which Jonathan intended to furnish with brass bedsteads and other fixtures unknown at sea. Her decks were fashioned of teak imported from the West Indies, and her saloon would be served by two stoves, one of wood and one of coal. She was the most luxurious vessel, by far, that had ever been built at the Rakehell yard, and Jonathan was using his own private funds for her construction, refusing to spend company money.

The reasons, now that Brad had been told by Judith, were easy to understand. Her nameplates were already in place on either side of her prow: *Lai-tse lu.*

Brad grinned sourly when he realized that the ship was being named for Jonathan's Chinese woman.

Even her figurehead, the head and shoulders of an Oriental girl, had been carved according to Jonathan's precise specifications, and he had spent many hours with the artist who had been responsible.

The man was a damned fool, Brad reflected.

That fact, however, was irrelevant. The information that Brad had gleaned from his wife could prove useful. Ever since Jonathan had returned from the East his brother-in-law had searched in vain for some weakness in his armor, and his love—or whatever it was he thought he felt for the Chinese woman—made him vulnerable.

Somehow that weakness could be exploited to Jonathan's disadvantage. Brad was uncertain how to utilize the knowledge, but he was in no hurry. By preparing and executing a careful plan he could shoot down Jonathan's rising star and gain the ascendency himself. His mood more cheerful than it had been in many months, Brad hummed under his breath as he walked jauntily to his office.

The *Elizabeth* was as trim a clipper as any that Jonathan had built, but Charles Boynton had to abandon any hope of breaking his cousin's speed record from Canton to New London. There were far too many distractions.

Chief among them was his small son. Each day Charles took David to the quarterdeck with him for an hour or two, and the child was fascinated by the sails, by the rising and falling of the ship as she plowed majestically through the South China Sea. "My boy," Charles proudly told his mates and boatswain repeatedly, "has the sea in his blood. He'll grow up to command a ship of his own."

Actually, he hoped that David would do far more than that. Ultimately he and Julian Rakehell would be direct inheritors of a family dynasty, and the child needed a careful preparation for his future. That meant growing up in a stable, loving environment, sending him to the best available schools, and indoctrinating him from early childhood in the mysteries of the sea, as Charles and Jonathan had been indoctrinated.

Somehow, after returning to England, Charles knew he would have to take steps to have David made legitimate and officially declared his heir. He would need the advice and help of a solicitor, of course, and was determined to do whatever was necessary. He continued to worry about his father's reaction, but there was nothing he could do while on the high seas, and he tried to push that future unpleasantness out of his mind.

Less than two days out of Canton Wu-ling fell prey to seasickness, and for the next seventy-two hours she was confined to her bunk in the one passenger cabin the clipper boasted. Charles was forced to take his son into his own cabin with him for those three days and nights, and necessity compelled him to learn a great deal about the care and feeding of babies. He was grateful to his boatswain, the father of five, for help beyond the call of duty.

Wu-ling gained her sea legs when she recovered, and the relieved Charles was able to return David to her care. He continued to spend as much of his free time as he could with his son, however, and Alice Wong was never far from his thoughts.

Immediately prior to leaving Canton he had been presented with a package by Lo Fang. He hadn't opened it until he had come on board and had been startled to find a cheap edition of the King James Bible, with Alice's name written on the flyleaf in large, childishly formed letters. It was his only memento of his son's mother, the woman who had given her life so he might live. Charles was not a religious man, but he found himself leafing through the Bible by the light of an oil lamp every night. He would save the book, and when David grew older he would present it to the boy.

In spite of the need to make many personal adjustments, Charles sailed the *Elizabeth* to an empty berth in the Rakehell-Boynton yard on the one hundred and eleventh day of his voyage from China. "With no thanks to me," the master told his mates, "the clipper made fairly respectable time."

If Jeremiah Rakehell was in any way dismayed or upset by his nephew's unexpected arrival with an infant son and a teenaged Chinese nursemaid he did not show it. "You'll stay with us, naturally," he said.

At dinner a short time later Charles told the story of Alice's death and his discovery of the son she had left behind. Jonathan was in complete sympathy with him.

"I've had a talk with Wu-ling, who was very happy to find someone in this benighted land who can speak fairly fluent Cantonese. She tells me she managed to pick up a bit of English on the voyage."

"She's doing well," Charles replied with a grin.

Louise sat rigidly at her place, and when she spoke her voice was stiff with disapproval. "We don't mind having her here," she said, her tone indicating the contrary. "But I assume you'll be sending her back to China on board the next clipper, Charles, and hiring an American nursemaid to take to England with you."

Charles shook his head. "Wu-ling is David's only link with his past," he said. "I wouldn't dream of taking her away from him. In the meantime, I'm grateful to all of you for receiving her hospitably. As well as accepting David as a member of the family."

Louise sniffed audibly but made no comment.

Jonathan glanced at her for an instant. Perhaps she was remembering the period when Julian hadn't yet been made legitimate. Whatever her feelings, he wanted to state the situation clearly. "David is your son," he said, "so he *is* a member of the family." His tone left no room for denial.

As they left the table, Jeremiah grasped his nephew's

arm. "I'm sure you've devoted a great deal of thought to the question of how to make your father aware of David's existence and gain his acceptance."

"I've thought of little else, Uncle Jeremiah. All I can tell you is that, if I must, I'll set up my own household."

"Well, you'll have a few more weeks to ponder. We weren't anticipating the *Elizabeth*'s arrival here, so it will take time to assemble a cargo for her before you sail her back to England." Knowing that Charles and Jonathan wanted to talk about the East, he left them together, Louise having already gone upstairs.

As the cousins went to the library they could hear shrieks of laughter from the nursery, where Julian and David obviously were well on their way to becoming acquainted, the year's difference in their ages providing no barrier. The men grinned at each other, recalling how close they had been in their own boyhood.

Jonathan's smile faded rapidly as he closed the library door behind him. "You saw Lai-tse lu in Canton?" he asked anxiously.

"I stayed at the Soong complex, for reasons I'll explain to you. She was a godsend in making the arrangements to bring my son with me. I saw her every day I was there, and her last words to me on the day I sailed were to send you all of her love and to tell you she counts the months until you will return to her."

Jonathan covered his gaunt face with his hands.

Charles felt for him and was embarrassed, too. "Soong Chao is well, and Sarah Applegate is completely unchanged."

Jonathan nodded and, rising abruptly, walked to the window and stared out at the placid waters of the Thames Estuary.

"Let me give you a chronological account of my trip," Charles said, and deliberately launched into a humorous story of his visit with the Fat Dutchman in Djakarta. "He was so pleased we kept our word and sent him a clipper," he said, "that he tried to give me a young Balinese slave girl named Molinda. Extraordinary girl, actually. I knew she'd be a delightful bedmate, but I didn't expect her to

507

speak several languages fluently. Or to have a mind like a whip. If I have problems now, imagine how much worse it would be if I had brought her with me!"

Jonathan chuckled and resumed his seat.

Charles discussed their business relationship with the Fat Dutchman in detail, then went on to talk about Canton, beginning with Admiral Sir William Alexander's warning that tensions between Chinese and Westerners were rising rapidly.

"I sensed as much when you told us about the murder of Alice, but I didn't want to go into too much detail in front of Papa and Louise," Jonathan said. "Do you have any idea who might have been responsible for killing her?"

Charles shook his head. "It could have been someone hired by Owen Bruce. I saw him only once, the day I arrived, and there was murder in his eyes when he looked at me. But it could have been anyone. A white man who resented my affair with Alice. Or a Chinese, for the same reason."

"The situation is as bad as all that?"

"Worse," Charles said. "The new viceroy is determined to stamp out the opium traffic, which is all to the good, but he's treading hard on Western toes, and something nasty is brewing. You feel it the minute you land. No white man can go anywhere in Canton without a heavy escort, and it's just a matter of time before there's serious bloodshed."

"What does Soong Chao think?"

"He's badly worried, Jonnie. He was careful not to criticize the new viceroy, but it was plain to me that Lin wouldn't listen to his advice to move gradually."

"You're saying there's a chance of war," Jonathan said.

"More than a chance. I regard it as inevitable." Not wanting to cause him needless suffering, Charles refrained from mentioning Chao's relief that his daughter would be coming to America to live and would be spared the dangers of life in Canton.

Jonathan grew pale. "My God, I'm paying for my sins," he said. "There's nothing I can do for Lai-tse lu. Or her father. Or Missy Sarah. I'm trapped here, with my hands and feet tied. And a gag stuffed in my mouth. No Chinese executioner ever invented a torture this exquisite. I think I'm slowly losing my mind."

He looked frightful; he had lost far too much weight, and there were dark smudges under his eyes. Charles well realized that his news of the situation in the East would place even more pressure on his cousin, so he changed the subject abruptly and launched into an account of his business dealings with Soong Chao.

Jonathan listened, commenting from time to time, and when Charles ended his recital he asked wistfully, "How does Lai-tse lu look?"

"I think we've talked enough about her for one day," Charles said firmly.

"No doubt you're right, but I must tell you what I'm doing. I've just finished building the clipper of clippers, which I've named for her." He described the *Lai-tse lu* in glowing terms. "I'm sending her to Lai-tse lu as a gift," he said, "as the only way left to me of expressing my love for her. With the ship I'll send her the letter I've delayed for so long, telling her why I can never return to her."

"You say you've just finished building the ship?"

"The fittings for the passenger cabins haven't arrived yet. They're being made to my specifications. But she's ready for her sea trials."

"You'll conduct the trials yourself?"

"I don't have the heart," Jonathan said.

"For old times' sake, why don't you and Edmund Barker and I take her out?"

"Eddie is in home port, as it happens," Jonathan said slowly. "Nothing would please me more than to have you two put the clipper through her paces for three or four days. But I'll bow out. I—I have too much work to do right here, with other ships in various stages of construction and all of them needing my attention."

Charles knew he had made up his mind and would not be persuaded to change it, even though he knew that a brief voyage would help relieve his unbearable tensions, at least temporarily. So, if Edmund Barker was willing, as Charles felt certain he would be, they would take the new clipper out on her trial run themselves. "How are Eddie and Ruth?" he asked casually, unwilling to reveal his continuing interest in the young woman. He had to remind himself that she was the wife of a friend and colleague, and he could not admit, even to Jonathan, that he frequently found himself thinking about her.

"They've been rattling around in that big house ever since Ruth's father retired some months ago and went to live with his older daughter and her husband in South Carolina," Jonathan said. "I believe Eddie would like to sell the place and buy something smaller, but Ruth seems to be too attached to it."

They went off to the yard together, and while Charles supervised the unloading of the *Elizabeth*'s cargo, Jonathan returned to his own labors, inspecting each of the new clippers he was building and somehow managing to neglect none of them, even though he was devoting most of his attention to the *Lai-tse lu*.

Charles's news disturbed him more than he was willing to admit. If relations between the Middle Kingdom and the nations of the West were becoming critical, Lai-tse lu, her father, and Sarah Applegate certainly would be in personal danger. But he wasn't in a position to urge them to escape to some safe place on board the new clipper. In view of his own inability to marry Lai-tse lu, the mere suggestion would be an impertinence. Besides, he knew Soong Chao well enough to realize that the merchant would not desert his duty post when his country was threatened.

The frustrations of his situation ate into Jonathan constantly. His vocational success was greater than he had imagined possible on that day long ago when he had first seen the *Ann McKim* and had made up his mind to devote the rest of his professional life to the building and sailing of clipper ships. He had won universal recognition in the United States, Great Britain, and Europe as the leading expert in the construction of the temperamental, graceful clippers, and he had more orders than he could fulfill. The Rakehell and Boynton merchant fleets were growing, their clippers showing remarkable profit margins. He had already established a solid place for himself as a worthy successor to the long line of Rakehell shipping men who had preceded him.

But his life had lost its savor. He was doing his best to rear Julian in the family traditions, but otherwise his day to day existence was flat. He and Louise performed the duties required of them, and on the surface they were amicable enough, but their relationship lacked depth, and it was impossible to believe they would ever grow closer.

Lai-tse lu continued to haunt him. He knew he would yearn for her until his dying day; he could not reconcile himself to her loss. His cousin's return from the East reopened wounds that would not heal; he realized he had to learn to live with his sorrow, but he didn't know how.

The following morning Charles decided to pay a call on the Barkers so he could discuss the trial voyage of the new clipper. But he had more than that lurking in the back of his mind and took David with him, the little boy sitting happily on his shoulder.

Edmund came to the door and, greeting his old comrade warmly, was not surprised to see the child. "News gets around fast in a town this size," he said. "David, you look like your father, and like your mother, too, so you're fortunate. If you have your mother's courage and your father's mind, you won't need anything else in this world."

Ruth came down the stairs soon after the two men and little boy went into the parlor. Handsome in a new dress that she had made of silk Edmund had brought back to her from his last voyage to France, she had heard Charles's voice and was looking forward to seeing him again. But she forgot all else when she caught sight of the small child, the part-Eurasian who would go through life without a mother and would be pressed into the mold that Rakehells and Boyntons demanded of their sons.

Instinctively dropping to her knees, she held out her arms.

David responded to her without hesitation and toddled to her, eagerly nestling in her embrace.

Charles thought she had never looked lovelier.

For a time Ruth, still holding the child, listened politely as the men discussed their coming sea trial, but their talk bored her, so she took David to the kitchen for a glass

511

of milk and one of the gingerbread cookies she had baked earlier in the morning.

David was eating a second cookie, joyously scattering crumbs, as Ruth returned to the parlor with him.

"I've been wondering," Charles said, "whether there isn't some way I can legitimatize my son before I take him back to England."

"I'm no lawyer, but it seems simple enough to me," the hard-headed Ruth replied. "Adopt him formally. The courts are never busy at this time of year, so it shouldn't take more than a day or two for a judge to give his approval. Then take the baby to Reverend Crowell, who will baptize him, I'm sure."

"Of course," Charles said. "That's precisely what I'll do. Provided you two will do David and me the honor of becoming his godparents."

Ruth's advice proved to be sound. The attorney who handled the legal aspects of the Rakehell and Boynton business drew up the necessary adoption papers. "This step may not be strictly necessary, since you're actually the boy's father," he said. "But it does answer any questions that might arise in the future."

The following day Charles made a brief appearance in court, and the New London county judge signed the documents.

That afternoon a small group went to the Anglican church, where Reverend Crowell duly baptized David. Jeremiah and Jonathan were in attendance, with the latter bringing his own son, and Judith Walker came with her three children. Jonathan asked Louise to go, too, but at the last moment she developed a headache that sent her to her bed.

Ruth and Edmund stood up with David and became his godparents.

The party then returned to the Rakehell house for dinner, and Louise recovered from her headache in time to come to the table. Charles suspected she had absented herself deliberately because she didn't approve of him or his son. But he was indifferent to her opinions. Jonathan's wife was an increasingly withdrawn, sour woman, and Charles took care to avoid her whenever possible.

Two days later the *Lai-tse lu* was launched quietly, and feverish preparations were made for her sea trial. Jonathan released Oliver from his other duties to act as her boatswain, and two young mates, both with clipper experience, were added to her staff.

"We'll flip a coin, Eddie, to see which of us is the master and which the first mate," Charles said.

"We shall do no such thing," Edmund replied. "You're senior to me, and I was your mate on a good many voyages. I wouldn't revert to a lower rank, even temporarily, for anyone but you or Jonnie, but I'll be happy to make this voyage under your command."

Jonathan selected the crew for the trial, all of the sailors having had experience on clippers, and early one morning the *Lai-tse lu* was ready to sail with a company of thirty-one on board.

Trials were regarded as routine, so no crowds appeared to watch the departure of the *Lai-tse lu*. Only Jonathan came to the pier, and as he stood alone, looking forlorn in the early morning light, Charles said, "It isn't too late to change your mind, Jonnie. Come with us and take the command yourself."

Unwilling to admit the pain of sailing the ship into which he had poured his love for the Chinese girl he could neither marry nor ever see again, Jonathan shook his head. "I'm going down to New York with my father for a few days. We're holding a series of meetings there with the merchants who use the services of our clippers." He did not add that he had arranged the meetings deliberately in order to keep busy while his new vessel put out to sea for the first time.

Charles was piped aboard and joined Edmund on the quarterdeck. Orders were given, then relayed to the crew by Oliver, and the great ship slowly moved out into the estuary.

Jonathan stood still on the dock, alert to every nuance of the clipper's movements, but the moment was taking its emotional toll, and his shoulders slumped.

This should have been an exciting hour for his two old comrades on the quarterdeck, but they were conscious of his loneliness, and that awareness robbed them of their sense of pleasure. They gave the routine commands mechanically, and not until the solitary figure on the pier faded from sight did they force themselves to put him out of their minds and devote their full attention to the tasks that awaited them.

Bradford Walker told himself that he was in luck. Jeremiah and Jonathan had gone to New York, Charles was at sea, and Louise was alone with her child and the servants in the Rakehell house. Brad couldn't have selected a more appropriate time for a quiet, confidential talk with Louise.

For weeks he had been thinking about the information Judith had given him about her brother's feelings, and the time was ripe for him to strike. Jonathan was dispirited and painfully thin, looking like a man on the verge of collapse. All he needed to destroy him was a slight nudge, and Brad was ready to give him a push over the edge. If Louise turned on him and created serious problems for him, the weight might be too much for him to bear.

Certainly there was everything to gain and little to be lost by going to Louise. There had to be more spirit in her than she exhibited, and the only risk he was taking was the possibility that she might reveal the identity of her husband's betrayer. Well, he had to take that chance.

Brad left the shipyard an hour earlier than usual, taking care to dismiss his coachman when he alighted at the Rakehell house.

Louise, who had just returned from her regular afternoon visit to her mother and was planning to dine with her parents because Jonathan was away from home, was slightly surprised to see Brad. But she greeted him cordially and led him into the parlor. She had always liked him because he, unlike the Rakehells, sometimes talked about subjects other than the shipping business.

He declined her offer of tea or coffee. Now that he was actually here, confronting her, he would have preferred a drink of West Indian rum, but he didn't want to go home to Judith with liquor on his breath. "I've been wanting to have a chat with you for quite a long time," he said, pausing significantly and adding, "a private chat."

Louise made no reply, her expression placid.

"You and I are in the same boat, you know," Brad said with an ingratiating smile. "Being married to a Rakehell means being married to the whole family. So to speak."

She smiled faintly. "I know what you mean, Brad. Their energies can be exhausting."

"I wasn't thinking in quite those terms. What sometimes concerns me is their blood-is-thicker-than-water attitude. Rakehells have a loyalty to each other that excludes everyone else, including you and me, I'm sorry to say."

"Oh, I don't think they're as clannish as all that." Louise's protest was faint.

"I hate to contradict you, but they are. In fact, that's why I'm here."

She looked at him uneasily, making it plain that she regarded any disturbance of the even tenor of her ways as a threat.

"Before I go into this matter," Brad said solemnly, "I must ask you to treat this conversation as completely confidential. I wouldn't want any of the Rakehells to know that we've talked."

"It's as serious as that?"

"Indeed it is. To you, especially." He allowed the significance of his statement to sink in. He could see that she was intrigued, even somewhat alarmed, and he was able to breathe more easily because he felt he had the situation under control.

"What could possibly concern me?" Louise asked in wonder.

"Do I have your pledge?" he countered. "I don't want trouble between Judith and me as a result of my having come to you."

"I give you my promise that I'll never mention a word to Jonathan. Or his sister. Or Papa Rakehell, either."

"Good." Brad leaned forward in his chair, looking sorrowful. "I've had a long, difficult struggle within myself, Louise. I've wanted to come to you with what I know, especially since I've seen the Rakehells closing

515

ranks and keeping silent. But I haven't wanted to upset you. As you can see, I've had to come. Because my conscience simply wouldn't let me shut my eyes. As the Rakehells have done."

"Whatever—"

"To be blunt about it, and I hope you'll forgive my candor," Brad said, "but your marriage to Jonathan hasn't been the happiest in the world."

"Oh, we get along well enough," she replied, her voice barely audible.

"I've seen you two together," he persisted, "at least once or twice a week. And aside from your joint concern for Julian, it has struck me that you have very little in common."

He was more perspicacious than Louise had imagined. "Some marriages need time to grow and flourish, as my mother so often reminds me," she murmured.

"In theory your mother is right," Brad declared, becoming bolder. "And in some instances I daresay couples do gain a greater appreciation of each other. But it won't happen in your marriage."

He was invading a territory she considered her own, a matter she had never discussed with anyone other than her mother.

He could see she was becoming indignant and struck still more firmly. "When is Jonathan going back to Cathay?" he asked abruptly.

Louise shrugged. "I have no idea. He hasn't even mentioned the possibility. We don't discuss such things."

"You can bet your last dollar he'll sail there again." Brad halted dramatically, then said in a low tone, "To see her."

"If you're joking, I can't say much for your good taste." For the first time she showed a spark of life. "Who is this person?"

"Her name," Brad said, speaking distinctly, "is Lai-tse lu."

"That's the name of his fancy new clipper, the ship he discusses day and night with his father—until I'm ready to scream."

"The ship is named for the lady, if I may call her that.

In fact, Jonathan intends to present her with it. As a gift."

"I don't believe you." Louise's voice suddenly became strident.

Brad knew he was scoring. "Perhaps you'll take my word if I show you the company ledgers, which I'm prepared to do. In confidence. That clipper hasn't been built with Rakehell and Boynton funds. Jonathan has paid every penny out of his own pocket. He's been working for months on this incredible, expensive gift."

She took a lace-edged handkerchief from her sleeve and began to pick at it, unaware of what she was doing.

"The Rakehells," Brad said somberly, "have been keeping a secret. I wouldn't swear to this, but I think that even our esteemed father-in-law knows the story and is keeping quiet about it. I haven't been able to glean much beyond the basics, thanks to the Rakehell conspiracy of silence. But I do know this much. Jonathan had a blazing romance in Cathay with a Chinese woman named Lai-tse lu."

Louise looked even paler than usual. "Who is she?"

Brad had no intention of mentioning that she was the daughter of the man who had become the Eastern trading partner of Rakehell and Boynton. It was better to let Louise assume she was an ordinary courtesan. Now that he thought of it, he quickly amplified. "No one has told me," he said, "but in a land where every man of substance keeps a whole harem of concubines, it isn't too difficult to imagine this woman's origins."

"Are you insinuating that Jonathan lived with her?"

"I insinuate nothing. I do know for a fact that they were at the same place in Canton. So you can draw your own conclusions."

Louise's handkerchief began to become frayed. "I'm not trying to defend him or excuse his conduct," she said, "but we weren't actually married when he was in Cathay."

Brad had heard about the secret marriage ceremony from Judith, but he thought it wise to change the emphasis. "That isn't my concern. I came to you because I know for a certainty that he's built this ship in the past six months as a gift for the woman. He's poured a fortune into it, I can tell you, what with teak decks and special fittings for

517

a row of passenger cabins. There's no ship in merchant service anywhere that's as elegant or expensive." He thought of mentioning the figurehead, but decided the impact would be greater if she hadn't already seen the figure of a young Chinese woman and discovered it for herself.

For a long time Louise was as stiff and unmoving as the chair on which she sat.

"I hope you'll forgive me for this intrusion into your personal life. But my sense of family duties and obligations is—well—more elastic than that of those with Rakehell blood."

Louise mouthed the words, "Thank you."

"Jonathan isn't the first man who has strayed, and he won't be the last, I'm sure," Brad said as he stood. "But the way I figured it, once you knew about this woman, you could find a dozen ways to prevent him from going back to Cathay. With half the world separating them, he's bound to lose interest in her eventually."

"I—I'm very grateful to you, Brad," the shaken Louise said, extending an icy hand to him. "And you needn't worry that I'll betray the source of this information. I won't tell it to a soul, not even my mother."

He patted her on the shoulder, then left her sitting in the parlor. Not until he reached the street did his somber expression change, and he walked jauntily toward his own home. He had no way of guessing what Louise might do, but he was confident she wouldn't remain idle. Not even the most mouse-like woman would tolerate such a situation without putting up a stiff fight, and Jonathan soon would have his hands full. So full that he well might collapse under the strain.

As the hunters who came from northwestern Connecticut to sell their wares so often said, there were a dozen ways to skin a wild animal's carcass. Brad's previous efforts to discredit Jonathan had failed, but the present situation wasn't his doing. Jonathan alone was responsible and would pay the consequences. And if those consequences forced him out of the company, he had a brother-in-law who wouldn't mind in the least. Brad had done a good day's work, and he looked forward to his first drink of the evening.

Louise continued to sit in the parlor, unmindful of the growing dusk and her own failure to light an oil lamp. She was shaken by jealousy, and gradually a sense of deep, bitter humiliation crept over her, threatening to inundate her.

In all of the long, loveless months she had spent as Jonathan's wife in name only, she had complained to no one except her mother. And she had accepted her mother's flat, repeated statement that if she showed enough patience her relations with her husband would improve. Well, they wouldn't. Because he was infatuated with someone else—a Chinese woman, at that!

In a sudden burst of unreasoning worry Louise wanted to turn David's simpering little Chinese nursemaid out of the house. But that would cause troubles with Jonathan and Papa Rakehell, as well as with Charles, when he returned from the sea.

Forced to examine her own feelings, Louise made an effort to understand where she really stood. She had denied, even to her mother, that she loved Jonathan, but that wasn't true. She did care for him, as much as she was capable of caring for any man. She wanted him to make love to her, not because she yearned for him, but rather because she regarded marital relations as a symbol.

Now, however, knowing that he was fascinated with some promiscuous heathen, the very contemplation of his lovemaking made her physically ill. To remain married to him would be a lie, but no one in New England ever sought a divorce, and she cringed at the thought of returning to her parents' home across the street and remaining there for the rest of her life.

There was Julian to be considered, too, but she couldn't even think about him at the moment. Since he was a Rakehell, she knew Jonathan and his father would look after the child. They were already trying hard enough to cast him in the family image. He would grow up to be like them and would think of nothing but the shipping business that obsessed all Rakehell men.

Not quite. She had to change her thinking on that score. Jonathan, in spite of all his hard work, had the time to contemplate his Chinese mistress—and to pour money into the magnificent clipper he had just built for her! Louise felt as though she were drowning in a sea of shame.

The present situation, now that she knew about it, was intolerable. She had to do something, but for the present she had no idea how to begin. Rising slowly from her chair, she made her way up the dark stairs to her bedchamber. Her supper was forgotten, and so was the existence of her son. She wanted to give in to the hysteria that engulfed her. Later, perhaps, she would be able to think more clearly and could decide what needed to be done.

The *Lai-tse lu,* her sails filled, sliced majestically through the sparkling waters of the Atlantic under a clear sky. Charles had been right last night, after they had spent sixty hours putting the ship through exhaustive tests, when he said, "This is the finest clipper Jonathan has ever built. Her balance is so perfect that I don't see how he can duplicate it. This ship is one of a kind, and there will never be another like her."

Edmund Barker vividly recalled his friend's words. Standing duty watch on deck, he knew the *Lai-tse lu* was unique because building her had been a labor of love. She cut cleanly through the swells of a moderate sea, her rocking motion gentle, rarely pitching. Her lines creaked and her tackles rattled rhythmically, and even with her skysails furled she was easily achieving a speed of almost twenty knots. Edmund felt he was fortunate to be sharing in the privilege of testing her.

What was more, he could understand the care that Jonathan had devoted to her. More in love with Ruth than he had been the day he had married her, Edmund could guess the extent and depth of his longtime friend's yearning for the girl he had left behind in Canton. Jonathan never mentioned her, but this ship bore witness to his love.

Scanning the horizon, Edmund had to admit he had been fortunate. When these trials ended he would return to his own clipper as her master. He knew more about sailing these spirited ships than anyone except Jonathan and Charles, and they had to spend a major portion of their time attending to other phases of the growing business. In fact, the Rakehell and Boynton merchant fleet soon would be so large that, for the first time, it would become necessary to name a commodore to direct the sea operations. Charles had volunteered, just last night, that Edmund was certain to be given the post. The idea of a commodore had been Jonathan's, and Jeremiah Rakehell had given his approval after his son and nephew had convinced him the promotion had to be made for the good of the fleet.

Ruth would be pleased when he returned. Or would she?

The thought that assailed him, ruffling his serenity, appeared as suddenly as the tiny black cloud that suddenly showed at the horizon. Like the cloud, Edmund's sense of uncertainty grew rapidly.

He had no reason to complain in any way about Ruth. She was a considerate, attentive wife, a splendid cook, and an immaculate housekeeper. Not once had she rejected his attentions as a lover, and if she failed to gain satisfaction from his lovemaking, he could not fault her for that. More than once she had explained to him that women's needs were unlike those of men.

Ruth had shied away from the prospect of having children, giving him no reason for her attitude, and Edmund had been content to wait, believing that in time she would change her mind. Her spontaneous reaction to Charles's small son had jarred him, however, and he realized now that she had a deeper love for children, a greater need for them than he had imagined.

Perhaps that was what had triggered his thinking in recent days. Occasionally Edmund had imagined that Ruth was in love with Jonathan, but he couldn't pinpoint any incident that would confirm his suspicions, so he had dismissed them. Repeatedly. They had returned again and again, however; perhaps it was the way she looked at Jonathan, perhaps it was the softer tone she used when addressing him.

Rubbish! Edmund told himself he was allowing his imagination to get the better of him, which sometimes happened when a man went to sea. Right now that black cloud was filling the whole sky, blotting out the sun, and there was work to be done.

"Bo's'n," he called, "turn up all hands. We're in for a blow."

"Aye aye, sir." Oliver put his silver call to his lips and the pipe shrilled.

Edmund sent to his cabin for his oiled raincoat and hat, then told the boatswain, "My compliments to Captain Boynton, and ask him if he'd like to join me."

Rain was falling steadily by the time Charles came to the quarterdeck a few moments later, buttoning his raincoat. "This is an odd storm, Eddie," he said. "The sky was clear five minutes ago."

"What I don't like is that the wind keeps shifting, and it gets stronger by the minute." He interrupted himself to give some sharp orders. "Stand by to go about!" The head and foresheets were let go, the jibs were sheeted to port, and coming round on the starboard tack, the mainyard was braced round.

Charles nodded approvingly as the veteran crew carried out the commands and the clipper headed directly into the wind once her headsails were set on the new tack.

"Would you like to take the watch?" Edmund offered politely, discovering he had to shout to make himself heard above the increasing roar of the wind.

"I know of nothing I could do that you aren't doing," Charles replied. "If you don't mind, old boy, I'll stay here with you. This storm is becoming positively nasty, and two heads may be an improvement on one, even if both of them are sopping wet."

The wind had already risen, seemingly out of nowhere, to a Force Seven strength, and the sea was reacting viciously, the moderate swells rising and becoming mountainous, unpredictable waves that seethed with white-capped anger.

The rain became a deluge so great that the men on the quarterdeck could see only a few feet beyond the carved figure of the Chinese girl on the prow.

Edmund fought to keep the clipper headed into the fickle, violent wind. The *Lai-tse lu* responded admirably, although she was rolling heavily and pitching so hard that foaming sea water washed over her main deck every time she plowed into a huge, oncoming wave. Occasionally a maverick wave slapped her hard on the hull, causing her to shudder, but she reacted gallantly, quickly regaining her perfect balance.

"This is quite a test!" Charles shouted, and grinned.

"Jonnie couldn't have devised a more severe trial if he had tried." A confident Edmund laughed aloud.

He and Charles, together with their mates and crew, were comrades who were pitting their skills against the raging, unexpected storm. This was the real fascination of the sea, the reason that men sailed the waters of the earth in frail wooden ships, the reason they challenged nature. There was no sensation equal to that of defying the elements and winning the battle.

Every precaution was taken, the most urgent task being that of shortening sail. The topmen worked furiously high in the standing rigging, their experience enabling them to keep their balance as the clipper moved erratically, buffeted by the wind and sea.

First the courses were taken in and the topsails were double-reefed. Then the head sails were taken in, and only one jib was retained. Sail canvas was made to be stretched, and the great danger was that it might split or that a yard might be carried away. Such disasters had to be averted.

The howling, swirling wind blew with even greater vehemence. By now the flapping canvas had been rolled up, and Edmund took the precaution of putting two helmsmen on the wheel.

The clipper wore and tacked again and again, the crew repeatedly responding to his orders to come round.

Her timbers groaning, her whole frame shuddering when a huge, vagrant wave slapped her amidships, the graceful clipper fought the storm, buoyant because of the expertise of her builder and the seamen who manned her.

The rain had turned into a cloudburst, drenching the entire company and sending torrents across the open spaces. Every man who went to sea was accustomed to such discomfort, to be sure; frequently their clothes were wet, as was their bedding, and they accepted the clamminess as normal. But this drenching rain was far worse than any they had known in a long time, and they had to squint continually, wiping rivers of rain from their eyes so they could see.

A storm such as this tested the mettle of the men as well as putting their ship on trial, and the seamen responded to the challenge as they clung to the ropes that had been rigged on the deck to prevent them from being washed overboard.

Edmund doggedly kept the ship facing into the screaming wind.

Gradually the rain became less intense, dropping off to a drizzle and finally dying away. The wind became less violent, too, and although it remained brisk it lost most of its sting. The movements of the ship gradually became smoother, less violent.

The two officers on the quarterdeck grinned at each other. The new vessel had come through with flying colors. Licking the salt spray from their lips and relishing the feeling of the more benign wind, they knew they had conquered the sea.

Soon they would hoist sail again and begin their homeward voyage.

"That was great," Edmund said.

Charles knew exactly what he meant. The experience had been nerve-wracking, at times terrifying, but as veterans they, too, had emerged unscathed from the vicious trial. The storm had lasted no more than two hours, but in that brief time the entire company had faced death without flinching.

All at once the clipper began to nose down into a deep trough.

Edmund instinctively looked back over his shoulder, and for an instant he froze in horror. Bearing down on the ship astern was a rare phenomenon of the sea, a gigantic tidal wave that towered above the vessel, seemingly shrinking even the high mainmast. There was no way to escape the grim power of the mammoth wave in so short a time, no opportunity to come about, no chance to increase speed in order to stay ahead of that wall of solid, surging water.

Edmund found his voice. "Hold the ropes," he shouted to Charles and the crew as he pointed at the enormous body of sea water that loomed above the frail ship like a living mountain.

Charles and the seamen obeyed instantly, grasping the nearest rails or lines and hanging on with all of their might.

The wave crashed down onto the clipper, and for a moment it seemed as though she would be torn to kindling and founder. Then the wave passed on, rolling swiftly across the open sea.

Edmund Barker had vanished from his place on the quarterdeck.

Charles Boynton caught his breath, knowing at once that the tidal wave had claimed a victim. There was no sign of Edmund anywhere, and it was plain that the wave had carried him away.

His timely warning had saved the lives of Charles and the crew, but in the brief moment before the wave descended he had lost his opportunity to gain a secure hold himself and had sacrificed his own life so the others might live.

As the seamen became aware of the tragedy they scattered, some running to the forecastle, others hurrying to the fantail while still others moved to the port and starboard rails. They peered out at the increasingly calm waters, now turning from an ugly gray to a complacent green-blue, but none caught any sight of Edmund. The ship's log would be forced to carry the grim notation that had been written on countless previous occasions: *"Lost at sea."*

The huge wave also had damaged the ship. The mizzenmast had been sprung at the cap, rendering it useless. So sail was taken in, yards were sent down, and the clipper would limp home, using her other two masts. Replacing the mast was a difficult task that could be accomplished far more easily at the Rakehell yard than at sea, and the ship was close enough to her home port to sail there safely.

Standing erect on his quarterdeck, Charles felt lonelier and more impotent than ever before in his life. He was alive and well, thanks to Edmund, but in a single moment of sheer horror he had lost a dear friend and close comrade. For the first time since he had been a small boy he wept, without shame, still standing erect as the tears rolled down his face.

Twenty-four hours later the *Lai-tse lu* limped into port. Word spread quickly that her Tree of Life pennant was flying at half-mast, and a silent crowd gathered on the shore as she maneuvered into her berth.

Jonathan came on board at once and raced to the quarterdeck.

Charles told him all that had happened, speaking succinctly. "There was no way to save him," he concluded. "Our one consolation is that this ship is sound and seaworthy."

For the present Jonathan was more concerned about the human tragedy. "I dread telling Ruth."

"I'll go to her at once myself," Charles said. "I must. I can never forget that Eddie saved my life." The knowledge that two people had given their lives so he might be spared was ever-present in his mind, and he knew that Edmund Barker and Alice Wong would be forever interwoven in his memories.

Jonathan gave orders for the new clipper to be returned to her drydock for repairs, and a carriage was provided for Charles so he could carry out his unhappy mission.

Ruth Barker came to the door in response to his knock, and her initial surprise immediately was replaced by a certain knowledge when she saw his face.

Charles accompanied her into the parlor.

The young woman had lived all of her life in a community where men went out to sea. Over the years friends had lost husbands, fathers, and brothers, and now it was her turn. She had never been truly in love with Edmund, but he had been kind, gentle, and considerate, and it had been her fault, not his, that she had been unable to return his deep and abiding affection for her.

She grasped the back of a chair for support and braced herself.

Strongly attracted to her, as he had been for so long, Charles told her of Edmund's loss in dry, clipped terms, for her sake making his story as unemotional as he could.

Ruth couldn't help seeing that his eyes were suspiciously moist as he finished his brief recital. She thought she was empty, incapable of feeling anything at this awful moment, but the realization flashed through her mind that here was a man as sensitive as Jonathan, a quality for which she had never given him credit. Now that she looked at him, her throat raw, her spirits numbed, it occurred to her that the Rakehell family resemblance was strong, that Charles looked strikingly like the Jonathan whom she had been unable to exorcise from her heart and mind.

No one knew what sparked the incident. By the time word reached Lin Tse-hsü at the viceroy's palace, thousands of Cantonese were marching through the streets toward the foreign concession at Whampoa, shouting, "Death to the Fan Kuei!"

One regiment of Imperial Guards, the only disciplined troops in all of Kwantung, were rushed to the scene. When they arrived, scattering the militants who were brandishing clubs, knives, and an assortment of homemade weapons, the foreign-owned factories had been closed and barricaded, with heavily armed white men waiting at the windows to open a barrage as soon as they were attacked. Merchant ships fled the harbor so hastily that many left their cargoes sitting on the wharves, and Rear Admiral Sir William Alexander was moving his squadron of Royal Navy warships into position to bombard the city.

The Imperial Guards were ruthless, using the butts of their weapons to strike the rioters, and the mobs were dispersed at a heavy cost. No official figures were released, but Lin informed the Tao Kuang Emperor in a secret report that eighteen Chinese died and more than one hundred were injured.

Soong Chao spent the entire day doing what he could to protect warehouses in Whampoa, and he arrived home at dusk, weary and discouraged. He had no appetite, even though he had eaten nothing all day, but he was persuaded by Lai-tse lu and Missy Sarah to sit down to a light supper before he bathed and retired. They joined him in the dining pavilion, and neither commented as he told them about the day's events.

"We defile the sacred memories of our revered ancestors when Chinese kill Chinese in the cause of maintaining peace," he said.

Lai-tse lu was reminded of the ancient myth about Kuan Yin, the goddess of mercy, who had destroyed the people of an entire province when they cursed their ancestors during a famine. According to the story, the goddess reasoned that death was preferable to allowing the people to spend the rest of their days on earth being ashamed of their shocking misconduct.

"The feeling against foreigners is like a fire that spreads until it can no longer be controlled," Chao said. "Lin Tse-hsü claims he is not responsible for these feelings of hatred, but he fools himself. He fans the flames while pretending they do not exist."

Sarah Applegate was deeply concerned. "When do you think the war with the British and whatever nations may join them will begin?"

The merchant shrugged. "Only the gods know. Another incident could take place tomorrow or the next day. I am certain of only one thing. I cannot imagine our present precarious state of peace lasting for more than another year."

"Perhaps, as you and I have discussed," Sarah suggested, "the time has come for Lai-tse lu and me to go off to the estate in the country, where we'll be safe."

The girl broke her silence. "Make all the plans you please," she said flatly. "But I will not go. I will not leave Canton."

Her father and the New England governess turned to stare at her.

"I told Jonathan I would wait for him right here until he returns, and so I shall," she declared. "If I go off to our country place, hundreds of miles into the interior, there is no way he could ever find me, no way he would be allowed to travel past farms and villages through territory no white man has ever visited. Every year missionaries from the West who try to push their way into the interior are killed, and the same would happen to Jonathan."

"We appreciate your concern for him, my daughter," Chao said, and exchanged a quick glance with Sarah.

"I know what both of you are thinking," Lai-tse lu said. "You believe he will not return to Canton and marry me."

"We want you to be reasonable," Sarah told her.

"In all of the many months since Jonathan returned to New England," Chao said, "you have received no letter from him. Even I, who do business regularly with his company, have had no word from him. Only Charles writes to me."

"Charles is in charge of the company's trade with the Middle Kingdom," the girl replied defensively. "Besides, he told us when he was here that Jonathan works day and night building new clipper ships."

"Any man who loves a woman finds or makes the time to write to her," Sarah Applegate said.

The girl's temper flared. "Do you dare to suggest that Jonathan no longer loves me?"

"We suggest nothing," her father said quickly. "All we ask is that you question for yourself the possible reasons for his long silence."

The girl's bravado crumpled. "I question and wonder and analyze every day of my life, but I have no answers. I do not believe that Jonathan has put me aside, as Westerners are said to do with their women in distant, foreign places. My love for Jonathan has not changed, and I would know if his for me had changed. I would feel it inside me."

Chao wanted to suggest that she visit one of the hundreds of soothsayers in Canton who predicted the future, but he realized she was too highly educated to believe in the powers of a fortune teller who undoubtedly could be influenced by her father's bribe.

"When Jonathan comes to me," Lai-tse lu said, "he will tell me why he did not write, and I will take his word. We believe each other in all things. So, until he comes, I will wait, and my faith in him will not lessen. Without that faith I would wither and die, as the fruit of the kumquat tree shrivels and dies when there is no rain and no sun." Tears came to her eyes, and she brushed them away in quick anger.

Chao and Sarah felt desperately sorry for her, but there was nothing they could do. Convinced in their own minds that Jonathan had developed a new romantic interest elsewhere, they were powerless to prevent the hurt he was inflicting on this girl who had given him her whole heart.

The *Lai-tse lu* was returned to her fitting out berth, where she would be given a new mizzenmast and the fittings for her luxurious cabins would be installed. And Jonathan privately began to comb the company rosters in his search for the right ship's master who would sail the clipper to Canton and deliver her, along with his letter of farewell, to the one woman he had ever loved.

As that day drew nearer he relied more and more heavily on the company of his son and Charles's son for distraction. He played for at least an hour every day with the two little boys, and because they embodied his hopes for the long-range future, they comforted him.

Certainly Louise was no help to him. Ever since he had returned home after his business trip to New York with his father, he had found her more withdrawn, more silent than she had ever been. Until recently she had chatted about inconsequentials at the dinner table and had willingly conversed with him about household matters. Now she was morose and sullen, and even her visits to her mother became less frequent. She seemed to be brooding. On the one occasion Jonathan inquired whether anything was amiss, she merely stared at him, her eyes expressionless, and shook her head negatively. So he asked her no further questions.

Meanwhile Charles escorted Ruth to the memorial service for Edmund. Waiting for the cargo he would carry to England in the hold of the *Elizabeth,* and with little to occupy him other than correspondence on behalf of Rakehell and Boynton, he began to pay daily calls on Ruth, taking little David with him because she was so fond of the child that she was able to put her sorrow out of her mind when he was present.

One afternoon, while David dropped off to sleep after

a strenuous time of play that wore out both Ruth and Charles, the adults adjourned to another sitting room.

"I've been wondering," Ruth said, "whether you'd consider leaving David with me for a year or two when you return to England."

Charles was too startled to reply.

"I've been thinking about the life he'll be leading there," she said. "Wu-ling is just learning English herself, so who will take overall charge of him?"

"I'll admit it's something of a problem," Charles said ruefully. "If my father turns David and me out, as he may, I'll have to find quarters for us somewhere, and in that event I'll need to hire a governess. Even if we live at my father's house it won't be too easy. Elizabeth is thirteen now, and I don't believe it would be fair to ask my mother, after rearing two children, to start again with David. Not at her age. So either way I'll need to hire someone."

"Obviously I think I can help David," Ruth said, "but my motives are partly selfish. I've learned to love him already, and with no one else to look after, he'll keep me busy."

"I don't quite know what to say," Charles told her. "Certainly I would never allow you to do it without giving you an appropriate fee."

"To be honest with you, Charles," she said, "that crossed my mind, too. I'd like to augment the widow's pension that you and Jonathan are being kind enough to pay me." She did not add that, if David lived with her, she would see Jonathan frequently when David played with Julian. Not that she had any intention of injecting herself into Jonathan's private life. He was a married man, so her own code of morality forbade it.

"If you will," Charles said, "give me until tomorrow to think about all this. It's too new an idea for me to make a judgment."

That evening, after a late supper at the Rakehell house, Charles mentioned the subject when he and his work-weary cousin went into the library for glasses of port.

Somewhat to his surprise Jonathan approved heartily. "Trust Ruth to find a perfect solution," he said.

"What makes you call it perfect, Jonnie?"

"First of all, there's the problem of your parents. I know Aunt Jessica would pitch in without being asked, but it wouldn't be right to burden her."

"I've already thought of that."

"As for Uncle Alan, there's no need for me to tell you that his reaction is totally unpredictable. Not that he could force you out of the new company. Papa and I wouldn't tolerate it, and we could out-vote Uncle Alan. But he could compel you to live somewhere other than in his house, and there inevitably would be hard feelings all around."

"How well I know it," Charles said with a sigh.

"Well, this plan of Ruth's gives you at least a year to prepare your father, little by little. Once your mother becomes your ally, as she most assuredly will, she'll work him around to a tolerant point of view."

"I hope you're right, Jonnie."

"There are other angles to consider, too," Jonathan said briskly. "Ruth can contribute far more to David's rearing than a governess for whom you'd advertise in the *Times*. She's a splendid woman."

"She's far more than that," Charles said slowly, "and there's no need for you or anyone else to sing her praises to me. I mean no disrespect to Eddie's memory when I say that I've had Ruth on my mind for a very long time. Eddie was on the scene and had the intelligence to act promptly while I was still drinking and whoring in London."

Jonathan smiled. "I intend no disrespect to Eddie, either, when I mention the obvious. If you want to develop a serious interest in Ruth, and vice versa, there's no better way to do it than to have your son in her care."

"I've thought of that, too," Charles replied, and looked guilty.

"There's one additional factor. Julian and David are still babies, but they represent the next generation of the Rakehell dynasty, which has become permanently intertwined with that of the Boyntons. I'm convinced that one reason you and I have become the closest of friends as well as business partners is because we spent so much time together in our boyhood years. It would give me great pleasure to know we were providing our sons with the same benefits."

"That alone would be a good enough reason for me," Charles said.

The next morning he went to Ruth's house immediately after breakfast and, telling her he had decided to accept her offer, promptly made a generous financial arrangement with her.

"I'm thrilled," Ruth said, "and overwhelmed. You need have no worries about David. I'll treat him as I would my own son. And I'll take good care of Wu-ling, too, the poor little thing."

Charles wondered if he should tell her that Wu-ling was Alice Wong's half-sister, but decided not to mention the fact. It was enough that Ruth sympathized with the adolescent girl and intended to befriend her, and he saw no need to complicate matters by telling a woman of high morality that Wu-ling was the blood relative of his late mistress.

"I don't want David to forget me, which is all too easy at his age," he said. "So I'll come over here much more frequently than I've done in the past. And when the atmosphere is right at home, I hope you'll bring him to London yourself."

"I'd enjoy that," Ruth said, and extended her hand.

Her touch jolted Charles, and he told himself it was just as well that he was leaving for England in a few days. He didn't want to disgrace himself by making advances, even proper advances, to a widow during her time of mourning.

A portion of the *Elizabeth*'s cargo arrived by sea from Baltimore, and the rest was delivered to New London by wagon train from the hills of western Massachusetts, a region that produced timber of a quality that commanded high prices on the English market. Charles canceled his crew's shore leaves, and while the cargo was being loaded, the clipper's company made ready for a swift trans-Atlantic crossing.

Ruth consented to attend a farewell dinner for Charles at the Rakehell house, and as he planned to spend his last

533

night in America on board his ship, she took David and Wu-ling home with her.

Louise seemed relieved that the little boy and the Chinese girl were leaving, but she remained glum and made no comment.

Most of the family went to the pier the following morning, and Charles came ashore for his good-byes. Although he had been reared in the belief that it was almost sinful for an English gentleman to show his feelings, he hugged David fiercely and, on sudden impulse, kissed Ruth on the cheek before returning to his ship.

Jonathan held Julian on one shoulder, and because it was easier for a small child to see more clearly from that elevation, he lifted David onto the other. Ruth stood beside them. Louise hadn't bothered to make an appearance and on this occasion didn't even offer a headache as an excuse.

Charles gave the order to cast off and, as his clipper began to move away from the wharf, he turned for a final wave. The thought occurred to him that Jonathan and Ruth made an exceptionally handsome couple, but he quickly conquered his absurd stab of jealousy. Jonathan was not only married, but had given his heart to Lai-tse lu. On the other hand, the Chinese girl was halfway around the world, and with a wife as drab and sour as Louise, any man would be tempted to turn to someone as vibrant and pretty as Ruth.

Enough, Charles told himself sternly, and raised his hand to his bicorne in salute as the *Elizabeth* sailed out to sea.

Jonathan promptly ordered some changes in the household routines. Julian and David were to play together daily, he said, with the former to be taken to Ruth's house on the days that the latter wasn't brought to the Rakehell house. The brooding Louise agreed without a murmur of dissent and no longer seemed to care.

The new mizzenmast was stepped, or emplaced, on the deck of the *Lai-tse lu,* and Jonathan was pleased that the special furnishings for the clipper which he had ordered from New York had just arrived.

"I'll soon be putting her into the water again," he

534

told his father at supper one evening, "so I'm organizing a crew, although I haven't yet selected a captain who'll sail her to China."

"Are you sending her loaded with cargo?" Jeremiah asked as a matter of course.

"I'd be stupid if I missed that opportunity, Papa. Hundreds of new cotton looms are being made for me up in Fall River. Soong Chao sells them as though they were made of gold, and we share in the profits."

Louise astonished father and son by looking up from her plate and joining in the conversation. "Your special clipper will be leaving port soon, Jonnie?" she asked.

"Within two to three weeks, if no new snags develop," the startled Jonathan replied. He couldn't recall a time when she had displayed the slightest spark of interest in anything concerned with the business.

"You've talked so much about this particular ship," she said, her stilted speech at least hinting that she had rehearsed the words, "that I'd like to inspect her. I—I'm curious about her."

"You're welcome at any time." Never, either before or after their marriage, had she ever gone on board one of his clippers.

Jeremiah stared at her, too, wondering if she was finally gaining enough of an understanding of the requirements of marriage to develop or at least feign interest in her husband's all-absorbing vocational life.

"Would tomorrow be suitable and convenient?" she asked.

"Certainly," Jonathan said. "Name your time."

"Well," Louise said, "Julian will be spending most of the day at Ruth's house with David, so I could go to the yard with you and Papa Rakehell right after breakfast."

Jonathan wondered if his hearing had become defective. Most mornings Louise came to the breakfast table in a bathrobe and didn't bother to dress until much later in the day. "That will be fine," he said. "I'll have the carriage pick us up. You wouldn't enjoy walking all the way to the yard."

"I suppose not," she said faintly.

That sounded more like her, and Jonathan couldn't

535

planned and plotted was actually at hand, Louise won-
of the ships on which he had labored so hard. It was a
subtle irony that she had chosen to make a tour of the
Lai-tse lu, but no matter. He would take her on the inspection himself because it was a courtesy he owed her,
and he doubted that he would lose much more than an
hour of his work time.

That night Louise found it difficult, almost impossible,
to sleep. It was true that she wanted to see the ship
Jonathan had built for his Chinese paramour, but her
reasons for visiting the vessel had far deeper roots. For
many days she had contemplated doing away with herself
in some way, perhaps jumping to her death from the ship.

She had come to the conclusion that she was of no
use to anyone. Even her mother didn't care all that much,
and Jonathan had taken her duties as a mother from her
by providing a substitute in Ruth Barker. Perhaps she was
being unfair to the woman she had so long regarded as
her closest friend, but the facts spoke for themselves.
Thanks to Jonathan's ruling, Julian would be spending
every other day under Ruth's roof and consequently would
no longer depend exclusively on his own mother's guid-
ance. And there was yet another angle to that unpleasant
situation that irritated her. For years Ruth had admired
Jonathan and now would see much more of him. Any man
who was living his daily life apart from his wife was vulnerable to the attractions of another woman, especially
one who was sympathetic to him and pretty.

As for Jonathan himself, Louise reasoned he would
be as pleased to be rid of her as she would be relieved
never to face him again. She was willing to admit to herself
that, perhaps, her love for him had been shallow, that
whatever affection she had felt for him had grown out of
the circumstances that had thrown them together rather
than a genuine community of interests. But whatever her
feelings might have been, they had changed sharply on
the day Brad Walker had told her about Jonathan's
Chinese mistress. Since that time she had positively loathed
him. At least he wasn't trying to make love to her; the
very idea made her flesh crawl.

All the same, now that the day for which she had

planned and plotted was actually at hand, Louise wondered if the solution she had chosen for her problem might not be too drastic. Death, although an escape, was permanent, and now that she faced the prospect squarely she knew it was unlikely that she had the courage to kill herself.

In fact, the serious contemplation of actually doing away with herself sent a chill up her spine. The realization that no one would miss her was a powerful factor in causing her to change her mind. Her father, like her husband, was absorbed in his work. Her mother always placed her father's welfare and happiness first, far ahead of that of their daughter. Julian was still so young that he wouldn't miss her for more than a short time.

The real key to her future was Jonathan, and she had no idea how he might react if she died. She was being inconsistent, but she wanted him to yearn for her. Something in her inner core demanded that he come to her, beg her forgiveness, and ask her to participate in a true marriage with him. Only then would she be fulfilled, only then would she be able to hold up her head again. And she would have to stay alive if she expected that dream to be realized. Suicide was not the answer.

Torn and confused, Louise slipped into her robe and went down to the kitchen, where a fire burned in the wood stove all night. She made herself a cup of hot chocolate, and as she sipped it she was more at peace within herself than she had been in a long time. She couldn't explain this new feeling, but that wasn't necessary. It was enough, she knew as dawn broke, that she no longer felt tormented.

Unexpectedly pert in spite of her lack of sleep, she appeared at breakfast wearing one of her more attractive dresses, and when she accompanied her father-in-law and Jonathan to the carriage she donned a cloak with a lining that matched her dress. She couldn't remember when she had last gone to the trouble of making herself this attractive.

When they reached the shipyard and walked toward the docks where the new ships were in their final phases of construction, Louise forced herself to look directly at Jonathan's unique clipper. It was huge, far larger than

537

she had anticipated, and when he led her on board she discovered it was even more impressive.

She had to feign interest in the tall masts, the hold where he had to light an oil lamp to enable her to see, and the quarters for the crew. Not until they reached the passenger cabins did she spark, and one in particular fascinated her.

It was twice the size of any of the others, and with its furnishings now complete, it looked more like a sleeping and living chamber in a private home rather than quarters on a ship. She couldn't have imagined anything this luxurious at sea. Oak paneling covered the bulkheads, a brass bedstead was bolted to the deck, which was covered by a thick rug imported from the Ottoman Empire, and the square portholes were covered by silk curtains that made them resemble windows. Two comfortable chairs faced each other, and a table could be lowered from the bulkhead between them. There was even a commodious clothes closet and chest of drawers built into one bulkhead.

"This must be the captain's cabin," she said.

Jonathan shook his head. "No, his quarters are aft," he said, and when he saw she didn't understand he added, "at the rear of the ship. That's traditional."

"Then who will occupy this grand cabin?"

"It's intended for a passenger," Jonathan replied. "I'm making an experiment with this entire row of cabins. The speed of clippers will make them attractive to travelers, especially on the trans-Atlantic route, and can earn a ship's owner appreciable sums. I'm seriously thinking of including passenger cabins on all of my clippers in the future."

Louise nodded, turning away slightly so he wouldn't see her expression. In spite of what he had just said, her instinct told her that he had lavished special care on this cabin because he intended it for the use of his Chinese mistress. She composed herself with difficulty.

The tour continued, and Jonathan showed her the officers' quarters, saloon, and galley, then took her to the quarterdeck, where he explained its purpose. "Now," he concluded, "I reckon you've seen just about everything."

"Except from up there, where I could get an overall view." She pointed to a high tower that stood on the dock beside the ship.

The tower, which could be moved up and down the length of the dock by yard workers who pushed it, was one of Jonathan's many experimental innovations. It stood several feet higher than the mainmast of his new clipper and could be climbed by means of a wooden scaling ladder built into one side. At the top was a platform where a yard foreman and one or more of his assistants were stationed when a new mast was stepped, or put into place. The purpose of the tower was that of obtaining greater precision in the various processes of the stepping operation, and Jonathan sometimes climbed to the platform himself.

But he didn't see how it would be possible for Louise to make the climb, and he shook his head dubiously. "It's a ladder," he said. "You'd have to go up hand over hand, and that isn't as easy as you might think."

"I wouldn't mind," she said, and smiled. "I'm not that old and decrepit."

He tried to protest again.

Louise laughed at him. "Really, Jonnie. Just because I'm married to a Rakehell doesn't mean I've got to be as sedate as my grandmother!"

"Well, if you insist."

"I do," she said firmly.

He gave in to her gracefully, surprised by her sustained interest in the ship. "All right. I'll stay close behind you, so let me know if you feel dizzy or change your mind."

"I won't," Louise said, hitching up her skirts and fastening them under her sashed belt.

Jonathan led her to the scaffolding that stood within a few feet of the deck amidships. "You'll have to go up hand over hand," he said.

"So I see." She caught hold of a crossbeam, planted her feet on a lower bar and began to climb.

He moved onto the scaffolding directly below her. "Take your time, and rest whenever you feel the urge."

"Oh, I'm enjoying this," she told him.

Jonathan was surprised by her agility.

Louise climbed steadily until she reached a point high above the deck and saw that the mainmast extended only a few feet above her.

"Far enough?" Jonathan asked.

"Just a little more," she said, and continued to ascend. Pausing for a moment, she looked down at the ship and marveled at how high she had climbed. Then she caught sight of the painted wooden figurehead, the head and shoulders of a Chinese girl, which she hadn't noticed previously.

Unexpectedly her eyes filled with tears, and she closed them for an instant, then reached for the rung above her. But she was still blinded and her hand missed the crossbar.

Louise groped for it, but it was too late. Losing her balance, she fell backward.

Jonathan reached for her, but her loss of balance was so sudden and swift that there was no way he could save her.

Scores of workmen saw her fall and crash to the bottom of the dock, landing only a foot or two from the hull of the *Lai-tse lu*.

Jonathan climbed down the tower even more rapidly than he had ever descended a line at sea.

By the time he reached the bottom a carpenter had already sent for the physician who maintained a small clinic in the headquarters building.

Sickened by what he saw, Jonathan stared at the broken, grotesquely sprawled body of the unhappy woman who had been his wife.

Jeremiah Rakehell raced to the scene with the physician, and while the doctor went through the routine motions of examining the still body, the older man joined his son.

"It wasn't like her to climb the scaffolding, Jonnie," he said. "Did she—do away with herself on purpose?"

"I have no idea," Jonathan said in a low tone. "We'll never know."

A short time later, before leaving the yard, he gave a brief, curt order: "Take down the observation tower, and don't build another."

A large company of mourners gathered around the Rakehell plot in New London's Old Cemetery, where the Reverend Crowell conducted a short graveside ceremony. Louise's parents had agreed with Jonathan that, as no one knew whether Louise had done away with herself, the funeral should not be elaborate.

Only Ruth Barker was absent, having deemed it better for Julian and David, both of them too young to attend, to remain behind at the Rakehell house with them and keep them occupied.

Bradford Walker stood at his wife's side, his face impassive. Like everyone else present, he didn't know whether Louise had killed herself, and he knew it was useless to speculate. Only one thought was foremost in his mind: he knew for certain now that Louise would not be able to reveal to anyone that he had told her a version—a highly colored version—of Jonathan's secret.

After the services everyone went to the Rakehell house for cold meats, bread, cake, and tea.

For a few moments Ruth Barker stood at a window and watched the black-clad Jonathan alight from a carriage with his father. A wicked thought lurked in the back of her mind, and she could not dispel it. Jonathan was free now, just as she was free, and perhaps, after he recovered from his shock, he would begin to turn toward her.

"I'll join you in the house shortly, Papa," Jonathan said. "I need some air." He went down to the beach and walked rapidly along the water's edge.

Not pausing until he reached the familiar cluster of boulders, he halted, sat, and stared out at the water. A question that burned within him had to be answered. For the sake of his lifelong peace of mind he had to determine whether he was responsible for Louise's death.

Certainly their marriage had been an ill-fated travesty, and neither could be blamed for its failure. Nor was it his fault that he had learned to love someone else.

It was even possible that Louise had guessed his true feelings and had killed herself deliberately in order to burden him with a sense of guilt for the rest of his days.

But he was too practical, too realistic to cripple himself. The Rakehell and Boynton Company needed him. Julian needed him.

Yes, he thought, and Lai-tse lu needed him, just as he needed her. It served no good purpose to brood over what had happened or what might have been. Life had to be lived to the full for the living.

Lai-tse lu was in danger, with the threat of war in the East growing more critical with each passing day. Only in a clipper ship might it be possible to reach her side before hostilities erupted.

Very well, the issue was settled. Jonathan stood, squaring his broad shoulders and, staring out at the sea, turned toward the East. He would go to Canton as swiftly as he could sail there and would join Lai-tse lu, his one true love.

OUTSTANDING READING FROM WARNER BOOKS

THE CULTURE OF NARCISSISM
by Christopher Lasch   (93-264, $2.95)

Have we fallen in love with ourselves? Have we bargained away our future for self-gratification now? With an unsentimental eye, Christopher Lasch examines our society and our values and discovers that we are in thrall in a new enchantment—self-involvement. We live today in THE CULTURE OF NARCISSISM.

**HOW TO PROSPER DURING
THE COMING BAD YEARS**
by Howard J. Ruff   (95-261, $2.75)

Will you survive this round of inflation? You will if you listen to Ruff. Now he tells you what you must do to keep your money intact, be sure of making intelligent investments. "I recommend this book to everyone," said the *Dow Theory Letter*.

PALOVERDE
by Jacqueline Briskin   (83-845, $2.95)

The love story of Amelie—the sensitive, ardent, young girl whose uncompromising code of honor leads her to choices that will reverberate for generations, plus the chronicle of a unique city, Los Angeles, wrestling with the power of railroads, discovery of oil, and growing into the fabulous capital of filmdom, makes this one of the most talked about novels of the year.

WARNER BOOKS
P.O. Box 690
New York, N.Y. 10019

Please send me the books I have selected.
Enclose check or money order only, no cash please. Plus 50¢ per order and 20¢ per copy to cover postage and handling. N.Y. State and California residents add applicable sales tax.

Please allow 4 weeks for delivery.

_____ Please send me your free
mail order catalog
_____ Please send me your free
Romance books catalog

Name_____

Address_____

City_____

State_____Zip_____